DEERFIELD PUBLIC LIBRARY
P9-DMS-571

Sticks and Bones

ALSO BY CAROLYN HAINES

SARAH BOOTH DELANEY MYSTERIES

Rock-a-Bye Bones
Bone to Be Wild
Booty Bones
Smarty Bones
Bonefire of the Vanities
Bones of a Feather
Bone Appétit
Greedy Bones
Wishbones
Ham Bones
Bones to Pick
Hallowed Bones
Crossed Bones
Splintered Bones
Buried Bones
Them Bones

NOVELS

The Book of Beloved
Revenant
Fever Moon
Penumbra
Judas Burning
Touched
Summer of the Redeemers
Summer of Fear

NONFICTION

My Mother's Witness: The Peggy Morgan Story

AS R. B. CHESTERTON

The Darkling
The Seeker

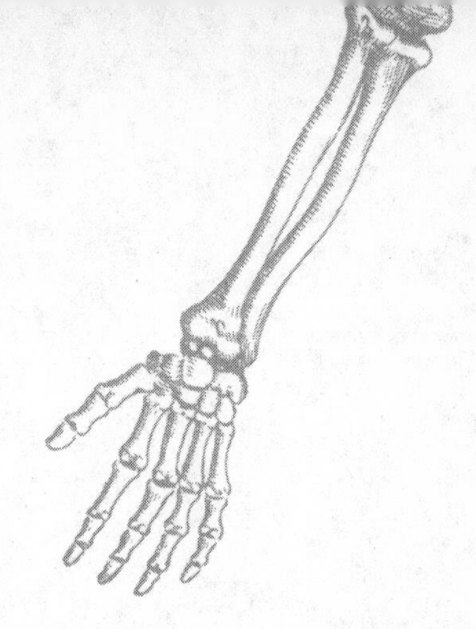

Sticks and Bones

CAROLYN HAINES

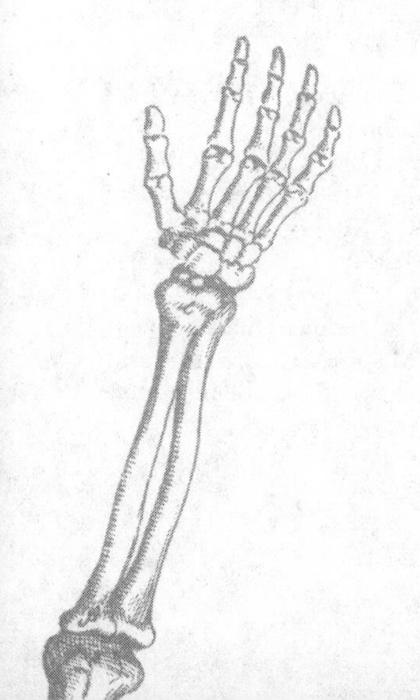

MINOTAUR BOOKS
NEW YORK

This is a work of fiction. All of the characters, organizations, and events portrayed in this novel are either products of the author's imagination or are used fictitiously.

Printed in the United States of America. For information, address St. Martin's Press, 175 Fifth Avenue, New York, N.Y. 10010.

www.minotaurbooks.com

Library of Congress Cataloging-in-Publication Data

Names: Haines, Carolyn, author.
Title: Sticks and bones / Carolyn Haines.
Description: First edition. | New York : Minotaur Books, 2017. | Series: A Sarah Booth Delaney mystery ; 17
Identifiers: LCCN 2017002188| ISBN 9781250085269 (hardcover) | ISBN 9781250085276 (e-book)
Subjects: LCSH: Delaney, Sarah Booth (Fictitious character)—Fiction. | Women private investigators—Mississippi—Fiction. | Murder—Investigation—Fiction. | Family secrets—Fiction. | BISAC: FICTION / Mystery & Detective / Women Sleuths. | GSAFD: Mystery fiction.
Classification: LCC PS3558.A329 S75 2017 | DDC 813/.54—dc23
LC record available at https://lccn.loc.gov/2017002188

Our books may be purchased in bulk for promotional, educational, or business use. Please contact your local bookseller or the Macmillan Corporate and Premium Sales Department at 1-800-221-7945, extension 5442, or by e-mail at MacmillanSpecialMarkets@macmillan.com.

First Edition: May 2017

10 9 8 7 6 5 4 3 2 1

For my friend Louise Bousquet. We are kindred spirits, bound by love and friendship. Our adventures together await, time and time again. In the season of butterflies.

Acknowledgments

Special thanks go to Barb Staub, who answered my call for help with a title. When I was stumped for a good title after my original idea proved to be unsuitable, Barb came through with *Sticks and Bones,* which is exactly perfect for this story. Sometimes, two heads are better than one!

I also want to thank all of the dozens of readers who responded with excellent title suggestions. I have them filed away for future use. You are all smart cookies with a lot of imagination.

Heartfelt thanks apply to the editing process. Thank you, Kelley Ragland, Elizabeth Lacks, and Laura Starrett for the hard work on this story. Every book is greatly improved with the help of great editors, and I've been fortunate to have that help.

Marian Young, another year and new contracts. Who knew we'd be such a team all those years ago when I stalked you? It's been a ride, hasn't it?

I've been fortunate to have smart friends who read and write and who also give generously of their time. Thank you, Rebecca Barrett, for your keen eye. I hope to return the favor for your next book.

Sticks and Bones

1

The chill December wind rattles the windows of my bedroom at Dahlia House. Old Man Winter had a grip on my ancestral home, but I'm not about to let the cold keep me from this evening. I lean into the vanity mirror that has reflected at least seven generations of Delaney women and adjust my mother's diamond and pearl earrings. They're the perfect accessory for the white tulle dress I've chosen. It is by far the most beautiful gown I've ever worn, and though I'm a bit long in the tooth to play Cinderella, I feel like I've been tapped by a fairy godmother's wand. I do a little twirl and watch the dress float around me à la Disney animation. It is perfect for the approaching celebration marking the end of one year and the beginning of a new one.

"Glamour is nothing without intrigue, Sarah Booth Delaney." A husky voice comes from the doorway.

Without looking I know it is Jitty, the ghost who shares the Delaney family home with me. During the Civil War, Jitty was a nanny, but since she's taken up residence at Dahlia House with me, she is more of a bane. Nurturing is far down her list of talents—way behind tormenting, torturing, annoying, bossing, heckling . . . Did I say bossing?

I turn slowly and discover that Jitty too is dressed for the occasion. She's encased from head to toe in a beautiful black and gold sequined gown with matching skullcap that reflects an era long past. I recognize her instantly. My nearly two-hundred-year-old ghost is vamping as Greta Garbo in *Mata Hari*, a film about a female spy. Oh, Hollywood, gird your loins.

"You look marvelous, darling," I say. "Where did you steal that gown *and* that body?"

Jitty is beautiful on her own, but she is something else as Greta. She moves and the gown is like warm, molten gold. There's no doubt she could worm the most secret information from any man. As she slithers across the room toward me, she is leaking sexuality all over the floor.

"You should practice your interrogation skills, Sarah Booth. I believe they'll come in handy."

"Is that a hint that I'm about to have a new case?"

"I don't give hints." She looks down her nose at me as I secure the last earring.

I stand up and reach for my wrap. "Good, because I don't have time for your hints and teases."

"My, my, my, but don't you look feminine." Jitty circles, me. "Sarah Booth, this is the dress that could do it. Uh, huh! This dress could offset that annoying mouth of yours. Wearing this, you should be able to throw a man to the ground and catch some little swimmers. I'll have me a Delaney heir before the new year even gets a jump-start."

Protesting would only make her more outrageous so I pick up my purse and walk to the door. "Happy New Year, Jitty. Don't wait up, and take care of Pluto and Sweetie Pie."

"The cat and dog will be just fine. Don't come back until you're pregnant," Jitty calls out, followed by a cackle.

As I get into the car, I look up at my bedroom window. Jitty is there, her silhouette classic Garbo. I'd have to give some serious consideration to what she was up to. Jitty never gives hints, but she often uses symbols. Was my haint trying to tell me something or just having a frolic? Only time would tell.

The drive to town was short but cold. The party was in the Prince Albert Hotel ballroom, and I stepped inside and stopped. "Winter Garden" was the theme, and Harold Erkwell, the best party thrower in the Southeast, had truly created an enchantment with billows of blue silk decorated with twinkling stars forming the ceiling and frosted foliage and tiny white lights everywhere.

The melody of "Unforgettable" swirled through the glittering ballroom on the strings of a small orchestra. Harold had done himself proud. This New Year's Eve party served a dual purpose—celebrating the coming year and the grand opening of the exclusive boutique hotel.

I was greeted with a chorus of good wishes from my friends and swept into the party where the champagne flowed and the orchestra took me back to the 1940s. I love the dances of that era, and I danced until my shoes were smoking.

At last I leaned against a marble column to catch my breath and watch the glamorous couples spin around the dance floor. The gowns were all white and the men wore white tuxes, giving the party an Old World elegance. I spotted Harold across the room and waved. He was at my side in an instant.

"Happy New Year, Sarah Booth. I've been trying to flag you down for a dance, but every time I get a break from my duties as host, I can't find you."

"It's almost a new year. Can you believe how fast time slips by?"

"It's terrifying how quickly the months roll past." He nodded toward the far side of the room. "There's your partner in crime."

Tinkie Bellcase Richmond, in a flowing gown of white silk with a diamond belt at the waist, was my partner in *solving* crime at the Delaney Detective Agency. She waved and came toward us. "Sarah Booth, you look beautiful."

"She does," Harold said, "and so do you, Tinkie."

"Ditto," I said.

"It's a lovely party, Harold. Millie is having a great time, and Cece has taken enough photos to fill the *Zinnia Dispatch* for the next year." Millie Roberts was the proprietress of Millie's Café, the finest eating establishment in the South, and Cece Dee Falcon was the society editor of the local newspaper.

Cece came toward us, a waiter in tow with a tray of brimming champagne glasses. "Grab a drink everyone. It's almost time to toast in the new year!" Cece, though she was once Cecil, was the prettiest woman in the room. She wore an off-the-shoulder gown that hugged her slender form. Millie wore a white sheath overlaid with gossamer lace. With her hair swept up, she looked ten years younger.

We each took a glass, and Cece was about to propose a toast when the door of the ballroom burst open in the tradition of all bad fairy tales—the grand entrance of the witch, sorcerer, villain, or in this case, troll. Frangelica "Sister" McFee stepped into the ballroom. Her gaze drilled into Tinkie.

"Well, well, if it isn't Stinky Bellcase Richmond." She sniffed the air. "Doesn't anyone else smell that awful stench?" She curled her lips in a nasty smile.

I'd never seen Tinkie intimidated by anyone, but she took two steps backward before she bumped into me. I tried to push her forward, but she balked.

"Oh, holy Christmas," I whispered. "It's Sister McFee." I pronounced the name properly for the Mississippi social elite—"Sista."

"What the hell is she doing back in Zinnia?" Cece asked just before she blinded Sister with some flashes of her camera. "Run, Tinkie, run, before she regains her vision."

Tinkie had finally found her backbone. "I'm not running anywhere."

"Frangelica," Harold said, trying to step into the breach. "I had no idea you'd be in Zinnia or I would have sent you an invitation to my party."

"I figured it was an oversight," she said. "I hate this Podunk town and this backward county, not to mention this third-world state. And call me Sister, please. Only my classy New York friends call me Frangelica. Right, Stinky?"

I looked around for Oscar, Tinkie's husband, but didn't see him. This confrontation was headed south at a rapid pace. Coleman was supposed to arrive before midnight, but he would be too late to stop the bloodshed. Tinkie hated Sister McFee. I didn't know the details, but my normally cool and collected partner couldn't talk about Sister without becoming spitting mad. Something had happened in the sorority house at Ole Miss that Tinkie couldn't forgive or forget.

"Get out." Tinkie squared her shoulders and walked over to Sister. "Get out right this minute."

"Or you'll do what, Stinky? Gas me to death?" She laughed like a sweet Southern belle. "You're too cute." She reached to pinch my partner's cheek, and Tinkie snapped. Her teeth clicked on empty air with an audible sound as she tried to bite Sister's hand.

"Stinky *and* rabid," Sister said with a merry laugh. "Good to know you grew into my predictions."

"Get out!" Tinkie roared the words.

Harold stepped between the two women and grasped Sister's arm. "It was so good of you to drop by, and I'm sorry you have to leave." He propelled her out of the ballroom like a paper sack before a hurricane.

Two hotel staffers closed the doors as soon as the witch's hasty exit was complete. I put a hand on Tinkie's trembling shoulder.

"I hate her," Tinkie said, almost in tears. "She is the biggest biyotch on the face of the planet!"

I couldn't argue with that assessment so I didn't try. At last Oscar noticed Millie's frantic attempts to get his attention, and he hurried over and immediately saw Tinkie's distress. "Are you okay?" he asked, looking at all of us.

"I'm fine," Tinkie said, and with those words she

seemed to expel the miasma that Sister had cast upon her. "Sister McFee made an appearance."

"She's a total bit—" He didn't finish because Cece elbowed him in the side.

"What is Sister doing in our 'Podunk town'?" I asked.

"Her new book about the death of her mama and brother has been at the top of the bestseller list for several months now. I heard some gossip about a movie," Millie said. "I thought it was just big talk, but maybe not. Maybe she's here because they are going to film."

"Refresh me on what happened with Mrs. McFee and Son." Cleo, Sister's mother, and her son Daryl, better known as Son, had driven into the flooded and raging Sunflower River during a terrible rainstorm five summers earlier. Cleo's body was found trapped in the car, but Son's body was never recovered. The presumption was that he had also drowned and then been washed down river. Son had been driving the car.

Millie gave the short version because she had the best memory for local history. "Son was known to use drugs and drink," Millie said. "His father, Colin, insisted that Son had killed his own mother and himself, either by accident because he was drugged up or in a murder-suicide scenario."

"What a terrible thing for a father to say about his child," Tinkie said. She'd regained her composure, and now she was about to lose her temper.

"How could Colin know that to be true?" I asked. "Son's body wasn't recovered. The investigators couldn't do a tox screen. It was raining cats and dogs. It could truly have been an accident."

Millie held up a finger, considering. "Colin couldn't

know anything for a fact, but it didn't stop him from publicly blaming Son. And Sister's book does the same. I've heard rumors for the past several weeks that the book has been optioned for a movie." Millie always had the scoop on Hollywood. She read tabloids religiously, and she consulted Zinnia's famous psychic and one of my best friends, Madame Tomeeka, a.k.a. my high school chum, Tammy Odom.

"Great," Tinkie said. "Just great. She'll be in town for weeks."

"Colin is running for the U.S. Senate from Mississippi," Harold pointed out. "This might be a manipulation to gain sympathy votes. You know, the poor guy whose loaded son killed his wife."

"Didn't he marry, like, six weeks after Cleo was buried? She was barely cold." Tinkie was no shrinking violet in the arena of gossip.

Before anyone could respond, the bandleader rapped for attention on his music stand. "And the countdown begins! Ten, nine, eight . . ."

The doors opened and Coleman walked into the room.

"Seven, six, five, four, three . . ." The bandleader marked off the time.

Coleman strode toward our little group.

"Two, one! Happy New Year!"

Harold swept me into his arms and laid a kiss on me that I wasn't likely to forget for the next twenty years. "Happy New Year, Sarah Booth."

"Happy New Year to you, Harold." I was flushed and breathless.

"You know, your aunt Loulane would tell you that whatever you do on this day, you'll do for the rest of the year." And he kissed me again.

I'd forgotten how powerful Harold's kisses could be until my thumb gave a strange tingle.

Just as he released me, I felt a hand on my shoulder. When I turned, Coleman lifted my face with a gentle hand. "In that case, I need to greet the new year myself." He kissed me too, but very chastely on the cheek.

"Happy New Year," I said to both men, because I was too flustered to think of anything original to say.

Tinkie at last stepped up to defend me. "That's enough, Romeos. Now let's forget about all the McFees and celebrate the new year. Oscar, can we contribute heavily to whoever is running for that Senate seat against Colin? Surely he doesn't stand a dog's chance of winning." But a tiny line of worry tugged at her lips.

When, an hour later, I managed to pull her away, I asked, "What's wrong?"

"It's Sister. Why is she back in town? Do you really think it's a movie deal?"

"I don't know, but I'm positive we'll find out sooner rather than later." I grabbed two glasses of champagne from a passing waiter. "Don't let her ruin this evening for you."

"You have no idea how much I loathe her."

"Why? I mean she's awful, but you handle awful people all the time."

Tinkie only shook her head, and her blue eyes teared up. "I have my reasons."

"Tinkie, I'm your best friend. You can tell me anything."

She shook her head harder. "I can't. I've never told anyone and I can't. Just know that Frangelica is the meanest bit—"

She never got to finish because Scott Hampton and his

band, including Cece's squeeze, Jaytee, burst into the party. "Happy New Year," Scott said grabbing me and Tinkie and pressing a kiss on each of us. "And the new year is off to a rip-snorting beginning."

Before we could finish our conversation we were pulled to the dance floor. It was impossible to stop Scott's infectious good spirits, so I let go and partied as hard as I could, dancing again and again with Scott, Harold, Coleman, and a dozen other men.

As Jitty would have told me had she been there, magical evenings don't come around all that often. I took full advantage.

Near Year's Day rang itself in with a hangover from too much champagne, but the wonderful memories from Harold's party offset the Thor-like headache. I'd picked up the phone to call Harold and thank him for the lovely evening when I glanced at the time: 11:10. I was due to meet Tinkie and the gang at Millie's Café for the traditional Southern New Year's Day fare of black-eyed peas cooked with hog jowl or a ham bone, greens, and cornbread. The peas were for luck and the greens for money. I wasn't about to miss out on luck or money.

I jumped in the shower, slapped on makeup and clothes, loaded my hound dog and cat into the antique Mercedes roadster, and tore down the driveway. The day was cold and I left the windows rolled up, much to Sweetie Pie's consternation. She kept nosing the cold glass, but I wouldn't give in. If I let the window down so she could hang her head out, my eyelashes would freeze and break off.

"Millie said you and Pluto could hang out in her

office," I told the critters. "She made a special dish for you both. A pesky-pet celebration for the new year. Roscoe will probably be there too." Roscoe was an evil little dog I'd ended up with while working a case. Harold adopted him—and adored him. Every vile thing Roscoe did, Harold enjoyed.

I whipped into the parking lot. The parked cars told me everyone was already there. Millie had closed the café for us to have a private lunch. She would reopen at two for her regulars. A lot of people didn't cook and relied on Millie's delicious and nutritious offerings to keep themselves fed.

"Happy New Year. Sorry I'm late," I sang out as I rushed into the warmth of the small café that faced an otherwise empty Main Street. The most delicious smells made me sigh with pleasure.

"Champagne?" Harold asked wickedly as he approached me with a crystal stem and a bottle.

"Back!" I made the sign of the cross. "Coffee. Please."

Everyone laughed and Cece pushed a mug filled with strong black coffee into my hand. "Caffeine and something greasy and filled with carbohydrates will do the trick."

Tinkie nudged me into a chair and Millie put buttered toast and a side of hot grits in front of me. "The New Year's food is on the way," Millie said. "Eat this now and you'll feel better."

Of course she was right. As soon as I ate, my stomach settled and the little man with a sledgehammer tapping on my optic nerve stopped. "Thank you," I told them.

"Too bad you can't have a toast with us," Harold teased.

"I can toast. There's no law that says it has to be alcohol." I raised my cup of coffee and clinked with my friends as Oscar proclaimed the word for the new year to be "positivity."

The lunch at Millie's had become a tradition since I'd returned to Zinnia. I looked around the room with gratitude. I was rich in friends. Good friends, and that was the greatest gift of all. But people were missing.

"Where's Coleman, DeWayne, Scott, and Jaytee?" Cece almost never left Jaytee's side.

"They're coming," Cece said. "I told the band to relax a little bit. After Harold's party they went back and closed down their club. The work of a musician is never done."

"Or a lawman," Millie threw in. "But here they all come."

Two cars pulled into the parking lot and the missing men entered the café to another round of hugs, greetings, and a toast.

Surveying the smiling faces of my friends, I saw the ghosts of the past standing close behind them. My parents, Aunt Loulane, the people who'd loved and cared for me. But I pushed those sad thoughts aside and lifted my mug. "To the best friends ever."

As we all raised our drinking vessels to toast, the door of the café slammed open so hard the jangling bell fell to the floor. Tinkie gasped as Sister McFee stepped inside. The Wicked Witch of the South grand entrance redux, and she eyed Tinkie like she was Toto.

"Well, well, if it isn't a little celebration, and they've let Stinky attend. What's with you? Have you all gone nose blind?"

Oscar put his glass down and stepped toward Sister. "Either apologize to my wife or get out."

"This is a private party," Millie said. "You should leave."

"The door was unlocked. If you want privacy, maybe you should lock your door." Sister sauntered deeper into the room and picked up the bowl of grits I'd been eating. She sniffed it. "Someone loves clogged arteries, don't they?"

"Leave now, before I arrest you." Coleman grasped her arm.

"For what? Entering a diner? Oh please, you might humiliate me by tattling to the tabloids that I set foot in a place like this, but you can't arrest me."

"This is a private party. You're trespassing." Coleman was deadly serious and Sister was a fool if she didn't heed his warning.

Cece pushed her camera in Sister's face and took at least a dozen photos. She checked the shots. "Very flattering. Have you checked your nose lately? I think I have photographic evidence you've been practicing obsequiousness with someone."

I couldn't help it; I burst out laughing. "Good one, Cece."

"What do you want, Frangelica?" Tinkie was the only one to ask the obvious.

"I was checking this dump for a location for my movie, but I can see that if I brought a camera in here, the lens would fog with grease."

"Making a movie of that awful book that paints your dead brother as a murderer?" Tinkie asked. "The dead brother who can't defend himself against your unfounded accusations?"

"So you've read my book." Sister grinned. "Like millions of others."

I put a hand on Tinkie to keep her from jumping the table and tearing Sister's throat out. The animosity between the two was palpable.

Coleman tightened his grip on Sister and escorted her to the door. When she was outside, he closed and locked the door and closed the blinds. "I took the trash out," he said to Tinkie, who burst into tears.

"She is just so damn mean," Tinkie said, wiping her cheeks angrily. "I shouldn't let her get to me, but she is the meanest person I've ever known."

"She's pretty mean," Cece said. Her wicked grin told me she wasn't above a bit of mischief. "So let's pay her back in kind."

"Do you have a plan?" I asked.

"Oh, you bet I do. We'll plot together at a later date. I think Millie is ready to put the food on the table."

In ten minutes we'd brought out the holiday fare from the kitchen, formed a buffet, and filled our plates. Sister and her attitude were forgotten. We laughed and joked and told stories of the past year. Scott rubbed my short—but growing—hair and thanked me and Tinkie again for saving his blues club. Everyone put Oscar's word, "positivity," to good use.

We'd just dug into the pièce de résistance, Millie's incredible Amaretto chocolate cheesecake, when we heard the sound of a glasspack muffler or a motorcycle in front of the café. A loud knock followed.

Millie went to the door saying, "We'll be open to the public at two—" She stopped in midsentence when she saw a tall, very handsome man wearing leather everything. Right behind him was a strikingly beautiful woman, also in black leather.

"Oh my god!" Millie squealed. "It's Marco St. John and his wife, Lorraine. Come in, come in." Millie ushered them into the room and to the table, where Harold pushed forward two more chairs. "Have a seat and join us in a New Year's Day celebration."

"Smells delicious," Marco said. "I love Southern cooking."

Lorraine walked around the café examining everything. "This is perfect," she said. "The light, the ambience . . . It's the place to bring Cleo alive. It's the perfect setting. This is a place she'd come and talk about her ideas for Mississippi education. She'd meet with the man on the street. She'd mingle with the real people here. Not at that old mausoleum they call Evermore."

"Cleo McFee often stopped by for breakfast or coffee and a slice of pie," Millie said. "She was a lovely woman."

"Who are those people?" I whispered to Tinkie.

"He's a movie director. She's a cinematographer. They're the hottest film couple in Tinsel Town. *Oblique, Touched, Fever Moon, Morgan Creek, Dead at Midnight.*"

I knew the movies and they were some of my favorites. "What are they doing in Zinnia?" I asked.

"I'm afraid I know exactly what this is about," Tinkie said. "It's Sister's book, *Dead and Gone.* They really are making a movie." She sounded defeated. "I thought it was all a big bluff, but it isn't. She's going to have a movie made of her book. How is it possible that someone who is such a bully could be so talented?"

Oscar brought his wife another glass of champagne and gave me a concerned look. I was worried too.

Marco and Lorraine dug into the holiday food with gusto. The moviemakers were surprisingly open about everything except the name of the movie. "We can't say," Marco said. "Once the deal is signed, we'll tell you everything, because we're going to need your help."

While Marco and Lorraine ate, we peppered them with questions. Finally, Marco pushed back from the table. "Thank you for such wonderful food, but I'm here on business. I'm looking for Sarah Booth Delaney."

I raised my hand. "Here."

"May I have a word with you? Outside?"

I followed him out the door amid a buzz of speculation. When the door closed, Marco leaned against the café wall. "I want to hire you to find out what really happened to Son McFee and his mother, Cleo."

"Hire me?"

"Are you deaf?" He wasn't being mean. He really thought I had a hearing problem.

"No, I'm not deaf, but why hire me?"

"You've read Frangelica's book?"

I rolled my eyes. "No. But you can bet it's a pack of lies."

"Exactly. I'm making a movie of what happened based on the book. But I have a hunch there's more to this story. I want to find out what happened to cause the accident, and to prove, beyond a shadow of a doubt, what happened to Son McFee."

"You're really interested in the truth?" I asked.

"Lorraine and I have our suspicions, but we want the truth. And I'm very serious." He brought out his wallet and withdrew a personal check for ten thousand dollars. "This is a retainer," he said. "I'll hire you as a location scout for the movie, so that will give you access to everyone and everything." He pulled the check back. "But this could be dangerous."

"Dangerous?" I realized I did sound deaf. "I mean this is a cold case. Do you really think there's danger?"

"Someone damaged one of Lorraine's cameras. It was deliberate sabotage."

"Okay."

"For some reason it's very important to Colin and Sister McFee to make Son a villain. My experience as a filmmaker tells me that when someone promotes one and *only* one version of an unproved truth, there's a reason for it. Colin has a lot to lose and something tells me he isn't the kind of man to go down without a fight. Are you still interested?"

This was a case I wanted. I hadn't been close with Son in college. He was a year or so older than me, but he'd always been pleasant. Where Sister was a total B, Son had been funny and kind. It might be true that Son was drunk or on drugs and lost control of the car. But right at the entrance to the Sunflower River Bridge? It didn't feel right. It never had.

"Let me talk to my partner," I said.

"Yes, we need Mrs. Bellcase on board. Tell her I'll give you both walk-on parts."

"She'd love that." Maybe Marco could cheer up my friend with a chance to be in a movie. It would be the best revenge ever against meanie Sister. "Let me ask her. I'll be right back."

Five minutes later, Delaney Detective Agency was on the payroll of Black Tar Productions. The new year was off to an auspicious start.

2

The second day of January was brisk and cold. Bundled up like an Arctic explorer, I hurried out the front door of Dahlia House when I saw Tinkie coming down the driveway. Sweetie Pie bounded gleefully at my side. Even Pluto, who disdained all excited movement, jacked up his normal saunter and put it in gear to jump into Tinkie's warm car. The cat might be covered in thick black fur, but he didn't like being chilled.

Tinkie drove toward the bridge on Highway 12 that linked Washington and Humphreys Counties. Cleo and Son met their fates attempting to cross the flooded Sunflower River. As we traveled, I filled her in on what I'd learned about the whole McFee clan, via a little Internet research and a few phone calls. It was an interesting story that paralleled the development of Mississippi. I pulled the papers I'd printed from my purse.

"Stuart McFee emigrated to America in the late eighteen hundreds as a young man. He left Scotland—and accusations of horse thieving, robbery, and murder—behind him."

"Well, I don't think the apple fell far from the tree," Tinkie said. "Colin's business practices have raised a few eyebrows."

"Nothing has ever stuck to Colin." There had been accusations, but never charges and certainly not convictions. He played hardball and some people admired him for that. "Anyway, Stuart avoided the hangman's noose and worked his passage to America on an immigrant boat. He discovered two things in New Orleans, his love of the Mississippi River and a young woman, a prostitute, named Amelia. Beautiful and cunning, she was notorious for rolling her customers. Stuart fell under her sway just as there was public outcry to imprison her."

Tinkie frowned, and it wasn't from staring into the sun. "I don't believe a person's ancestry should be held against him, but there seems to be a component of that gene pool that includes aggression and chicanery." Tinkie slowed and turned onto another two-lane highway. The fallow land seemed to stretch around us forever. Soon the giant tractors would be out turning the earth, preparing for planting.

"Aggression, chicanery, and a streak of genius for making money, but not necessarily good luck. Stuart was a savvy businessman and he worked hard. Before long he had his own steamboats and a beautiful home in Natchez.

Stuart and Amelia managed to put their pasts behind them. They had three children, but two died of fever. Only Jamie survived." Tinkie and I both remembered Jamie McFee, a bearded thundercloud of a man who was greatly respected by adults and feared by children because of his booming voice and constant scowl.

"So Jamie's siblings died. People lost children all the time back then," Tinkie said quietly. "It must have been terrible."

Tinkie's sudden softening caught me by surprise. I shot a quick look at her. She was still suffering from the episode with little Libby Smith. That baby had stolen her heart, and while things had worked out and there had been a happy ending, Tinkie still missed being the baby's mama. "Yeah. It affected Jamie a lot. He grew into a serious young man, a devoutly religious man. He believed the death of his siblings was punishment for his father and mother's sins."

"That's ridiculous," Tinkie said. "People aren't punished like that."

"You and I know that, but when Jamie was a child, people believed a lot of superstitious things. He felt he was left alive to bring his family to heel, show them the path of righteousness. Sadly, he was destined for failure."

"Where did you learn all of this?" Tinkie glanced over at me. "You didn't get this background off the Internet."

"You are correct. I called Mrs. Harris. She's been working on the genealogy for every family in the Delta since I can remember."

"Teasie Harris?"

"Yes."

"Good work, Sarah Booth. I'm impressed. Now tell me the rest."

"Okay, so it seems Jamie grew into a very stern man who married a very stern woman, Margaret O'Day. He expanded the McFee holdings to Europe and had one son, Angus, who proved to be a bitter disappointment. Angus was an excellent businessman, but he was a womanizer. He married and a few years later moved to Switzerland to run the European interests of the McFee family. He was shot to death in his own home when his son, Colin, was eighteen."

"Colin, as in Son's and Sister's father?"

"Yes, the big man himself."

"No wonder he's so driven. I feel a little sorry for him."

I sighed. Tinkie had a big heart, but Colin, as we both knew, was the kind of man who crushed anyone who stood in his way. He owned a development company that had a global reach. He'd bought and renovated some of the world's most famous buildings, and everything he touched turned to gold. The Midas touch hadn't prevented the loss of his wife and a son. It seemed the McFees, while able to turn dross into silk, were not lucky in family. There had not been a generation without tragic loss.

"It's dangerous to feel sorry for someone like Colin. What if he had his wife murdered? It's possible."

"Very true, but it's more likely Sister did it. She inherits Son's half of the vast McFee estate."

"Interesting that Jamie skipped Colin in dispensing his estate." It was something to ponder, but I didn't see how killing Cleo or Son might improve Colin's chances at inheritance. Everyone in Sunflower County knew the primary points of Jamie McFee's trust—because Jamie had not been shy about publicly stating his intentions. The estate would go to his great-grandchildren. Sadly, Jamie died only months before Cleo drowned and Son disappeared.

Tinkie sighed. "Jamie disparaged Colin constantly. He would come in the bank and talk to Oscar, saying that Colin was a whoremonger and a thief, that he didn't understand what a vow meant."

"I guess that explains why Jamie skipped his grandson Colin and left his estate straight to Son and Sister. They were the only alternative for heirs." Inheritance by default.

"If Jamie had ever really known Sister, he would have given his estate to the Humane Society before he let her get her greedy fingers on it."

"Rich people do crazy things." I could say that since I was a long, long way from ever being rich.

Tinkie laughed, and her good humor seemed to be restored. "There's the bridge. Let's take a look."

She pulled to the verge, a good distance from the bridge, and we got out to walk the area where the accident had occurred.

"How did Son miss this bridge?" Tinkie asked.

"Good question." I surveyed the side of the road. A road crew had recently shored up the shoulder and widened the roadbed. It would be impossible now to figure out what really happened.

"And why were they even on Highway 12?" Tinkie asked. "I thought they were going to Jackson for a meeting. They should have been on 55. This doesn't make sense. Why were they even on the west side of the state?"

She was right about that. As I recalled the event, Cleo had spent the night in Oxford, Mississippi, meeting with community leaders about her Delta education initiative.

She was seeking local businessmen to commit to funding preschool and kindergarten for counties with low tax bases. Her next stop was Jackson—so it didn't make sense that she was on Highway 12. No one knew why she was there or how her big Cadillac Escalade, driven by Son, went off the side of the bridge. The Sunflower River was swollen and coursing with a dangerous current. Once the vehicle hit the current, it was swept rapidly away, tumbling and smashing into trees, docks, and other debris.

I surveyed the river, now lazy and shallow. "How did they miss the bridge? It was raining. Hurricane Elsie hit the Gulf Coast and the back end of the storm flooded the Delta. But I still don't see how Son went off the road and into the river."

"Car failure? Maybe the steering went out."

Tinkie made a good point. The problem was that Colin had hired one of the best private investigators in the Southeast, Hoots Tanner, to look into the wreck. Tanner had come up with zilch. And we wouldn't have a chance to examine the physical evidence. By now, the Escalade was a cube of crushed metal, either recycled or in a landfill. Still, we'd have to pursue this angle as far as we could.

Although I wasn't the photographer Cece was, I took dozens of shots with my cell phone documenting the shoulder, the approach to the bridge, and the car's likely angle when it left the road and entered the floodwaters.

The banks of the river were covered in small scrubby trees and bushes, but it was a heck of a drop. The Sunflower had been well above flood stage. I'd checked the weather for that date in August. If the river hadn't been flooded, the accident would have been minor.

I'd just climbed up the bank when the sound of a rifle

shot made me drop to all fours. Tinkie did the same. A bullet smacked into a tree behind me.

"What the hell?" Tinkie asked, swiveling to look in all directions. "Let's make a dash for the car."

"Maybe it's hunters." Only a fool would shoot toward a highway, but it happened all the time.

Another bullet thwacked into the dirt beside me. "Run!" We dashed the fifteen yards to the car and hid behind Tinkie's heavy Cadillac.

"Did you see where the gunshots came from?" Tinkie asked.

"I didn't see anything. Whoever it was had to be east of us in the brake along the river." The trees and underbrush were thick and someone could easily have hidden there. The one thing I couldn't speak about was my deepest fear. That Gertrude Strom, a former B&B owner and the woman who wanted to destroy me, had reappeared in my life. She was my Jason—the unkillable monster.

"Do you think this is our new case or . . ." Tinkie wouldn't say it either. Gertrude was the person whose name we dared not speak.

"Listen." I heard motorcycles approaching. I wasn't surprised when Marco and Lorraine, both riding the baddest looking choppers I'd ever seen, pulled in behind Tinkie's car.

We stood and brushed off our clothes. "Someone was just shooting at us," I said. "Maybe now isn't the best time to be here."

"Are you okay?" Marco asked. He spun around, surveying the area. "Where did the shots come from?"

I pointed in the general direction.

"Let me take a look."

Before I could say anything else, he was across the road and disappearing into the thick woods. "Should we stop him?" I asked.

Lorraine's long leg swung over the bike and in less than ten seconds she had a camera out and was filming. "If someone is hiding, Marco will find him." She worked with precision, commenting to us as she captured the area. "It must have been a helluva storm for Son to miss the bridge entirely," she said.

"Our thoughts exactly," Tinkie said.

She worked another ten minutes before Marco returned. "Whoever it was is gone, but I found marks on a tree. Looks like someone was sitting up there waiting."

"For us?" Tinkie asked, a little surprised.

Marco shook his head. "Maybe for a deer. I don't know." He thought for a moment. "Who would know you were coming here at this time?"

Tinkie shrugged. "I mentioned it to you and Lorraine. I thought you might like to scope out the bridge."

"I may have let it slip," Lorraine confessed. "I like to get Sister in a snarl. She's furious that anyone questions her version of the truth."

"Chances are it was a hunter," Marco said. "When he realized how dangerous his shot was, he took off."

I nodded, but I didn't really agree. Not at all. But if the person was gone, there wasn't any point in belaboring the incident.

"Hey, Marco, come take a look at this angle," Lorraine called out. We all went to the side of the road where Son had to have gone off.

"I don't think that car crash was an accident," Marco said. "I don't think Son was loaded on drugs or alcohol.

From what I've heard, Cleo McFee was nobody's fool. She wouldn't have gotten in the car with Son if he'd been out of control."

Another good point in the "this wasn't an accident" school of thought.

"Colin inherited a nice insurance policy when Cleo died," Marco said. In his leathers, he looked like a taller, handsomer version of Marlon Brando. If the words, "I coulda been a contender" came out of Marco's mouth, I wouldn't have been shocked.

Lorraine embodied the sultry beauty of Natalie Wood and glamour of Lauren Bacall. She could have continued her career as an actress, but the call of working behind the camera had been too strong. I could tell by the way she handled the equipment that it had become an extension of her own body.

"And Sister inherits Son's share of the McFee trust effective February 5," Tinkie said. Her inside sources at the bank had been talking.

"What's the trust worth?" Marco asked.

"Billions." Tinkie shook her head. "I don't really know, but it's land, investments, a huge stock portfolio, you name it. Colin built his own fortune, but the McFee estate is generations of innovative McFee planning and investing."

"So, very soon our little author will be a fabulously rich woman." Lorraine held the camera at her side.

"Yes," Tinkie said glumly. "It's a shame. She's so awful, and Son was nice. I only knew him a little—they didn't go to public high school. They were sent away to boarding school. But I knew Sister from parties and from college. We were in the same sorority."

Tinkie almost dripped dismay. Whatever had happened at the sorority had left a permanent scar. I intended to make Sister pay for that.

"If you ladies haven't read Sister's book, you need to," Marco said. "Roon Talley, the screenwriter who optioned the book, is working on a script based loosely on *Dead and Gone*. We intend to start filming as soon as the script is complete. That's where you come in. You have to find the truth and find it fast."

"I can't promise we'll find anything," I cautioned him. "There may be nothing to find."

"You're better PIs than you think," Marco said, winking at Tinkie. "I have complete faith in you."

"So what's your first step?" Lorraine asked. "Maybe I should come with you and film."

"We'd better try this without a camera," I said. "Somehow I don't think the Washington County sheriff's office is going to want to be on film."

"Because you think they gummed up the investigation?"

"No." I couldn't say that without evidence. "But it's very possible they were helped along in their decision to so quickly call it an accident."

"Colin bought them off!" Marco had a handle on what Colin McFee was capable of.

"Maybe. Let me see the reports and we'll take it from there."

"Be safe, ladies. Watch out for hunters." Marco waved a hand and covered his black hair with a helmet that gave no view of his features. Lorraine followed suit. In a moment they were buzzing down the highway like slender, lethal insects.

"They're deeply invested in making this film," Tinkie said.

"Yes, they are." From what Millie said, Marco and Lorraine were eccentric artists. Who was I to question how they approached moviemaking? Going all-in seemed like the best way to do anything, especially investigate.

"Do you think someone was trying to shoot us?" Tinkie asked. "Marco was a little blasé about the whole thing."

The director's attitude did give me pause. "I don't know. It could have been an accident, a hunter who overshot. Or it could have been someone trying to warn us off this case. You know by now everyone in ten counties knows we've been hired to investigate what happened to Son." I couldn't pretend I wasn't worried, but there was a ray of sunshine. "It seems if they'd really wanted to hit us, they could have. We were sitting ducks."

"Somehow, that doesn't make me feel better," Tinkie said. "We have to be really careful."

"Agreed. Look, we're already at the county line. Let's go to Greenville to visit the Washington County sheriff's office. We can file a report there."

"A brilliant idea," Tinkie said. "Head 'em up, move 'em out."

I whistled up Sweetie Pie and Chablis, Tinkie's little dust mop of a canine. The two dogs had hit a scent and were romping along the riverbank. Pluto, who was smarter than your average black cat, had remained in the car. Sitting on the side of an empty highway in forty-degree weather wasn't Pluto's thing. But when the dogs and I jumped in the car, he was on my lap in a flash.

"I wonder what really happened that night when Cleo

died," Tinkie said as she pulled onto the empty highway. "Why were they on this road and what happened to send them into the river?"

"That's exactly what we have to find out."

3

The sheriff of Washington County wasn't in, but the dispatcher, Hattie Fagan, took our report of the gunshots.

"I hate to say it ladies, but a lot of folks carrying guns these days don't have sense enough to pour piss out of a boot. They get trigger happy. What do they call it, 'buck fever'? But I'll have the sheriff check it out. He'll have a few of the usual suspects to talk to. I'm just glad you weren't hurt."

"Me too." Hattie had made me feel better in one way and worse in another. Everyone assumed it was a careless hunter. What if it wasn't? I couldn't allow "what if"s to control me. We'd filed the report in the proper jurisdiction, which relieved me of having to report it to Coleman. Now it was time to get busy with our case.

When I told Hattie what we needed, she pulled up the file on the cold case and gave it to us as we sat at Sheriff Bud Lenton's desk.

"I can't see why the sheriff would care about you seeing this," she said, "but don't get me in trouble, okay?"

"Yes, ma'am," Tinkie said with an angelic smile. She could play ninety percent of people like B.B. King could play Lucille. The dispatcher was putty in her hands.

"Why are you looking up that old case?" Hattie asked. "They never found that poor boy who washed down the river. He's crab bait in the Gulf."

Not the image I wanted in my head as I contemplated lunch.

"Were you working here when the accident happened?" Tinkie asked.

"Been here fifteen years. Ever since the sheriff took the oath. I told him just last week he ought to deputize me. I handle a lot of things around here."

"He should," Tinkie said. "I'll bet he couldn't get along without you."

"That's a fact. So what are you two so interested in the McFee accident for?"

"They're going to make a movie about what happened to Cleo and Son," Tinkie said. "We're scouting locations for Black Tar Productions, and the director asked us to take a look at the accident report. He wants to get everything right."

Hattie's interest increased. "A movie? That's exciting."

"A big Hollywood film. Marco St. John is directing and Lorraine St. John is the cinematographer. It's going to be fabulous."

I studied the accident report as Tinkie chatted up the dispatcher. We made a good team.

From the photographs taken at the scene, it was easy to see the Sunflower River was way out of its banks and raging across the flat delta land. One mystery solved. When the SUV went off the road, it would have impacted with the water about four feet down the bank. The car would have instantly smashed into trees and other debris in the flood. The photos showed the driver's door was torn off the car. Son could easily have been pulled out of his seat belt and taken down river, never to be found. Chances were, he'd been battered into pieces.

Cleo, in the passenger seat, had been somewhat better protected.

The car had traveled at least a mile downriver, bumping and tumbling until it hung up in some fallen trees that had partially blocked the river. It had taken searchers two days to find the vehicle, due to the heavy rains, flooding, and the fact that Cleo wasn't reported missing in that area. The search for her had focused on Highway 55 South. It wasn't until the car was found with Cleo in the passenger seat that another person was added to the list of the missing. At first, no one suspected that the driver was Son. Not until a young waitress at a gas station diner had finally identified Son as the man with Cleo McFee. The man who must have been in the driver's seat.

By the time a search party was out looking for Son, the odds of finding him were slim to nothing.

From what I could tell, the investigation into the accident had followed the regulations play by play. The lawman hadn't skipped a step—but there was no way to tell if anyone had unduly influenced him. Sheriff Lenton came to the same conclusion I'd come to—Son had missed the bridge. Whether it was the storm, drugs, homicide, carelessness, or perhaps a deliberate desire to end his life and his mother's, the sheriff couldn't tell. Official pronouncement had been death by accident.

Son was the only person who knew the truth, and I believed he was dead. Now it was my job to find the evidence that supported my belief. If it wasn't an accident, we needed to find the person responsible.

"Do you remember anything about that night?" Tinkie asked Hattie.

"I do. It was terrible. I remember when Bud found the skid marks. It was like the SUV went off the road and the driver fought to get it back on. Anyway, that's what Bud said. There had been some serious accidents on Highway 49 South and Highway 82 was under water near Indianola. All those coastal people trying to evacuate north had the main highways jammed for miles—it was a freaking nightmare. I'm surprised more lives weren't lost."

"Did you know the McFees?" Tinkie asked.

"My mother worked for Angus McFee."

I lifted my head and looked at Hattie Fagan. I'd tuned out the conversation between the dispatcher and Tinkie as I'd focused on the report. Now I was paying attention. "What did your mom do?"

"She took care of Colin and Liam."

"Liam?"

"Colin's brother. He died in a terrible accident when the family was living in Switzerland. They were camping in the Alps. That's why Mom took the job. She wanted to get out of Mississippi and Switzerland sounded like paradise. Too much *Heidi*, I think. Mom had a real obsession with the Alps."

"What happened?" I asked.

"Colin was seven or eight, I think. Liam was ten, but he was slow. Something happened when he was born. Mom said he was sweet and loving, but Angus kept him hidden away. Folks around here never even knew he was part of the family."

"What kind of accident?" Tinkie asked.

"An ice shelf broke and fell on Liam. He and Colin had left the camp and gone exploring. Colin did everything he could to dig his brother out, but he was just a kid."

A kid alone in dangerous territory. And another tragic death. Either the McFees were slow learners, or they had a real passion for losing family members.

"Your mother knew Colin as a young person?" Tinkie asked. We were obviously thinking along the same path.

"Would she have some time to talk with us, do you think?" I asked.

"She's in the Loving Arms Nursing Home. She'd probably enjoy a chance to talk about the good old days. I go by every morning and afternoon, but that leaves twenty-two hours when she's mostly alone. She doesn't sleep well."

"Thanks so much, Hattie."

"Her name is Aurelia Fagan. Tell her I'll bring her a milkshake when I get off work."

"I could do that," I offered. "There's an ice cream shop just down the street."

"She'd like that. It's an easy way to get some calories into her. Thanks."

I'd learned all I could from the accident report, and Hattie had given us an unexpected lead. I wasn't keen on a visit to a nursing home, but that's exactly where we were headed.

The visitor's parking lot was all but empty when we pulled in. Walking in the door, I saw two older women in wheelchairs looking out at the bright January day. They called a greeting as we entered, and Tinkie stopped to speak with them while I took the vanilla milkshake to Hattie's mother. I found her in the community room working a jigsaw puzzle.

"Mrs. Fagan?"

When she looked up at me, I continued. "Hattie said you might be able to help me with some information. She also said you'd like a vanilla milkshake." I put it on the table where she could reach it and offered my phone. "You can call Hattie to make sure I'm okay to talk to."

Aurelia only laughed. "You look okay. I'm a pretty good judge of character."

"I'm glad to hear that." I eased into a chair. The puzzle was a Monet painting of water lilies. Aurelia's eyesight had to be pretty darn good to piece those intricate shades into place. "Would you mind telling me a bit about your experience in the McFee household?"

"Oh yes, Mr. Colin said some movie people might be around to talk with me. You want to know about Angus McFee. That was a good time in my life. I was a young woman, unsure of what I wanted to do with my future. Travel was the big lure. Travel to Switzerland and the Alps. It was my dream. And it was wonderful for a while. Until the accident." Her eyes brimmed with tears. "The time with the McFees, while lovely, made me realize the role of governess wasn't for me."

"Because the children were so difficult to manage?"

"Oh no, Liam and Colin were lovely boys. Sweet-tempered, kind, considerate."

I couldn't believe she was talking about Colin McFee. Ruthless, willful, take no prisoners—those seemed more appropriate descriptions. "We are talking about the developer, Colin McFee of Sunflower County?"

"Yes, I was with them in Europe, but I also spent time at Evermore with the family. Now Jamie, the grandda, he was a love. I wasn't too fond of Angus, and his missus wasn't my cup of tea, either. They weren't hard to work for and the pay was superb, but there was tension in the house. Bethany, Colin's mother, was cold and a real bit—bad person. I don't approve, mind you, but I can see how Angus might have been driven to find love in other places. In fact, I'd say all the terrible things that came started with Bethany. But that's just my opinion."

Aurelia wasn't the judgmental older woman I'd expected.

"What did you do after you left the McFees?"

"Oh, I went on to school and became a teacher. Taught fifth grade for decades over at the Greenville Middle School. I worked on Saturdays at McCormick Book Inn. I've always loved books, and Hugh and Mary Dayle McCormick know books and Mississippi. It was a wonderful time in my life."

"Tell me about Colin and Liam. What were they like?"

"Liam was the quiet one, always busy with his projects. Engineering was what interested him, though he could never have gone to college. He was . . . slow. But smart. Just a little slow. He wanted to build tunnels and bridges and such. Lord, there was one time he and Colin decided to dig a tunnel under the creek in the back of

Evermore. The thing collapsed on him and I thought he was dead." One tear moved slowly through the rouge on her cheek. "Scared me nearly to death. I dug and dug in that muddy water. I was afraid to run for help and I was terrified I wouldn't get him out. But I did. That time I saved him. When the ice fell on him, there was nothing I could do."

"What was Colin like?" I asked gently.

"Now that boy was wild from the moment I met him. He brimmed with mischief and grand ideas. He didn't see danger because he was fearless. He was always dragging poor Liam into trouble, but Liam adored Colin. One time Colin found some dynamite in one of the farm sheds at Evermore and blew the dam on the pond." She laughed. "It's funny now, but at the time I was terrified. I guess you could say those two cured me of illusions of being Jane Eyre and made me realize I was closer to that poor governess in *Turn of the Screw*. Those boys took years off my life, but they weren't mean. Colin was all boy and filled with endless energy."

She told her tale of woe with a smile. It was clear she loved Colin and had loved Liam. "So Colin was the bad one."

"Bad only in the sense that he thought up more mischief and compelled poor Liam to participate with him. Liam was older, but Colin was the leader. He seemed to really love his brother. And me. I was the surrogate mother who gave him affection and played with him. I never believed he'd forget that. But he did. The boy I knew and the man I see today are miles apart."

"There's some thought that Colin might not be such a . . . good person." There wasn't any easy way to say it.

"I remember him as a child. I don't recognize the man

he grew up to be. The McFee house was always in emotional turmoil. Angus and Bethany fought, and they took no prisoners. There were physical altercations, and they both hurt each other. In front of the kids. That takes a toll on any youngster. If Colin is the angry, ugly man I see on those television ads today, talking about how the Russians are the great Satan, then I blame it all on Angus and Bethany. He started out sweet. They turned him into what he is today."

"Do you think Colin is capable of killing his wife?"

Another tear slipped down Aurelia's cheek. "I do. I hate to say it, but I do. Colin became a man driven by the need to succeed. That was all that mattered. He buried those tender feelings and became so cold and unpleasant. When he came here—it was like he wanted to shake the words out of me, as if we'd never been close at all."

"He visited you here?"

"Only for a minute to ask if I would keep quiet about the past. He tried to give me money, but I wouldn't take it. What would I do with money? I can't be bought."

"Is there something Colin would want you to keep secret?"

She folded her hands together. "Possibly many things. But I don't need to be paid to keep my mouth shut. I told him to leave me alone. The last time he dropped by was five years ago, just before Son disappeared. He wanted me to sign something saying Jamie wasn't fit to manage his own affairs. He said because I'd lived in Evermore with Jamie and Angus, it would hold weight. I refused to do it, and he told me he had no more use for me. Not until four days ago, I guess."

"Why was he here four days ago?"

"It's his campaign. He wants the past in the past. He

didn't want me talking to the media about the family. Of course, I had no intention of doing that anyway."

Colin McFee was a callous moron. There had been one person in the whole world who believed in him. Who stood up for him. And he treated her like she was a used tissue. "He might have been decent once, but he isn't any longer."

"I fear you're right." She inhaled shakily. "What if I'd stayed with Colin after Liam's death? I ran home. If I'd stayed, everything might have been different. I could have protected him."

I put a hand over hers on the table. "He grew to be the man he chose to be. You aren't responsible for that."

"Perhaps not, but it's the only thing that gnaws at me late at night when I can't sleep. Somehow, I failed that boy."

"You didn't." I nudged the milkshake closer to her. "Hattie said she'll be by to see you as soon as she gets off work."

"And she will. Daughters are the blessing at the end of your life, Sarah Booth. Some sons step up, but always the daughters."

I gave her a hug and left before I started crying myself.

Walking down the long corridor, where several elderly women toddled about their business, I heard "Coat of Many Colors" in a clear soprano. I turned a corner and saw Tinkie playing a zither and leading a sing-along in the community room. I leaned against a wall and watched her play and sing, making the residents laugh. She was Zinnia's own Dolly Parton, without the big breasts. When she saw me, she finished the song and returned the zither to the table.

"I didn't know you could play one of those things."

"I have many talents, Sarah Booth. Many." She grinned. "I'm coming back next week to play again. I have lots of songs, but I need a bit of practice."

"You sounded perfect to me." And that wasn't a lie.

Tinkie dropped me and the critters off at the front of Dahlia House, and then she hurried home. We'd been gone longer than expected, and she'd vowed to have a home-cooked meal ready for Oscar when he got home from the bank. Tinkie's cooking was more threat than reward, but I chose not to say that. Oscar would have to figure out how to avoid being poisoned without hurting Tinkie's feelings.

I stepped into the chilly foyer and stopped. At the foot of the stairs, a woman in an old-fashioned military dress suit stood at attention, her brown hair just off her shoulders and her penciled eyebrows arched.

"I killed a Nazi with a judo chop to the throat," the woman said in a British accent as she came forward. "I can certainly handle you."

"Who are you?" I asked. "And why are you in my foyer?"

"You have to learn better strategic tactics, Sarah Booth. I was one of the most decorated women in the war. I helped save my country. I helped save England. But I lost my husband and so much more."

I wasn't all that well versed in World War II history, but a tiny little bell in the back of my brain was jingling. "You were a spy?"

"And a good one."

"So, who?" I couldn't put my finger on it. Jitty loved these guessing games, but I wasn't in the mood.

"Nancy Wake. Like your friend Cece, I was a journalist, working for the Hearst papers. But when I saw what the Nazis were doing, I had to fight."

I walked around her, taking in the very neat suit, the military posture. "I can see where you'd be a threat."

"I was the Gestapo's most wanted person. They called me the White Mouse."

"Why are you on a spy kick, Jitty?"

She began to morph and shift into the more familiar figure of my haint. "You got to learn to be sly and work undercover. Frontal assault isn't always the ticket."

"Why?" I went to the decanter in the parlor and poured a Jack Daniel's. "This is a cold case. There's not really any reason to be sly."

"You never know," she said. "And if it's such a cold case, why was hot lead flyin' today?"

"Is that a hint?" I could torment her as much as she could torment me.

"The hint is that terrible things happen in this world, because terrible people are on the loose. Take advantage of all the love showered on you, Sarah Booth. Find someone to love and grab hold. Don't let loose until it thunders."

"I'm not a snapping turtle."

"No, you aren't, but I wish you were. You're a solo turtle. And the years will pass and that's how you'll end up. Solo. Alone. Solitary. Hunkered down in that shell you built to keep from gettin' hurt again. You've been home comin' on two years—no man, no baby."

I was unprepared for the impact Jitty's words had on me. It felt as if some mean person had thumped me in the heart. I had to change the course of the conversation. "Hold on there, White Mouse. I'm not sure how romance and spying mix, though I do love me some James Bond. Sean Connery is hot stuff."

"Danger makes the little swimmers move faster."

I burst into a laugh. Jitty always said the most outrageous things and would stonewall if I called her out as a liar. "I'm going to call Doc Sawyer and ask him if danger makes sperm more active."

"Do it, and he's going to think you've lost your mind."

Doc had taken care of me since I was a child, and he *would* think I was insane if I asked such a question. I couldn't say I was checking on Jitty, my resident haint. If I mentioned her, then he'd *know* I was nuts. "You win, this round."

"I always win," Jitty said, and once again she was the brave British spy whose head the Nazis had graced with a five-million-franc reward.

"Yes, we win, don't we, Jitty. And at what cost?"

I left her pondering the answer to that and went out on the porch to sit in the sun and sip my drink. I'd started drinking early, but as the old saying went, it was five o'clock somewhere, and I needed to unwind. The Son McFee case, technically a cold case, shouldn't be loaded with stress and worry. And it sure shouldn't be loaded with danger, but it was.

The McFee family was like a tar baby. If anyone touched a single one of them, he, or she, was permanently stuck to all the dysfunction, cruelty, and meanness. There was no getting away from them. And I had a terrible feeling that both Tinkie and I were now tightly stuck. We had put ourselves in a position where we would be forced to deal with Sister every day. I had no doubt we would pay a high price.

4

I woke up the next morning raring to get to work. I had several excellent leads, but one might take considerable more finessing than the others. I knew just who to see to make the magic happen.

Getting records from Switzerland on Liam McFee's death would require some badge power. And I required me some Coleman. He'd been busy with work and, aside from a Fred Astaire New Year's Eve, he'd been avoiding the holidays, much as I had been. We were both alone—and both scared of taking another romantic risk. Essentially, we were cowards, and the holidays made us even more skittish. So much pressure to be a couple, to be with someone, to be home for the holidays with family. For those of us without family, the expectations made us hide under the bed. But now the holidays were over, and I needed to reestablish my relationship with the sheriff of Sunflower County. Would we remain friends or become friends with benefits? I found myself thinking of Coleman at odd times. We'd come very close to taking that step from friends to "more than friends" in the past, though circumstances had sent us in different directions. But I fantasized about a more intimate relationship. I'd die before I'd confess such things to Jitty, but friends with benefits sounded delightful. And dangerously wicked.

Dressed, coiffed, and accompanied by Sweetie Pie and Pluto, I drove to the courthouse. The place was bustling, especially the tax assessor's office. In such a rural county as Sunflower, property owners came to the courthouse to pay their taxes instead of mailing a check or paying online.

The queue at the tax assessor's window was long but folks were laughing and chatting, a real social gathering. Coleman had given DeWayne the week off, and he was alone in the office. The dispatcher had taken off to run a few errands.

"We haven't had much chance to talk," I said as I closed the door behind me.

"We're always busy during the holidays. Kids are out of school and looking for trouble. They find it, and then we find them."

Coleman had a way with young people. He could set them straight without making it contentious. Maybe he could handle Sister. Though I feared she would be a challenge even for his skills.

"Any interesting cases?"

He shook his head. "I have a sneaking suspicion things will soon be a lot more active. Colin McFee is moving his campaign headquarters back to the McFee estate, Evermore. Sunflower County won't be the same for at least a year, until the election is over."

"Oh no." Politics weren't my favorite part of being an American, especially since things had gotten so crazy and candidates had Twitter wars, no restraint, and no fact-checking. Though I did my best to avoid the political fray, I knew about Colin's campaign. A snail living under a rock would know. Colin was everywhere. Staking his claim to become one of the U.S. senators from Mississippi, he'd decided to focus on his expertise in foreign affairs—which centered around his personal hatred of Vladimir Putin, the Russian leader. That was his campaign strategy. He intended to show he could out-macho Putin. It was insane.

To his credit, Colin had taken the high road with the other two candidates running for the Senate seat. He hadn't aired a single negative ad about his fellow contenders, but Putin and all things Russian were on Colin's hate list. So far, Colin had vowed to halt the import of Russian vodka, caviar, and babushkas. He'd been getting pushback on the vodka since Stolichnaya was popular with some constituents. Caviar and babushkas weren't in high demand in Mississippi.

"Why does Colin hate Putin so much?" I asked Coleman.

He chuckled. "You think I'm privy to Colin's mental processes?"

"Does he have mental processes?"

"He's a smart man. The renovations he did on the library in Belgium. Incredible. And Memphis is beautiful now since he renovated most of the downtown. I hear he's reimagining the Chicago skyline. If his plans are accepted, it will be stupendous, much like the work he did in Dubai."

Colin's designs and renovations were almost divinely inspired. "Why does he want to be a senator? He's wealthier than a god."

"Power. Control. He wants to put his stamp on the state in a way his grandfather never could. This goes back to the breach between Colin and Jamie. He's still trying to show the old man that he's worthy."

"Jamie is dead. He died shortly before Cleo's wreck."

"Doesn't matter. Colin thinks he still has something to prove."

"Men. All that testosterone and competition and proving of things." I sighed. "It can be so tiring."

Before I could catch my breath, Coleman was across the room and had me pinned to the high counter. "Testosterone can be a really good thing, Sarah Booth."

Even if I'd wanted to argue, which I didn't, I couldn't have. Pressed against his chest, I put my arms around his neck. "I'm really glad the holidays are over."

"Me too." His kiss was both demanding and tender, and my bones melted. When he had me at the point of total surrender, he drew back. "But I'm sure you're not here to be kissed. You're here on business. What can I do for you?"

I stomped his toe hard and pushed free of his arms. "You're right. I'm here on business, and I don't have time for your kisses."

He laughed. "I love that little flush that climbs up your neck when you get all hot and bothered."

I glanced down at his uniform pants. "Keep talking, wiseguy."

He closed the distance between us again. "I could be sweet-talked into one more kiss. Maybe. Why don't you give it a try?"

"You should be seducing me, not the other way around. I don't have to sweet-talk men for a kiss."

"But can *other* men kiss like this?"

I resisted for maybe three seconds before I kissed him back. With each kiss, I came closer and closer to losing my self-control.

The office door started to open and we jumped apart like we were red-hot. I turned away from the door, hoping for a moment to compose myself.

"Well, well, looks like our fair sheriff has been playing naughty with the local dick." Sister McFee's grin made me think of a rabid skunk.

"What can I do for you, Frangelica?" Coleman asked.

"Someone is following me. It's a black sedan, dark tinted windows. I believe they mean me harm."

"Really? Some widow you kicked out of her home? Or some war veteran whose prosthetic legs you stole?" I couldn't stop myself.

"Sarah Booth," Coleman said softly. "Now, Frangelica. What kind of car?" Coleman was all business.

"I can't be certain of the make or model, but something bigger, maybe a Chevy SS. The car lurks in the background, but I know they're following me. I'm afraid." Sister looked up at Coleman like he was Zorro, Superman, and Deputy Dog all rolled into one.

"What do they want, Sister?" I asked acidly. "Maybe they want to steal your bullying techniques."

Coleman snorted and tried to cover it up with a cough. Sister turned on me. "You went to New York and failed, but I took the city by storm. I'm a winner, and you're what, a third-rate private dick who has a partner with body-odor problems?"

The remark about Tinkie was more than I could take. I stepped so close that I was right in her face. Sweetie Pie came from around the counter and stood at my side while Pluto paced down the counter so that he was within a swat of Sister's face. "What is this stinky business with my friend?" I demanded.

"Ask her. All I can say is that she really was quite stinky." She laughed.

"Stop saying that—"

"Or what? Are you threatening me?"

"I don't make threats. I'm just giving you some facts. Stop talking about Tinkie like that or we're going to have a serious problem."

"Ooooo, 'serious.' My! I'm shaking in my boots."

Sister wasn't a person who could take a hint. She was going to have to learn the hard way, and I wanted to be the teacher for that lesson.

"Next time you see the car behind you, give me a call," Coleman said. "Or if you could snap a photo of it. Maybe get the license plate. That would give me something to work with."

"Thank you, Sheriff. I knew I could count on you." She reached out and took his hand and squeezed it. "I always liked you, Coleman."

He extracted his hand. "If I can do anything else for you, just give a call."

Sister walked past me as if I didn't exist. And she was out the door.

"She is such a capital *B* with an *itch*," I said.

"She has a real high opinion of herself." Coleman agreed. "Now, what really brought you to my office?"

I told him about the death of Liam McFee in Switzerland some fifty years ago. He agreed to get a copy of the investigation, with pertinent parts translated into English, and any relevant paperwork that could be found. I mentally checked the item off a long list of things to do, places to go, and people to talk with. I wanted to stay in the sheriff's office, but I knew I'd get Coleman—and me—in trouble. Walking away was hard, but I did it, taking the critters with me.

Pluto took a leap, swatting my butt with a claw. I couldn't tell if he was congratulating me or giving me a spanking. I didn't know which one I deserved.

Tinkie met me at Millie's Café. The chow was so much tastier at Millie's than my house. We ordered a late breakfast and filled each other in on what we'd discovered. Tinkie had been doing a little online research into Colin's campaign, and into Susan Simpson McFee, Colin's former mistress and now his wife.

"Colin doesn't actually need campaign donations. He's very rich. Give the devil his due, he's a fabulous businessman. Cleo was insured for five million dollars, but I can't even see that as a motive because he's so rich. Five mil is nothing to him." Tinkie bit into a buttered biscuit and bliss infused her features.

"I wish I had a life where five mil was nothing." Five *grand* was a hefty sum to me. "So has anyone invested in Colin's campaign?"

"Some of the in-state politicos have started a PAC for

him. It's impossible to find out how much they've collected or who contributed. No one has to report anything these days."

"Don't you love how elections can be bought by the man behind the curtain?" I was only a little bitter. My father had been a judge—an elected position—in Sunflower County. He'd been very touchy about the idea that elected officials could be owned by the rich. He'd refused contributions to his campaign from interests outside the state, but before he died he saw the direction things were headed. And he had not been happy.

"There are several big investors who've made noises about contributing to Colin. Oscar has talked with one of them, and the man says that Colin is a genius in foreign affairs."

"Affairs, maybe, because he has the reputation of a real horn dog, but he hasn't said anything about foreign policy except that Putin is the great Satan."

"Exactly," Tinkie said. "This investor—Oscar wouldn't tell me his name—thinks that Putin is behind all of the woes of America, because Colin says so. And if Colin can knock Putin out, then America will be on top again." She rolled her eyes. "According to this contributor, Putin controls the weather because he's put weather satellites into space that have the capability of manipulating El Niño. There's no such thing as climate change—it's all Putin." She rolled her eyes again. "Putin is responsible for the mess in the Middle East because he's going to take over Mecca and turn it into a brothel. *And* Putin is responsible for the drug problem in America because he's the head of a big pharmaceutical enterprise that ships narcotics here. The contributor believes all of this without reservation. Because Colin says so."

I couldn't fathom or change Colin's bizarre political message so I refused to worry about it. "So what about Susan Simpson McFee, aside from the fact she was sleeping with her boss who was also married? Anything good there?"

Tinkie finished the last bite of her omelet. "She's been with Colin for at least six years and the relationship began when Cleo was very much alive. Susan was a secretary in his development company, a native of Memphis, graduate of Christian Brothers University, and a real party girl. Word on the street is that Susan can do things with her body that a contortionist would envy. She trained for acrobatics and contortion with a troupe of performers like Cirque de Soleil."

Millie stopped by and poured coffee for both of us. "Cece called to see if you were here. She's on the way."

"Great! And thank you."

Millie gave me a hug and then went around the table to hug Tinkie. "So, Marco and Lorraine St. John are going to film a movie in Zinnia. Can you believe it?"

"You should sign up for craft service, Millie."

Her eyes widened. "That's a great idea, Sarah Booth. I will." Another customer came in and she started toward him but turned back. "I took some chicken and dumplings out to the car for Sweetie Pie and Chablis and a little bit of amberjack for that cat. He is such a handsome creature."

"You are worth your weight in gold," Tinkie said. "Hey, Millie, what do you know about Susan Simpson?"

"I know I'd like to have her body. Well, before she got pregnant. She had the best figure I've ever seen. I hear she's a gold digger and she wouldn't hesitate to screw a man right out of his money and family, but he'd love every second while it was happening."

"Was she involved with anyone you know of before Colin?"

Millie shook her head. "She's not from around here. I'll bet if you could talk to some of the other female secretaries at McFee Enterprises, you'd get a bucket-load on her job . . . qualifications."

"Thanks, Millie." It was another good tip. It shouldn't be too hard to find someone at McFee Enterprises who hated Susan. Women like her, the home-wreckers, created a lot of enemies.

Tinkie pushed her plate back. "I'm so stuffed my pants hurt."

"Me too." The holidays had packed on a few pounds. Jitty would be making caustic remarks if I didn't put the brakes on my appetite.

Tinkie leaned in closer. "The interesting thing I found out was that Susan was Colin's alibi the night Cleo died. I called Hattie, the dispatcher over in Washington County, and she asked Sheriff Lenton, and he said Susan and Colin were together in Memphis. The file only said Colin was with someone who verified his alibi. It was Susan, which to me makes his alibi worthless."

"Damn. Sheriff Lenton should have put who Colin was with in the file." I was miffed.

"I mentioned that to Hattie, and she said the sheriff didn't want the tabloids chewing on that piece of fat. It would hurt Cleo's memory as much as Colin, and the major point was that Colin had an alibi." Tinkie grinned. "And it was some alibi. According to Susan, they were together, *all* night. Susan was very clear about that. She's not the brightest lamp on the street."

"Illumination isn't her first concern. If she's as good in the sack as people say, she doesn't have to be smart."

"Why don't men see that they're just a chow wagon for some women?" Tinkie's question encompassed more men than Colin McFee.

I shook my head. "Ego dancing with the Little Head makes for a bad combination. I don't blame Susan. She took advantage of a man who was ripe for the plucking. If it hadn't been her, it would have been someone else. Colin is just that kind of man."

"Poor Cleo. And in a way, poor . . ." she made a face, "Sister."

"Don't feel sorry for her." I told her about the encounter in the sheriff's office. "She's toxic. What is the deal with her calling you Stinky?"

Tinkie ignored my question. "Why don't we check out the McFee estate, Evermore? I've always wanted to see the house."

"Maybe Cece will want to accompany us." I nodded toward my journalist friend, who entered the café wearing denim leggings, boots, and a red pullover. She looked like a million dollars.

"Maybe I'll accompany you where, dahlink?" she asked, air-kissing both of us.

"To Evermore."

She waved Millie away. "No time for food right now, we're going exploring. I'll be back for lunch." She grabbed our elbows and we were off.

Evermore was east of Zinnia on some of the most fertile land on the planet. The McFee holdings in Mississippi were vast. In the near future, Sister was destined to come into a big bundle, including Evermore. The Neo-Renaissance Italianate house rose like a giant birthday cake from the flat lawn. Tall, slender cypress trees flanked the white shell drive. It wasn't a house that struck me as beautiful—it looked a bit like an Old World prison—but it screamed wealth. Three stories, at least twenty arched windows on the first floor, tall windows on the second floor, and small square windows on the third. A quick calculation told me there were at least seventy rooms in the house.

Jamie McFee had built it, and in many ways the perfect symmetry matched what I knew of the man. He lived a morally correct life, disdaining drink, womanizing, and gambling. He went to church every Sunday and believed in philanthropy. That was one of the reasons the old man had loved Sister and Son's mother, Cleo. She'd also been devoted to good deeds and shared Jamie's passion for helping others.

Son had inherited his mother's desire to make the world a better place, but I wasn't certain Sister had ever drunk from the milk of human kindness. She was a lot more interested in Sister than she was in anyone else.

Somehow, they'd all managed to live within the walls of Evermore until Son and Sister went off to college. Freed of the children, Colin had moved his development business to Memphis, and Cleo had, for the most part, remained in Zinnia at Evermore with Jamie. I could understand that. Though Jamie was strict, he was a kind man with a white beard and a hearty laugh. When I was a young child, he reminded me of Moses, which was a little scary. My parents had liked him, and my father said he was a man who earned your respect.

As we drove down the drive, Cece whipped out her camera. "I heard they were going to film inside Evermore," she said. "I'll get a few shots of the house."

A few was more like several hundred. Cece got out of

the car and went to work. I noticed the two motorcycles parked at the front steps. Marco and Lorraine were inside.

We left Cece snapping photos as we knocked at the front door. To my surprise, Colin opened the door. He was dressed for success. No matter how nutty his campaign might be, he was a good-looking, older man who epitomized a statesman.

"Why, Sarah Booth Delaney and Mrs. Richmond," he greeted us. "Did you come to volunteer on my campaign?"

"Wouldn't that be fun, Sarah Booth?" Tinkie said, shifting in front of me before I stepped on my slack jaw. "What kind of volunteer help do you need, Mr. McFee? I have a lot of talents."

Tinkie reached back and snatched me through the door with her. "Sarah Booth is very talented too, though she's going to catch flies if she doesn't shut her mouth."

The door slammed behind me and I found myself in the paneled foyer where dozens of Vote McFee signs in red, white, and blue leaned against a delicate table. Red-blazered men and women hustled around, talking into Bluetooth headsets. The first floor of the house was in constant motion.

"I'm sure I can find some exciting work for you. And when I'm elected to the Senate, you'll have a friend you can call on."

"Thanks." I didn't know what else to say.

"Let me get Adele to put you to work," Colin said.

"Wait!" Tinkie linked her arm through his. "Would you give us a tiny tour of Evermore? My whole life, I've wanted to be here. It's like a dream come true."

"It's a beautiful old home," Colin said. "It's my permanent address, by the way. Sister has given me permission to stay once she inherits. My business is in Memphis, but my home is in Mississippi. I don't want any confusion about that matter when it comes time to vote."

I finally had a clear grasp on why Evermore had suddenly become campaign headquarters. As far as I knew, Colin hadn't been back to the house for years. Now it was important to validate his residency in Mississippi if he meant to run for the Senate seat.

"Shall we tour?" Tinkie looked up at him and pulled her bottom lip into her mouth. When it popped out, I knew she had Colin exactly where she wanted him—eating from the palm of her hand.

"Of course, Mrs. Richmond."

Arm in arm, they set out for the parlor. I brought up the rear. I didn't mind. It gave me a chance to really look around. The house was an architectural delight. Colin had made building his trademark, but he'd inherited the talent from Jamie McFee. Each room held some unique bit of beauty, whether it was tigerwood flooring, built-in book cases, or marble fireplaces—the place was elegant and darkly masculine.

As Tinkie chatted up Colin, I hung back. When I slipped away to a small morning room off the front parlor, I saw a gun case. Most plantation homes boasted an assortment of hunting rifles, and that's exactly what was contained in this glass case. No one was about, so I tried the door, which opened with ease.

A rifle with ornate workings, including etchings in silver of a falcon and a lever with a falcon's claw holding a crystal, immediately drew my attention. I'd never seen a gun with such craftsmanship. I lifted the gun out and smelled the barrel. It had been recently fired.

The gun was a work of art, but it was also a weapon. I put it back and snapped a photo of it. Someone had taken a shot at me and Tinkie—and they might have been using that rifle. There was no way to prove it, and no way to disprove it.

Footsteps came toward the morning room, and I bolted out the door and caught up with Tinkie.

"Sarah Booth, Colin is showing me the kitchen. Come along."

The kitchen stopped me in my tracks. While it held the charm of the 1920s, it was thoroughly modern. The appliances were designed for a commercial chef, and a glass-fronted built-in bookcase held dozens of cookbooks. My gaze rested on *How to Please a Demanding Man*. I almost reached for it, but Tinkie and Colin moved on through an enormous pantry filled with enough foodstuffs to last through World War III. Chatting a mile a minute about his plans to bring Russia to her knees, Colin led Tinkie to the gardens in back of the house.

He paused to look back and saw me malingering on the steps. "I would take you upstairs, but Susan is resting. She's in a terrible mood, too. The baby keeps kicking and she can't sleep. Have I mentioned I'm going to be a father?" Colin said. "A boy. Another McFee to carry on the name."

Colin was sixty if he was a day, but he'd used his pregnant wife and even the sonogram of the baby to good effect in his national TV ads. "It's a boy for McFee," was another campaign ad that made my skin crawl. Not because it involved a fetus, but because in the ad, Colin pointed out the baby's genitalia and challenged Putin to produce a male heir. It was way over the top.

When I started to turn back to the kitchen, Colin cut the garden tour short and followed me back inside. "It's wonderful to think of being a father."

"Yes, it's so sad about your first male heir, Son." I struggled to contain my sarcasm.

"Son wasn't a fit heir. He was a drug abuser. He killed his own mother." Colin's brow warned of an impending storm.

"He was your son," I said softly but with an edge of steel. "You ruined his name without any evidence. You and Sister."

"Are you here to defend a dead man?" Colin asked, his voice rising so that several of his staff members scurried toward us.

"No, not necessarily," I said. "We're here—"

"We're here to work with the film people," Tinkie interjected, giving me a look. "Sister said they needed some extras, so we thought we'd come over and see if they could use us. Are you going to be in the movie?" she asked.

"Over my dead body." He moved on to new terrain. "That film will never be made."

"If they follow Sister's book, it paints Son as the drug-addled killer," I said. "Isn't that what you want?"

"I know enough about Hollywood to know they don't have to follow the book." He grinned. "But I'm not worried. I have some pull at the studio. I can't have a film digging into my family's tragic past while I'm running for a national office. Once I'm elected, they can do whatever they want."

"A film all about you. What would Putin think?" The words were out before I could stop them.

"I'm sure Mr. Putin would be eaten up with envy," Tinkie said, and this time she followed her look with a quick stiletto stab to my big toe. It was all I could do not to scream and hop up and down.

"Putin can kiss my—biscuits," Colin said. "He's the biggest threat to our country and no one else seems to see it but the people of Mississippi. I'm digging into information that indicates he was involved in the Kennedy assassination."

I was stunned. "Was he even alive then? He was like, twelve. Which assassination?"

"John and Bobby. Both of them!"

Tinkie nudged me away. "Colin, would you mind showing me the second floor? We'll be quiet so we don't wake Susan. Sarah Booth is supposed to meet the film people right now." She tapped her watch face. "Hurry along, Sarah Booth. You don't want to keep important people waiting."

She was ditching me, and I didn't blame her. I wasn't helping her question Colin, I was just making it more difficult. But this would clear the way for some serious poking about the house. Tinkie was the best partner ever.

5

I scuttled back through the kitchen and headed for the stairs I'd seen earlier. If Colin's campaign headquarters had taken the first floor, then it made sense the film crew was on the second or third floor. How hard could it be to find a film crew? And besides, I really wanted to explore the place without Colin eagle-eyeing my every move.

The second floor landing was big enough for a complete house, and I found sofas, tables, magazines, and a series of photographs in ornate frames on the walls and tabletops. As I glanced through them, I was stunned to find all of them pictured Son as a young man. He was a handsome boy who grew to be a fine-looking young adult. His talents, activities, and awards had been captured in photos.

He'd captained track and baseball teams, and he held huge trophies from his winning seasons. He posed with certificates of scholastic achievement and with pretty girls in formal gowns. He'd starred in theatrical productions in high school and college, and the framed playbills proved it. Dozens of moments in time showcasing the handsome young boy had been captured. In contrast, there were only five pictures of Sister. In all of them she was chubby and petulant, a frown her only expression.

Son was the star of the family. He won top honors at whatever he turned his hand to. Sister had no trophies, or at least if she did, no one had bothered to photograph them. A glimmer of compassion for Sister touched me. Maybe I'd judged her too harshly. Growing up as the redheaded stepchild might account for her meanness. It didn't excuse it, especially not the way she goaded and bullied Tinkie, but it might explain some of her animosity toward those who were well-liked and loved.

"Snooping again, Sarah Booth?"

I almost peed my pants, but I managed to turn slowly to face Tinkie's nemesis. Sister had gotten the drop on me, but I'd never let her know. "That's my job. Professional snoop. I thought you knew that."

"But what are you snooping for? And who?" She walked around me. "I thought you told Daddy you were here as an extra."

"I am. An extra snoop." I shrugged. "You caught me. I'm curious to see what you'll inherit when the trust goes to you. Cece is going to do a big spread in the newspaper about the passing of the McFee banner to a female. After all, you're the first female to inherit the dynasty. Cece's taking photographs now. I'm helping her."

"How delightful. All she had to do was ask. I'm happy

to tell her I'm getting *all* of it." Sister waved her arm to encompass, well, everything. "All the McFee land and money *and* all the money my bestselling books make. I'll be the most powerful person in this county."

"More like the biggest bi—" I stopped myself and smiled, deciding to play the Hannibal Lecter card. "So, show me the rest of the house. All the little hiding places where you hoarded your toys. You didn't like Son to play with any of your things, did you? He got all the love and attention, and you got crumbs."

A flush of anger touched her cheeks. "You are insane. I wouldn't show you anything except the door. And I'm going to tell my daddy on you."

I couldn't stop the laughter. "Oh, do that. He'll be amused. Keep in mind your father doesn't like weaklings."

"Sister!" Colin's voice came from the first floor. "I thought you were taking my campaign aide to Jackson for the Women's League of Voters meeting? Why aren't you gone?"

"Coming." Sister started down the stairs but turned back to face me. "Don't try to steal anything. I'll know."

"Oh, I don't doubt you've counted every knob and drawer pull in this house. You're the type to guard every penny. That's why no matter how much money or how many exquisite things you have, you'll always be a miserable person."

"Only a person without two nickels to rub together would say such a stupid thing." She trotted down the stairs.

She'd gotten the last word, but I had things to do. The hallways were paneled in dark wood with the doors recessed, reminding me of the old Overlook Hotel in Stanley

Kubrick's classic film *The Shining*. It was with trepidation that I pushed open the first door I came to, the film clip of the dead woman in the bathtub clear in my mind. I didn't plan to look in any bathrooms for any reason. My heart couldn't take an ambulatory floater.

The door creaked softly and swung open to reveal an enormous suite where Colin and Susan had nested. I'd expected the Colin McFees to stay on the ground floor in Jamie's old quarters, but I'd been wrong. And Colin had lied. Susan wasn't resting—and a good thing. A bassinet had already been set up by the window, and when I stepped inside, I found a complete adjoining nursery with a huge bath, at least twenty by twenty feet. Evermore offered every accommodation.

I had no qualms about poking through Colin's and Susan's belongings, but I didn't want to be caught. Sister might be lurking around, and she could move like a mouse. I checked the obvious places and came up empty-handed. If I had time, I'd return for a more thorough investigation.

Exploring the east wing, I found the cameras and equipment belonging to the film crew. A large suite contained a mountain of Marco and Lorraine's luggage, but no one seemed to be about.

I'd just turned to leave when I heard raised voices. Marco was talking to a woman. The sultry Southern accent did not belong to his wife. Being a true snoop, I eased down the hallway where I could hear better. Susan McFee, Colin's young wife, stood in the door of a gym that included every piece of exercise equipment imaginable.

"I'll pop this baby out and be back to my slender self in a week. Two, tops. I've maintained an intense exercise regime. I'll be ready for my chance to be in a movie by the time you start filming. I swear it. I won't look like a pudge."

"I can't promise you a part in a movie." Marco leaned away from her, but she shifted toward him, invading his personal space. "You've never been screen-tested. I don't even know if there'll be a part for you."

"It's the story of the McFee family. Of course there's a part for me. I'm a member of the family, and I'm carrying the real McFee heir. The only male heir."

"What?" Marco turned to look at her. "Sister inherits in less than a month. She's the heir. Believe me, Sister made a point of that in her book. Repeatedly."

Susan's jaw snapped shut. "I meant the heir to Colin's dynasty. Since that old prude, Jamie, disinherited Colin, my husband has done very well for himself. He has plenty. We don't need Jamie's ugly old house and land. Let Sister have it. We have a mansion in Memphis where they have the opera and theater and culture. Not like godforsaken Mississippi."

"So, you're a culture vulture?" Marco asked. If Susan didn't hear the condescension in his voice, she was tone deaf.

"I don't really like the word *vulture*, but I think culture is the most important thing in our universe." Her voice had turned dreamy.

"More important than medicine?" Marco was an absolute devil.

"Yes."

"More important than religion?" He took his torment up a notch.

"Culture can be a form of religion, don't you think?

The movies you make always express a philosophy. You make your audience think about everyday things we simply accept as normal. But they aren't normal. They don't have to be. I'd give anything to be in one of your films."

I wondered how much of Susan's butt-kissing was an attempt to secure a part in the movie, versus sincere admiration for Marco's films. He was an exceptional storyteller, and actors loved to work with him because he'd begun his career as an actor. He knew how to give them freedom with support. His wife was able to reimagine every scene with her camera. The old became new again. Her lens captured the characters and the setting and told an exquisite story.

With Lorraine as the cinematographer, Marco had the big names begging for work. Money wasn't the draw—the privilege of being in a St. John movie was what the top tier of actors desired. As much as I despised Sister, I had to give her credit for snaring the best Hollywood film team working.

Footsteps came toward the door where I was hiding and I nearly broke my neck hurrying down the hall to a recessed doorway. I wasn't safe from discovery, but I didn't have another option.

"I have work to do." Marco stepped into the hallway. He wore sweats and a T-shirt with a towel draped across his neck. Susan, wearing completely inappropriate workout clothes, followed him. Her beautiful chestnut hair was pulled into a ponytail. She carried the baby all in her stomach. Her arms and legs remained slender—just the basketball of a baby right in the middle. She looked to be in terrific shape for an incubator.

"Just give me a chance, Marco. Please."

"Susan, everyone will have a chance. There are many things that have to be settled before we even decide to film. Lorraine and I are here to scout for locations, to get a feel for what's possible. The crew is here to take some initial location shots. Nothing more. Just because Sister's book has been optioned doesn't mean a film will be made."

"I know the studio is hot for the story. Colin told me there's a screenwriter on the project."

"That's true. It's also true that Colin doesn't want this movie made. At least not right now. In case you've missed it, he's running for public office. This movie might not be good for his campaign."

"Hogwash. All publicity is good publicity for a politician. The great ones all knew that."

"Colin doesn't share your view. In fact, he flatly stated he was going to shut this project down. So before you worry about a part in a movie that might never be made, you should talk to Colin."

"If he ruins this for me—" She put her hands on her hips. "He'd better not." Her voice was grim. "He'd just better not. He doesn't know . . . I have to have this part. It's my best shot for a career."

"I never thought I'd feel sorry for Colin," Marco said, "but, man, your hormones are a mess. You'd better hatch that kid and get some balance back in your life before you end up a single parent. Spawning a McFee baby is only significant if Colin designates the kid as his heir. It's not a birthright."

"You're right. One hundred percent right. I am overwrought. I feel like a whale, and I'm ugly and tired all the time. I want to eat chocolate truffle ice cream nonstop.

Colin has to lock the door and hide the key to keep me from escaping to the kitchen and gobbling a gallon." She sobbed softly. "My life is totally out of control."

"It's not that bad," Marco said. "You've only got a few more weeks before the baby comes. Once that happens, everything will right itself."

"You'll consider me for the part?"

"I can't promise."

"But you might? Just say you might. I'll take that and leave you alone, but I have to have something to hold on to." She sniffled. "Please."

"Okay. I might." Marco threw in the towel.

"You are the most brilliant filmmaker ever born. I'll make you proud. As soon as I have the baby, I'll return my body to the limber, sexy tool it's always been. You'll see. Thank you, Marco. Thank you."

Footsteps came toward me and I pressed myself deeper into the shallow recess.

"Hello, Sarah Booth." Marco stopped and leaned against the doorframe. "That's not a very good hiding place."

I sighed. "I'm not very good at hiding today. First Sister, now you. At least Susan didn't see me."

"Don't be so sure. That little scenario might have been just for your benefit."

"Dammit."

"I saw you talking to Colin. Any leads into what happened to Son?"

"He's sticking to his story. I left Tinkie to see what she could weasel out of him. She's a lot better at that than I am." I pulled out my phone. "I did find a gun that was recently shot." I showed him the photo of the beautiful rifle.

"I'll say. I saw it down in the morning room. It's a VO Falcon." He stared at the photo I'd taken. "The price for that gun, which is Swedish-made, is close to $900,000."

I was stunned into silence. "For a gun?"

"What's money to Colin? He has more than he'll ever spend." Marco was right about that. "So, what's the next move?"

"We've examined the scene of the accident, as you know. We've looked at the accident report in the sheriff's office. Next, I'm going to check the insurance claim to see what the adjustor had to say."

"That's a damn good idea. Get a copy of the report, okay?"

"Sure." I could photograph it with my phone, like a spy.

"What's after that?"

"They found Cleo's car about a mile downriver. If Son remained in the car until then, he could have drifted farther downriver. Maybe someone saw something. I'll talk to folks along the riverbank. Maybe put up a poster offering a reward."

"Colin tried the reward thing, didn't he?"

I shook my head. "I honestly don't know. I was in New York at the time. Surely there was a reward offered. What kind of man wouldn't try to find out what happened to his son?"

"Colin is a narcissist. They're a dime a dozen in Hollywood. Nothing matters except *his* needs. He'd written Son off, and so Son's disappearance didn't trouble him at all. He looked at it like a problem solved. Colin wouldn't have to fight to keep Son from his inheritance, and believe you me, Colin will control Sister. She'll do whatever he says."

Sister *was* desperate for Colin's approval, and Marco

seemed to have a good grasp of psychology as well as movie directing. "Desperate people are dangerous."

"You speak the truth."

Marco turned to leave. "Let me know what you find."

"I will. After all, you're footing the bill."

6

Tinkie and I left Cece at Evermore. She said Jaytee would pick her up when she finished the photo shoot. Colin had welcomed her inside, and since Sister was on her way to Jackson, Cece had an open field to get as many photos as possible. When Sister returned, I had no doubt the journalist's access would be squelched, so Cece was making hay while the sun shone.

Tinkie and I stopped by Hilltop to pick up Chablis and Dahlia House to get my critters. Judging by the way Chablis cuddled into Tinkie's chest, I could see that the damage done by Tinkie's obsession with a little red-haired infant had been repaired. Chablis, with her lion-sized heart, had forgiven.

"I think about Libby every day," Tinkie said, as if

she'd read my mind. "You are right, Sarah Booth. She is better off with her mother. And you were also right that Pleasant brings her over a lot."

"I knew she would. When the baby's older, I'll bet you'll have some extreme spend-the-night parties for her."

Tinkie's smile was slow, but luminous. "I'd like that. Oscar too."

"So would I."

Tinkie's phone buzzed and she checked it. "Harold sent the property map for the land along the Sunflower River with the names of the landowners. At least we'll be able to ask for the owner by name."

"Excellent. Want to start with the Washington County side first?"

"Yes."

We crossed the bridge and traveled down Highway 12 for a mile before I turned down a driveway that I hoped would take me to property that abutted the river. The land ownership map that Harold had sent to Tinkie's phone said the property belonged to Benjamin and Sally Westeros. I knew nothing about them except their names. I hoped for a friendly reception, but some landowners could be extremely sensitive about trespassing, and some would consider an uninvited visitor to be trespassing.

The small cottage, built high on stilts to prevent flooding, was made of weathered cypress. Potted plants on the wraparound porch added vivid color against the gray wood. Birds trilled and chirped at a big feeder in the front yard, and a yellow tabby lounged on the steps. Tinkie and I left our critters in the car as we walked up the high staircase. The dogs and Pluto would behave, but it would be rude to turn the gang loose.

A lean man in camouflage answered our knock. "Can I help you?" he asked. He wasn't friendly, but he also wasn't unfriendly.

Tinkie explained our mission, and he opened the door for us to enter. "Have a seat. Sally, put on a pot of coffee, we have visitors."

The house was snug and warm with incredible views off the back porch, where Benjamin seated us with mugs of coffee. The day was brisk, but the bright sunlight warmed us. Below, the Sunflower River, lazy and low, meandered around a bend, winking through leaves in the sunlight. The woods crowded up to the edge of the water. "Serenity" was the word that came to mind.

"So, you're investigating the disappearance of that rich man five years ago? The one who was swept out of his car and never found?" Sally perched on the arm of her husband's chair, a petite redhead whose mannerisms made me think of a cardinal.

"We've been hired to find out what caused the wreck and what happened to Daryl 'Son' McFee."

"For the movie?"

"Yes," I said. It was pointless to try to stop the gossip. Marco and Lorraine had gone to a lot of trouble to be so visible in the community.

"I don't know what happened, but I can guess. That boy was pulled under by the current and got caught under a tree or something. Feast for the catfish and the 'gators." Sally sighed. "He was a good-looking young man and now his daddy wants to be a senator."

"From what I knew of Son, he was a nice guy," Tinkie said. "That is not true of his sister. She is a total bit—"

"Businesswoman," I cut in. "It's her book they're basing the movie on. The director wants a conclusion about what happened to Son. Did either of you see or hear anything during that time?"

Sally frowned and looked at her husband. "We searched the banks for the missing man. A lot of us went downriver for miles on land and by boat. Benjamin and I walked the bank on this side of the river. Of course there were places we couldn't cross, but we were very thorough. Mr. McFee had offered a big reward. Twenty-five thousand, as I recall. That money would have made a difference for us, but we didn't find anything. Not a trace of that man."

"There's still a reward," Tinkie said. "Not from Colin, but from the movie people."

"Colin McFee made it pretty clear he blamed his son for the accident. Said he was a druggie and had terrible judgment." Benjamin watched us for a reaction.

"That's what Colin believes," Tinkie said.

"But you don't?" He was sharp.

"I knew Son in college." I fielded his question. "Son had issues with drugs, but it's my understanding he'd gone into rehab and cleaned up his life. We believe his mother called and asked him to drive with her."

"Why?"

"We don't know," Tinkie said. "We're searching for answers. The number one question is what happened to Son. Did he drown? Was he injured? Did he wash into the Mississippi?"

"Folks have been drowning and disappearing for a long time," Sally said. "The river can look so shallow and placid, but it's dangerous. That night, when the accident happened, the Sunflower was way out of her banks. It was almost to our floorboards," Sally said. "I saw a lot of debris go past the house. Each time a tree or dock or boat came floating by, I was terrified it would ram into our pilings and knock the house down. But I didn't see a car or a body."

Son, pushed down the river by the floodwaters and hidden by the dark night, might have passed right by Sally and Benjamin as they sat on the porch. It was depressing to think about, that they'd watched the surface of the river unaware of the subterranean currents tugging a body along.

"Do you know your neighbors?" I asked.

"They're like us, folks who love the river and the land. There are sometimes houseboats tied to the bank of the river, but not during a flood. River people find safe harbor."

"Is it possible for us to leave our vehicle here and walk downriver and talk to some of the other residents?"

"Let me make some phone calls," Sally said. "River folks don't like someone showing up without warning."

"Thanks," Tinkie and I said together.

Benjamin refilled our coffee cups as Sally made some phone calls. We talked about the river and the upcoming Senate election. Or at least Benjamin talked and Tinkie and I listened. He was a supporter of Colin. "The man is a business genius, and Mississippi needs some industry to come in here. Some good jobs in the Delta would go a long way to help the people."

He was right about that. The Delta had been agricultural forever, but with the implementation of machinery to do the work, only the very wealthy benefited. The state prison was one of the biggest employers. It was farm or work at the prison. Things were changing, but the progress was mighty slow.

"If Mr. McFee can bring some automotive jobs or

manufacturing or something where a person can make a living wage, I'd vote for him twice. His spat with that Russian fellow is silly, but what politician today doesn't do a bunch of silly things?"

"What do you do for a living, Benjamin?" Tinkie asked.

"Mail carrier. Thank goodness. It's a good job. Benefits, too."

"Good for you," Tinkie said.

The conversation hit a lull, and Sally returned. "The next four houses are expecting you. The Weltons and the Pennebakers weren't in. I'm not surprised the Weltons aren't home. They have a house in Clarksdale and the house on the river is more of a getaway, but the Pennebakers are usually home. Walking along that riverbank can be difficult, though, so I think you should drive. Just take the next four driveways to the left."

"Thanks," I said, rising. It was time to move along.

We took Sally's advice and drove, and a good thing. Some of the houses were a mile apart. And none of them had any information for us. While we were in the area, I suggested we try the next property, owned by the Pennebakers. Maybe they'd returned home.

We'd just pulled into the yard when a big pickup rolled past us and parked under the house, which was also on stilts. A gray-haired man got out of the truck, came over, and introduced himself as Grant Pennebaker. "Can I help you ladies?"

Tinkie filled him in on what we were doing.

"I remember that night," he said, looking past us at the river. "It was a tragedy, but I can't help you. My wife and I went to visit our kids in Helena, Arkansas. We don't stay on the river when the water's up. Too dangerous.

Back before I retired, we stayed through tornadoes, storms, freezes. Hell, we spent a month without electricity during an ice storm. But we aren't young anymore. Now we can go to Helena or, if the weather looks really rough, on down to Florida. The job doesn't hold us here anymore."

We thanked him and headed home. The afternoon had been a bust, but that was par for the course for an investigation. You had to kiss a lot of toads before you found a prince.

Tinkie dropped me off at Dahlia House. I wanted to do some Internet research on the whole McFee dynasty thing and particularly on Colin's campaign. Tinkie, who was far more involved in campaign awareness and financing—since she had money and I didn't—said big money from outside Mississippi was perched on the sidelines waiting to commit to Colin. He needed one homerun PR campaign, a sign that he could take the election. A success to prove he was a winner.

As Tinkie cruised down the drive toward home, little Chablis looking out the driver's window at me, I waved goodbye and she lifted a paw. She was a smart little thing.

I opened the front door on a slender black woman in a white summer dress belted at her waist. She wore a straw boater and carried a parasol.

"Who the hell are you?" I asked. Of course it was Jitty, but I had no clue who she was impersonating.

"I'm just a slow-witted slave named Mary Bowser. My mistress, Mrs. Elizabeth Van Lew, sent me to help you out."

"Thank goodness you're here to help. I have a ghost

named Jitty who's supposed to watch over me, but she is lazy as sin." I waited for her reaction, but she held to character.

"I'm good with cleaning and cooking, but I can't read or write."

"Is that so, Mary Bowser." Because I intended to do some research, I started toward the PI offices. Delaney Detective Agency was housed in a part of my home. "Come with me, Mary," I said.

She followed obediently, and I had some misgivings that this was truly Jitty. She was never obedient, silent, or tractable.

"Have a seat and I'll be right with you," I said as I googled her name.

The information that popped up had me looking over the computer screen at her inscrutable face. "What is it with the spy thing?" I asked her.

"When you believe in something, you do what you have to do."

I read more. Mary Bowser, a slave, was freed by her mistress and joined the Van Lew spy ring that infiltrated the Confederacy. At one point, Mary worked in the Confederate White House for the Jefferson Davis family. Since it was assumed that she was slow-witted and couldn't read or write, important papers were often left in plain view. Mary had a photographic memory and would memorize the documents and then report to her Union handler.

"My, my," I said. "I don't think I'll leave you alone with any of my valuable documents." Which wasn't a problem since I didn't have any.

"A girl has to do what a girl has to do." Jitty slowly revealed her own features.

"Jitty, did you know about Mary Bowser when you were alive?"

She shook her head. "No, I didn't. Miss Alice and I were hard at just tryin' to survive. And there wasn't any news source. I didn't even know that Mary tried to burn down the Confederate White House when they began to suspect her as a spy."

"She was a brave woman, right in the lion's den."

"That she was."

"Okay, so this is the third time you've shown up as a spy. What's going on? Am I supposed to commit espionage?"

"You know I can't tell."

"Of course not. You just show up and torment the devil out of me, but you can't tell me why."

Jitty nodded. "That's pretty much it." She stood up. "But while I'm all dressed up, I think I might pay Madame Tomeeka a visit and perk up her day." She grinned wickedly. "I could send her spinnin'."

"Don't you dare. Tammy doesn't need you meddling in her psychic business." I had a sudden thought. "But you know, it might not be a bad idea to see if Tammy can help us figure out what happened to Son. We're not having a lot of luck asking the living. We may as well ask the dead."

I abandoned the PI offices and headed to the kitchen. Sweetie Pie was asleep in the sun on the floor, and Pluto had curled up in a sunny window. I considered waking my sidekicks, but I let them snooze while I made a quick run to Tammy's house. I'd planned to meet Tinkie and Cece later at Millie's Café.

The day was perfectly crisp, a cold January without humidity. When I inhaled, my lungs ached. The winter vista made me stop the car at the end of the drive and revel in the natural beauty of the Delta. The brownish earth, fallow until the spring planting, met the blue, blue sky at the horizon. Clouds, puffed white but rimmed with pale gold, contrasted against the blue. It looked like an Ascension painting. I absorbed my fill and turned the car toward town. Tammy would have a message for me. I felt it in my bones.

7

Tammy had a small cottage surrounded by incredible white oak trees. She lived in a part of Zinnia known as the Grove. When Zinnia had been segregated, the Grove was where black people lived. I hadn't been aware of such things as a child, when I'd gone home from school with Tammy and played in her front yard, swept bare of leaves by her grandmother. I never thought to ask what had happened to Tammy's mother. She seemed happy and safe with her granny, and, like most children, I'd accepted the situation without question. Now, as an adult, I knew Tammy's early life held tragedy.

My memories of childhood were good ones, of being safe, protected, and loved. There wasn't a problem in my world that my parents couldn't solve. Fear was unknown to me. What a shame that all children didn't have the same.

I tapped on her door and waited for her to let me in. "I had a cancelation," Tammy said. "Come on in and I'll put on a pot of coffee."

"Sure." After all the coffee I'd drunk, I probably wouldn't sleep for a week, but I loved sitting at Tammy's kitchen table drinking coffee and talking.

Tammy's business as a psychic medium was booming, and I was positive she could have bought a brand-new house in any part of town, but she liked it where she was. The house had belonged to her grandmother, and Bessie Odom had been a force to be reckoned with. She'd marched with Dr. Martin Luther King and changed the life of many Americans. Just as Dahlia House was home to me, this was Tammy's touchstone, the place that grounded her.

While Tammy made the coffee, I picked up a tarot deck and shuffled the cards.

"Do you want a reading?" Tammy asked.

"I didn't come for a reading, but I sure wouldn't mind. Good way to kick the new year off."

"You sure?" She looked at me over her shoulder with an amused expression. She knew I was afraid of what she might tell me.

"I'm sure, but first I want to ask about Daryl 'Son' McFee. I need to know what happened to him and if we can possibly recover the body."

"I remember when he and his mama ran off the road just before the Sunflower River Bridge. She drowned in the car and his body disappeared."

"Exactly."

"I've always wondered if someone made him take that plunge."

"Like forced him off the road?"

"That, or damaged a tire or maybe shot out the windshield."

Tammy had a handful of violent possibilities. "Do any of them feel right? Can you call him up and ask?"

"Yeah, sure. Nine-one-one, I'd like to speak to a dead person."

"You're a riot." I took the steaming cup of coffee she offered.

"And you can't seem to learn the rules of the Great Beyond. I'd think you're acting deliberately obtuse if I didn't know better. You'd never do that to a friend."

I rolled my eyes. "Okay, I was being pushy. But can you help me?"

"Hold on." She sipped her coffee, then set it down and closed her eyes. "I'm scanning the Sunflower River." She nodded, made a little humming sound, and opened her eyes. "I can't get any sense of Son McFee."

"Would a picture help?"

"I know what he looks like. Cleo used to visit me sometimes, and Son would pick her up. He was a handsome boy who always came to the door to collect his mother. He didn't sit in the car in the yard and blast the horn like some people."

"I know what you mean." I searched Tammy's face. Sometimes she tried to protect me, but this wasn't one of those times. "It's just a blank?"

"If his body were underwater in that river, it would seem that his spirit would remain close. Now, that's not true in all cases, but a violent death like that, the body, even if it's just bones, is like an anchor to the ethereal spirit. But it could also be true that he died and instantly transitioned. It's different for each soul."

"So he could be in the river, or he might not be?"

"That's pretty much it. Sarah Booth, I can't command the spirits to tell their secrets. But I have a sense Cleo is around me."

"Cleo?" I sat up. "Can she tell us what happened?"

Tammy closed her eyes. She inhaled slowly and seemed never to exhale. Finally, she let out her breath and a soft, cultured voice said, "Save Son. Please. Save him."

Tammy's posture returned to normal, and she looked at me. "She was barely here," she said. "Some spirits come through strong, but it takes so much energy. Others are like a wisp of smoke or fog. They pass through me. I'm surprised she could speak so clearly."

"'Save Son.'" That was what she said. "Was she saying this now or was she still at the river, knowing her child had been swept from the car?"

Tammy shook her head. "I didn't really get a sense of her; a muted umber suit of some type, a sense of lightness, of air. She wasn't dripping water, like someone who obviously drowned should. I don't know, Sarah Booth. This spirit business confuses me as much as anyone else. Let me read your cards."

Cowardice was such an unattractive trait that I smiled and held the cards out to her. "I already shuffled them for you."

Tammy signaled me to move closer, and I did. She shuffled once and offered the deck for me to cut. She laid the cards out carefully in a pattern she'd told me was the Celtic Cross. I knew some of the images and symbols, but the cards held no true meaning for me. Some looked scary, but often those only meant change.

Tammy tapped the first card, the Page of Pentacles. "New case, new adventure." She went on to stop at the image of a woman, a queen, sitting on a throne in the middle of a river as the water rushed all around her. "Cleo."

When she stopped at the Knight of Pentacles, she looked at me. "This card represents Son, and it's in the position of the future. The cards don't tell me where Son is, but they tell me he's a part of your future. The final outcome is Apollo, the Sun. Apollo was the messenger of the gods, the most handsome of the gods."

"I'm going to meet a handsome man?"

She laughed. "Is that your concern? I thought you were searching for a lost son?"

"Sad to say, but Son is lost only to a dead woman. His father and sister are just glad he's not there to take his part of the inheritance."

"He'll plague them and you for the next bit of time. He may be dead, but his presence is everywhere."

"Thanks, Tammy."

"I wish there were specific answers, Sarah Booth. I do. I'd love to be able to tell people, 'Oh, sell that piece of property. It's the perfect time.' Or, 'Your son will grow out of his rebellious drug use and lead a happy life.' I wish I had the answers for you and all the other people who come to me because they're troubled and afraid."

"I do too, Tammy. You'd share with the world, because that's who you are."

"How is Tinkie doing since you found Libby Marie's mother?"

"She's okay. She doesn't talk about it a lot, which I understand. I know the Smiths have brought Libby to visit more than once. Oscar and Tinkie were at their Christmas party. I think it will all work out."

"Good." Tammy nodded. "Time will ease the pain for Tinkie, and soon each moment with that child will bring only joy."

"Wisdom, Tammy. That's wisdom."

"Time doesn't heal all wounds, but it does make the wound less painful."

I knew from personal experience she spoke the truth. "Thanks for your help."

"Tell Tinkie to stop by for a complimentary reading."

"Sure." Tammy never charged either of us. "I'm surprised she hasn't been by, but I guess we've been a little busy."

"Busy is good. Keeps you off the streets and out of the bars."

"As if I had time to go cavorting around the clubs. I haven't been to Scott's in over three weeks. Now that's just wrong."

"We'll plan a girls' night out. Soon."

"Why not?" I agreed. "It's a date."

I took my leave, still thinking of the things I'd seen and heard at Tammy's kitchen table. Cleo wanted someone to save her son. From the river, from himself, from eternal wandering? I couldn't say what Cleo feared for her son. The one takeaway I had no doubts about—Cleo loved Son and she blamed him for nothing. She could have said, "Son caused the accident." Or, "Forgive Son." But she wanted him saved.

My visit with Tammy put me right on time to meet my friends for an early meal. I already had my menu planned—fried chicken, green beans seasoned with Millie's secret ingredients, and a bowl of mustard greens with some cornbread. I intended to show my tick nature, meaning I was going to eat until I almost popped.

When I pulled into the parking lot, my friends were already there.

"Sarah Booth!" They stood up to greet me with hugs and air-kisses. They acted like we hadn't seen each other in a hundred years.

I settled at the table and we placed our orders. The café smelled like heaven, and waitresses bustled around putting heaping plates in front of hungry customers. My mouth watered as I waited for my food.

I filled Tinkie and Cece in on Tammy's observations. "I wish the spirits would just tell us what we ask."

Cece laughed. "Then you'd be out of a job, silly. If folks could just go to Tammy, why would they need an investigator?"

I hated it that Cece was right, yet she was. We gabbed a bit about Jaytee and Oscar and the men who made up a big part of our lives. "Scott has an offer to tour the Netherlands, France, and England next month," Cece said. "He should take it. Even though I'll miss Jaytee a lot."

"He should. Scott's doing great here with the club, but if he tours, he'll really boost his business here. Europeans would swarm Sunflower County."

"He won't go anywhere if he thinks he'll miss the chance to win your heart." Cece looked hard at me.

"I'm not in a place to consider letting my heart out for a walk, much less a marathon." I caught both of their hands. "I refuse to jump into bed with Scott or Coleman or Harold or Tom, Dick, and Harry. I can't. I have to be certain this time that I can trust my lover with my heart, and I have every right to demand all the time I need to make sure."

Cece patted my hand. "You do, dahlink. You do."

"Good for you, Sarah Booth. We shouldn't be so pushy. Hey, here comes Marco. And he looks a bit frazzled."

Cece sat up taller. "I got a terrific photo spread at Evermore for tomorrow's paper. Even some shots of Colin nosing around the production. And that Susan! Holy cow, she came down in this slinky dress and was all over Marco. She looked like a spider with that big baby-belly and her skinny arms and legs. And she's physically fit. She did a backward flip over the sofa. It wasn't pretty, but she managed it."

"She wants to be in the movie," I said.

"She's got a beach ball in her dress," Cece said. "Not meaning to be unkind, but she's at the lumbering stage of pregnancy. She should cool it until she delivers."

"Right." We halted the conversation when Marco came our way.

"Join us," Tinkie said.

"My god, I had to get out of that house. That woman is driving me insane."

We laughed out loud. "I was just telling them how desperate Susan is to be in the movie."

He sighed. "You wouldn't believe . . ."

But we all would.

When Millie spied Marco at our table, she hurried into the office and came out with a pen and a black-and-white photo of the director from one of his movies. "*Mafia Don* was a great film. Would you mind autographing this photo?"

I leaned in to see the black-and-white of Marco when he'd been a young actor, a hot ticket on the Hollywood scene. He wore a flashy suit and a fedora tipped slightly over his right eye. "Handsome."

He signed the photo with a flourish. "Thank you, Millie. How about a vegetable plate and some cornbread?"

"Coming right up."

Before Millie could leave, he captured her hand and kissed the back of her fingers. "You're a true lady and a godsend to this hungry man who has come to love Southern cuisine."

"Marco, once more of the crew arrives, would you need me to take on the craft service?" Millie shot me a quick look seeking reassurance. I nodded.

"A brilliant idea! You are not only the best cook in the Southeast, but you are a damn genius. You're hired. Starting Friday. If you could cater lunch and some snacks. For about a dozen people. There's a full kitchen at Evermore."

"You'll adore the kitchen," Tinkie chimed in. "It has everything you could want and more."

"The weather is supposed to be glum. I'm thinking chicken and dumplings," Millie said. "I do have one question, Marco?"

"What is it?" He gave her his full attention. Contrary to the behavior normally associated with powerful directors, Marco had lovely manners. He and Lorraine had charmed most of the town. They were eccentric and a bit wild, buzzing around Zinnia on low-slung motorcycles in leathers and helmets. But they were kind and considerate. Sister, on the other hand, had created nothing but enemies.

"I just read an article in the *National Enquirer* that

said Leo DiCaprio breaks up with women when they hit their twenty-fifth birthday. Is that true?"

Marco's eyes widened. "Lorraine keeps up with Leo better than I do. He has dated a bevy of beautiful young girls, but I've never asked their age. They are young though. And there seems to be a new one on a regular basis."

Millie arched her eyebrows at Cece. "I wish you'd write stories like that in the *Dispatch*. I love my tabloids, but sometimes they just make things up."

"Maybe we could do a weekly celebrity column," Cece said. "Nothing would be more fun than bird-dogging celebrities. So, Marco, who's going to play Son in the movie?"

"I have a long list of potential candidates, but I will tell you that Ian Somerhalder is my pick right now. We could film *Dead and Gone* while he's on break from *The Vampire Diaries*. Ian's from Covington, Louisiana, so he'll have the Southern drawl down perfectly."

"He is a very handsome young man who puts me in mind of Son," Millie agreed. "Who for Colin?"

"That's a tough one," Marco said, perfectly willing to play the game of casting the film with her. "What about Liam Neeson?"

"Perfect!" Millie almost squealed. "And Cleo?"

"Because the film will feature a number of juicy flashbacks detailing the McFees' lives prior to the accident, I've put out feelers to Sandra Bullock."

This time Millie's squeal caused customers to stop eating. "Oh, this is going to be the best time ever."

"If the screenplay is as good as I anticipate, it will be a great time. Filming on location is always exciting."

"And you want to finish up before the heat hits," Millie said. "Humidity will make you cry for your mama."

Marco laughed, and I loved him for the way he treated Millie. Someone had raised him right.

While we had Marco at the table, Tinkie and I made our report, which consisted of a bunch of failed efforts.

"What's next?" Marco asked.

"I'll go to the newspaper to pull all the old stories about the accident. Then we'll try to find the private investigator that Colin hired, the insurance agent, a few more leads."

"If Colin hired a pirate investigator, it seems he would have turned up something."

Millie shook her head slowly. "The word was that Hoots didn't find anything, not a shred of evidence. But that didn't stop Colin from painting Son as a villain."

"Why would Colin do that?" Tinkie asked. "He was the golden child, the heir to the McFee dynasty when he was a young man. I knew a girl who dated Son in college, and he was always talking about the things his father expected. He got a business degree so he could work in the family business."

"Why did Colin grow to hate him so?" I asked.

Millie picked up the story. "After Son left school, he moved to Memphis and did very well. Colin made him start at the bottom of McFee Enterprises, but before long he was a VP of investments or something like that. He was doing well. I heard he was engaged to be married. A Memphis belle. And then things went to hell."

"Drugs," Tinkie said. "Do you know how many people from all walks of life are hooked on prescription pain killers?"

I frowned. "No, and why would you?"

She grinned. "Doc Sawyer gave a talk at the Rotary Club last week. Oscar reported back to me. Doc is on a tear about all of this. He's blaming the pharmaceutical companies and the doctors who are too free with a prescription pad."

Coleman had been fighting the movement of drugs and guns through the Delta for years. Gangs from Memphis had moved south, using the outlying buildings on the big farms for storage until the shipments were dispersed. It was a serious problem, but not my problem at the moment.

"Who was Son engaged to?"

"Bess Billingsworth. Of *the* Billingsworths." Millie was on top of the gossip, I had to give her that.

I didn't have Tinkie's command of the blue-blood name list. "Who is that?"

"They're a pillar of Memphis. Cotton, shipping, a chain of barbecue joints, a record company." Tinkie ticked each item off using her fingers. "You name it, the Billingsworths are involved in it."

"Do you know Bess?"

She shrugged. "I knew her in school, but we weren't friends."

"But you can get her phone number and set up an interview in case we need to talk to her?"

"Can do."

"Good. I'll check the newspaper articles. Hoots lives in Hollywood, Mississippi, so I'll head there after the paper. Maybe we can kill two birds with one stone." I said it and then clapped a hand over my mouth. I was turning into my aunt Loulane, spouting adages and bits of wisdom culled over the past two hundred years.

Tinkie's beautiful laughter bridged the awkward moment where Marco looked at me in confusion. It would take too long to explain to him how I'd lived with my aunt who had a saying for every single moment in time.

"If we can figure out why Son fell off the straight and narrow, we might learn something valuable," I said.

"He had everything. Why get involved in drugs?" Cece asked.

"That's what we need to find out." I stood and stretched, ready for action.

Cece put a hand on Marco's wrist. "Can I print the story of the actors you're considering?"

"Absolutely," he said. "There is no bad news when it comes to a film getting made. The more press we have, the more likely the studio is to green light the project."

One thing troubled me. "Can Colin really pull the plug on this?"

Marco's big laugh caused the diners to glance his way, most of them smiling. "No, not Colin. He has plenty of money, but it just happens that the head of the studio is a personal friend of mine. If Colin tries to push or influence him, Rodney will just dig in his heels and be more determined than ever to make the film. What could really hurt is a bad script."

"That will never happen if Roon Talley is the writer," Millie said with great confidence. She passed behind Marco with an armload of lunch plates, then stopped in her tracks. "Is he coming to Zinnia too?"

Marco grinned. "He'll be here shortly. He likes to get a feel for the locale, and say what you like, the South is a place you have to experience."

"I am dying!" Millie put down the tray and fanned herself with some napkins. "Roon Talley in Zinnia! But before I die, I have to finish up in the kitchen."

"I'm going to dig into McFee Enterprises," Tinkie said. "While you're at the newspaper, I'll go to the bank and enlist Harold's skills."

"Great idea."

As we adjourned, the table was swarmed by Zinnians savvy enough to know who Marco St. John was. We left him signing napkins and shaking hands with his many fans. It put me in mind of Graf Milieu, my former fiancé, who was also an actor. I hoped things were working out in Hollywood for Graf. I wished him well. Graf had not done anything dishonorable or given me cause to hate him, which would have been easier in some ways. But he was the past, and right now I had a case to solve and no time for moping around thinking about what might have been.

Cece had walked to Millie's from the newspaper, only a few short blocks away, and since I'd eaten my weight in Millie's fine cooking, I waddled back with her.

"Any progress on finding out what happened to Son?" she asked.

"I even stopped by Madame Tomeeka's. No dice. Tammy did a little session and got something from Cleo, who said to 'save Son,' but that was it. I didn't want to bring up our psychic friend in front of Marco. He probably already thinks Southerners are nuts."

"Marco's a smart man. He *knows* we're nuts." Cece stopped in front of her favorite boutique to check out a mannequin wearing a turquoise colorblock sweater, skinny black pants, and a pair of knee-high boots with incredible leather work. Instead of going inside for a more personal inspection, Cece remained on the cold sidewalk. "I had a chat with Lorraine this morning. She's one of us, Sarah Booth. Wicked sense of humor, determined to tell this story. She and Marco are a great team. This is going to be a bang-up movie."

"What if I can't find out what happened to cause that

accident? If Marco moves forward with his movie plans based on the assumption my skills will give him answers, he might lose a lot of money. What if I can't deliver the resolution Marco needs?"

Cece rounded on me. "I'm a lot more worried about you and Tinkie getting shot than I am about a movie. Tinkie told me about the gunshot incident at the Highway 12 bridge. And don't hand me that 'it was a warning' bull-crap. Maybe the homicidal maniac with a gun is just a terrible shot. Maybe next time you won't be so lucky."

"Calm down. It was probably a deer hunter." I didn't believe that for a minute, but I also realized that if some-one had wanted to kill Tinkie and me, they could have. Easily. We were sitting ducks on the verge without a bit of cover.

"You'd better come up with a better story than that for Coleman. He's not an idiot and neither am I."

"Okay, the shot *was* probably a warning," I conceded because it was pointless to lie to Cece. She was a Geiger counter of truth and could easily detect a plutonium lie. "The question is, from whom and what did they hope to accomplish?"

"What does Coleman say?" When I didn't answer in-stantly, Cece's expression went from considered worry to outrage. "You didn't tell Coleman about someone shoot-ing at you and Tinkie."

My face had given me away. "I will. I have to. Cole-man and I have a deal and I won't break my word."

"You'd better tell him, and soon. If he finds out before you spill the beans, he's going to be pissed. Omission is also lying." It was too cold to stand on the sidewalk bick-ering. We started forward side by side. "So, who do you think is taking potshots at you?"

I told her about the rifle at Evermore—the close-to-one-million-dollar rifle that had been fired recently by someone in a household of people who probably couldn't load a gun—with the exception of Colin McFee. It would be just like Colin to use an expensive weapon to shoot at people he considered a nuisance. "I think it was Colin trying to spook us, but he can't really kill us. He's running for office, and a potential murder charge would blow up his chances."

"He would just blame it on Putin." Cece was only half kidding.

"There's no need for anyone to try to scare us off. Tinkie and I haven't hit a hot lead yet, and I don't know that we can find out anything about Son."

"Look at it like this. If someone is shooting at you, you're getting too close for comfort. Besides, have you ever failed?"

"I've been saved from failure by the loyalty of my friends." And sometimes at a high cost. My friends sometimes put themselves in danger to help or protect me. "The whole potshot incident doesn't make any sense. That's why I haven't told Coleman."

"You should drop the case right now, but I know you won't. You're pigheaded. But you can still count me in. I'll help. The arrival of Black Tar Productions has given me some great stories and photos that have been picked up internationally. And to be honest, I'd like to know what really happened that night. I didn't know Son well, but he was one of the few people who was kind to me when I was still Cecil but longing to be Cece."

"Do you have any theories about what happened that night?"

"Follow the money." She opened the door of the

newspaper and I stepped into the familiar chaos that was her everyday life. Reporters pounded out stories and threw caustic remarks at each other as editors went over photos and copy. I loved the paper.

I knew where the newspaper's morgue was, so I went there and let Cece work in peace. The accident had happened five years earlier, so I had no trouble finding the archives and going through the film that contained the news of Sunflower and surrounding counties.

Cleo's tragic death and Son's disappearance had been front-page fodder for weeks. The initial accident, the later investigations and reports, the photos. I'd seen some of the crime-scene photos at the Washington County sheriff's office, but the newspaper shots were better. The photographer had hired a helicopter and took excellent pix of the flooded and swollen Sunflower River. The devastation of the flood, as the river expanded miles outside of its banks, left no doubt that Mother Nature couldn't be controlled. It was no wonder Son's body hadn't been recovered.

It could have been swept into a tree line or brake miles away from the point where the SUV entered the river. The land was awash with water at the Highway 12 bridge. With the wide, swift flow of the floodwaters, I was actually surprised something hadn't crashed into the bridge and taken it out.

I studied every inch of each photo, looking for indications of what had caused the accident. In one shot, there were deep ruts off the shoulder where the car had lost the road. Several attempts had been made to wrest the vehicle back onto the blacktop, but the car had veered right and gone into the river.

Why had Son lost control? Weather, accident, human failing, or intervention?

There were no answers to my questions in the newspaper accounts. The *Dispatch* reporters had been careful not to assign blame. They didn't have to. Colin and Sister did it themselves, giving interview after interview about how Son had destroyed his life with drugs. They painted Cleo as the ever-forgiving mother who simply couldn't accept that Son was a lost cause.

"'Save him.'" The words echoed in the small, musty newspaper morgue. While Colin and Sister might not be fair or just in placing the blame for the accident on Son, they were correct about Cleo. She had loved Son. And still did.

Whether it was my imagination or the true echo of Cleo's request, my determination to find out what had really happened to Son was renewed. If I couldn't recover his body and see it placed in a final resting place, I intended to clear his name if he was innocent.

Still thinking about the tire marks, I stopped by Cece's office and said goodbye. I was almost out the door when another thought occurred to me. If the rain had been coming down in sheets, as everyone had described, wouldn't the tire treads have been washed away? They were so clear. They looked almost as if they'd been made *after* the rain stopped.

If there was foul play in Son's death, then the rifle shots at Tinkie and me were serious warnings. The next attempt might not be merely an attempt. It could have a very different outcome.

8

The shorter days of winter left me with the blues as I drove home from the newspaper. Dusk settled over the barren fields, and, far in the gloaming, the lights of distant houses began to blink on. I would find my haven inside Dahlia House, but the fading light reminded me of all the endings in my life. Melancholy was a disease to some, but not to the poet Keats—or to my spinster aunt, who had walked away from love and marriage to care for me in my family home.

When the blue hour dropped over us, Aunt Loulane would sometimes grow still as she looked out the window of Dahlia House. This was the time I most intensely missed my parents. She would repeat Keats's "Ode to Melancholy." I remembered some of the lines.

But when the melancholy fit shall fall
Sudden from heaven like a weeping cloud,
That fosters the droop-headed flowers all,
And hides the green hill in an April shroud;
Then glut thy sorrow on a morning rose,
Or on the rainbow of the salt sand-wave,
Or on the wealth of globed peonies

Nature was the balm for sorrow, and there was no running away from emotions. Aunt Loulane was right about both things—up to a point.

I stopped in front of the house and was greeted by the wonderful baying of Sweetie Pie. Pluto got into the act and came to rub against my legs. It was good to be home.

I raced the critters into the house and hurried to the kitchen, which I flooded with light, and turned on the oven. Keats's remedy for sadness was to look upon beauty. I had another solution. Carbohydrates were the best medicine. I would make us something sinful and bad, because when the gut was full, all the blood rushed from the brain to aid in digestion. Without fuel, the brain would turn off.

Though no one else supported my theory, I didn't care. I would make pasta with a cheese sauce. Carbohydrates *and* fat. I would shut down my melancholy brain, and soon I would be in the best of moods, which I would maintain with a bit of Jack Daniel's.

For a moment I saw Aunt Loulane at the kitchen door, frowning. She would not approve of my self-medication. I was about to tell her I'd be fine when I heard another voice.

"Once on the lips, forever on the hips. I can't have fat spies."

I whirled around to discover that Megan Follows, in

her Queen Catherine getup from *Reign*, stood in my kitchen. Begowned, bejeweled, and a true badass, Queen Catherine de' Medici of France was not someone I wanted for a foe. Her reputation for espionage—and ruthlessness—had survived the centuries.

"I'm not your spy." I wanted to kick myself for answering as if she were real. Jitty had surprised me, but I wasn't a total goober. I knew this was one more appearance on her theme of espionage.

"And you never will be if your butt spreads any more. My ladies are quite accomplished at the art of bedding a man and learning his secrets. So far, you've provided me with nothing useful. My ladies were known as the Flying Squadron. Beautiful, smart, talented in the ways of the bedroom. I trained them well."

"Jitty! Stop it. I've had a hard day. I've been beset by Sister McFee, and I'm stalled in my case. I don't need you haranguing me."

"Yesterday you were in a bad mood because someone took a shot at you and your partner." Jitty was all over it.

"Thanks, Sherlock. Brilliant deduction."

"Do you think if you got shot in the head and lived you could still produce an heir?"

Now that was a Catherine de' Medici question if ever I'd heard one. "Get out of my kitchen. That's a terrible question to ask."

"The world operates on information. Either you provide it or . . . you die." She came toward me, her upswept 'do and crown perfectly set upon her regal head. "You'll spy for me, Sarah Booth. You'll discover what I need to know."

She was so commanding in her role that I almost agreed. Sweetie Pie came to my rescue and barked at Jitty as if to say, "Back off. Don't be so pushy," and I regained my balance. "If we had a dungeon in Dahlia House, I'd put you there. Now stop it. What is with you and this spy business? Who should I spy on? What is it you want to know?"

Jitty's gown slowly disintegrated and she morphed from the queen of bad back to my beautiful haint. "Secrets are more powerful than coin."

"Great. How about a hint as to whose secrets I need to be plundering. I'm not opposed to a bit of spying if I know what I'm seeking. What do you want to know?"

But there was no answer because Jitty had vaporized. She was gone on a puff of regal sounding bugles.

The knock at the front door was almost instantaneous. When I pulled it open, I was delighted to see Harold and the impish Roscoe. Harold arched an eyebrow. "Are you okay?"

"Just a little frazzled, but fine."

"I thought I might take you to dinner at the Prince Albert. A little wine, some candlelight, maybe a dance or two . . ."

The invitation tempted me, but I'd begun preparation for my own carbo-blast dinner. "Come inside and open a bottle of wine. I'm making pasta."

"Even better." Harold and Roscoe followed me into the kitchen. Before I could get the wine, Roscoe and Sweetie took off out the doggie door and disappeared into the night. They were perfectly safe, with nothing but acres and acres of farmland to romp on. Pluto stretched out in front of the stove, which I'd turned on to heat some bread.

Harold was handy in the kitchen because he loved to entertain. As I finished cooking, Harold opened the wine and then grated fresh Parmesan cheese to put atop the pasta. I made enough for the two dogs, and I found some fresh grilled chicken for Pluto. He was more of a Paleo-diet kitty than carbs, though he did enjoy a taste of buttered bread every now and again.

"I'm glad you came over." I topped off Harold's wine. "I was going to call you anyway."

"So, you have ulterior motives toward me. I hope they're romantic."

"In a way. But probably not the way you're thinking." I tossed the pasta in the cheese sauce and added some fresh steamed broccoli. "Do you know Bess Billingsworth?" It was a fair question. Harold was hooked into the world of society belles and since he was one of the most eligible bachelors in the Southeast, he had a very busy social schedule.

"I do." He went to the stove to retrieve the bread.

"Avoiding eye contact for a reason?"

He looked at me. "I dated Bess a few times. I was her escort to the Memphis Cotillion."

"Holy cow, Harold, she's my age or close. I didn't think they let anyone our age be a debutante."

He laughed long and hard. "She wasn't a debutante, Sarah Booth. We attended the dance as guests of her niece. You know, your aunt Loulane would turn in her grave at your total lack of knowledge of how female society operates."

Red flushed my face. I felt like a fool. The rules of society had never interested me, but that was a pretty silly gaffe. "Oh, that makes more sense. Did you date Bess before or after her engagement to Son?"

"After."

Now that my embarrassment had passed, I had a

multitude of questions. "How did you come to date her? Not that you aren't one of the best catches in the Delta, but she lives in Memphis."

"Which is an hour away, not on the far side of the moon." Harold's amusement made me laugh.

"True. But how did you meet?"

"At a museum opening. She's a beautiful woman, but she has her share of issues."

"Did she talk about Son?"

"A lot." He grinned wickedly. "Feed me and I might tell you. I have to withhold the juicy parts or I fear you'll be done with me."

"You make me sound heartless." I knew he was teasing me, but it was a sore tooth.

"And I know you aren't ready for romance. No problem. I enjoy your company, so let's leave it at that."

I cut the toasted French bread and served the pasta with a fresh spinach salad. We ate in the kitchen, which was far cozier than the big dining room. Harold, adept at small talk, kept me amused as we ate. Sweetie Pie and Roscoe tore through the kitchen, gobbled their food, and went back outside.

When I'd brought out some bread pudding from Millie's café, Harold agreed to tell me about Bess and Son.

"At the time of their engagement, Son and Bess were *the* couple in Memphis society. Son had all the credentials and was a hotshot in McFee Enterprises. It wasn't just the prestige and money, either, Bess really cared for Son."

"He deserved someone who loved him. He didn't get a lot of that from Colin and Sister."

"No, but he and Cleo were close. Bess said they were a lot alike. They both shared a desire to put the McFee money to use to help people. Son was involved with building homeless shelters in Memphis. He spent a lot of his personal money funding housing projects. And Cleo was all involved in literacy, especially in the Delta."

"So what happened with Bess?"

"They started dating when Son was rising in the company. They were the perfect power couple. But something went wrong with Son. He started using drugs. I know Bess fought hard to bring him back, but when he fell into a circle of friends who did a lot of drugs, she had to break off the engagement."

"I understand." And I did. It was too hard to watch someone you loved destroy himself. "But why did Son start using drugs? That's the real question. He'd worked his way up in McFee Enterprises and he rose through the ranks. He was raking in the big bucks and his daddy was proud of him. His star was ascending. So what happened?"

"Bess never understood. Or at least that's what she said. In the beginning, Son was the apple of his father's eye, and he was deeply involved in the business. It was clear Colin was grooming him to be the heir to all things McFee. Sister was the neglected child. She was the one Colin never had time for. But Son. He was everything. Where Colin's talent was in renovating space and creating something wonderful, Son's talent was with business and investing. They should have been perfectly matched as a team."

"And Son gave it all up for drugs? That doesn't make sense. He never stuck me as someone who wanted to escape his life." My dealings with Son in college were minimal, but the few times I'd been around him, he'd been thoughtful and kind. We'd taken a drama class together, and Son had gone out of his way to befriend a freshman from Leakesville, Mississippi, who flubbed a line in a production. Son didn't seek the spotlight, but it always seemed to find him.

"Bess said the same thing. He enjoyed his life."

"And she had no clue what provoked him to take drugs?"

"She had an assumption that Son found himself in a moral quagmire. She described Son as a throwback to Jamie McFee. True moral rectitude, and no tolerance for liars, cheats, whoremongers, and such. Bess felt that Son found out something that he couldn't accept. He was put into an untenable position. Whether it was at McFee Enterprises or in a secret part of his personal life, he never told her."

"It must have been something big to push him into using drugs."

"Or it could be that he started out on a lark, a recreational binge, and it got out of hand. Disposable income can be deadly for some personality types."

"We need to check his medical records. Maybe there was an illness. If he was into pain killers, maybe his drug use had a medical origin. Some of those are highly addictive."

Harold stood up to clear the table. "I'll wash if you'll dry. You can't check medical records tonight. Let's take a glass of wine to the porch." He frowned with the plates in his hand. "If he had a terrible disease, maybe he did deliberately drive off the road."

"You're saying he might have committed suicide."

"If he was really sick . . ." He offered a spoon of leftover sauce to Pluto, who licked daintily.

"But he wouldn't kill his mother, would he?"

"It doesn't sound like the Son Bess described, but it's possible. People who use drugs for a long period of time sometimes don't think clearly."

"He'd been in rehab." Sadness settled over me. "I don't want him to be guilty of killing Cleo."

Harold ran hot water into the sink. "Neither do I," he said.

I had a dishwasher, but it was fun to do the dishes together. I thought about the possibility that the wreck was a suicide as I cleared a few dishes from the draining rack. "I don't see Son killing his mother. I don't."

"I hope that's what you find out. So, what's next?"

"I want to talk to Bess and to Linda Thorne, the insurance adjuster who paid out on Cleo's insurance policy."

"Good idea. I'll give you Bess's number."

I gave him a sidelong glance. "You kept it?"

He laughed. "Jealous?"

"No." But maybe I was, a little.

"Bess married two years ago. She's happy and very pregnant."

"Good for her." And I meant it.

Harold wisely said nothing and washed the plates.

"You know, I—"

A shadow darker than the night ran through the barn's booger light that I'd set up after Gertrude Strom's last attempt to shoot me. The outdoor light illuminated the area on the side of the barn and I could easily see it from the kitchen window.

"Did you see that?" I asked Harold.

"What?"

He'd been looking down into the dishwater. "There's someone outside."

Harold dried his hands. "Are you sure?"

"Someone ran into the barn."

He dialed his cellphone. "Coleman, someone is in Sarah Booth's barn."

He hung up and put his arm around me to draw me away from the window. "He's on the way with DeWayne."

"The intruder will be gone by the time they get here." I went to the parlor and got my gun from the antique hunt board. I kept it in a drawer. I'd been better about remembering to bring it out of the car trunk.

"You are not going out there to hunt trouble." Harold took the gun from me.

"We can apprehend the trespasser."

"*You* can get yourself shot. Not going to happen on my watch. Let's just hope it was a moon shadow."

"We need to check." I was sick of people coming on my property and threatening me. "My horses and the dogs are out there. If someone mean is out there, they can hurt the animals. We have to go look."

While Harold was always going to put our safety high on the list, protection of Sweetie and Roscoe was at the top. "You stay here." He gave me a look that brooked no disobedience.

"I will not." I wasn't about to let Harold face danger while I hid in the house.

"Promise me or we'll both wait until Coleman gets here." I stepped around him and ran into the mudroom and cracked the back door.

"Sarah Booth!" His hand settled heavily on my shoulder.

Sweetie's long, mournful howl echoed on the crisp night air. Roscoe's wicked bark followed. The dogs were onto something. And I wasn't waiting for Coleman to make sure Sweetie was safe. Harold had the same idea. He bolted out the back door and I followed.

"There!"

A tall person ran from behind the barn and across the pasture. As I watched, the dark figure climbed the pasture fence and took off across the fallow cotton fields. Sweetie was in hot pursuit, but when I called her back, she returned with Roscoe at her side. Since I couldn't tell if the fleeing figure had a gun or not, I didn't want to risk Sweetie Pie and Roscoe getting shot.

I'd just grabbed her collar when I heard the wail of a siren and flashing blue lights turned down the driveway. Coleman had arrived.

"Could you tell who it was?" Harold asked as he caught Roscoe in his arms. Together we walked to the front of the house to meet Coleman.

"I couldn't."

"They didn't appear armed."

"No." I hadn't seen a weapon, but that didn't guarantee the trespasser wasn't armed. "It wasn't Gertrude. Too tall."

"That's a good thing."

Coleman jumped out of the car and came toward us, hand on his weapon.

"The interloper is gone," Harold said, pointing in the direction the figure had run. "We could tail him with Sweetie Pie, but he's probably got a vehicle hidden on a farm road. We'll never catch him."

"Everyone okay?" Coleman's hands grasped my arms. He was a bit angry at me and Harold. We'd disobeyed and run toward danger.

"We're good," I said gently. "It's just frustrating."

"Was it Gertrude?" His mind had gone down the same dark path as mine.

"No. Not her," Harold reassured him. "Too tall."

Relief touched Coleman's features. Gertrude's potential for serious injury bothered him almost as much as it did me. "We'll check it out tomorrow in the daylight. Maybe we'll find some clues."

"Then let's feed the horses and get back inside. It's cold." I was shivering, but I wasn't about to let the horses go unfed.

"I can't stay long," Coleman said briskly. "Someone is defacing Colin McFee's signs along Highway 8. He's threatening to send an armed security team, which is the last thing I need. An O.K. Corral shootout over billboards."

"He wants to shoot someone over a billboard?" I asked.

"Colin thinks Putin wants to destroy his chances to be a U.S. senator. He believes the defaced signs are part of a larger Russian conspiracy."

"Why would Putin even care about a road sign on a two-lane road?" I knew once the question was out there, I would regret asking it.

"Because Putin and Colin, at least in Colin's mind, are locked in a deadly battle for male dominance." Coleman was amused, but only a little. "DeWayne is out there preventing Colin and his thugs from igniting World War III." He looked beyond me at Harold. "I'll check the barn. Can you get Sarah Booth inside and keep her safe?"

"I may have to use force," Harold said. They both acted as if I weren't standing right in front of them.

"You have my permission to use necessary force."

Coleman reached behind his back and brought up a pair of handcuffs. He tossed them to Harold. "Do what you must."

"Hey!" I didn't have to pretend indignation. "Hey, you can't treat me like a balky mule."

"You're right," Harold said as Coleman strode toward the barn. "A mule can be trained. A Sarah Booth is another story."

I took a fake swing at him, but he easily dodged. "Go inside. I'll take care of the horses. I'm right behind you. Coleman is making sure the property is safe." He leaned closer and whispered, "I think it was a spy from Colin's camp."

I thought of Jitty and her latest obsession with spies. I had to agree with Harold. "Lurking around the barn won't give a spy any useful information."

He turned me toward the door and nudged me forward. "But if they're Russian spies, they might not know that. Go inside while I finish in the barn. We can talk by the fire."

The truth was, Coleman and Harold could handle the barn check, and I was freezing. "I'll make some coffee and call that insurance adjustor, Linda Thorne. Maybe she'll be able to tell us something about the policy that will shed light on Son's and Cleo's death."

9

Linda Thorne's annoyance at my evening call came through the phone loud and clear, but I pressed forward. Because Tinkie had a talent for soothing people's ruffled feathers, she could have handled Linda with one hand tied behind her back. I muddled through as best I could. I propped my feet on my desk in the detective agency office and let Linda rant at me for my lack of consideration. While Linda's words assaulted one ear, with the other I heard the distant sound of Coleman's and Harold's laughter. They were in the parlor mixing drinks. DeWayne had called in with the welcome news that he'd defused the highway sign situation. Now Coleman wasn't going to leave. Each man insisted on staying at Dahlia House because of the intruder. I was both flattered and annoyed. And they seemed to be having a good time without me.

"Ms. Delaney, surely you understand that a person needs some time away from the job?" Linda continued. "I'm in my office at eight sharp, and I don't leave until six. It's almost nine now and I want to relax. People don't work after six o'clock in the evening."

"I'm working," I replied.

"That's your choice. I choose not to work at nine o'clock at night."

She had a point, but I had a case to solve. "Time stands still for no man, Linda. Could you just tell me about Cleo McFee's insurance policy?"

"Why didn't you say you wanted to talk about Cleo and Son!" All hesitation was gone. "Two words. Double indemnity."

"Are you kidding me?"

"The death was ruled accidental and that meant we had to pay double. Of course, the way Colin was blathering on about how Son was hopped up on drugs and ran off the road, I insisted we fight the double indemnity because, I mean, if he was loopy on drugs, wouldn't that be murder?"

"I don't know." Actually, I was stunned by this new tidbit of information. Ten million was a lot of hot cash. Cece had said, "Follow the money."

"I warned the home office against taking out a five-million-dollar policy." Linda had been wanting to get this off her chest for a long time. "Cleo was in great health, but the monthly premium was just over a thousand a month. It was foolish to offer that kind of policy. I told the home office that, but they wouldn't listen. It was on them, not me."

I was still calculating double indemnity. "You paid out ten million?"

"We had no choice. We tried to fight it, because Cleo only had the policy for a year. They'd paid in just over twelve grand and got ten million. But Colin brought a preponderance of evidence—that's the legal wording for 'you're screwed.' We had to pay."

No wonder she wanted to talk about Cleo McFee's policy. "That's a big policy."

"We no longer write for that amount, because of Cleo's death. A day late and a dollar short. But it's on the home office, not on me."

"Colin took out the policy?"

"No, actually, Cleo took it out herself. The funds were to be used for her literacy initiative. Of course, we can't dictate what happens to the money, but that's what Cleo told me when she bought the policy."

"Is that what happened?"

Linda sighed. "I can't say."

"Oh yes, you can. If you know." I suspected Linda knew the whole story and had made it a point to keep up with the facts.

"My children go to public schools. Cleo had big plans for pre-K programs, new libraries, art and music classes resumed in the schools, visiting scientists and artists, and renewed physical education programs. Those were things we once had in public schools that have all been cut due to lack of funding and the fact wealthier families send their children to private institutions now. Not a single one of those things have happened in any of the public schools in the Delta."

Cleo's big vision had never gotten off the ground. "When was the policy purchased?"

"Ms. Delaney, there are certain ethics involved."

But she was itching to dish the dirt, I could tell by the tone of her voice. "Look, I'm a private investigator and I've been hired by Black Tar Productions to look into the matter of Son's death. It's for a movie."

"A movie?" Now she was really interested.

"They're going to film here in Zinnia. Marco and Lorraine St. John are on-site now scouting for locations. For the film to be accurate, I need to know what you know."

"Can you keep my name out of it?"

"Absolutely." At least she hadn't asked for a movie part.

"The policy was purchased twelve months before Cleo died, a year and a few days.

You know the policy has to be in effect a year *and* a day, don't you?"

I hadn't before Linda told me, but now I did and it was an interesting fact. "Was Cleo alone when she bought the insurance?"

"She came in with Sister, and she took out the policy and set up the beneficiary."

"And the money went to Colin, not Sister?"

"Yes, she was very clear. Colin was to use the money to continue the literacy programs Cleo was working to put in place."

She made her point. "And Sister was good with Colin as the beneficiary?"

"She didn't say anything except she was glad Cleo had finally come to her senses about Son and how he couldn't be trusted. She said something about how if he got hold of a large chunk of money, he'd put it up his nose and kill himself."

At the time Cleo had taken out the insurance policy

on herself, Son had been using heavily—according to gossip. Sister's statement made sense. "Did Colin know about the insurance policy?"

"I couldn't say," Linda said. "Maybe Cleo or Sister told him. Maybe they didn't."

If Colin didn't know about the payout and Sister wasn't a beneficiary, they had no motive to kill Cleo, at least not for the ten million. Of course there were plenty of other motives for murder, and the McFee family seemed to suffer from hundreds of dysfunctions.

"Thanks, Linda. I appreciate the help and I'm sorry I disturbed your evening."

"Since you're working for the production company, do you think you might get me an audition? I always wanted to be an actress. It's my dream. The insurance company is just a way to pay the bills."

"Sure. I'll speak to Marco." What would it hurt to give her a shot at her dream? Everyone and his brother would be trying to get a part. Why not Linda too?

"I do remember one thing."

"What?"

"When Cleo was setting the terms of the policy, Sister was grousing about Son and how worthless he was. This was when Sister's fourth novel hit it big. She had begun to rake in a lot of money and she was full of herself."

"Sister is always full of herself."

"Yeah, but Cleo said something."

My interest piqued. "Yeah?"

"She said people who live in glass houses shouldn't cast stones."

Now that was an old saw Aunt Loulane had used a million times when she felt I was getting on my high horse about someone else. "Did she say more?"

"Yeah, she said Sister was not in a place to disparage Son because people with secrets were always on the verge of exposure. She didn't use those exact words, but something to that effect."

"Any hint as to what Sister's secret might be?"

"Not anything solid, but it had to do with Sister riding high about her publishing successes. Rubbing people's noses in her achievements."

Maybe Sister had slept with a publisher to get her books published. Or maybe she'd pulled a trick a lot of politicians had tried—buying up books from booksellers who reported to the bestseller lists. In fact, Colin had been accused of that very thing when he'd published his book about his war with Putin, *How I Fought the Sleeping Bear—and Won*. The book had hit the bestseller list, but I'd never found a single person who admitted to buying or reading it. I'd always suspected he'd bought all the copies himself.

"Thanks, Linda. If you think of anything else, give me a call."

"I'll be in touch for my audition time."

"Sure thing."

Linda had given me a few things to ponder. Colin had plenty of money. He didn't need Cleo's insurance policy, but he'd failed to put the money where Cleo had asked. He'd betrayed her trust, and what *had* he done with the ten million? And why didn't Cleo just make the policy payable to a foundation? Why trust Colin, whom she knew was a cheater and a liar? It didn't make sense. Yet I didn't believe Cleo had been coerced by anyone. Linda would have said if Cleo had acted odd.

And what was Sister's big secret in the land of books and fame? That was something worth pursuing, because if she had a weakness I could divine, I would absolutely use it as a club to beat her off my partner. She belittled Tinkie every chance she got, and it would give me immense pleasure to squeeze her back—hard. I'd like to see Sister dancing to my tune for a change.

I was on my way to the parlor when I heard a voice whisper, "The red fox trots quietly at midnight."

I knew it was Jitty with some of her crazy spy foolishness. I ignored her and ran to the parlor where I was safe from her torment. Coleman and Harold were on another round of drinks, and I decided to join them. Sometimes it was good to drink away my worries. I would pay the piper in the morning, but tonight it was good company and good conversation.

When Tinkie pulled up the next morning, she took one look at me and put on a pot of coffee. "A Bloody Mary might be a better idea."

I only groaned at the mention of alcohol. "I think I hurt myself."

"I hope you weren't drinking alone."

"Coleman and Harold."

She laughed out loud. "Drinking with not one, but two men. You could have put that time to better use and not have a hangover."

"You sound like Jitty." The words were out before I could stop them.

Tinkie stood in front of me. "Who is this Jitty?"

I had to think fast. "My imaginary friend." I was in it deep. Tinkie was not going to let this go. Her blue eyes held my gaze.

"You've said her name a few times, always in reference

to someone who tries to make you do things that might actually be in your best interest."

"Not necessarily." Why would she think Jitty's advice would be in my best interest? The things Jitty wanted me to do were primarily focused on creating an heir.

"What does 'not necessarily' mean? That is a non-answer."

"Not necessarily in my best interest."

"Quit dodging. *Who* is Jitty?" She pushed me back into a chair. "Tell me now or else."

"Else what?"

"Tell me."

I couldn't keep ducking Tinkie's questions. She was like a dog with a bone. "Jitty's the woman who helped my many-greats-grandmother, Alice, through the Civil War. She was a nanny, a slave, and Alice's best friend. Without each other, neither would have survived."

"You talk as if she's in your life now. A black woman from the Civil War." Tinkie put a hand to my forehead. "I'm calling Doc. You're hallucinating."

"I'm not. Jitty is sort of like my subconscious. She nags me and tries to make me conform. It's a mental thing. Like an angel on my shoulder." I actually shuddered as I said the word *angel*. Devil would be more accurate, but truth wasn't my business right now. Getting myself out of the hole I'd dug with my big mouth was my foremost concern.

"You're not telling me the truth."

"I'm telling you as much truth as I can." I had one truly terrible thing on my conscience regarding Tinkie. When I'd first come home to Zinnia, I'd dognapped Chablis and then ransomed her back to Tinkie for five grand. It was the money I needed to save Dahlia House from a tax sale and foreclosure by the bank. But the end didn't justify the means. Tinkie had paid the ransom and then hired me to dig into Hamilton Garrett V's background. And she'd paid me again. She'd praised my talents as a PI and helped me find cases. So I wasn't about to add to the wagonload of guilt I was already carrying by lying to Tinkie. She was loyal and smart, and I owed her more.

"You act like she's a real person."

"She was. Once."

She tapped her toe with impatience. "I don't know why you won't just tell me the truth, but I'll figure this out myself. After all, I am a private detective."

"If you did figure it out, maybe that would be okay." My fear was not that Tinkie would think I was insane, but that Jitty would disappear if I told anyone about her. There were stringent rules in the Great Beyond, and I wasn't clued in to the one regarding revelations about spirit guides. What if I blew Jitty's cover and she was recalled? I couldn't take the risk, no matter how much I wanted to tell Tinkie. Jitty was a constant torment, but I relied on her.

"I'll find out who Jitty is, and then you'll have to come clean."

"Can we just work on the case?" I had to get away from this dangerous ground. Jitty linked my present to Dahlia House's past, to the generations of Delaneys who'd farmed the fertile acres of the estate. Jitty was also my friend and counselor. I couldn't imagine staying in Dahlia House without her. Therefore, I had to be careful.

"Sure, you have your secrets. Everyone has secrets. I'm the only open book in this equation, but what the heck. Let's just pretend we're all truthful."

"Hold it right there! If you're such an open book, what's with the 'stinky' talk from Sister?"

"That's the past. Your Jitty is the present. But I'll let it drop. For now."

This was going to be a hair shirt for me for a long time to come. I'd just have to wear it and go on. "Okay, here's what I learned from Linda Thorne last night."

And I caught Tinkie up on all the things I'd put together.

"What is Sister's big secret?" she asked. At last she'd moved on from me to someone with the potential for a juicier secret.

"I don't know."

"Have you read any of her books?"

"I'm reading *Dead and Gone*." I had bought the book and was digging through it. Sister painted her family with a palette I would not have chosen. Colin was wonderful; Son was a worthless addict; Cleo was a naïve woman who led with her misguided emotions rather than logical thought; Susan Simpson, the mistress and now wife, was the person who held Colin's many interests together. I would have painted Susan as a greedy home-wrecker; Son as a lost boy; Cleo as a woman with a mission to help Mississippi; Sister as a b**ch; and Colin as a man who let nothing come between him and his ambitions.

"The book is interesting because of what happened to her family, but her romantic stories are the best. She's a very good writer. I don't understand how a woman who seems to hate everyone and everything can write about love so beautifully."

"She writes love stories?"

"Pretty much, yes."

"Do you think anyone has ever really loved Sister?"

"Don't you dare try to make me feel sorry for her." Tinkie was instantly defensive. "She is mean. If she were nicer, maybe someone would risk caring for her."

"I don't feel sorry for her. If love came around the corner, she'd toss kerosene on it and set it on fire. But how can someone like her write a beautiful love story?"

"Beats me," Tinkie said. "How can Agatha Christie, who was reputedly very nice, write murder mysteries?"

"Touché. What's our next step?"

"How about we check with the tow company that hauled the vehicle out of the river?"

"You're a damn genius, Tinkie Bellcase Richmond. Let's do it."

I grabbed a cup of strong, black coffee and my jacket. Sweetie Pie and Pluto were waiting at the front door, along with Chablis. We were off for our sleuthing session.

Cleo McFee's SUV had been dragged out of the river by Jimmy's Wrecker Service and Dismantling Yard. The junkyard doubled as a spare-parts place and had a compression service. Old cars, stripped of any usable parts, were crunched into cubes and shipped to steel mills for recycling. The old junkyard, where abandoned and sometimes dangerous old cars and trucks spread to the horizon in rusting heaps, no longer existed—at least not where Jimmy Deets was concerned. There were plenty of junked cars, but each one was in a different stage of recovery. He recycled every possible part. Jimmy was more businessman than junkyard owner.

Jimmy's place was across the county line, and we pulled up just as he came out the door of his office. He was a tall, good-looking man close to my age. Muscles bulged in his arms and thighs. He was seriously in shape.

"What can I do you for?" he asked as he went to Tinkie's window.

Tinkie put on the charm. "I hope you can help us," she said and made the introductions. "We're working for a movie company and we need any information you can give us on the McFee accident five years ago."

The phrase "working for a movie company" was a magic elixir. "No kidding. I heard we might have a movie made around here. This is the film about Cleo and Son and the accident?"

"Yes." Tinkie batted her eyelashes. "We're working for Black Tar Productions."

"Will they film in the Delta?" He glanced over the property, which was filled with neat rows of vehicles in various stages of dismemberment. Jimmy ran a tight shop. There was a minimal number of vehicles on the property, and they were stripped, compressed, and recycled without delay. A huge crane fed the compactor.

"That's the plan. Sarah Booth and I are also scouting locations for possible filming. We thought the dismantling yard had great potential."

"It would be better if we could restage the way I pulled that SUV out of the river. It was hung up on a tree, a big poplar that was pulled down by the floodwaters. I had to use two wreckers simultaneously to get it out. It was a hairy situation and there was more than one time I feared me and my wreckers would be pulled into the current."

"I'm sure Marco and Lorraine St. John will want to hear all about how you did it."

Tinkie was masterful, but she also wasn't lying. I could see where that scene might be great in a movie. Tinkie had an eye and a great imagination. Other talents to add to her long list.

"That old SUV wouldn't happen to still be around here, would it?" I asked. "It might make a great visual for the film." A fleeting expression passed across Jimmy's open face. It was gone so quickly I couldn't tell if it was uneasiness, unhappiness, or worry.

"That's pretty strange." He looked out across the vista of cars.

"What's strange?" Something was up with him and the McFee vehicle.

"I towed the car here and there were cops, insurance adjustors, news reporters, and all kinds of people who wanted to take a look. I let the cops and adjustors in, but no one else. A woman died in that car and another person was swept away and likely drowned. Son was still missing, and no one knew if he was dead or alive. I just thought it was inappropriate to let the media splash that torn-up car all over."

"That's very considerate of you," Tinkie said. "Were you thinking Son had managed to get out alive?"

Jimmy tucked a hand in his jean pocket. "The driver's side was totally submerged. I don't see how Son could have gotten out. The car would have crushed him against the tree trunk. Anyway, I didn't want pictures and such all over the place, so I kept folks out."

"I agree. That was the right thing to do," Tinkie said. "So, what happened?"

"After I brought the car here, it was stolen."

"What?" Tinkie and I spoke in unison.

I wouldn't have been surprised to know the SUV was a cube of metal long shipped to be recycled, but stolen was something else altogether. "Who took it?"

Jimmy shook his head. "I have no idea, and the sheriff couldn't find out either."

"Someone hauled off a junked car? How could that happen without leaving a trace?" Tinkie asked.

"That crane lifts the cars onto the crusher. I guess someone used it to load Mrs. McFee's wrecked SUV onto a flatbed and hauled it off."

"Who would do that?"

Jimmy shrugged, but he wouldn't meet my gaze. He knew something.

"And the vehicle never showed up anywhere? Not as a point of curiosity or in photos for a tabloid or anything?" Tinkie asked.

He shook his head.

Tinkie and I exchanged a glance. If it wasn't someone trying to capitalize off a piece of gruesome history, then only someone who was afraid evidence would be found would go to the trouble of stealing a wrecked car. But evidence of what? A crime? A tragic accident? Someone protecting Son? Someone protecting Cleo? It could be anything.

"Jimmy, how did the thieves get into the yard?" I asked, and my tone clearly indicated I had trouble believing his story. The entire place was surrounded by a ten-foot chain-link fence.

"They cut the lock on the gate with bolt cutters. Anyone could have done it."

"But you suspect someone in particular?" I pressed.

"I don't have any evidence, but I do suspect someone. The SUV was stolen and never seen again. Who would do that? My bets are on Colin McFee."

"*Why* would he do that?"

"To keep the buzzards from feeding off his tragedy for the next months. I'd do the same thing. If he could get in with bolt cutters, some of those tabloid reporters could too. So I think he took the car and disposed of it. His wife died in that car and his son disappeared. That had to be hurtful. Colin could have hired anyone with heavy-equipment knowledge to come in and take it."

Jimmy's reasoning could be accurate, but I didn't view Colin as a man with tender emotions about the tragic death of Cleo and Son. He married only weeks after Cleo's death, and he accused his son of murdering his mother. Not very tender at all.

"Had the crime-scene people finished their investigation?" Tinkie asked.

"They had. I'd offloaded the car behind the office, sort of out of the way. I was going to tear it down and then crush it. Best thing to do with painful memories."

Now Jimmy was right about that. I'd like to crush a few of mine. "Did you notice anything suspicious about the car?"

Jimmy thought a minute. "The driver's seat belt was intact."

"Son was pulled out of the car by the current." I frowned. "Or at least that's the assumption."

"Either he wasn't wearing his seat belt or he managed to release it. It wasn't buckled and the belt was intact."

"You believe Son survived the impact and was trying to get out of the car?" Tinkie asked.

"I do. Let's say he wasn't wearing his seat belt. It's possible he did manage to escape the car before it rolled into that tree. Possible. But I've always wondered why Son wasn't wearing a seat belt. What seems more likely to me is that someone got to the wrecked car before the law did and took Son's body."

Now that was another whole can of worms. "You think someone snatched Son's body?"

"I didn't say I really thought that. I said it had occurred to me to wonder about it."

"Meaning that's what you really think," Tinkie said dryly. "Was the seat belt the only evidence?"

"Folks are afraid of Colin McFee. He's a powerful man. He said Son was using drugs and missed the bridge, so that's what everyone else agreed to."

"Even if it wasn't true?" I held his gaze.

"Even if it wasn't true," he repeated.

"When you pulled the car out of the river, did you happen to stop by the bridge and check the evidence there?" Tinkie asked.

"I'm not a cop. But I will tell you it was raining cats and dogs that night. It had been raining hard for at least twelve hours. I saw some photos of tread marks where the vehicle was supposed to have gone off the road. The way it was raining, there was no way those tread marks would have been visible the next day. That's just a fact."

"So you're saying whoever took the photos of the treads in the mud probably made them."

"The thought has crossed my mind. Now if there's nothing else I can do for you . . ."

He was ready for us to leave. "Thanks, Jimmy."

"I hope you find the answers you're looking for. And I hope Son didn't suffer. I met him a few times and he was a decent guy."

Tinkie turned the car around and we drove back toward Zinnia. "Someone tampered with evidence," Tinkie said. "And why? If it was just an accident where Son was high and drove off the road, why would anyone bother to steal the car or create tread prints?"

"Good questions," I said. "Let's take a ride. I think it's time for a visit to Hoots Tanner."

10

The drive to Hollywood, Mississippi, and Hoots's horse farm took us north up Highway 61, the same route Cleo and Son must have taken south five years ago. That August day, roads throughout the Delta had been flooded. Wrecks on the major highways had blocked traffic for miles. Cleo and Son had taken a circuitous route toward Jackson because of road conditions, but what in the heck had they been doing on the west side of the state? No one could answer that question.

In contrast to the wretched day of the accident, the January weather today was beautiful, with crisp sunshine and the smell of fresh-turned dirt as a few farmers began preparing the land for the spring planting. I loved the winter vista, where the brown earth met the blue sky. Far on the horizon, small, dark clouds warned of a coming storm, but for now, the day boasted perfection.

Tinkie and I chatted about our friends and future plans for the detective agency. We'd been asked to speak at several private-investigator conferences, and we had to decide if we wanted to participate. The miles disappeared beneath the Cadillac's wheels. We took the turn off Highway 61 and drove to the unincorporated community of Hollywood. Not far away, the Tunica casinos drew tourists from around the region, but the little community we sought was quiet and rural. There wasn't much to mark the spot, but Hoots Tanner had retired from PI work and taken up raising Tennessee Walking Horses there.

The long drive to the house ended at a wrought-iron gate that included the image of a Walking Horse doing the famed running-walk. We pulled through the arch and drove to the house. Tinkie and I had debated calling Hoots and letting him know we planned to stop by, but we'd decided not to. We didn't want prepared answers—we hoped to catch him off guard. Assuming there was anything to catch.

We parked and walked to the door of the beautiful ranch-style house with a wraparound porch and inviting rocking chairs. The exterior was milled cypress, giving the house a dark, restful profile. Before we could even ring the bell, the front door opened and Hoots Tanner stood before us. He was a slender man who wore jeans and a snap-button flannel shirt. His chestnut hair, streaked with gray, was short and neat. I estimated he was in his late forties or early fifties, and he was in great shape. He wore the lean-cowboy look well.

"Ladies," he said, "I don't believe you're Jehovah's Witnesses or Avon salesladies. What do you want?"

"We'd like to talk about an old case," Tinkie said. She didn't even try her feminine wiles on Hoots. Something told her—and I agreed—that he was immune. As a private investigator, he'd seen his share of women who were aces at male manipulation.

"Forget it. The past is gone. I don't talk about it."

He started to close the door but I stopped it with my hand. "We need your help. Please."

"I'm out of the private-investigator business."

"But we're just getting started. I'm Sarah Booth Delaney and this is my partner Tinkie Richmond. We're the Delaney Detective Agency in Zinnia."

His grip on the door relaxed as he gave us the once over. "I have to say that maybe I retired too soon. I never saw PIs who looked like you two. The private dicks I know are crusty men who smoke and drink too much. You ladies are a different breed of cat."

"Thank you," Tinkie said, seizing the opportunity. "Don't let our looks deceive you. We're pretty good detectives."

"And you're here about the Son McFee disappearance."

"How did you know?" I was surprised he'd put two and two together so quickly.

"It's all over the Delta that someone is digging into what happened to Son McFee and what caused the accident. I expected someone to show up and ask." He grinned. "Plus, the movie is hot news. Everybody wants a part."

"Even you?" I asked, thinking that Hoots could actually pull off a part in the film.

"Not me. I have no urge to be in a movie. I just want to ride my horses and enjoy life while I still can. Which means I don't need to be digging into the past. Especially not the Cleo and Son McFee accident."

"Do you know what happened to Son?" I asked.

"I gave Colin my complete report. That was the end of it for me. Now ladies, I have stalls to clean."

I stepped in front of him. "You never believed Son was high and wrecked the car, did you?"

"It's in my best interest to believe what the man who hired me believed."

"That doesn't make it true."

He considered for a moment and then waved us into the house. It was a very masculine place with horse tack and training equipment scattered about, boots neatly placed in front of a small fire, and the smell of something good cooking. My stomach growled.

"I see you came hungry," Hoots said, but he was smiling. "I have a pot of stew and I was just about to eat lunch. Care for a bowl?"

"Yes." I was hungry and it would give us a chance to stay a little longer. "Why are you talking to us?" I asked.

"Sometimes a thing eats at your craw." He turned his back as he stirred the pot of stew on the stove.

We settled into chairs at the kitchen table and Hoots spooned up three steaming bowls of stew. He'd already cut a loaf of fresh bread that looked suspiciously homemade.

He saw me eyeing the bread. "I like to bake," he said. "It calms me down. Gives me a chance to think things through when I need something to keep busy."

"And you need calming down why?" I asked.

"Some cases never leave you. You see some terrible

things in this business. Folks are capable of dirty deeds, and sometimes there's no justice. That's what you have to look forward to if you continue in this line of work." He sat down and motioned for us to dig in. "I got tired of seeing the terrible things people do to each other for the craziest reasons. If my thoughts go back there, baking bread helps me refocus."

"Was the McFee case one of those cases?"

He didn't answer immediately. "That case bothered me. Why did that young man drive off the road? It just never sat right."

"There are possibilities," I said. "Because he was blinded by heavy rain, or because he was loaded, or because he was suicidal. That's what Sister and Colin believe."

For a long moment, the only sounds were our spoons against the stew bowls. Tinkie and I were just going to have to wait Hoots out.

He wiped his mouth with a napkin. "It was made very clear to me what the remaining McFees believed, Sister, Colin, and Susan. And there was no evidence to the contrary. Since Son's body wasn't recovered, there wasn't a tox screen or autopsy to check to see what chemicals were in his system. Son had come out of rehab, and all the sources I checked said he was clean and intended to stay that way. I couldn't find evidence to prove Son was high, but that didn't stop Colin from promoting the story that best served his purposes."

"Why did Son start using in the first place?" I asked.

Hoots sighed. "There was something going on at McFee Enterprises. I wasn't given access at the business to really poke around, but I would have liked to have had a look. I never understood how Son, the golden heir, became an addict. And then there was Susan Simpson.

I'm sure having his nose rubbed in that upset Son. He adored his mother."

"And Susan was playing mattress tag with his father." Tinkie waited for Hoots's reaction.

"True, she was a woman who saw an opportunity and moved on it. I'm shocked she and Colin are still married. And my god, she's pregnant. It all over television in those ads Colin is running. Have you ever seen anything worse than him standing beside that giant monitor of an ultrasound with a pointer directed at his unborn child's penis? It's an outrage."

"The sad thing is that he had a son. A really nice guy, from all I've been told." It angered me that this new baby was like the second coming and poor, dead Son was forgotten.

"I'll tell you what I found. It might save you a bit of legwork, but it won't answer the question about what happened to Son. He had issues with his father cheating on his mother. Everyone said Son was a throwback to Jamie McFee. He had rigid moral rectitude, and when he discovered his father's antics with Susan Simpson, he disapproved and did so vocally. Son created turmoil at McFee Enterprises. That much I learned before Colin interfered and told me to stop that line of inquiry. I argued with Colin and told him that if Son was making waves at McFee Enterprises, there might be room there to look for someone who wanted to hurt Son, someone who killed him. Cleo could have been collateral damage."

It was a hard way to look at Cleo's death, but it made sense. "Other than Susan, was Son after anyone else at the company?"

"One of the secretaries, Hannah Martin, said that Son

was poking around in one of the McFee developments. He was asking questions that had people upset."

"What kind of questions?" Tinkie asked.

"I never found out. Ms. Martin clammed up when she found out I was working for Colin. She told me I should ask Colin. Of course when I did, he told me to drop it."

"Impropriety in the company." Tinkie was all over the financial aspect.

Hoots passed the bread around again. "Other than Hannah Martin, I couldn't find anyone else who would talk. Colin told me to look in another direction, that I was barking up the wrong tree."

"And he was paying your bill. Of course he'd say that if he was doing something illegal." Tinkie's cheeks were pink with annoyance.

"Is Hannah Martin still at the company?" She was a possible lead.

"She disappeared about three months after she talked to me. No forwarding address. She just packed up her stuff and was gone."

"Sounds like someone scared her off."

"You think?" Hoots leaned back in his chair.

"Do you think Son died in the crash?" I had to figure out where Hoots's loyalties lay. He worked for Colin, but he didn't seem overly determined to protect his former boss.

"I don't see how he could have survived," Hoots said.

We told him about the seat-belt evidence we'd acquired from Jimmy Deets. "Jimmy said Son's seat belt was intact."

"Inconclusive. Do you know how many men don't wear a seat belt? About forty percent."

I couldn't argue those stats. "So you think Son was swept downriver."

"I do. And I'm not certain he wasn't dead before the car hit the water."

We both sat up even though we were so full of stew we'd have to waddle out the door. "Why?"

"The windshield in the SUV had shattered and was completely gone. That's not unusual. Anything could have knocked the window out—a tree limb, something floating in the river. And any obvious blood that might have been in the car was also washed away. I wanted to run some Luminol tests, but someone stole the car before I could convince Colin it was necessary. There's just a lot of funny business with the whole scenario."

"What do you think happened, based on your years of experience?"

"I have no evidence, only a theory based on a hunch. And the fact that the car disappeared, Hannah Martin was suddenly gone, and someone made new tire ruts at the bridge to support the theory Son went off the road and struggled to get back on, like he'd lost control. You and I both know those ruts were made after the fact."

"So, what's your theory?" I asked.

"I believe someone shot Son as he was approaching the bridge. The bullet shattered the windshield and went straight into Son's head. When he died, he slumped to the right, turning the wheel in that direction and sending the car plummeting down the side of the road and into the swollen river."

"You think Son was murdered."

"I do," he said. "I just couldn't prove it. And Colin didn't want me to prove it. I told him what I thought, and he obstructed me every step of the way. Which made me believe I was on to something." He stood up and went to the counter. "Coffee?"

We both declined, but I watched Hoots. He was antsy about something. "What haven't you told us?"

"You might as well hear it from me." He faced us. "Colin gave me a huge paycheck for the work I did, essentially for finding nothing. Enough money that I could retire as a PI and turn my hand to raising the horses I love. I'd had enough of the worst of human nature, so I took the money."

"He bought you off." Tinkie said it before I could.

"You could look at it that way. Or you could say that I was ready to quit and Colin gave me the key to a different future. I didn't find anything that could be used as proof against the way he interpreted events. Nothing. If I had, I would have made it public, but Colin shut down every single path to new evidence or a different theory of what happened."

I stood and took our dishes to the sink. I stopped in front of Hoots. "Nobody can fault a man for doing his best. May I ask who you think had Son killed?"

"Someone from McFee Enterprises. Someone who had something to hide and who thought Son was about to discover it."

"Colin?" I asked.

He put the lid on the pot of stew. "I can't accuse a man without evidence, and I didn't find anything that I could use. My gut tells me that Son was an inconvenience to Colin, and Colin is a man who doesn't like inconvenience. But it doesn't mean he'd kill his son and wife."

"Did you ascertain who knew Son was in the car with Cleo? Was their trip together planned in advance?"

Hoots shook his head. "Not to Colin's way of thinking. He said he was shocked when Cleo called him and said Son had unexpectedly decided to ride with her because of the bad weather. That upset Colin. He asked me to find out if the two of them were telling secrets. But how could I do that? They were both dead."

"A secret of what magnitude?" Tinkie asked.

"Colin's infidelity, financial misappropriation, corruption. It could be anything. Or Cleo may have been planning to leave Colin. She was a proud woman who knew Colin was a cad. But we'll never know for certain now. The only people who could tell us are dead."

"So Colin knew Son was in car with Cleo." This was something to ponder.

"Yes, he did."

"Why was Cleo on the west side of the state?" That nagged at me.

"The best I could come up with was that Son had been in Memphis. Maybe Cleo drove over to pick him up so they could talk. There was no other reason for Cleo to be there. But Colin knew the route she'd taken. Chances are if he knew, others knew as well."

"You really think someone set up at that bridge to put a bullet in Son's brain?" Tinkie asked.

"Let me just say that when I'm sitting down on my porch to have a drink at the end of the day, my thoughts go to Son McFee and those last five minutes of his life. I'd give a lot to know what really happened. I know better than to hope the guilty are punished."

"You have our word. If we discover evidence one way or the other, we'll let you know. And the guilty will be punished." Tinkie picked up her purse and keys. "If you think of anything, will you call us?"

"Absolutely." He walked us to the door. "Keep your eyes open. When I was in Memphis asking questions, I parked in the garage that belongs to McFee Enterprises. My brake lines were mysteriously nicked. Thank goodness I was in a residential area when the brake fluid bled out. I only hit a utility pole. It could have been fatal and I could have killed someone else."

"Who do you think cut the lines?"

"The same person who killed Son. You know, Son didn't have to be shot. Don't think I didn't consider the possibility of a slow leak in the brake lines of the SUV Cleo was driving. Maybe Son was never the target. Maybe it was Cleo all along. After she was dead, Colin had a clear path to marry his mistress. And with Cleo dead, there was no one nagging him to do good deeds with all of his money. Those are troubling thoughts. You two take care."

"Thanks, Hoots." He'd been good enough to warn us.

"My best advice—don't trust anyone. I could never get a feel from Colin that he was part of the accident, but he's a politician. He's trained to hide things. Just watch out."

Tinkie and I were both quiet on the drive back to Zinnia. The storm clouds had moved a little closer, but the day was still beautiful. We had a lot on our minds. Hoots warning us about his cut brake lines reminded us that someone had taken potshots at us. And it wasn't over. Digging into Cleo's and Son's deaths threatened someone. They had died five years ago, and nothing had changed. As long as we pursued the truth, we were in danger. We had to be vigilant. And careful.

"It doesn't make sense that Colin would try to kill Hoots," Tinkie said. "He could just fire him. In fact, why hire him in the first place? Sheriff Lenton's reports were good enough for insurance purposes."

She was right about that. "But it would look odd if Colin, this wealthy, powerful man, made no effort on his own to get to the truth. And, as you can see, by hiring the best investigator in the Southeast, Colin was able to control the investigation. If Hoots found something, if Colin didn't like the direction the case was taking, he could just shut it down. Ultimate control of the outcome."

"So why try to kill Hoots?" Tinkie asked.

"Maybe Colin was afraid Hoots had already found something."

"So he would buy him off. Sort of like he did."

"Except Hoots didn't have any solid evidence."

"That he told us about." She turned left off Highway 61 toward Zinnia. "Just saying. We don't really have anything on Colin except dark suspicions. Someone at McFee Enterprises could easily have cut Hoots's brake lines because Son uncovered a thief in the company. We don't have enough to even accuse Colin."

"Not yet."

I called Coleman and let him know what Hoots had told us, and I told him about the potshots in Washington County. As I expected, he was angry. That I'd delayed telling him increased his ire. "I reported the incident to the sheriff there. Be mad at me, but don't tell Oscar until Tinkie has a chance."

"I can't believe you two. I could have investigated the scene. Now there's not a chance to find or gather any evidence, and there's a bad storm coming."

"You couldn't have probed into it. It happened in another county, and I didn't want to drag you into another jurisdiction. Besides, it was probably some idiotic deer hunter who wasn't careful where his shot went." I had to change the direction this was going. "How bad is the weather supposed to get?" The clouds had been massing on the horizon for the past twenty minutes. Judging from the way they'd blown in from the south on the warm, moist gulf air, we could expect a big blow with lots of lightning. I had to get the horses up for sure. Nothing scared a horse owner more than lightning and fire.

"There's a danger of tornadoes. You need to get home and stay there. They're expecting at least twelve inches of rain to fall by eight o'clock."

That would create flooding and a lot of other dangerous situations, a parallel to the very night Son and Cleo went into the river. Coleman was correct. I needed to stay home for the evening. "I'll go straight to Dahlia House. You have my word."

"You'd better."

I looked at Tinkie, who was smiling. She didn't have to hear the conversation to know Coleman was giving me the dickens. "I promise." I hung up.

"Let me guess. He was pissed and worried."

"Yes, just as Oscar will be when you tell him."

"No need. Coleman is the sheriff. He had to know about the gunshots. Oscar is just a banker. He doesn't have to know. I refuse to give him needless worry. As you say, probably a deer hunter."

"Oscar is your husband."

"And there's no need to get him all wound up. Trust me. I know what I'm doing."

Tinkie had a great marriage. Who was I to coerce her into telling Oscar things that would only make him anxious? "Okay."

My phone rang and I expected Coleman was ready to heap another load of guilt on me, but it was Cece.

"Where are you?" she asked.

"Just turned off Highway 61, headed home."

"Come by the newspaper. Now. Don't go home. Come by here."

"Okay. What's this about?"

"Just come as quick as you can. You are not going to believe this." Her voice was laced with excitement. "It's better than a catfight at the Black and Orange Ball."

This I had to see. "We're on the way."

Fifteen minutes later, we walked into the *Zinnia Dispatch* and found the entire newsroom gathered around a big-screen TV in stunned silence. "What?" I asked, but no one answered. They were all watching something on the screen.

We joined the crowd. Tinkie grabbed my arm. "This can't be happening."

"Unbelievable," I agreed as my gaze followed the antics of Colin McFee. He stood shirtless on a Mississippi beach, with a casino in the background. The camera panned beyond him and captured the sandy, man-made beach, the neon signs of the casino, the trolley trundling tourists from the parking garage to the casino.

"That looks like Biloxi," I said.

"It is." Tinkie said it with dread. "This is going to be awful. Why is he topless?"

"It's a Putin thing," one of the male reporters said. "See, Putin shows his chest on horseback and hiking in the mountains. Manly man and all of that. McFee can't let Putin be more macho than he is."

"I hate this." Tinkie was truly distraught.

"Shhhhhhh. Colin's talking." I wanted to hear what he had to say.

A breeze rumpled Colin's hair as he continued. "Mississippi moves forward with every new casino, every job opportunity. We produce. We work. We are strong people. And we challenge the Russians to a competition. You claim to be the sleeping bear. You claim to be strong. But you are weak. Can you do this?" Colin stepped closer to the camera and his nipples began to jump. In the background, the music to "Go, Mississippi" began to play and Colin's man-nipples jumped in time to the music.

"Mississippi is gonna roll all over you, Putin." He jabbed a finger toward the camera lens.

"Vote McFee" were the final words on the screen.

No one said a word. The reporters slowly dispersed and went back to their cubicles. The only sound was that of fingers pounding keyboards.

"Why isn't someone saying how awful that was?" Tinkie asked me.

"I think their brains have refused to register the whole thing. Did he really make his nipples dance to 'Go, Mississippi'?"

"He did. And I don't ever want to know how. Not ever. If you try to tell me, I will cut out your tongue. I think I've been damaged for life." She covered her eyes. "See no evil, see no evil, see no evil."

I burst out laughing. I couldn't help it. I went to the TV and picked up the remote. I was thrilled to see that someone had taped the ad. I hit replay, and Tinkie slumped into a chair and hid her face. "You're a sick woman, Sarah Booth."

Cece entered the break room and leaned against the door she closed. "Dahlink, that is some wicked crap. I knew you had to see it."

"My eyes are melting," Tinkie said.

"Look, look." I pointed at the screen. "He has perfect timing. His nips are choreographed."

"Stop it!" Tinkie jumped up and unplugged the television. "You are a sadist, Sarah Booth. I can never get the image of his chest out of my head. That pale chest with the line of hair descending . . . I may never be able to have sex again."

Cece gave her a hug. "You'll recover."

"You called us over here to see that ad?" I asked.

"Don't you think it speaks to Colin's character? If he'd do that, he'd do anything."

She had a point. "Bad taste. I mean really, really bad taste doesn't mean he'd kill his first wife. And his son."

Cece motioned us into her office where she closed the door and waved us toward chairs. Well, I assumed they were chairs because they were covered in files and books and different research materials. I sat gingerly on a stack and waited.

"Marco called me today," she began, almost whispering. "The screenwriter, Roon Talley, has almost completed the script. He's coming to Zinnia soon to scope out locations so he can polish the settings. He'll need to know what happened to Son."

"We don't know." I said it calmly, but I was a little annoyed that Marco would go through Cece to try to push us harder. "I don't know that we'll know anything more in the next week. We're working as hard as we can."

Cece held up a hand. "Stop, in the name of . . . just stop. Marco wasn't trying to get me to gig you to work harder."

"Then what was he trying to do?" Tinkie asked.

"Set you up to install surveillance cameras at Evermore."

"It won't be admissible. I'm sure any judge would throw out anything gleaned from hidden cameras." Tinkie didn't like the idea at all.

"I shared your reluctance. At first." Cece grinned. "Marco convinced me this is the right step."

"It's such a violation . . ." And way, way creepy. "I don't think we can do this."

"You're saying exactly what I said. At first," Cece said. "As a journalist, I'm always torn about confidential sources and printing information obtained through . . . unusual means. But this is only a way to gather information that there's no other way to get. No one can use it for anything—except maybe to more sharply focus the investigation that would *then* have to produce *facts*, not illegal tapes."

She had a strong argument, but not strong enough to convince me. Or Tinkie.

"That just isn't right, Cece." Tinkie's frown was impressive. "Would you secretly video someone?"

"Each case is different. If someone in Evermore is guilty of killing Son and Cleo and I could know who it was for certain, I would. Think of the good Cleo would have done in Mississippi. Now if I could find the truth—even if I couldn't print it—I would go after it. If Colin, Susan, and Sister have nothing to hide, then the videos won't surface. Ever."

"Any evidence gathered in this way can never be used in court." Tinkie was still reluctant.

"This isn't about legalities. It's about justice. Does it matter if Colin is found guilty in a courtroom?" Cece made a great devil's advocate.

"If we get the goods, can Marco use it in his film?" My eyes widened. "What if Sister confesses?" I let Tinkie's imagination do the rest of the work.

"Where do we pick up the cameras?" Tinkie said. "Colin's bedroom and the gym are the obvious places to bug."

"Marco will let you know when he has the equipment. And you'll have even more opportunities to check out Evermore. Millie will start preparing food for Marco and the crew tomorrow. We can go in to help her."

"We?"

"Of course I'm going," Cece said. "Think of the stories I can write. Marco has been feeding me information, and tomorrow I have the front page above the fold. Ron Howard of Imagine Entertainment has come onboard as a producer. This is big! Very big! And I'm breaking the story."

"The town is going to go nuts," I said. "Opie is producing a movie here."

"Oh, this is only the beginning. And tonight, we're going to celebrate at Playin' the Bones. Madame Tomeeka said you'd promised her a night out for some fun. You can get a little dancing in and see Scott."

"We'll be there," Tinkie said. "I'll call the rest of the gang."

I'd promised Coleman I'd go home and stay there, but a chance to go jukin' couldn't be ignored. "You call Coleman," I said to Cece.

"My, my, Sarah Booth, I didn't realize you took direction from any man."

"Shut up and call." They could tease me all they wanted, but I didn't want Coleman mad because I'd broken my word. He shouldn't object to my plans since I would be in the middle of a huge group of people.

Two minutes later, the evening plans were set. Coleman would meet us at the blues club. Now I had to run the critters home, feed them, and put the horses in the barn before the bottom fell out of the sky. Then it was time for some blues.

11

When I arrived at Playin' the Bones, Scott Hampton's hot blues club outside of Zinnia, the music escaped the building and sparked across the parking lot like an electric current. My body responded with a mad desire to dance. Scott's establishment honored a tradition—the juke—which was as much a part of the Mississippi Delta as cotton. Smoke from a faraway chimney wafted to me on a brisk wind that was the forerunner of the pending storm that lingered, unmoving, to the west.

The scent of burning wood transported me backward in time to a cold winter night in the early 1900s. From far down the long dirt road that led to the weathered juke, I heard people coming my way. Footsteps, laughter, a dare called out, and a flirtation dipped in the honey of an evening free of labor. In the magic of a stormy night, the past had come alive. Phantoms appeared in the distance, a gaggle of men and women, walking slow and steady. They talked and laughed, tired but eager for some pleasure after a day in the fields. The blues combined the history of sweat and hard work, of slavery and prison, of the hope that love brings and the pain that often follows.

The figments of the past came, eager for music and dancing. At the juke they could hear music, have a drink, eat some home cooking, and maybe meet a romantic partner. Clubs like Playin' the Bones, which had once been the province of blacks, had populated the rural dirt roads of the Delta. From them, a unique form of American music had been born and it had influenced the course of music around the world.

I listened to Scott's wailing guitar while chill bumps danced across my skin. I could almost feel jealous of his relationship with that piece of wood and steel strings, because his touch evoked so many emotions. As I pushed through the door and stepped into the light and laughter, I realized I'd unconsciously steered clear of Scott for the past few months. Looking at him on stage, his white blond hair falling over one eye as he squeezed sound, feeling, and a story out of the instrument he held, I knew why. He could be dangerous to my carefully guarded equilibrium.

"Sarah Booth!" Lorraine pulled me from my dangerous thoughts and waved me over to the table where she sat with Marco, Cece, Tinkie, Oscar, Tammy Odom, and Millie.

"I love this club," Lorraine said. "Scott is the best blues musician I've ever heard."

"He's good."

"And he's in lust with—"

Scott seemed to know we were talking about him. He broke into "Big Legs, Tight Skirt," a John Lee Hooker standard. The bar went nuts as folks crowded to the dance floor. Marco grabbed Lorraine's hand and whatever she'd been about to say was lost.

Scott was a master showman as well as the best blues guitarist ever. He read the mood of the audience, and as soon as the band finished "Big Legs, Tight Skirt," he led them into "Cry to Me." The old tune was a favorite dance song of mine, and obviously of Marco's and Lorraine's. They tucked in close to each other and the other dancers cleared the floor for them as they moved so suggestively that sweat popped out on my forehead.

"Were they part of the cast in *Dirty Dancing*?" Millie whispered to me.

"Maybe." I'd never seen two people go through the dirty dance moves with such intensity and precision.

"Get a room!" Someone in the audience yelled, but it was with appreciation. Marco and Lorraine used every inch of the floor. At one point she wrapped a long, slender leg around his waist and leaned back until her hair swept the floor. With a wrench of his hips, Marco tossed her upright and into a lift.

"Dance with me?" women began to scream. "Dance with me, dance with me, dance with me." The chant was taken up and the whole place cheered and stomped.

Scott and the band went right along with the moment and didn't even break before going into "Hungry Eyes."

"Get some water, quick," Cece said. "Marco and Lorraine are going to burst into flames." But when the song finished, Marco stepped over to the stage and said something to Scott. "I wonder what song Marco will request."

Cece sounded wistful, and I realized that with Jaytee in the band, she often had to sit out the best songs.

I didn't get a chance to answer because Scott was signaling Cece to the stage. She hurried over and he pulled her up. A moment later, the keyboardist ran the opening of "Pussycat Moan." Tinkie and Oscar jumped up and began dancing. They didn't have the flair of Marco and Lorraine, but they had a special bond that came through. When Cece began to sing, she sounded better than Katie Webster and that was saying something.

Marco and Lorraine split up and began dancing with people from the audience. Several women almost swooned, and I worried some of the stronger men might try to abduct Lorraine. Monty Earl, the mortician, grabbed hold of her and showed some dance moves I'd never have thought possible. The man who wore somber like an everyday suit had rhythm. "Holy Christmas," I said. "This is better than a soap opera. Who knew?"

Millie took the hand of a gentleman and hit the dance floor, followed by Tammy. They were having the time of their lives. I was completely unprepared when Marco offered his hand, but I gave it everything I had. He was a strong lead and easy to follow. It was pure joy to dance with him. Lorraine was a lucky woman, and vice versa.

When I finally sat back down, someone had replenished my drink, and I needed it. My blood was jumping.

Cece went into "Red Negligee," and it gave everyone a chance to calm down and drink. The line at the bar was five deep. When Cece finished her song, the band took a break, and Scott hopped down and came to our table. With my nod, he lifted my drink and took a sip.

"I don't like to drink when I play, but that dance business made me thirsty."

"And other things," I said knowingly. "Marco and Lorraine have got belly rubbing down pat."

"And other things," Scott said and lifted my glass again.

"Cece was superb." I waved at her across the room where some of her fans were asking for autographs. Millie and Tammy flanked her like the guard-friends they were.

"We should hire her, and we've tried," Scott said. "She won't take any money for singing. I'd be happy to put her on the payroll."

"She sings because she loves it. If it became work, it would be different. Millie loves cooking, but sometimes it's just work. Don't do that to Cece. Let her sing when she feels it."

"Good advice," Scott said. "How about I get another round of drinks?"

"Excellent. I'll help. They'll all be back at the table any minute and dying for a libation." I followed Scott behind the bar and helped fill the glasses with ice as he mixed for the table.

"What's going on with the movie?" Scott asked. "Sister came by before we opened and warned me that someone was trying to make trouble for her film. She made veiled promises and a few threats." He grinned, and I loved the way his eyes lit up when he was amused.

"Threats like what?"

"Like the movie would make me an international star and bring business to the club. It's clearly in my best interest to make this movie happen."

"That's probably true."

"She said the 'snoop,' as she referred to the person

who was going to gum up the works, would destroy my chances of being a celebrity on a global scale."

"Tragic." I sipped my drink.

"Was Sister talking about you?"

"Maybe."

"I know she's awful to Tinkie, but would you go so far as to derail her movie to get even?" Scott knew me. He knew I'd do whatever was necessary to protect Tinkie, so I was only a little miffed he'd think I was that vindictive.

"No." I thought about it. "This isn't personal. I can't stand Sister, but I have no reason to ruin her film just because she's a mean girl. I'm working for Marco, who wants to find out what really happened to Son. I don't see how the truth would ruin the film. Of course, it might not have the ending Sister envisions. Maybe she's in here whining to you because she's afraid of what I'll discover." I told him about our visit with Jimmy Deets and Hoots Tanner. "Both men believe something happened that sent Son off the road and into the raging river. Hoots thinks Son could have been shot. Jimmy got the SUV out of the river and had it at his recycling plant. The car was stolen. Son's body was never found. No real evidence was collected."

"If you can prove there was foul play, I'd say that angle would destroy what Sister hopes to accomplish with her film."

"And that is?" I'd never been completely clear on what Sister hoped to accomplish.

"She wants to paint Son as the villain and to win her father's undying love."

"How do you know this?" Scott was perceptive, and

he'd twigged on Sister's deep, deep psychological wounds quicker than I would have thought.

"It's easy to see if you know what to look for. She came in here last evening and talked to me for a few moments. She mentioned that she was single and even though she knew I had a thing for you, maybe a little fun could be had."

"You have the right to do whatever you want," I said, "but please, not Sister." I was asking for something I had no right to ask for, but I couldn't help myself.

"No worries. She's not my type. Spoiled rich girls don't do it for me. I let her down as gently as I could, but I think she holds a grudge."

"No doubt. So what happened after that?"

"She set up at the bar. There was one older guy drinking and she was on him like a fly on a turd."

I liked his description. "Maybe they were friends. She lived here once, and her family has connections."

"Or maybe she was looking for Surrogate Daddy's love and approval. You forget I've spent a lot of time in bars around the world. I've seen that tableau play out time and time again. There are some girls who never get over paternal neglect. Their whole life is a quest for approval and love from the father who ignored them. Sister is one of those women."

"Did she leave with the man?" I was curious about Sister's social life. She'd never been a part of the Sunflower County community, so I wondered whom she might show a romantic—or at least sexual—interest in.

"I thought she would, but she didn't. A woman came in and it was clearly a shock to Sister. She was angry. They huddled in a corner for a little while. Jaytee was helping Travis behind the bar, and he went over to see if they wanted to refresh their drinks. They were in a heated argument and Sister told him to beat it. So he did. The two women left together."

"Who was the woman?"

"Never saw her before."

"Help me out, here, Scott."

He only laughed. "I'm not your spy, but I promise if she comes back in, I'll snap a photo of her just for you."

"Did Jaytee say what they were fighting about?"

"A contract. Maybe it was someone from her publishing house."

She had some kind of power if publishers had followed her to Zinnia, Mississippi. I was impressed. "I wish Jaytee had eavesdropped a little more."

Scott stood up and stretched. "I'll chastise him and tell him to get his tin ear closer and memorize every word."

I rolled my eyes. "Clever. And don't mention it to Jaytee. I'll talk to him when I get a chance. He's always helping me when he can, and I don't want him to think I'm ungrateful."

"He knows Cece and I both would skin him if he didn't do what he could."

"Speak of the devil."

Jaytee came toward the table with Cece on his arm. Millie, Oscar, Tinkie, and Tammy tagged behind.

"I'm returning Queen Cece to her tribe. Honor her." Jaytee was only half-kidding.

I pretended to bow and scrape. When I finished teasing, I sat up. "You did great, Cece. You have some bluesy pipes."

"Thank you, dahlink! I love singing 'Pussycat Moan.' It may be my favorite blues song."

"It may be mine, too." I turned to Jaytee. "Could I

talk to you a moment about Sister and the woman she ran into here earlier?"

"Cece said you'd want to know all the details."

We excused ourselves and stepped out the back door. The stars glimmered with a brightness only seen on a winter night. At a picnic table beneath a leafless tree, we found seats. Our breath frosted in the air. "What happened with Sister and the woman?"

"I don't know for certain. Sister was at the bar talking to some guy when this woman walked in like she owned the place."

"Describe her?"

"Tall, dark curly hair, slender, wearing a black minidress and a black wool coat. She was a hot number."

"Did she know Sister?"

"Had to. She went right up to her at the bar. Demanded that she talk to her."

"Demanded?" This was good.

"I heard this part of the conversation because I was mixing some Long Island Iced Teas for a table. I took my time so I could eavesdrop. Cece told me Sister had been cruel to Tinkie, so I'm on the lookout for anything you can use."

"Bless you, Jaytee. You're a great friend."

"Thanks. So the woman said, 'You'd better talk to me or you'll be sorry. You've cheated me.' Sister wasn't shocked, but she was very angry. She warned the woman to be careful about slanderous statements. Then the woman called Sister a cheap cheat."

That was a delicious tidbit and knowing how cheap Sister was, I didn't doubt she'd done exactly as she was accused. "She's always going to be the girl who feels someone is trying to take her toys. The sad thing is she's the person trying to cheat others."

Jaytee eyed me. "That's pretty much what the woman said."

"Did she have an accent? Was she from around here?"

"Naw, she was a city girl. She had the look, the walk, the attitude, and the voice. I'd say Manhattan. She wasn't a Southern girl at all."

"What else happened?"

"They went to a table in the corner and talked, really low and quiet. Sister got something out of her purse and they looked at it. Then the woman said something, and Sister laughed and said loud enough that I could hear, 'We have a contract. Violate it and I'll own everything you ever hoped to have.' The woman was pissed and she stood up. Sister said something I couldn't hear, then the woman yelled at her and said she'd be sorry. Then she left."

"What did Sister do?"

"She left about a minute later. She was in a big rush. Left a fifty-dollar bill on the table to cover the bar tab."

"What about the man at the bar Sister was talking to?"

Jaytee's eyes widened. "He had a few more drinks then said he was hitting the sack. He had to be in Memphis early the next morning. He said he worked with computers."

"He didn't show any interest in the McFees?"

"He asked about Colin's political aspirations. He had some skepticism that Russia was the issue Mississippians had at the top of their list of concerns, but he'd seen the nipple-dance ad and loved it."

"Loved it?" The idea creeped me out.

"Loved it like it was great entertainment. He wasn't seriously interested, as far as I could tell. Just a guy at a bar talking to a pretty woman. Too bad Sister McFee is such a shrew. She's got looks and money. She could be having fun instead of constantly trying to make others miserable."

I thought about Scott's assessment of Sister and her desperate need for a father's love. It was kind of sad. She truly was the poor little rich girl.

"We're up," he said, tossing back his club soda with a twist of lemon.

The band took the stage again and set off into a raucous honky-tonk number to get folks up and dancing. They were a versatile band, focused on the blues, but out of nowhere they'd crank it up with a country foot-stomper or a torch song. The variety made an evening at Playin' the Bones unpredictable. I was headed to the table when strong arms swept me into a hug.

I smelled starch and sunshine, and I knew Coleman had finally joined us for a little fun. He maneuvered me to the dance floor where we did a fast swing that left me panting when we finally sat down.

"What's on the agenda for tomorrow for Delaney Detective Agency?" Coleman asked Tinkie and me when we'd sat down, caught our breath, and fortified ourselves with a sip of Jack.

I looked at my partner. "So far we have zilch. Nothing except theories." I ran down Hoots's suspicions. "Marco will expect some answers soon. Any suggestions?"

"Hoots quit his PI business after the Cleo-Son case?" Coleman frowned.

"He said Colin paid him handsomely, enough that he could invest in the horse farm."

"If you made a windfall on a case, would you quit detecting?" Coleman asked.

The question caught me by surprise. "No, I wouldn't. It's what I do." His arched eyebrow told me he'd made his point. "So you think there was more to Hoots quitting than he let on?"

"His reputation was rock solid. He was hired by folks all over the country. Then he suddenly quits? Either he was paid a whole lot of money, which would indicate he knew more than he ever let on, or he was coerced. That's how I read it."

"Thanks, Coleman."

"Don't mention it. Just keep in mind that someone has already made an effort to scare you off the case. The next time it might not be a *scare* tactic. Keep that in the back of your mind."

"You bet."

12

An entourage followed me back to Dahlia House, but it was Millie who stayed the night with me. I insisted that I didn't need a babysitter, but powers above me held sway. And truthfully, I was glad for the company. The storm, pregnant with rain, had finally opened up and thunder crashed around Dahlia House. Wicked forks of lightning turned the sky into Frankenstein scars. It was good to be home, protected by the walls that had withstood nearly two centuries of the worst nature could throw at us. The horses were safely in their stalls, and Sweetie Pie, replete with some chicken and brown rice Millie had brought her, lay at our feet. Pluto had curled between us on the sofa in the den.

I scurried to the front door to double check I'd locked

it and peeked out the sidelight at the pouring rain that looked like a curtain of gray gauze pulled across the landscape. The fat drops fell quickly and in a dense wall. I couldn't see five feet from the porch. This was the type of deluge that Son had been driving in when he'd missed the bridge. It was possible the wreck had been an accident caused by the weather conditions. But because no one had really examined the vehicle—or Son's body—the plunge into the Sunflower River could also have been deliberately caused by another human.

And possibly by someone who was Son's blood.

"Come help me select a movie," Millie called out, and I stepped back from the front door. Staring at the rain gave me no answers, only a sense of a setting for a tragedy.

We'd had plenty to drink, so Millie and I made popcorn and hot chocolate and searched out a Bette Davis movie, *What Ever Happened to Baby Jane?*, a classic tale of sibling rivalry and ultimate revenge.

"In a twisted way, that movie could be about Sister and Son," Millie said, plopping another marshmallow in her cocoa.

"You're right. Who would be Blanche and who would be Jane?" I loved playing Hollywood games with Millie. She knew all the gossip and all the history. She was a deep resource for factoids real and fabricated, old and new.

"Blanche was the desperate one, the one who begrudged Jane her success, but it was Jane in the end who was so cruel and horrible." Millie dropped another marshmallow and stirred her chocolate. "I guess they are both Sister."

"A double dose of crazy."

"Sarah Booth, you can't let Sister get away with besmirching Son's reputation in a movie. The book is bad enough. People read that and believe that Son was high on something and killed his mother and himself. That's never been proven, yet no one refutes her accusations, even though she has not one shred of evidence to support her lies."

"I know."

"I think about Cleo, and it makes me very sad. She loved both her children. Sometimes when she stopped by the café, we'd talk. She said Sister was more difficult to love. Cleo was such a decent person, and she cared about Mississippi. If she were alive, *she* should be running for Congress, not Colin. This is all about his ego."

"I can see that."

She pointed at the TV screen. "Did you know that Bette Davis and Joan Crawford actually hated each other? Both of their careers were waning, and this movie, which was rated *X* in England in 1962, revived their stock as Tinsel Town stars."

"No kidding, Ms. Encyclopedia Brown."

Millie laughed. "I am a little OCD about celebrities. Look, here comes the parakeet scene. By the standards of the day, this was a shocking film. It won an Oscar for Costume Design."

"What other tidbits have I missed?"

"The film created a new subgenre of movies, the hag horror flick, which includes elements of black comedy and camp."

"You should write a column in the *Dispatch*." Once I said it, I realized it was a great idea. "Really, Millie. People would love it. What a great opportunity to remember some of the classics and the actors who made Hollywood the epicenter of film. I'll speak to Cece about this."

"I would love it, Sarah Booth, if you think people would really be interested."

"You could do a movie review of an old classic each week. Recap the careers of the actors, talk about what you loved or hated. It would be excellent. So what is your takeaway from *Baby Jane*?"

"Jealousy is the incubator for a monster."

I faced her. "Oh, my." Thoughts raced around my brain until I felt dizzy.

"What's wrong?" Millie put her cup aside and put a hand on my forehead. "Are you sick?"

"No, *you* are profound." I sighed. "I think Sister killed Cleo and Son. I've always thought Colin was behind it. But he didn't really benefit. Ten million is nothing to him. He doesn't really gain financially. And neither does Sister. So what was the motive if not money?"

"To be the star. The only star." Millie licked a bit of chocolate from her lip. "She did it so she would be the only one to orbit her daddy. If Cleo and Son were gone, Colin would have to finally see her."

"And then Colin married Susan, so there was no clear path to his affections. As soon as Cleo was out of the way, Colin found a replacement, and it wasn't Sister."

"You think Sister actually ran her mother and her brother off the road that night?"

"That's what I have to find out. And I think Colin knows."

I'd loaned Millie a pair of my sweatpants and a warm, comfy shirt. The storm had played itself out, leaving a thin moon to light our way to bed. Climbing the stairs, we looked like twins, except that she was six inches shorter and my sweatpants bunched around her ankles. Sweetie Pie and Pluto followed behind us, ready for their own adventure down the River Lethe.

I'd gripped my bedroom's doorknob when my cell phone rang. It was nearly three in the morning. There was no good reason for someone to call me at this hour. It could only mean an emergency.

Millie had the same thought, and she instinctively moved closer to me. I pulled my phone from the pocket of my pants to find Coleman on the line. "What's wrong?" I asked.

"Be sure your doors and windows are locked." Coleman was tense and not kidding around.

"What is it?"

"We got a tip. There's a body at the bottom of your driveway, Sarah Booth. A young woman has been murdered and the body dumped on your property. It's a message for you."

My heart hammered so hard it hurt to breath. "Who is it?"

"I don't know. She's a stranger to me and DeWayne. Brunette with curly hair, about your age."

"I'll be down to help." I dreaded telling Millie. She'd be sixty shades of upset.

"You will not! You will stay in the house with the doors and windows locked. There is nothing you can do here."

He was right, but I couldn't hide in the house. A body had been dumped on the property of Dahlia House, a place sacred to me. My home had been defiled. "Let me tell Millie." I quickly filled her in and was relieved that Millie agreed with my assessment. "Coleman, we're getting dressed and coming down no matter what you say."

"If you get yourself or Millie shot, it'll be on your head." He hung up because he was furious.

"He's right," Millie said gently. "We should stay here. It will be daylight in another three hours. You can wait that long."

"Sure." But I couldn't. The body would be gone, the scene destroyed. Coleman would show me the crime scene photos, no problem, but it was never the same. I had to see it, no matter how much I didn't want that memory in my head. But I wouldn't risk Millie. "I'm going to bed. I'm about to drop in my tracks."

Millie kissed me good night on the cheek, and I went into my room and closed the door. I stepped out of my sweat clothes and pulled on my black jeans and a heavy black sweater and barn coat. I found my black toque, and a pair of heavy gloves. With Sweetie pressed against my leg, I put my ear to the bedroom door and listened. If I was being a fool, at least I wasn't endangering Millie by taking her with me. And I certainly wasn't going to call Tinkie out of her safe, dry house.

The hallway was quiet. In the back of my head, a little voice said that this was way too easy.

"Hello. Hello." The male voice came from behind me and almost made me pee my pants. I whipped around to find a man in a tuxedo talking into a shoe.

"What the heck." It took me a minute to recognize Maxwell Smart, the inept spy on the 1960s TV show, *Get Smart*.

"I must have reinforcements. The agents of KAOS are all around. They're dumping bodies right on my doorstep, figuratively speaking. It's actually in the driveway near the county road. Hello? Hello? It's Agent 86. Send Agent 99."

I'd watched reruns of the comedy about an inept spy battling the Russian forces of KAOS. A parody of James Bond, Maxwell had plenty of gadgets, like a telephone shoe that never really worked. He was a danger to himself and anyone in his vicinity.

"Take cover!" Maxwell yelled, and I ducked instinctively. When I stood up, I was more than annoyed.

"Jitty, stand down." I knew it was my haint, deviling me with her crazy obsession with spies, real and fictional. "You are going to get me hurt!"

"Sorry about that, Chief. There's a dead body in your driveway."

"Stop it. Do you understand?"

"I missed the part after 'do you understand.' "

I wanted to wring her neck. "Jitty, I'm warning you." I had to get out of the house, and she was goading me into arguing with her. Thank goodness Millie couldn't hear Jitty, but she could sure hear me.

"You need my help." "Smug" best described Maxwell.

"Oh, no I don't." I edged past Agent 86 and grasped my bedroom doorknob. "I'm leaving and you are not to follow me."

"Ah, it's the old sneak-out-the-door trick. You don't want my help. Would you believe I *can* help you?"

I opened the door and fled into the hallway. I rushed down the stairs as quietly as I could and out onto the front porch, where Millie sat wrapped in one of the heavy coats I'd left hanging in the mudroom.

"What are you doing out here?" I asked.

"Waiting for you. I knew good and well you'd go down to the crime scene. I'm not stupid."

"No, you aren't, but it's obvious you're just as hardheaded as I am."

"Let's go, if we're going. It's cold."

I let her have the last word as I slammed into the car to drive to the place a woman's body had been dumped. Jitty-Maxwell had not been far off. It was indeed in the middle of my driveway.

Although I didn't know the dead woman's identity, I recognized her from Jaytee's description—she had to be the woman who'd had an argument with Sister in Playin' the Bones. She had on a chic black wool coat over a black minidress. Her dark hair spread across the white shells of my driveway. Her hair was damp but not sodden, so she'd been dumped after the rain had ceased. She'd been laid out, her hands crossed over her chest, as if she were awaiting burial. As soon as we arrived, Millie grabbed my arm. "Do you think Gertrude did this?" she asked.

"No. I think this has to do with the McFees."

"But why is she in your driveway?"

"I could hazard a guess, but I think I'll wait to see what Coleman says."

"*If* he'll talk to you," Millie said.

She had a point. Coleman was so angry that I hadn't stayed safely in the house that he only glared at me. He and DeWayne were waiting on Doc Sawyer to come before they loaded the body and took it to the hospital.

"How did she die?" I asked DeWayne.

He looked at Coleman, who turned away. Reluctant to answer, DeWayne finally said, "Blunt force to the back of the head. All that curly black hair is hiding the wound."

"How long has she been dead?"

"Doc will be able to say for certain, but it's been a few hours. She's stiff as a board."

Rigor mortis had set in, so the woman had been dead longer than three hours. She hadn't been there when we came home from the blues club. It was now just after four in the morning. Someone had known that I was out and waited for me to get home to make this hellish deposit.

"You said you got a call." I confronted Coleman. He had to talk to me eventually.

"Yes."

"Would you mind sharing the details?"

"Yes." He turned away and spoke to DeWayne, who was walking down the road to light the way for Doc with his flashlight.

"Coleman. Stop it."

"Sarah Booth, you delight in putting yourself in danger. For no reason."

I knew why he was so worried. "It isn't Gertrude Strom's work. This is related to my case."

"How so?" He could barely contain his skepticism.

"I think this woman had an argument with Sister at the blues club. Jaytee overheard them making threats to each other about some contract."

"Who is she?" Coleman was at least interested now.

"I don't know, but somehow she's connected to Sister. I'll find out as soon as it's daylight."

"I'd have more luck bringing Sister in."

"A capital idea." If Coleman could force Sister to talk, I might be on the trail of the person who shot at me and Tinkie. I had no doubt all of the incidents were connected, and they all led back to the McFee family.

"Doc is taking the body to the hospital for an autopsy. DeWayne is going with him. Do you want to ride with me to pick up Sister?"

It was like my fairy godmother had waved her wand and given me the best gift ever. "Oh yes. Can I?"

Coleman watched me. "I should say no, simply because you're so pigheaded. But you did help with identifying the dead woman."

"Is that a yes?"

He nodded. "We'll drop Millie at her house on the way."

"Thank you."

"Why don't I stay at Dahlia House with the pets while you two pay a visit to Sister?" Millie said.

"I'd appreciate that." Sweetie Pie and Pluto loved Millie. They would be happy for her company.

"I have to open the café and that means at least an hour of prep work. Remember, I don't have a car."

I reached into my pocket. "In case we aren't back, take my car. I'll pick it up later."

We were all set. Millie drove the critters back to Dahlia House and Coleman and I left for Evermore.

The first floor of Evermore was ablaze with light when we pulled up. I'd thought the campaign workers might be gone, but apparently Colin's key to success involved working his staff day and night.

As we approached the front door, I heard yelling inside.

"You can't do that!" Colin roared. "It's invasion of privacy."

There was a quieter male response, and then I heard Lorraine St. John. "My goodness. The camera *is* on. I had no idea."

"You can't film a man in the privacy of his home."

"Uh, it was an accident. I just forgot the camera was on." Lorraine was totally unrepentant.

"It's no accident and you know it." Colin was furious.

"Think of it this way, Colin. This footage is going to add a human element to the film."

"I'm human because I drank too much? I won't allow you to portray me as a drunken fool."

"Of course not. Drunken isn't where I was going at all. You and Susan go at it like a mongoose and a viper. Great television."

"I will sue you into next year."

"He will, too!" Susan's honey-slow drawl kicked in. "If you want to finish this film, you'd better back off."

Susan wanted that film to be made. She clung to her ambitions for a part in the movie.

"Try suing me," Lorraine said calmly. "Waste of your money, but hey, you've got plenty to waste. Or did I overhear you telling Susan to back off the spending? Seems our major braggadocio capitalist is low on capital right now."

I started to knock, but Coleman caught my hand. "Let's see if this goes any further."

He was right. We might learn more eavesdropping than we ever could through legitimate interrogation. I leaned in to whisper, catching the scent of starch and sunshine that would forever be linked to Coleman in my olfactory memory. "So Lorraine has been filming Colin and Susan in their private moments. This could be juicy."

"And it might reveal motive."

Coleman hit the nail on the head. Unfortunately, the argument between Lorraine, Susan, and Colin ended when Colin and Susan left the room in a huff. Since there wasn't anything to gain by eavesdropping in the dark, Coleman knocked and Lorraine opened the door.

"It's nearly five in the morning," she said, as if we might not be bright enough to tell time.

"We need to talk to Sister."

"She's the only one who's still asleep. Let me wake her." Lorraine was far too pleased with the idea of waking Sister. "I'll have her down here in a jiffy." She opened the door and led us to one of the front parlors. "Have a seat. If the cook is in the kitchen, I'll have her put on some coffee. Your friend is due to begin catering at lunchtime, but I think the kitchen help has coffee and some Danishes."

Coleman took a wing chair and I sat on the edge of a beautiful Victorian sofa. We stared at each other, and I was glad to see his anger at me had burned itself out. "Are you taking her to the courthouse?"

"Depends," he said.

"On what?"

"On her reaction."

Our conversation was cut short as a red-faced Sister came in the room. Her hair was wet on one side. "What do you want?" She spoke to Coleman and ignored me.

"To talk."

"What happened to your hair?" I asked. She looked like someone had poured water on her head. And then I realized that was exactly what Lorraine had done to wake her up. Bravo for Lorraine!

"Bite me," Sister said to me, then turned to Coleman. "You're here at my house at five in the morning to talk? Don't you find that a little strange? I mean, Sarah Booth has all the indicators of a vampire, so I'm not surprised she's up all night and afraid of sunlight, but you?"

"This is official business," Coleman said. He stood and indicated she should take his chair.

"What in the hell is so important that you couldn't wait until daybreak?" She sat down as she complained.

"This." Coleman held his phone so she could see a photograph of the dead woman. "Recognize her?"

"Oh no." Sister put a hand to her throat and went pale. "How did you find . . . is she—"

"Dead? Yes, she is. Who is she?"

Sister's features shifted to those of a trapped rat. I could almost see the cogs turning in her brain as she tried to figure out if she should lie or tell the truth. "What makes you think I know her?" she asked, playing for time to think.

"Because you were seen arguing with her in the blues club."

That was stretching the truth. I'd told Coleman the body had to be the woman Sister was arguing with, but Jaytee had not positively identified the corpse as that woman. Coleman had skipped several steps, and I loved it.

Sister's expression hardened. "I won't lie. I know her, and I was arguing with her in that rat-infested bar. Judging from the fact she's dead, she got what she deserved."

"Who is she?" Coleman's jaw clenched. If Sister had good sense, she'd realize she was skating on thin ice, as my aunt Loulane would say. Coleman would cuff her and take her to a cell without any hesitation.

"It's Krista Yost." Sister dismissed her with a wave of her coral-tipped fingers. "She's a third-rate writer."

"She's dead, Ms. McFee."

"Not my problem."

"You were arguing with Ms. Yost about a contract?"

Even cornered, Sister was a complete jerk. "Yes, we

were. We were collaborating on a book idea, and Krista felt like I'd abandoned her to come here and make the movie. She was upset with me and I blew her off. I told her I had bigger fish to fry than some piddling series. I'm the bestselling author, the name. She was riding *my* coattails."

"What book idea?" Coleman asked. "Tell me about it. Why would a bestseller take on an unknown writing partner?"

"We, uh, we were talking about a . . . fantasy. A young-adult fantasy. We were going to write as a team. Krista had experience there. I didn't. That's the only reason I considered working with her."

"I'd like to see a copy of the contract," Coleman said.

I thought for a moment he'd nailed her, but she slithered around the question.

"There wasn't a contract. That's what Krista was annoying me about. She wanted a contract, and she wanted me to sign it. She wanted it all down in writing."

"Sounds reasonable to me," I said. "So she was the person shadowing you around town. And it sounds to me like you were lying just to get attention."

"Of course it would, because you're stupid. No writer of my stature would commit to a series of books with a person like her. I agreed to coauthor the first one and see what happened."

She was lying through her teeth. I knew it as well as I knew my name, but I couldn't prove it. I started to argue, but I noticed Lorraine sitting across the room with her camera rolling. She was filming the whole interview. Sister's lies would eventually come back to haunt her.

"Do you have any information about Krista Yost's family?" Coleman asked.

"She lived in New York. She wasn't a friend; she was

a business acquaintance. I don't really know anything about her. She was a nobody."

"Sarah Booth, it might be time for that tune-up you're always talk about."

"You want me to slap her silly?" I asked Coleman. Her total disregard for a woman's death was . . . exactly like her. She'd been that way as long as I'd known her, totally self-focused and without compassion for anyone else.

"I've never wanted anything more." He closed his notebook. "But I can't let you, and it's a crying shame." He stepped back from Sister. "I'm not going to take you in right now, but don't leave Sunflower County."

"I don't have to pay any attention to what you say. My daddy is going to be the next U.S. senator from Mississippi. I'd be careful what restrictions you try to impose on me." Sister didn't have a brain the size of a pissant's. Coleman wanted to pop a knot on her head, and she didn't have sense enough to stop goading him.

"I'd be careful of my conduct. It would look bad for your father if you were arrested as a murder suspect." Coleman wasn't the least bit intimidated by threats of big bad Putin-heckling Colin.

A young man wearing a red blazer and navy slacks and looking like he'd been groomed for the part of back-room political muscle, stepped into the room. The overhead light reflected off his shaved head, and, when he flexed his muscles, I thought the arms of his suit might split. "Ms. McFee, your father wants you to stop answering questions."

"Shove it," Sister said eloquently.

"Who are you?" Coleman asked him.

"Johnny Dan, Mr. McFee's campaign security manager in Mississippi. Miss McFee, please come with me."

"I don't have to do what you say and you'd better stop following me around. I see you skulking behind me all the time. I won't be followed like I'm a child. Note what happened to the last person who tried to sneak around after me."

Sister was dumber than a post. This man had come to save her from her own blabbermouth, and she'd climbed up on her high horse and kicked him in the face.

"It's not me telling you to be quiet. It's your father." Johnny Dan never looked at me or Coleman. He drilled Sister with a dark gaze. "Shut up now."

Sister stood up. "How dare you talk to me like that?"

"Shut up or I'll pick you up and carry you to your room." He turned to Coleman. "Please leave. Now.

I had no doubt Johnny Dan would follow through on his threat, and I wanted to see it. I reached for my cell phone to record the momentous event. With any luck he'd throw Sister over his shoulder like a sack of 'taters. Tinkie would love it. Before I could get my phone out, Johnny advanced toward Coleman and me. "Get out. If you want to speak to Ms. McFee again, you'd better have an arrest warrant."

Coleman chose not to push the matter. He'd get a warrant if he needed one. He motioned toward the door. As I turned to leave, Lorraine shot me a thumbs up. She was going to play hell with the McFee family. Colin, in his quest for fame, had allowed the asp to his bosom. His man-nipple dancing bosom.

13

Coleman was deep in thought on the way back to Zinnia. We both knew that somehow, Sister was involved in Krista Yost's death. Could Sister have actually wielded the bat or pipe that killed her? I believed she could and would. But that was merely a suspicion. I needed proof. So who was Krista Yost, really, to Sister? That question warranted a lot more investigation.

As Coleman drove, I googled the name and came up with—surprise—the fact that Krista Yost was a published YA fantasy writer, just as Sister had said. Color me perplexed.

"Sister wasn't lying, at least about Krista's writing credits."

"There's a lot more to their relationship." Coleman

asked me to read the Wikipedia information on Krista. It was short and sweet. She'd published two YA fantasy novels to limited success. She lived in New York City.

We stopped by the Sunflower County Hospital to see if Doc had any autopsy results. I'd known Doc my entire life, and he often administered medical care with a big dose of advice that my parents might have given. Doc had adored both my parents, and he'd taken care of the cuts, scrapes, and minor broken bones of my physically active childhood. After I became a PI, he nursed me through gunshots, poisonings, and my miscarriage. I could count on him to tell me the unvarnished truth whenever I asked.

We found Doc in his small office with a pot of coffee that looked and smelled like it had been brewed in the 1700s. Even Coleman, who could drink anything, refused a cup when Doc offered.

His white hair a wild cloud, Doc looked at me with frank unhappiness. "Sarah Booth, I don't like it that the body was left in your driveway. That's deliberate. She wasn't killed there. Someone went to a lot of trouble to haul a dead body to your driveway. Why?"

"I don't know."

"Her name is Krista Yost," Coleman said. "She's a writer from New York, someone involved with Sister McFee. We're still trying to figure out why the body was left at Dahlia House. Do you have a time of death yet?"

"Around two a.m. Wherever she was killed, there should be a large pool of blood. The killer cracked her head open with something like a bat or a pipe."

"Could a woman have done it?" I asked.

Doc gave me a sour look. "Someone like you, sure. An athletic woman could have easily crushed her skull in. It's all in the swing. I'd say the person who did this absolutely meant to kill her. There was great force. I'll know more when the autopsy is done."

"Anything else?" Coleman asked.

"She was healthy and in the prime of her life. It's a tragedy. Does she have next of kin?"

"That's what Sarah Booth is going to find out for me." Coleman's gaze told me he meant business.

"Sure thing." Better to work *with* Coleman than have him sitting on me like a two-hundred-pound guard dog.

"Then let's get 'er done."

Coleman dropped me at Millie's to get my car. He grabbed my hand as I was getting out of the car. "Thanks for helping me, and I should tell you I gave Cece a hot tip for a story. Don't be mad."

Before I could answer, he drove away. I went in for some coffee and grits. I hadn't slept a wink, and it was catching up with me. As I sipped coffee and tried not to slump, I thought about the work I needed to get done before lunch. A nap was out of the question. I had to catch Tinkie up on the busy night. She'd be upset that I hadn't called her when the body was first found. I should have, but I didn't want to endanger her if someone was out there intending to hurt us.

I'd call Tinkie as soon as I got home. Coleman had given me my marching orders. Some Internet research would likely yield the information he needed. And it was info I needed, too, because whatever affected Sister might have a bearing on what had happened to Son.

I'd just dug into my cheese grits when Millie came up beside me. "Did you see the big story in the newspaper?" She refilled my coffee cup.

"What story?" I hadn't had a chance to pick up the *Dispatch*.

"Colin was a suspect in the murder of his brother in Switzerland. It's all over the front page. Cece broke another national story."

I started to stand and then fell back in my chair. That was the information I'd asked Coleman to get for me. And he'd given it to Cece—that's what he'd meant when he drove off. I started to get mad, but I immediately saw the genius of his plan. Colin would have to combat the newspaper story, even if he wouldn't talk to me.

Millie whipped over to the counter and returned with a newspaper. She slapped it on the table with pride. "Cece rattled the bones of Colin McFee's skeletons. His campaign is going to be scrambling like mad to bury this. And by the way, Sweetie Pie and Pluto are in the back office. They didn't want to stay at Dahlia House alone, so they came with me. I already fed them."

"Thanks, Millie. You're like their fairy godmother." I opened the paper to a glaring headline. "Mississippi Senatorial Candidate Questioned in Brother's Death." Cece hadn't pulled any punches. Colin would be out for blood.

"I called Cece and told her you were here," Millie said. "And Tinkie, too. We should have called her earlier. No one likes to be left out, and she should have been given the chance to exercise her judgment."

"Yeah. I'm just tired of the taint of death around me all the time. I'm tired of my friends being in the line of fire just because they're my friends. Besides, we have no way of knowing how a dead woman figures into the McFee case."

"Right." Millie didn't look like she believed that reasoning would pass muster. "Maybe Cece can come up with a better excuse." The bell over the door jangled and Cece entered the café. She was elegant in a spice corduroy miniskirt, boots, and a longish forest-green sweater.

"My phone is on fire, dahlink!" Cece slipped into a chair at my table. "Colin must have called fifty times and his campaign workers are threatening to protest in front of the newspaper."

"I'll bet."

"Colin has issued a statement saying he was innocent of any wrongdoing in the death of his brother." Cece held my gaze. "Look, I published the facts from the crime report without embellishment. Circumstantially, Colin could have killed his brother. But I tend to believe him, Sarah Booth. And no charges were ever brought by the Swiss authorities. That's all in my story, too."

It was interesting to see that tiny shred of guilt nagging at Cece. She was a tough reporter, but she didn't like to falsely accuse. "You printed the facts. It would be wrong if you'd buried the story. Besides, all publicity is good publicity for a politician." I paraphrased the words of P. T. Barnum. "Coleman needed you to break that story. He had to put Colin on the defensive, and the story you printed is based on facts and the investigative reports of the Swiss police. Think of it as karma. Colin and Sister have done much worse to Son. They've labeled him a mother-killer for the past five years—without a shred of evidence. They never held back."

"True."

"You're darn tootin' it's true." Tinkie had slipped into the café with a gaggle of farmers. She sat down and picked up the newspaper. "I heard something about this on the radio driving over," she said. "You've broken another national story, Cece. Congrats."

"I haven't had a chance to read the story," I said. "What did the police reports from Switzerland show?"

Cece was more than willing to oblige. "Colin and his brother went exploring. The brother, Liam, was a little . . . he wasn't quick mentally. According to Colin, an ice sheet collapsed and buried Liam. Reports indicate that Colin tried to dig him out but couldn't. By the time he got help, it was too late, but there were also suspicions in the report that Colin's version might not be totally true."

I thought of the story Mrs. Fagan had told me about the boys tunneling by the creek and how Liam had almost died then when a bank collapsed. Was this happenstance, a penchant by the dead brother for caves and exploration, or something darker? "How old was Colin when Liam died?"

"Twelve."

"He was a kid. I mean, was he even old enough to think about killing his brother?" Tinkie asked.

"The *Global Enquirer* ran a story last week about a new generation of killer kids." Millie's eyes were wide. "They murder on a whim, and some of them are as young as nine. They mostly target siblings or weaker children in their neighborhood."

"Colin is certainly a narcissist," Tinkie said. She shuddered. "What if he's killing off his family? And what if he's elected senator?"

"Would that be so bad?" Cece asked. "There're a lot of people in Congress who just need killing. Maybe Colin can accomplish what the voters can't."

I didn't want to laugh, but I did. Everyone joined in. "Did you get a comment from Colin?" I asked. I'd never been a journalist, but I knew that a good reporter always gave each side a chance to have his say.

"He wouldn't speak to me." Cece finished the last bite of her French toast, maple syrup dribbling. "I gave him every chance."

People who refused to talk to the media were foolish. Colin had an opportunity to explain and didn't take it. "Lost opportunity."

"I did learn something from one of the ranting calls he left on my voicemail." Cece had played us like a cheap fiddle. She'd been holding out all along.

"What?" We all leaned in closer.

"Cleo had been receiving threatening phone calls for about six weeks prior to her death."

This was big news. "What kind of threats?"

"I have the message." She put her phone on speaker, and Colin's voice came through, a little tinny but clear.

"You reporters are a scourge on the face of the earth. My greatness makes you so jealous. And you're lazy. I've seen welfare mothers who worked harder than you. You're not a journalist, you're a nuisance. I didn't kill my brother, and I didn't kill my wife. If you did your homework you'd know someone had been terrorizing Cleo for weeks before she died. You call yourself a reporter. Well, get off your butt and dig for some facts."

"Wow." I was shocked. Colin had gone off the rails. Nowhere in the police report I read at the Washington County sheriff's office was there a mention of harassing or threatening phone calls made to Cleo prior to the wreck.

"Do you believe him about those calls?" Tinkie asked.

"I don't know," Cece said. "It's easy enough to make that up. Unless he kept a recording of the calls."

"Wouldn't he have brought that out when the wreck first happened?" Tinkie asked.

"Not if he meant all along to put the blame on Son."

"But if there was someone stalking Cleo, what if they're back? What if that's the person who took a pot-shot at Tinkie and Sarah Booth?" Millie looked upset. "There could be a homicidal nutcase out there after the McFee family and anyone connected to them. You know politicians attract fruitcakes. Garfield and McKinley were killed by maniacs. Teddy Roosevelt was shot on the way to deliver a speech. He survived and gave the speech anyway. Lincoln was killed by a Confederate sympathizer *after* the war was over. And . . . Kennedy!" Her eyes looked like Orphan Annie in the comics. "There's the connection. Colin has been talking about the Kennedy assassination. What if it *is* Putin behind all of this? What if a Russian operative is embedded in Zinnia?"

Tinkie pulled out her phone without blinking an eye and made a call. "Hello, Doc, I need a prescription for some Xanax for Millie. She's totally flipped out."

I snorted I laughed so hard, and even Millie joined in.

"Girlfriend, you are running on some high-octane fuel, aren't you?" Cece said.

"I was having a moment of connectivity," Millie said. "And now I have to connect some apple pies to the oven or I won't have dessert for my lunch regulars. But if there was someone after Cleo, and that person is still around, maybe they killed that poor woman who wrote children's books. There's a lot of strange stuff going on in Zinnia, and I believe it's all inter-connected."

Millie was right about one thing. A lot of strange things had happened in the past few days. Krista Yost's murder was at the top of the list. Was she connected to

Cleo and Son's accident? And if so, how? There was only one link I could find. Sister McFee.

"It had to be Sister who killed Krista Yost," Tinkie said as she read over my shoulder. I was at my desk at Delaney Detective Agency. The front windows gave a sweeping view of the long driveway and the side pasture where Reveler, Lucifer, and Miss Scrapiron grazed. "This woman was a young-adult fantasy writer. Who could hate her enough to bash her skull in?"

"I don't know." I'd found only the basics of Krista Yost's career, little more than what I'd already found on her Wikipedia page. Her personal life was sadly empty. No husband. No kids. No close friends that I could find. Her parents lived in Wyoming, and I left it to Coleman to tell them their daughter had been murdered. Thank goodness that wasn't something I had to do.

"It's after nine in New York. Her publishing house is open now. Want me to call and talk to her editor? Maybe they can shed some light on what Krista was doing down here in Mississippi."

"That would be great." Tinkie was over her huff about my not calling her to a murder scene at zero dark thirty.

I leaned back in my chair and listened to Tinkie's side of a very interesting convo. She'd taken hold of the Krista Yost angle and was shaking it like a rat in a terrier's mouth. In fact, she reminded me of her lionhearted little Yorkie, Chablis. She had hold and wasn't letting go.

"Does Ms. Yost have an agent who might be able to give us more information?" Tinkie asked. A moment later she said her thanks and hung up.

"I didn't get a lot. Her editor wasn't aware of any YA

fantasy collaboration in the works, but she said it wasn't uncommon for authors to flesh out ideas before presenting them."

"So we can't prove Sister was lying."

Tinkie shook her head. "Not yet. I got Krista's agent's name. Let me make a call there."

I went to the kitchen, made coffee, and brought two cups back just as Tinkie hung up the phone.

"Better!" She took the hot coffee and sipped. "Lindie Bosch, the agent, was shocked to hear of Krista's death. She said Krista was loaded with talent, but hadn't been able to achieve that breakout book that would set her career. She also wasn't aware of any collaboration in the works with Sister McFee."

"So what contract was Krista Yost so upset about?"

Tinkie pondered her answer. "I don't know, but you can bet Sister was screwing her out of something. That's just who Sister is."

"Surely we can find out." I chewed my bottom lip, and not with the same effect that Tinkie could evoke. "I wonder where Krista was staying and if Coleman has searched her room."

Tinkie dialed the sheriff and handed me the phone. "You call him."

I didn't have a chance to refuse because Coleman answered the phone. "Tinkie and I want to search Krista Yost's hotel room. Are you finished there and where is it?"

Coleman's baritone held amusement. "It's at the Prince Albert, room 305. And yes, DeWayne and I have been through it. You aren't going to find anything."

"Because you found it already?" I asked.

"Not exactly. Because someone beat us to the room. It

was totally trashed. Whoever searched it didn't care what they destroyed in the process. And I have no way of knowing if they found what they were looking for or not."

"Because Krista is dead and can't tell us if anything is missing." I didn't hide my disappointment. "Damn." I told him what Tinkie had found out from the editor and agent. "So if there was a contract between the two women, Krista Yost's agent and editor weren't aware of it."

"Since you're sharing facts, I'll tell you something I learned from Susan Simpson McFee. She stopped by for a visit. I have to say, she sprinted up the steps and down the hallway like an Olympic contender. Never mind she's about to pop with baby."

I wasn't interested in her preternatural athletic abilities. "She just showed up at the sheriff's department?"

"She said she'd been meaning to have a conversation with me. She likes my uniform."

"Don't get too excited. She's in perpetual heat." I couldn't believe Coleman was simple-minded enough to fall for Susan's flirtations.

"She is a hot number. Colin must have his hands full taking care of her needs. She knows how to make a man feel . . . manly."

Coleman was deviling me, and I refused to bite. "I concede, she's oversexed. Not of interest. Move on to the important stuff. What did she tell you about the case?"

"I just thought you'd want my assessment of her. She's one hot number. Even pregnant. I'll bet when she's lithe and limber she could turn a man inside out."

A flicker of green crossed my vision. Coleman was working on my jealousy button. "You can test that theory for yourself in about three weeks, once she's spawned.

She's like a carrousel horse. Anyone who pays a quarter gets a ride." My voice crackled with heat that I couldn't tamp down. Coleman's chuckle was so self-satisfied it made me angrier. "Either tell me or hang up. I don't have time for this."

Tinkie grinned. They were both enjoying my torment.

"Simmer down, Sarah Booth." Coleman paused to chuckle. "Susan has no love lost for her stepdaughter. Anyway, Susan said Sister left Evermore last night about nine o'clock. Colin had put a tail on her, that big galoot Johnny Dan. According to Susan, Sister slipped her leash about nine-twenty. So Sister has no alibi that I can discover for the time of Krista Yost's murder." When I didn't immediately respond, he said, "I thought that would cheer you and Tinkie up."

"Any idea where Krista was killed?" That would tell us a whole lot.

"Not yet. My hopes are high, though. Krista Yost was a striking woman, and she drew attention wherever she went. Someone is sure to have noticed her after she left Playin' the Bones. She did come back to the Prince Albert. She told the hotel clerk she didn't want to be disturbed because she had pages to write for her next book, and she went to her room. She scheduled a massage for ten o'clock, but she didn't answer the door when the masseuse knocked. The valet said she paid him to arrange for a rental car, and she left the hotel about nine p.m."

"So wherever she went, she intended to be back by ten." Tracking Krista's activities would give us at least a blurry picture of what she'd been up to.

"The kicker is, there's no evidence of any writing and no laptop. Which doesn't make sense at all."

"So that's what they took! The laptop. The evidence

of what she and Sister were working on. No blood in the room?"

"She wasn't killed there. My best guess is that she went to meet someone and that's when she was murdered."

"But who?" That was the question we both wanted answered. "Tink and I are going over to check her room."

"Be my guest. It's trashed, and we've taken prints and done what we could. Just let me know if you happen upon something. Or someone. DeWayne interviewed the desk clerk and two bellboys. We tried a door-to-door in the hallway, but the place was empty. A lot of the guests are following the blues trail, looking up locations and history, not hiding out in a hotel room."

"We're on it." I hung up and motioned Tinkie into action. "Let's head for the Prince Albert. I'll tell you what Coleman said on the way."

"And I'll tell you what Bess Billingsley had to say about Son." Tinkie had truly played her cards like a master.

14

The pale January sunlight bounced off the brick street in front of the Prince Albert Hotel as Tinkie and I exited the revolving glass door. Our search of Krista Yost's room, as Coleman predicted, had been fruitless. And Tinkie's talk with Bess Billingsworth had yielded only facts we knew—Son was a great guy who torpedoed his own career due to some personal torment.

As Harold had indicated, Bess loved him. But she hadn't spoken to him since she broke off the engagement. She'd married and built her own life.

Another dead end.

We stepped into the brisk day and left the lobby's warmth behind. I inhaled the sharp, cold air that made me think of new beginnings. Last night's heavy rain had washed the streets clean, and the ochers and mustards of the clay bricks shone like new copper pennies in a few remaining puddles.

We'd parked the Cadillac behind a dress shop and were on foot. As we passed the storefronts and displays, I saw Tinkie staring at the cutest little purple swing minidress. Amethyst accents sparkled from a prim lace collar to the short hem. Sexy schoolmarm came to mind.

"That's adorable. You want to run in and try it on?" I wasn't a shopper, but hunting the perfect outfit was like crack to Tinkie.

"Not the dress! Behind the dress."

I shaded the glass so that my reflection disappeared and stared into the interior of the boutique. Susan Simpson waddled toward a dressing room clutching at least ten dresses. All of them were too short, and all of them were not designed for the body of a woman who had swallowed a beach ball.

"Maybe she's shopping for after the baby is delivered," Tinkie said as if she read my thoughts.

"Come on. This might be a good time to ask her some questions." I pushed open the door and stepped inside the shop. Tinkie went straight to the purple dress and disappeared into the dressing area. In a moment I heard the murmur of conversation. It sounded friendly enough.

"Oh, that dress is adorable on you," Susan said. I peeked over the saloon-style doors and saw Tinkie modeling the dress in front of a full-length mirror. It was indeed adorable on her. Not so much with Susan. She'd chosen a red V-necked jersey that would have been perfection—had she not been pregnant. Susan had had the hottest body in the Delta, and I had no doubt she'd be back in fighting form minutes after she popped that baby out. But right now . . . that dress did not fit.

"When are you due?" Tinkie asked.

"I have another month. February 5." Susan put a hand at her back. "It's like being a prisoner in someone else's body. I can't believe this has happened to me."

Tinkie laughed merrily. "It's not like you don't understand *how* it happened. And Colin is so very proud. It's almost as if he didn't have children with Cleo. He acts like this coming baby hung the moon."

"Son was a disaster. Sister isn't much better. Needy, needy." Susan sighed. "I'm sorry, I'm just a big *B* today. Hormones and backache. And did I mention living with a political campaign *and* a movie production company. It's total bedlam at Evermore."

"No need to apologize. Sister is unkind to me every chance she gets. For no reason at all." Tinkie's frank admission shocked me a little, but it was tonic to Susan.

"I've noticed how cruel she is. What happened in college?"

"Tell me something first. Why doesn't Colin just toss the film crew out on their ear?" Tinkie asked.

"It's the estate settlement. Colin was cut out. That old puritan Jamie left everything to Sister. But she doesn't inherit until February 5. So essentially they've agreed to share the house. Colin had to have a Mississippi address for his campaign headquarters. Evermore is perfect. Sister invited the film crew, and I honestly don't think she knew that she'd opened the door to Satan's playhouse. That Lorraine films everyone all the time, always pretending it's an accident. I keep expecting her to kick in the bathroom door when I'm taking a tinkle." She heaved a sigh.

"But Colin says we have to get along. At least for right now. Once he's elected we'll buy our own estate north of Sunflower County."

"That makes sense." Tinkie examined another dress that would look fetching on her. She had an eye for fashion.

"You said you'd tell what happened in college." Susan was nothing if not persistent.

This was fish or cut bait. If Tinkie meant to make a friend of Susan, there was only one way—to share the public humiliation that would give Susan the upper hand. Susan would know her secret. Something she wouldn't even tell me.

"I'll tell you part of it," Tinkie bargained, which only made her sound more sincere. "And the rest later. It's not all that big a deal, except it really hurt me. You know, childhood wounds and all of that. Would you like to grab a coffee or brunch? The Prince Albert has a lovely little dining room."

Susan looked at her reflection in the mirror and sighed. "Yeah, sure. Why not? I'm wasting my time trying to look good in this condition. I'd pay someone to carry this little parasi—bundle of joy for the last month, if I could. I'd pay them handsomely. I'm dying to get back in shape before Marco starts filming. He's considering me for a part."

"Acting is so exciting, and this is right in your backyard and all about the people you know. I think you'd have emotional access that another actress wouldn't."

My god, Tinkie was good.

Susan flipped the dress off with a practiced move and returned to the dressing room to find her maternity clothes, if the tight yoga pants and top could be classified as such.

I skedaddled out of the shop and hied myself over to the Prince Albert. A corner table by the kitchen door gave me seclusion. A half-wall with chives, sage, oregano, and dill growing in planters along the top provided good cover. If Tinkie could wrangle it, she'd invite me to her table, but if not, I'd be close enough to get some photos and hear a portion of the conversation.

When Tinkie and Susan arrived, Tinkie made sure Susan's back was to my table, clever partner that she was. She ordered iced tea and salad plates and settled in for a gossip. The restaurant was quiet, the rush over. I occasionally missed a comment, but I caught enough of the conversation to keep up. Using my phone, I snapped away, documenting the meeting, though I was only getting Susan's back.

Tinkie got right to the confession. "When I was a freshman and I pledged the same sorority as Sister, I'd hoped we could be friends. We were from the same county, though I didn't go to high school with Sister because she and Son went to a private school. She was two years older, too. But I looked up to her, and I was so excited that we'd be part of the same noble organization. I took all of that stuff very seriously back then. You know, legacy pledge and all."

"No, I don't know. I went to business school," Susan said. Though I listened hard, I couldn't detect any jealousy. "It was the quickest way for me to find a good-paying job, and I did. I made up my mind I wasn't going to live the life my mother had, cutting coupons and scraping for months to buy a prom dress for her daughter."

"Because you're smart," Tinkie said. "Brains trump background every time."

I couldn't see Susan's reaction, but she leaned forward. "I have to feel sorry for Sister sometimes. Colin can barely tolerate her she's so desperate. And she's crap to everyone in his campaign. They loathe her. I'm surprised she hasn't pushed me down the stairs trying to end this pregnancy. I watch her shooting daggers at my baby." She put her hands over her ripe abdomen. "She's so afraid someone will try to take something from her."

"Would she really try to hurt the baby?" Tinkie was all concern.

"I wouldn't put it past her. She hasn't been as nasty to me as she is to everyone else, but only because she wants Colin to adore her. So what did she do to you?"

Only I noticed the hesitation in Tinkie's face. This was a very difficult memory for her.

"Sister had a boyfriend. He was the kicker on the Ole Miss football team and had incredible prospects of going pro. Guy Neely was handsome and wealthy and popular. He was the pick of the litter at Ole Miss. He played football but was getting his undergraduate degree in international business, just like Son."

Susan was intrigued. "I heard Son mention this Guy Neely before. At McFee Enterprises, the men were always talking sports. Testosterone bonding."

Tinkie nodded in sympathy. "Yes, male bonding. Anyway, Sister had everyone believing Guy proposed to her. He was Son's good friend and Sister had finally done something that caught Colin's approval. Colin liked Guy. I think he liked him better than his own son. Colin invited Guy to a family vacation and began to talk about a job at McFee Enterprises. It was clear Colin saw Guy as a potential son-in-law."

Tinkie painted a complex picture of those long-ago days at Ole Miss. I'd forgotten the drama of dating and popularity and who was who and why they mattered in the college hierarchy. I had a sudden gut-churning memory of a boy I had a mad crush on and how his glance across a classroom could rattle every fact right out of my head. Those were crazy days of hormones, hangovers, and heady hope. The future hung at the edge of the campus, and we were all waiting to graduate and step into our dreams.

As a theater major, I'd been protected from the sorority/sports competitions. Theater had its own egos and battles, but nothing like the Greek system and athletics. Nothing like the cliques where ready money made too many things too easy and sincerity too hard. That had been Tinkie's battlefield, and though I'd never realized it, she hadn't come out of it unscathed.

"So why didn't Sister marry the boy with the golden foot?" Susan asked, eager for ammunition against her stepdaughter.

"Because Guy came to the sorority house one day to pick her up as I was leaving to go to class. I bumped into him at the door. We chatted for a few minutes, and then I went to my American history class. Guy started calling me. I never went out with him. I wouldn't do that because I knew he was Sister's beau. But Sister hated me. She told everyone I broke them up, that I slept with him and tricked him—and every girl in the sorority believed Sister. No matter what I said, they wouldn't listen. The truth is, I never even shared a coffee with him. I adamantly refused to see him, but sometimes he waylaid me at campus events or when I was leaving a class. Sister blamed me because Guy dumped her, and I honestly had nothing to do with it."

"Of course Sister would blame you. It has to be someone else's fault, not her own. She never looked in the mirror and saw the relentlessly unhappy creature that she is. No one wants to spend time with a spider."

Tinkie's face fell. "She really doesn't see it, does she?"

Susan's laugh was brittle. "She can't see it because she's a narcissist and can't see beyond her own needs. Don't waste your compassion on her, Tinkie. She'd stab you in the back, slather you with barbecue sauce, and roast you on a spit. And never lose a wink of sleep."

That Susan didn't like her stepdaughter was an understatement. Just how much did she dislike Sister? More than a wagonload. It would seem Susan had a lot of influence over Colin, and perhaps Sister's hard road with her father was because someone was ahead of her digging trenches. If there had been no money to inherit, would the bitterness between the family members be so intense? I honestly doubted that it would. Money had turned family into foe. And, in the grand scheme of things, Susan was only an in-law. The baby she carried was her only link to a direct claim to the McFee fortune.

While Tinkie and Susan bonded over salad and iced tea, I had a Bloody Mary and googled McFee Enterprises. Hoots Tanner had given us a solid lead, and I needed to pursue it. I eavesdropped on Tinkie with one ear but went down a list of corporate offices and the people who held them on McFee's website. Hannah Martin wasn't listed as an employee, but I finally found a name and bio that looked interesting. Dorinda Posey was listed as chief administrative officer of the clerical staff.

Somewhere in the back of my mind, I knew Dorinda's name, and a Google search brought up that she was an Ole Miss graduate just a few years younger than I was. She'd been vice president of the SGA and held a number of other campus-wide positions, which is where she met Son and fell into his sphere. She'd majored in public administration, with an emphasis on employee relations and a minor in theater. Hence her position at McFee *and* my knowledge of her. I remembered her as moderately talented in theater but nice and very pretty.

Cold-calling anyone was a risky business, but I didn't have a mole in McFee and I needed to check out Susan Simpson McFee's background there. More importantly, I needed someone to tell me what had driven Son from the up-and-comer to the down-and-outer. What had torpedoed him? Someone with an Ole Miss connection might be more willing to talk. It was at least worth a phone call.

Tinkie had finished a general conversation about the accident that claimed Cleo's life and Son's sticky relationship with his father. Now she was digging into Sister's inheritance, obviously a sore subject with Susan. "You know, my son-to-be is just as entitled to part of the estate as Sister, but that old zealot Jamie never liked me. My baby will be a McFee just like Sister, but he won't get any of the trust or estate. Do you think that's fair?"

Tinkie didn't say it, but I knew what she was thinking—Colin's extramarital behavior went against everything Jamie held dear, and Susan couldn't be colored an innocent party. She'd known Colin was married. No way in hell would Jamie McFee have left a cold penny to a homewrecker like Susan, or her offspring.

"So you met Jamie," Tinkie said, adeptly turning the

question aside. "I was always scared of him. He seemed so stern."

"Colin always disappointed him. No matter what he did or didn't do, it wasn't good enough. Jamie used to come by Colin's company when I was working as Colin's private administrative assistant. He took one look at me and he knew that I was involved with Colin. It was like he could read my thoughts. Old codger. He could sniff a sin a mile away. And he loved Cleo. That really hurt Colin. That his grandad preferred his wife, a non-McFee, to him."

Tinkie moved in with delicacy. Her tone was totally sympathetic. "I saw the headline in the newspaper about how Colin was a suspect in his brother's death in the ice cave when they were in the Alps. He was only twelve. That was unfair."

"Tell me about it. The media will do anything for a headline. Anything. And that reporter, Cece Dee Falcon, is around Evermore all the time. Marco invites her there to help with the movie publicity, and Colin can't seem to get her banned. Sister won't listen to reason. She doesn't want to make the editor at the *Zinnia Dispatch* angry. The St. Johns and the movie have given that Falcon woman national headlines. Now that craft service will be there, even more strangers will be roaming about. I wish Colin would give up this political run and just go back to Memphis. We were happy in Memphis."

"You don't want to be the wife of a senator?" Tinkie asked. "That's a lot of power, and I think you'd be terrific at it."

"Since Colin started this Putin thing, his business has taken a few hits. Some of his business partners have backed away. They think he's over the edge. Frankly, I'd prefer we go back to Memphis and work on the San Francisco Bay development. There's a lot of money to be made on that project. We should get back to doing what McFee Enterprises does best."

I couldn't see Susan's face, but her tone of voice was upset.

"Why does Colin want to be a senator?" Tinkie asked gently.

"It's Jamie. Even though he's dead, Colin has to do something extraordinary to prove that Jamie's assessment of him was wrong."

"That's going down a long hard road to prove something to a dead man." Tinkie caught me peeking through the dill over the half-wall that hid my table. Her look sent me scuttling down.

Susan sighed. "I just want our lives back. The pregnancy, the run for political office, the book—these things have destroyed our lives. Now the one thing I want to happen, the movie, is something Colin wants to fight. It's just not fair. I've done everything to support him, but he thinks the movie will be bad for him, and as long as he's acting like a bully, I don't think Marco will seriously consider me for a part."

"I could put in a word for you." Tinkie offered the magic elixir.

"Would you?" Susan would have climbed on top of the table and danced had she not been pregnant.

"Sure. Once the baby is born, there's no reason you shouldn't audition."

"I just want a chance. Just a swing at the ball. I might not get this part, but if Marco will only let me show what I can do as an actress—I would be forever grateful if you could help me. I've been working out the whole pregnancy.

I've gained muscle tone and strength. I broke the Thigh-Master last week. My inner thighs are killer!"

Tinkie signaled for the check. "You have the perfect attitude for success. I'll definitely speak to Marco." She gave the waiter her credit card. "Susan, I've run across some rumors that indicate someone might have deliberately run Cleo's car off the road. I know Colin hired an investigator. Did he find any indication of foul play? Were those rumors thoroughly checked out?"

Susan drained her tea glass and sat back. "I was with Colin in his condo at Oxford that night. He didn't have a clue what Cleo was doing. Colin wants to believe Son was high and simply went off the road. Without a body, there wasn't a way to check for drugs in Son's system. There wasn't a way to see if years of hard drug use led to a stroke or heart attack."

"But Colin and Sister are so determined to say it was Son's fault. I don't understand why."

Susan rubbed her stomach. "Colin tried to find out the truth. He hunted for answers, but when he couldn't get any he latched on to the explanation he wanted. I tried to convince him not to blacken Son's reputation, that it would just reflect poorly on the McFee name. He wouldn't listen to me. And Sister was the cheerleader for blaming Son, even though there really wasn't a shred of evidence." She pushed herself out of her chair. "It made me very sad."

"The movie will further blacken Son's name."

"And I've accepted there's nothing I can do to stop Colin and Sister from going down that road. If you think you can, you're welcome to try. Now I have to find a ladies' room before my bladder pops. Then I'd better head back to Evermore. Colin is having another of his press conferences. I came to town to buy a new dress for it, but I'm a whale." She sniffed and then straightened her back as if she'd found a burst of energy. "If Colin takes his shirt off one more time to taunt Putin, I'm going to dump a bucket of cold water on him right in front of the TV cameras. Thank you for lunch, Tinkie."

Tinkie said her goodbyes and we slipped out of the restaurant while Susan took care of business. "She's got good sense," Tinkie said. "She wants to stop the political campaign, and I don't blame her."

"I heard most of what she said. Not a lot of sympathy for Son."

"No. Her ambitions outstrip her compassion. A lot of people suffer from that, but it isn't a crime."

15

We called Cece and alerted her to Colin's press conference as we headed to Dahlia House. Tinkie agreed that I should call Dorinda Posey and set up an appointment for the next morning. It would be better to question her face-to-face if she would allow it.

In the meantime, we made a quick detour to the courthouse to check on Coleman's progress with the investigation into Krista Yost's murder.

We'd just arrived when Coleman and DeWayne came barreling out. A disaster was averted when Tinkie yanked me out of the way. "What's going on?" Tinkie asked before I could get the words out.

"I think Junior Wells found the murder site by his office."

Junior was the bail bondsman who had a shop on one side of the courthouse quadrangle. "Right on the street?"

"Come on if you want, but I don't have time to chit-chat."

Since we were invited, we followed behind the lawmen. They didn't stop for a vehicle but walked across the grass to Junior's business. Junior was a tall, slender man with a face so wrinkled he reminded me of a sad Shar-Pei—in the best possible way. He'd been a friend of my father's, and I liked him. He was no nonsense about his job and he'd always been up front with me, even when I disagreed with some of his decisions.

"I called as soon as I found the blood," Junior said, leading us down a narrow alley to the back of his business. The pool of blood made Tinkie inhale sharply. We stopped, making sure not to get close to the evidence. Contaminating a crime scene would endear us to no one.

"Someone or something died here," Tinkie said. "The amount of blood . . ."

She didn't have to finish. No living creature in Zinnia could survive that blood loss. When Coleman found a pipe stained with blood, dark hair, and a fragment of scalp thrown into a weed patch at the very back of the property, I knew he had the murder weapon. Someone had struck Krista Yost in the head behind the bail bondsman's building. But what on earth was Krista, a New York writer, doing behind Junior's business? How had she come to be at that location?

DeWayne and Coleman went to work collecting the necessary evidence. Finding the location of the actual murder was a step in the right direction for the investigation.

It would help in numerous ways. But there were still plenty of unanswered questions.

Junior came to stand beside me and Tinkie. "The day the young lady was killed, I got a call. Woman didn't identify herself, but she was a Northerner. City gal. I recognized the accent. She wanted to know if I'd provided bond for any of the McFees."

"Assuming that was Ms. Yost calling, why would a fantasy writer care about that?" I wondered aloud.

"Better question, have you provided bond for any of the McFees?" Tinkie asked.

"I was asked to make bond for one of them."

My head whipped around as if I were possessed. "Who?"

"Sister McFee."

"When?"

"It was just before the accident that killed Cleo and Son. Before Coleman took office."

Coleman frowned. "I checked the record. There were never charges brought against Sister or any McFee."

"Cleo dropped the charges and it was all swept under the rug."

"Cleo!" We all spoke in unison.

"Better give me the details," Coleman said.

"Cleo was staying at Evermore and organizing her Delta education initiative. She'd been down in Yazoo City and returned home. She and the old man, Jamie, were close. She found Sister there, trying to coerce her great-grandfather into changing the will to exclude Son. Of course, Jamie being Jamie, he was having none of it and apparently accused Sister of working as Colin's agent."

I could easily imagine that scene, and it was one I was glad I hadn't had to witness.

"Anyway, Cleo and Sister got into an argument, and Sister spilled the beans about Susan and how Colin had bought her a mansion in Memphis."

"Oh my." Tinkie looked stricken. "That must have hurt Cleo. It's one thing to know your husband is a cheating sack of . . . well, you know. But to be slapped in the face with it by your daughter, and in front of Jamie, too. How awful. She must have been humiliated."

Junior looked sadder than I'd ever seen him. "Harsh words were spoken. Jamie was furious with Sister. Cleo told me that Jamie slapped Sister in the face, and she turned around and pushed him. Hard. Had Cleo not caught him, he would have fallen to the floor and possibly hurt himself. He was ancient, and his bones were brittle. Cleo was so undone by Sister's temper and lack of control, she called the law and pressed charges against her. The sheriff had no choice but to go out to Evermore and bring Sister back to the courthouse. In the end, Cleo dropped the charges."

"No official record," Coleman said.

"Right," Junior said. "That was very important to Cleo. She knew Sister for what she was, but she loved her anyway." He stood a little taller. "You might check back at Ole Miss. It seems Sister got into an altercation there. It was hushed up, too."

"So Sister has a pattern of violence?" Tinkie made it a question, but we both knew the answer. Another strike against her—*if* someone did harm Son and cause the accident.

"What kind of altercation?" Coleman asked.

Junior shrugged. "I didn't get any details, only that

Cleo was concerned about it. She tried to convince Sister to get professional help. Sister held to her bluster and said she'd been justified."

"I know what she's capable of." Tinkie put her hands on her hips. "She's a mean person. And she likes to hurt people."

"That's two documented incidents of aggressive violence." I counted them off. "Jamie and Ole Miss."

"Three." Tinkie said, but refused to be pushed for more details. "Suffice it to say, I'll tell everyone what happened if I have to, but until I have to, I prefer to keep the details to myself."

"While you've uncovered a pattern of bad conduct, we have nothing tying Sister to this crime scene," Coleman reminded us. "I wish we did, but we don't. We'll process what we find. Maybe there'll be some trace on the pipe, but Sister isn't stupid. If she did this, I'm sure she was wearing gloves. I'm sure the clothes she was wearing are history."

"Maybe we can trace the pipe," DeWayne said. "It looks like a used water pipe. See the build-up inside. Someone changed out their pipes, and maybe we can find out where."

"We'll check around at the local hardware and see if there have been any renovation projects," I offered.

"Excellent," Coleman said. "Just as long as you understand, even if they just replumbed Evermore, that's no guarantee that any McFee is involved. They could have hauled the pipes to the dump and someone picked it up from there. It won't hold up in court as evidence that a McFee was involved unless there is DNA on the pipe."

He was right. But at least if we got that close to Evermore and the McFees, and lit a bonfire of fear, we might be able to flush a rat.

"Will you let us know what you pick up at the crime scene?" Tinkie and I weren't really helping here. We had other fish to fry.

"Sure thing."

Since the hardware store was only two blocks away, we bade Junior farewell and walked over to Happy Jack's Supplies. Zinnia had not yet attracted one of the huge chain hardware stores, and I hoped it stayed that way. Jack Sullivan had a vast supply of things I had no clue how to use, but he was always available to explain and help me with repairs at Dahlia House. Special orders came in every day, so while inventory at the store might be slim, all needs could be met.

"Sarah Booth and Mrs. Richmond," he sang out when we entered the store to the sound of baby chicks. "Just got some Rhode Island Reds in. Great laying hens. You should start your flock and have fresh yard eggs every morning." Jack was all about going back to a clean, personally sourced food supply.

"Sarah Booth has three horses and a dog and cat. She doesn't need chickens," Tinkie said. "She'd have them in the house, too."

"No doubt," I said. "On those cold winter nights they'd have to come in and roost in the parlor."

Jack laughed at my foolishness. "What are you ladies looking for? A bathroom remake? Maybe a new stove?"

"Has anyone made any home improvements to their plumbing lately?" I asked.

He frowned. "Why are you asking?"

"We're working on a case."

He went behind the counter and fiddled on the lower shelves, and I knew he was buying time before he answered. Jack was an open and friendly man, but he wasn't a snitch. He knew everyone in the whole county, but tended to his own life, not others'.

"You know I don't like to talk about my customers," he said. "Folks like to keep their business to themselves, and I like to oblige."

I propped myself against the counter. "A woman was murdered. Galvanized steel water pipe smashed her skull. Only the older homes are plumbed like that now. Don't most use PVC?" I'd learned to be up front. Jack could find his way through a moral quagmire.

He considered. "Couple of people have come in for a few repairs. A pipe here and a pipe there. Colin McFee replumbed Evermore last fall. He was moving his campaign headquarters there and needed bathrooms added and so forth. He had a carpentry crew from Memphis, but he bought his supplies from me. And I appreciated it."

I held up a hand. "This doesn't implicate Colin or anyone else. The pipe used to kill the woman could have been pulled from a trash pile or dump. This just gives Coleman a direction to look."

His frown eased a bit. "Colin is a brash, arrogant man, but he wouldn't harm anyone. He's had his trials and tribulations, like everyone else. Just 'cause he's got money doesn't mean he doesn't have troubles too."

"We're not accusing anyone of anything. I'm sure Coleman will get to the bottom of it," Tinkie said. "Could I see those carpet samples? My bedroom is looking threadbare. Maybe some new carpet would perk it up."

For the next twenty minutes, Tinkie compared the different carpets and finally put in an order for a delicious jade green. Jack agreed to send a carpet team to measure the room and have it installed the next day.

When she'd settled her business, we found the car and returned to Dahlia House. Five minutes later, I had Dorinda Posey on the phone, and Tinkie and I had an appointment in Memphis at eleven the next morning. Dorinda hadn't even asked why we wanted to talk to her. And for that I was glad.

The day had been long and tomorrow promised to be as busy. Tinkie gathered Chablis and headed home to dinner with Oscar. I prowled the kitchen and finally settled on a tuna fish sandwich. My cupboards were all but bare. In contrast, Sweetie Pie had a serving of hamburger steak that Millie had sent to her. Pluto snacked on some of my tuna fish. He had plenty of dry food and sometimes enjoyed his kibble, but he wanted what I ate, and because I was a pushover, I obliged.

I considered a brief ride but settled for feeding and grooming the horses. Pluto and Sweetie Pie frisked in the dying light of the day as I plied the curry comb. I loved brushing the horses' thick coats, and they enjoyed the attention. I fed them apples and carrots while I worked.

I unsnarled manes and tails and listened to the contented sounds of munching as the sunlight faded and the dusky lavender of twilight slipped around me. In the east, the dark navy of night blinked the stars into existence. Dahlia House glowed like a birthday cake in the darkness, beckoning me inside. Somehow I'd managed to slip Coleman's protective custody. He'd been adamant that someone had to stay with me at Dahlia House at night because of Gertrude Strom's unrelenting attacks on me.

Gertrude, a former B&B owner, had taken it into her head that my mother had betrayed a secret. And Gertrude was determined to even the score by hurting me and my friends. I'd accidentally run Gertrude down on the side of Highway 3 when she'd leaped in front of my car in an attempt to waylay me. The thud of flesh meeting metal led me to believe I'd killed her.

When Coleman went to check, though, her body was gone.

And so Coleman had begun his attempts to keep a watchdog at Dahlia House at night, even though Sweetie Pie was the best watchdog ever and had come to my rescue more than once. Since Gertrude hadn't put in a resurrection appearance in recent weeks, I fervently hoped she was dead. Because I believed that to be true, I was glad for an evening alone. Though I adored the company of my friends, I wanted to sift through the myriad of details of Cleo and Son's accident.

I'd first believed Colin had bumped off his wife so he could marry Susan. Then it had seemed Sister might be the ultimate villain who'd killed her mother in an attempt to prevent Son from inheriting his portion of the McFee trust. Or simply because she'd had a temper tantrum, a theory based on her bad conduct in the past.

With Krista Yost's murder, Sister seemed even more likely to be the villain in Son and Cleo's tragedy. Not a single other person in Sunflower County even knew who Krista was. Unless her death was an act of random violence—which was belied by the fact her body was dumped at the bottom of my driveway—then Sister was the only person in Zinnia who might benefit in any way from the fantasy writer's death.

The noose was tightening, and soon Sister McFee might be swinging to Tinkie's tune. And it would be just payback for whatever she'd done to my partner.

I blanketed the horses, put out two bales of hay because the night promised to be cold, and opened the stall doors. I didn't like to shut up the horses in the barn when it was freezing. They could stay warmer moving about, and the insulated turnout blankets would help. The barn doors were open in case they chose to munch the hay I left in their stalls.

Tinkie hadn't been far off about my penchant for bringing the animals inside. I would have them snug in the kitchen if I thought they'd like it. Horses were grazing animals, though, and they preferred the cold night and the freedom of pastures to romp and roam.

As I skipped up the back steps my cell phone rang. I answered as I entered the warmth of the kitchen, a sensual pleasure after the cold outside.

"Marco St. John here. Sarah Booth, I'm taking the film crew into Memphis for some barbecue, blues, and booze. We're picking up the screenwriter at the airport, too."

"That's great, Marco." I wondered why he was passing his calendar by me.

"Colin has a rally in Jackson."

"I'm happy for him," I said, perplexed at this information.

"Evermore will be empty. Lorraine has purchased highly sophisticated cameras and recording equipment. If we're ever going to get to the bottom of what happened to Son, we're going to have to play dirty. I want those cameras in Colin's bedroom, the gym, his office, the library, and anywhere else you feel Colin might discuss his secrets."

I'd been dreading this request. "Are you sure—"

"Don't worry about the legal repercussions. It's taken care of."

"How?"

In the background I heard Lorraine telling someone to lock and load, it was time to party.

"No worries. You set up the equipment. I'll worry about how we use the footage."

I had a bad feeling about this. A really bad feeling. But the truth was, Marco had paid Delaney Detective Agency ten grand for information on what had happened to Son and Cleo McFee. While I'd done a lot of legwork, I had little to show for it. If this was the route Marco wanted to travel, I could either do the work or return his advance.

And at the bottom of my black little heart, I just wanted to know the truth.

"When is Colin leaving?" I asked.

"He's gone. Sister and Susan went with him, as did his campaign staff. They took a bus to prove he was a 'man of the people.' "

"Where are the cameras?"

"In our bedroom. Look in the bottom dresser drawer. They're top of the line, very discreet. They'll feed into a recorder in my room. Lorraine has them set up. All you have to do is install them somewhere with a good range and low chance of detection." Marco laughed. "Colin will hit the ceiling if he finds them. Then again, he'd probably blame Putin."

"No doubt." I actually cringed at the thought. Though

I wanted to say, "This may not be the best idea," I said, "I'm on it." Best to get the job done before I gave it too much thought. "Is there a ladder in the house?"

"I'll have one in my bedroom. Good thinking, Sarah Booth."

This job required speed and stealth, but I knew there would be no leaving Sweetie Pie behind. If I tried, she'd follow the car. I debated calling Tinkie, but remembering her hissy fit over not being called when Krista's body was found, I punched in her number.

When I told her what I was doing, there was a long silence. "What if you get caught?" she finally asked.

"Colin will probably ransom me back to the KGB as a spy."

"You won't be laughing if we're charged with espionage."

"We?"

"Of course I'm coming to help. I'm your partner. We haven't turned up a useful bit of evidence about Son. If this is what Marco wants, we're obligated."

Thank goodness she saw it the same way I did. "Want me to pick you up at the Sweetheart Café?" Millie's was closed, but I was suddenly starving. I could grab a milkshake.

"I'm on the way."

"Sorry about dinner with Oscar."

"He was coerced into attending Colin's political rally in Jackson. It's a bank thing. Daddy said he had to go." Tinkie's father owned the Bank of Zinnia, which Oscar ran. Normally, Mr. Bellcase stayed out of the banking business since his son-in-law had taken over, but sometimes he requested that Oscar represent the bank at functions.

"Poor Oscar," I said. "Hey, maybe Colin can teach Oscar how to make his nipples dance."

"That's crossing a line, Sarah Booth. I love Oscar, but if he *ever* did that . . ."

I knew she could hear my laughter as I hung up.

16

I had a chocolate milkshake in hand when Tinkie pulled up beside me. Along with Sweetie Pie, who'd inhaled a small vanilla cone, I jumped into her car and handed her the chocolate mint milkshake I'd ordered for her and a tiny cup of vanilla for Chablis. With her underbite, Chablis had issues with the cone. Not so, Sweetie Pie. She'd slurped the ice cream down to the cone and then opened wide and ate the whole thing. Crunch, crunch. The wolf in *Red Riding Hood* had nothing on Sweetie Pie when it came to ice-cream cones.

I held Chablis' cup as Tinkie drove and Sweetie settled into the backseat for a snooze. The car was warm and the night was dark. Sweetie loved to ride in the car and, like many babies, sometimes went right to sleep.

"Thanks for the milkshake." Tinkie's Cadillac tore through the night. "I'm kind of glad to have something to do. I hate the long, dark nights alone. Oscar said he'd be back about midnight."

"That gives us plenty of time." I filled her in on Marco and the imminent arrival of Roon Talley, the scriptwriter.

"Sarah Booth, we have to come up with some idea of what happened to Son. We're at the same place we were when we started. Except now we have a woman murdered, and we're about to break and enter and install hidden cameras."

I rubbed the place between my eyebrows hard. "We haven't found any evidence to indicate what happened to Son. All we have are a dozen theories from murder to accidental death."

"I'm uncomfortable with bugging Colin, but I don't see another choice." In the pale light of the dashboard, Tinkie's features were drawn. "Someone disappeared the physical evidence of Cleo's wreck. I can't believe they stole a car, a big car. And anyone who might have seen something helpful can't remember squat. Convenient memory loss." Tinkie expressed my frustration perfectly.

We pulled up to the gate of Evermore, which was standing wide open. Creepy. "Remember the old stories of this house being haunted?" Sweetie heard the reluctance in my voice and put her front paws on the back of the seat. Her head popped up between Tinkie and me. She was checking it out, and a low, worried moan escaped.

"Who could forget the ghost stories about Evermore? I had a hot high-school date on a dirt road that runs parallel to this property. We planned to leave the car and sneak across the property and kiss on the front porch. You know, a dare."

"Did you sneak on the premises?"

She shook her head. "Jamie was living here then. If he'd caught me he would have called Daddy, and I would have been grounded for the rest of my life. Daddy wouldn't have seen the fun in that episode."

"Jamie *was* viewed as a sinister figure by a lot of the teenagers, living alone, in this huge house. And he had that long beard and blue eyes as hard as flint. My father loved him."

"I really was intimidated by him. He looked like Moses with those fierce eyebrows. I always thought he kept a staff he could hurl to the ground and turn into a snake." We laughed softly, the car idling at the gate. We were procrastinating, and we both knew it. It didn't feel right to sneak into someone's home and put up spy equipment. "When Mr. Jamie shot a look at someone, they felt it like a punch."

"Jamie was stern, but he was known to be a fair man with impeccable ethics. How did Angus and Colin turn out to be such . . . wastrels?"

Tinkie shook her head. "Too much pressure, maybe. Or a family gene for dysfunction. Not our problem." We pulled through the gate and drove across the empty grounds. The house was as still as the proverbial tomb. Marco had disabled the surveillance cameras across the grounds and around the house. He'd also told us of a gravel path behind the farthest outbuilding. We were to drive down the path and park. The road led through a copse of trees and across some fields to a gate that fed onto a county road. The back gate would also be left open for our exit. All I had to do when we left Evermore was hop out and close the gate after Tinkie drove through. No one would ever know we'd been on the premises.

Tinkie followed Marco's instructions to the letter and turned off the car. "Let's get this done so we can leave. I don't like being here."

"I second the emotion."

The car was toasty warm but I put Chablis in the curl of Sweetie Pie's body and covered them with a warm blanket. They'd be fine. We would be gone twenty minutes, tops.

A weak crescent moon rode the night sky, and we slipped among the gathering shadows that guarded the house in twisted shapes and differing degrees of darkness. The idea that the shadows were alive—watchful even—made my skin dance and pucker. The old stories of Evermore and the headless gardener who prevented trespassers came back to me. Best not to mention that to Tinkie. Still, I was high-stepping as we made it to the entranceway.

Marco had left the front door unlocked for us. He was actually a pretty good mastermind. He'd thought of everything. Five minutes later we had the tiny cameras and were scouting Colin's bedroom for the best angle.

We placed the first one in the recessed television cabinet, which was left open. I figured Colin kept the TV on when he was in the room. CNN never stopped, and that was coverage he needed to stay on top of. The repetitive nature of the twenty-four-hour news cycle drove me batty, but Colin would thrive on it. He could watch clips of himself over and over and over again.

The king-sized four-poster bed was in the angle of the camera, and that was just plain creepy. Good thing Marco and Lorraine would preview the footage. My sex life, which was sad at the moment, would shrivel and die at the thought of watching intimacy involving Colin

McFee. My eyeballs would melt in their sockets, and my ovaries, decrepit at best, according to Jitty, would shrivel and fall out on the floor.

"Let's go," Tinkie whispered, as if there were anyone close enough to hear us.

We put a camera in the baby's room, and I couldn't help but wonder what it would be like to grow up with parents like Colin and Susan McFee. The child would want for nothing, but Colin's public brashness and buffoonery would be a thorny cross for a sensitive child such as Son had been.

"Good idea on the nursery," Tinkie said. "Soon Susan will give birth. I envision Colin and Susan cooing over the child and talking about the future—and how they'd bumped off Uncle Son and Grandma Cleo to clear the path for the new arrival." Her sarcasm hit the target perfectly.

"If only it would be that easy to get a confession," I said. We hustled on to the gym, the library, and Colin's office, where we installed cameras in places no one would think to look.

"What about Sister's room?" Tinkie asked.

We had one camera left. "Let's do it. I think she's behind the Sunflower River accident if anyone is. We've covered every room on Marco's list, but I actually think Sister is the best bet."

"The bad thing is she's alone in the room," Tinkie pointed out. "She doesn't have anyone to talk to or confide in, so she may not say anything useful."

I shrugged. "Let's place it, and if it doesn't yield anything, Marco can turn off the feed. We might not get a chance to do this again."

"Good thinking."

We scampered into Sister's room, dragging the aluminum ladder Marco so thoughtfully provided for us. Instead of helping me place the camera at the top of the heavy draperies, Tinkie poked through Sister's drawers.

"Looking for something incriminating?" I asked. "Or just being nosy?"

"Both. Look at these matching bra and panty sets. Her undies say she's having hot sex all the time. Her cranky attitude says she hasn't been laid in a month of Sundays." She tossed a rainbow of undies to the top of the dresser.

"Remember, you have to put everything back just like you found it."

"Pox on her. Surely there's something here that links Sister to a crime. I'd prefer the murder of her mother and brother, but any crime will serve my purposes. There must be evidence."

I put the camera in place and prayed Sister wasn't the type to throw the curtain back and welcome the sun. I had her pegged as more of a rise-at-noon-and-stumble-to-a-coffeepot kind of gal. "Let's get out of here. We have that meeting with Dorinda Posey tomorrow."

"Memphis, right." Tinkie brought up something hidden in a drawer. She walked it to me. The photo of Son and Sister was taken when they were in their early teens. Son had his arm around Sister, a clear sign of affection. In fact, it was the only photo I'd ever seen where Sister looked happy.

"What happened to them?" I asked.

"Money. The root of all evil."

The sound of the front door slamming made my body jerk straight so fast I thought my head would pop off.

Tinkie replaced the photo, and I shoved the ladder under the bed. We ducked into the puddled draperies, praying that it wasn't Sister and that she hadn't come home with the intention of going to bed.

Footsteps came up the staircase, slow and ponderous. Whoever it was carried some weight. Judging from the sound of the steps, I thought it more likely to be a man than Sister. That didn't relax me a bit. Tinkie's hand found mine and squeezed as we pretended to be part of the fabric we hid behind. I wished I'd checked to see how the windows latched. If push came to shove, we could jump from the second floor if the ground was clear.

The bedroom door creaked open and someone slipped through the room toward the far wall, which was paneled and contained a beautiful marble fireplace. I couldn't see a damn thing, but I heard a latch open and a sigh of relief. A minute later a compartment closed and the footsteps left the room. The bedroom door latch snicked into place.

We waited five minutes before we dared to peek out. The room was empty.

"Who the hell was that?" Tinkie whispered.

"I don't know, but we have to get out of this house before we're discovered. But *not* before we check out whatever the intruder was looking at." I went to the walnut paneling and pressed the surface. Something had opened. I'd heard it.

"Secret compartment?" Tinkie said.

"We have to find it."

I pressed along the wall, tapping. I hoped to find a secret hidey-hole. Tinkie, because she was shorter, worked below me. "He was in this area, based on what I heard,"

Tinkie said, "but I can't find a dang thing. The wall sounds like it's three feet thick here." She moved and tapped lightly against the beautiful paneling.

As she moved closer to the fireplace, I moved up the wall. "Who do you think was in the room?"

"I don't know, but it wasn't Sister. I don't like her, but she moves with a degree of grace. This was someone heavy. Maybe that Johnny Dan character, Colin's campaign security guy."

"So someone other than us is watching Sister and trying to find her secrets."

"Or making sure her secrets are still safe."

"I wish we'd caught a glimpse of him. It had to be a man, or a really, really big woman."

The sound of something shifting downstairs stopped us in our tracks. "What was that?"

"Let's get out of here." Tinkie was already moving toward the door. "I don't want to end up trapped in this bedroom."

I pushed off the wall to catch up with her when I heard a click. A small painting beside the fireplace moved away from the wall on a hinge. "Crap." I had to stay now. Tinkie, too, returned. I looked at the face of the little wall safe.

"We don't have time to open it," Tinkie warned. "There's someone downstairs, and they could come up here any minute. We need to hide and figure out an escape route. I'm worried about Sweetie Pie and Chablis. They're in the car. If someone finds the car . . ." She left the rest unsaid but I knew what she was thinking. Someone might harm them.

I fiddled with the dial of the safe for a minute, trying to think what might be significant to Sister. To my surprise, the safe opened. It had never been locked. I reached into the opening and brought out a manuscript. *The Dawn of Eros* was the title. And there was a note. "Here's the manuscript, delivered just as I promised. Please initiate the payment." The note was signed, "Krista."

Tinkie arched one eyebrow. "I may be jumping to conclusions, but—"

"I don't think Sister is writing her own books," we said together. We'd stumbled on the mother lode of best-ever reasons for someone to murder another person.

I snapped a photo of the note and typed pages, stuffed the manuscript back in the safe, and put the painting flush with the wall. Tinkie was right. It was time to cut and run.

The front door opened and voices drifted up the stairs. I recognized one that sent chills through me. Johnny Dan was in the foyer. "I've got men on the perimeter," he said. "Mr. McFee was very specific. He said someone had threatened to burn Evermore down. Get the searchlights and weapons."

Well nuts! What a night for some kook to make a threat against another kook.

Tinkie clutched my hand. "What about the ladder?"

"Leave it. Marco can retrieve it later. What are the chances Sister has ever looked under her bed? She has a servant to fetch her slippers."

Tinkie nodded. Tiptoeing, we made our way to the door and cracked it open to listen. As far as I could tell, the coast was clear.

I signaled Tinkie toward the gym. There were back-stairs on that wing, and I certainly didn't want to go traipsing through the parlor if Johnny Dan was there. He could crack our heads like raw eggs.

I had a million thoughts buzzing through my brain, but we had to focus on silence and escape. Laughter came from the front parlor, and I paused when a deep baritone said, "I love that rifle. Took it out a few days ago and did some target shooting. The trigger is sweet. Just the right amount of pull."

Were they discussing shooting at Tinkie and me? I had no way of knowing. I wanted to demand an answer, but I wasn't a total fool. We slipped down the dark servants' stairs, which would likely end in the pantry or kitchen area. I hadn't noticed a staircase in the brief tour with Colin.

"Johnny, the surveillance feeds are all down. Did you turn them off?"

"Oh no," Tinkie whispered, pressing against the stairwell wall. "It won't take them long to figure they've been breached."

She was right about that. "Let's go." We sped blind down the dark staircase and luckily avoided breaking our necks. We hit the first floor in a dark room that smelled of fresh paint and a bit of mildew. I used my phone for a flashlight and discovered we were in a cleaning pantry with mops and buckets and two large sinks. The walls glistened a pale yellow or white, I couldn't tell by the light of my phone. Five pieces of galvanized pipe leaned against the wall in the far corner.

Exactly the kind of pipe used to kill Krista Yost.

"Sister did it," Tinkie said, not moving toward the pipes. "She did it because Krista was writing her books for her and wanted more money or credit or something."

"I know Sister is a catty overgrown brat, but do you think she'd really bash a person's brains out?" Sister had a sharp tongue and a quick checkbook, but it took a level of fury or fear I wasn't certain she had in her to crack a skull with a pipe.

"She'd do it in a heartbeat, or else she'd pay someone to do her dirty work." Tinkie didn't hesitate. "She was a monster at Ole Miss. She forced everyone to do things they didn't want to do. She humiliated people with such pleasure that even the older girls were afraid of her. Bitsy Mopes had twiddles that—"

"Had what?" I had no idea what she was talking about. I thought for a moment she might have succumbed to a McFee fever or something.

"Bitsy had two littles, two pledges with one big sister are called twiddles. Anyway, Bitsy liked the girls she was in charge of. Sister set them up with frat dates who drove them out of town and left them in the woods saying they were hunting a local legend, the DeSoto witch. Those girls were terrified. They dropped out of school. Neither one would report Sister for setting them up or the frat boys who followed her instructions. Sister escaped punishment. She always did."

Hiding in a dank room of Evermore with pipes that resembled a murder weapon wasn't the time for true confessions, but I had to ask. "The things you told Susan. Were they true? How Sister hates you because she thinks you stole her fiancé?"

"All true. Sister never married. I think she cared for Guy. The problem was he didn't care for her. He told me she was manipulative and mean, and he wasn't getting caught in that trap no matter how much money her old man had."

"But he pretended to like her." Or at least that was how I understood the story.

"Guy was as mean as Sister in his own way. Too bad he

dumped her, because they were a match made in heaven. The only difference was that he wasn't as well funded. He couldn't create as much mischief because he didn't have the bankroll. But he did his fair share of damage."

I didn't know the person she spoke of, and I was glad I didn't. "Let's get out of here." I snapped a photo of the pipes in the corner. I knew better than to actually touch what might be evidence.

We pushed open a heavy door and moved through a series of rooms, including a wine cellar. There had to be a way to the outside. We should have planned this escape better. Marco probably knew every nook and cranny in the house by now, but I hadn't anticipated anyone returning so soon.

Our wandering led us to a dead end, and we returned to the mop room and found another door. We must have been beside the kitchen because I heard a familiar voice. Millie was at Evermore.

"I wanted to bring in supplies and my cooking pots," she was saying. "Could your men unload my van? I catered lunch today, but trying to haul hot food is foolish when the Evermore kitchens can accommodate all of my needs."

"Sure," Johnny Dan said. "What's for lunch tomorrow?"

"Pork roast and dressing," Millie said.

My mouth watered at the thought, and I'd never been gladder to hear my chef friend's voice. Millie was our ticket out of a sticky spot. "If we can get to the kitchen, Millie will pretend we're her helpers."

"No," Tinkie said. "We let them unload the van and then we hide inside until Millie gets us out. It's like a prison break."

"The dogs! We can't just leave them in your car."

"Millie can circle around to the back gate and let us out. We'll walk in and drive out."

Her plan was the best. "So where the hell is the door?" I asked. We'd found ourselves in a maze with no exit.

"There." She pointed to a faint glimmer of light. And when we got there, she was dead on. We turned a glass knob and stepped into the big pantry Colin had shown us on the house tour. Behind a closed door was the kitchen and the bustle of Dan's men bringing in Millie's supplies. We were saved.

Half an hour later the van had been emptied. Johnny and his men had returned to the parlor and Millie went to speak to them. Tinkie and I dashed through the kitchen, out the backdoor, and into the parked van. I'd never been so glad to be outside in the cold in my life.

17

The van was out the gate and rolling before Tinkie spoke. "Don't freak out, Millie." She pushed the bubble wrap we'd hidden under off her. "Sarah Booth is here too."

Kudos to Millie's great nervous system and her driving, she didn't even swerve off the road. "Tinkie Bellcase Richmond, I should spank you. I almost had a heart attack when that mountain of bubble wrap began to move. I thought a critter had gotten into the van while we were unloading."

"Just me and Sarah Booth."

I popped up too. "We got stuck in Evermore and couldn't get out."

"I don't even want to know what you were doing. And

how would you have gotten off the premises if I hadn't come along?"

"But you did," Tinkie said with such gratitude that Millie's mood changed.

"What in the world were you doing creeping around Evermore at ten o'clock at night?" Millie asked.

"Long story, and the less you know the better for you."

"Listen, you two, you can't take risks like this." Millie mother-henned us, and to be honest, I was glad to hear it.

"They wouldn't have hurt us," I said. "Not like as in hit us or shot us . . ." The longer I talked the less assured I was of my statement. "But we would surely be arrested. Then Coleman would have hurt us for being reckless."

"In the end you get hurt—that's the thing that worries all of us. And just so you know, Coleman would be right to throw you both in the pokey." Millie pulled the van to the verge. Evermore was several miles behind us and the road stretched long and empty in both directions. "How did you get inside Evermore? You need a gate code and there are surveillance cameras." Awareness dawned. "Someone on the inside helped."

"We can't confirm or deny," Tinkie said with an impish grin.

"You two need a keeper. I hope to goodness you found something worth all of this danger."

"First of all, the house was supposed to be empty. And we found out Sister has a ghostwriter for her books. Krista Yost, the dead woman."

"Now she really is a 'ghost' writer," Millie said. "Do you think Sister actually killed her?"

"We found pipes just like the one used to hit Krista in

the head." I showed her the photo I'd taken with my phone.

"What did Coleman say about this?"

"We decided to wait until we were clear of the property."

"Right." Millie adjusted the mirror so she could see us. "You haven't figured out how to tell him without giving away the fact you broke in and entered at Evermore."

"This requires some finessing," Tinkie admitted.

I gave her the bad news that we had to fetch the car and the dogs. Millie only grunted as she put the van back on the road and drove us to the gravel path that led through field and woods. It was going to be a hike across the property to the car, but there was nothing for it but to set out.

"I could drive you in," Millie offered.

"Not a chance. If we get caught, that's on us. If you get caught, you'll lose the catering job and get in a lot of trouble." I turned to Tinkie. "In fact, you go with Millie and I'll retrieve the car and dogs."

"Oh, noble one," Tinkie said, pretending to grovel. "I live to obey."

"Stop it."

"Then stop acting like an idiot. It's my car. If something untoward happens, at least I can sacrifice you and drive the dogs out."

"Okay, okay." She'd made her point. "Millie, please let us out. We'll text as soon as we clear the property."

"I should get Coleman to go in there and keep them occupied with a search warrant or something until you make your escape."

"We're good." My desire was to delay the confrontation with Coleman as long as possible. "The car is in a place where no one can see it. The moon is bright enough to drive without lights. No need to involve Coleman. He's exhausted, I know."

"Yeah, it's his sleep patterns you're worried about." Millie was nobody's fool. "I'll give you thirty minutes. If I don't hear from you by then, I'm calling Coleman."

"Good plan," Tinkie said. "And the clock is ticking."

We waved goodbye and headed down the gravel path, which was easy to follow in the moonlight. I hadn't anticipated a long walk in the cold night, but I found I enjoyed the exercise and the company.

Once Tinkie agreed to call Coleman and tell him what we'd learned, we planned our activities for the next day. We'd made no progress on finding out what had happened to Son, but we had a hot lead in Krista Yost's murder. That had to count for something.

At last we arrived at the car where Sweetie and Chablis were still curled under the blanket, snug and safe. As soon as we cleared the property I sent Millie the all-clear text. Twenty minutes later, Tinkie deposited Sweetie Pie and me at the roadster in the Sweetheart Café's parking lot. Our mission was successfully completed. Now, I could only hope the cameras worked and someone gave up some secrets.

I slept the sleep of the innocent and woke the next morning to sunlight and Tinkie's knock on the door. Thirty minutes later I was dressed and walking out with a cup of coffee. Memphis wasn't far, so we decided to leave Chablis at Dahlia House with Sweetie Pie and Pluto. The cat was annoyed that he'd missed the adventure the night before, and he let me know it with cold contempt. I would surprise him with a remote-operated rat that I could send scuttling all over Dahlia House. Memphis was the place to buy such cat-bribe toys.

The day warmed as we passed the empty fields and hit the highway. The McFee Enterprises building rose twenty-eight stories in downtown, and we parked in the attached multilevel parking garage. The same parking garage where Hoots Tanner thought someone had tampered with his brake lines. My spine gave a little tingle, but, as far as I knew, Dorinda was the only person anticipating our visit, or at least that's what I hoped. Paranoia was my companion, but not my friend.

The McFee building had been an old bank with floors of rental offices. It was constructed in the 1960s, a time when "institutional" design bowed to utilitarian lines, which translated in my non-architecture lingo to "ugly." It had been a Memphis eyesore until Colin McFee took it over and completely revamped it. Gothic flourishes, arches, fountains, beautiful tiles—all had given the old building a new look. Colin might be an egomaniac with a delusional Putin feud, but when it came to working with brick and stone, he had an amazing talent.

"This place is beautiful," Tinkie whispered as we crossed a lobby with a black marble reflecting pool that captured a deep lavender ceiling twinkling with stars. The reception area was designed as an intimate pod with desks and chairs so clients could sit down and talk quietly with the person helping them.

"May I help you?" a young woman asked. She wore her long hair in braids and the nameplate on her desk said Ann Marie Deerstalker. There was a small plaque that explained the role her Native tribe had played in the history of the Mississippi River region.

"We have an appointment with Dorinda Posey." I looked around the reception area to find that many nationalities were represented, each with a small plaque telling their role in Memphis's growth. In the back of the room, on a constantly changing screen, was the story of the McFee family and their role in the development of America—carefully edited to leave out horse thieving and prostitution. But it was Colin's story to tell, and I didn't blame him for selecting the facts about his family he wanted history to remember.

Ann Marie made a discreet call and pointed to two club chairs. "Please have a seat. Dorinda will be down in a moment. We have fresh coffee, herbal tea, scones, bagels. May I get you something?"

"No thanks." But I was impressed. They treated someone off the street as a valuable visitor.

"This place is phenomenal," Tinkie said as we settled into the chairs. The reception area was busy, but the acoustics of the room were so superb, the noise was muted.

Classical music filtered in as subtly as a subconscious urge. "I could spend an hour just walking around to the different desks and meeting the receptionists. Colin really is something of a genius. Why would he want to abandon this for a life in politics?"

This was evidence that Colin was completely nuts. The man had built an empire to be proud of. And he wanted to duke it out with a bunch of greedy, grubbing political animals.

"Ego," Tinkie said. "All about ego."

I didn't have time to comment before a tall redhead

with bright blue eyes came over and held out her hand. She had the grace of a dancer and the composure of someone used to handling difficult situations with ease. "I'm Dorinda Posey." We shook all around. "Please come with me. Did Ann Marie offer you some refreshments?"

"She did and we're good," Tinkie said as we walked to a bank of elevators and ascended to the eighteenth floor.

Dorinda gave us a business promo as the elevator doors opened. The McFee employees were flawlessly trained. "You might remember that once these offices were rented to a host of Memphis businesses, but now McFee Enterprises uses all the floor space, and at the rate we're growing, we could use more."

When we stepped into a hallway, it too was quiet except for soothing background music. We followed Dorinda to a suite of offices decorated with railroad memorabilia, including a model of the rail yard in Memphis with each track labeled and a brief history of the different lines included.

She saw our curiosity. "The railroad played a huge role in how Memphis grew. The railroad bridge over the Mississippi connected the Southeast with the Southwest, and it was key to the growth of the West. Cotton is a remarkable crop, but it doesn't mean anything unless it can be transported to market. Getting the cotton to the Southern ports for shipment to England was crucial."

We settled around a small table and she looked from Tinkie to me. "So, you mentioned Ole Miss on the phone, and I certainly remember both of you, even though we weren't friends. What can I do for you?"

My partner and I had settled on our approach. We would begin with questions about Susan and then work our way to what we really wanted to know—Son's relationship with Colin and Susan and how he'd fallen from grace at the company. Dorinda struck me as a straightforward person, so that's the way we went. "We want to know about Susan Simpson McFee. Her employment, her relationship with others in the office."

"You want me to talk about Colin's wife?" She smiled like a shark. "Why in the world would I do that?"

"Because you can possibly eliminate her as a suspect."

"A suspect in what?" Dorinda was unrattled.

I gave it a beat. "Susan gained enormously by Cleo McFee's death. We're not accusing her of anything because we're still sorting evidence. Cleo's death may have been the result of foul play. *If* that is true, Susan has a very strong motive to want Cleo dead. So if you have information, you can help exonerate her or you can move her higher up the list. It depends on what you tell us. Did you know Susan before she married Colin?"

I would have bet a hundred dollars she did. She was the same age. She'd worked for McFee during the same time period. They were both in the personnel area until Susan transferred to the job of executive administrative assistant for Colin. A position created just for her.

"Yes, Susan and I went to business school together. We also went to high school together. I've known her for a while, if anyone can really know her."

We had hit the jackpot! If she would talk about Susan, we would gradually shift the conversation to Son and his tumultuous tenure at McFee.

"Were you friends?" Tinkie asked.

A shadow crossed her face for a split second. Dorinda knew how to keep her cool, but she had that one tiny tell. No matter what she said, she didn't like Susan. "Answer a question for me first. Who are you working for?"

"Black Tar Productions," Tinkie answered. "We've been hired by the movie company that's filming Sister's book about Cleo and Son's . . . about the accident."

"That other PI, Mr. Tanner. He worked for Colin. He came around asking for Hannah Martin, and the next thing I knew, she'd disappeared. People who gossip don't do well at McFee."

"We don't work for Colin. I promise."

"Right, like that means anything."

"If you know something, please help us. We're trying to clear Son's name in the death of his mother before the film is made."

Dorinda blinked away the sheen of tears. "Five years have passed. If Son were alive, he'd have shown up." She shrugged. "What does it matter if I tell the truth? Susan Simpson and I were not friends. I don't know that Susan can be friends with anyone. From the minute she was hired, her sole focus was bedding Mr. McFee. It took her three months, but she did it. From there, she began to unravel his marriage with single-minded purpose."

I appreciated her bluntness, but there was never just one villain in a triangle. "It takes two to tango."

"Oh, Colin was a willing participant. Men are weak, and Susan is strong. Very strong. And cunning with her sexual power. She would do things like buy a mink coat. When the day was over and the staff was gone, she'd change into something sexy, slip on the coat, and go into Colin's office for dictation." She snorted. "The next day she'd take the coat back to the store and return it. It had served its purpose. Colin would probably have bought it for her if she'd asked, but she was smart. She never asked for anything. Not at first."

"How do you know this?" Tinkie asked.

"Susan's big weakness is that she has to brag about how smart she is. She confided in me, because I wasn't in a place to do a thing about her. I couldn't report her to the head of human resources because Susan knew things about me that would cost me my job. I couldn't tell Mrs. McFee—why would she pay any attention to me? Susan lorded it over us."

"And Son? Couldn't you have told Son?" Tinkie moved the conversation with such skill I almost gave her a high five.

"I would have died before I told Son his father was cheating on his mother. Son adored Cleo, and he wanted to please his father." She inhaled and lifted her chin. "Colin got what he deserved when he married that succubus, but Son, he broke my heart."

While Susan had set a hook in Colin, Dorinda had fallen for the powerless son, the high school hero who'd suddenly become persona non grata in the empire he was due to inherit.

"I went to school with Son," Tinkie said. "I liked him. He was kind and generous and always had time for people."

Dorinda swallowed, the only sign of her emotional distress. "I didn't know him at Ole Miss. I saw him around campus, and I ran into him a lot around here after I took the job. When he started coming to work drunk, I tried to help him. I covered for him when I could. I signed him up for AA meetings. There were times I bailed him out of jail, sobered him up, and brought him back to work. Not because I had the vaguest idea that he was romantically interested in me. I did love him, but he never saw me as anything other than a coworker and friend. He loved Bess. He really loved her." Her defenses lowered for one brief moment. "I would have given a lot to have him love me that way."

"After college, Son was a rising star at McFee Enterprises," I said. "What happened?"

"Something between him and Colin. I never knew, but I can tell you what I saw."

"Please."

"Son started drinking before the board meetings. At first it was just a highball in his office before he left for the boardroom. Then it was two highballs. Sometimes I took the minutes for the meetings, and I watched the progression. After a few months, he was drinking before he came to work. And more at work. I don't know how he got into the pills, whether it was a doctor or a street buy. Once those had a hold on him, it was like watching a slow-motion earthquake."

"Do you think it was just the pressure?" Tinkie asked. "Running a company like McFee would be stressful."

Dorinda's brow furrowed. "No. I don't think it was pressure. Son was doing great. Colin gave him control of the future-projects department the year before, and he'd turned up some amazing possibilities. He loved it. He told me there was nothing better than going to a city, finding a center or zone that had fallen into neglect, and working with his design department to rehabilitate it and bring it back. His passion was reusing urban space so that cities didn't sprawl into the countryside."

"And Colin approved?" My impression of Colin was that he was all about display and having his name on things. Environmental concerns were far down his list of priorities.

"Colin didn't care what Son did as long as money came in. That was Son's genius. He could renovate, rehabilitate, revive urban space, *and* make money."

"He was doing what he loved. He'd found the woman he was to marry. What happened?" Tinkie asked.

"He refused to talk about it."

"He never hinted?" I asked.

"I gave him every opportunity, and I think if he'd been able to tell someone, the burden would have been lighter. But he wouldn't. Or maybe he couldn't. Son would never unload on someone and put them in danger. He carried his own weight."

"Any chance his computer is still here?"

"Colin had it removed the day after he fired Son. That was about eight months before the accident."

That computer might give us a lot of answers, but it was gone, just like the SUV. Someone had gone to great trouble to collect every particle of physical evidence that might bear on Son's watery death.

"Did Son really give up the pills and booze?" Tinkie asked.

Dorinda went to her desk, opened a drawer, and brought out a framed photo. She sat down as she handed it to us. "He sent me this."

In the picture Son held up a trophy for a 10k race. The young man in the photo reminded me of the golden child in the pictures on the second-floor landing of Evermore. Son was back on top. He was winning again.

Dorinda took the frame and stared at the image for a time. "He'd moved to Idaho and was working for a design firm there. Urban planning. Nothing on the scale of McFee, but the note he sent said he was healthy and happy. He thanked me for being his friend but said he'd never return to Memphis."

I didn't have the nerve, but Tinkie put a hand on her arm. "I'm sorry."

"Pipe dreams. He never encouraged me to believe we were anything but friends. He loved me in a platonic way and appreciated all I did for him. He was a good person. A good man."

She stood. "If that's all, I need to work. If Colin finds out I talked to you, he's going to be angry, so I'll show you a back exit. He should be in the office by now if he's coming in, and he stampedes around here showing up in the most unexpected places."

"I don't know that he'll be in for a while. He's taking this Senate run seriously." Tinkie rose and gave Dorinda a hug. "Remember, a good friend is often better than a good lover. Love can fall apart, but friendship is forever."

"I tell myself that every day. And I tell myself that five years have slipped from me and I haven't really participated in life. It's like until Son's body is found I refuse to believe he's dead, even though common sense says otherwise."

"The heart has its own timeline," Tinkie said. "Honor it, but don't accept that grieving is natural for you. Don't let that emotional gloom become your only reality."

"Wise words," Dorinda said. "Now, I really must get to work."

"Would you happen to know if anyone associated with McFee Enterprises might have been interested in donating money to Cleo McFee's charitable works?"

"Maybe. A lot of companies wanting McFee contracts would do that. They wouldn't care about the charities, but it would open the door a little here. I wouldn't have access to that information, though."

"Thanks," I said, prepared to leave.

"One more thing," Tinkie said. "Did Sister McFee ever visit the offices?"

"Once in a while, when she needed money or wanted to complain about something. Once her writing career took off, she hardly ever came back South. From what Colin has said in passing, she loves New York City. She's the toast of the town."

"Did Son ever say anything about his sister?"

"He felt sorry for her."

"He said that?" Tinkie asked.

"More than once."

"Did he elaborate?"

"Only that she never got enough attention or love. He said Colin was responsible for her character, and Cleo tried hard to make up for it, but the die was cast. Sister grew up feeling like the unwanted child, and Son believed she'd never outgrow it. He went to great pains to remember special days and to call or send flowers. He was a wonderful brother."

"I know you have work to do, but has McFee Enterprises been in any trouble?" I asked.

"I'm not at a level where I'd have access to that information. I'm in charge of the staff. The secretaries, janitorial, clerical, mail, drafting. We're the worker bees. As

I said, I often take minutes for the board of directors' meetings, and nothing like that was ever mentioned in a meeting." She smiled. "But then it wouldn't be, would it. The stockholders would go crazy. Those things are always discussed in private meetings. If there was a problem, it was hushed up."

"How would we find those records?"

"There wouldn't be records. What corporation keeps records of a screwup?"

"This is the last question. I promise." We were standing by a bank of elevators and it was clear Dorinda was ready to move on with her day. "Did you ever meet a woman named Krista Yost?"

She nodded immediately. "She had an appointment with Colin last week. Very chic, and very angry."

"What was the meeting about?"

"You'll have to ask Colin. They talked for twenty minutes and she left."

"Was she satisfied?"

"I couldn't tell. She didn't make another appointment." She put out a hand to stop us from the elevator. "Ms. Yost didn't return, but a Hollywood director took several meetings with Colin back before Thanksgiving."

"What?" Tinkie and I looked at each other, dumbfounded. Surely it couldn't be Marco.

"What was his name?" Tinkie asked.

She thought a minute. "Marco St. John. He and his wife are a hot Hollywood team. Lorraine is her name. I don't know what they were discussing, but it was friendly. After Mr. St. John left, Colin remarked that he'd had a very productive meeting. It's odd that you work for a movie production company and a director was here to talk to

Colin. I guess they really are going to make Sister's awful book into a movie."

"Do you have any idea what St. John and Colin discussed?" I asked.

"Very hush-hush. That's why I'm hoping whoever you work for wants to tell the real story, not some crap Sister made up to blacken Son's name."

We had to tell her. There was no way to leave without doing it. "Black Tar Productions is Marco and Lorraine's company. We're working for them."

She paled and put a hand on the wall. "You deceived me."

"Only because we were deceived," I said. "I swear to you, the things you told us will never get back to the St. Johns or to Colin or Sister. We had no idea Marco was in cahoots with Colin. We were hired under false pretenses."

"And we're not giving that advance back," Tinkie said. She put her hands on her hips. "Who does he think he is to lie to us that way?"

"Colin always comes out on top. That's what Son told me. He wouldn't tell me what he was talking about, but he said that no matter how wrong, his father always got what he wanted. Now I must go, and you should leave before one of Colin's minions sees you."

She was right about that. "Thank you for your help. And we swear we'll protect what you told us."

"I hope so. When Colin settles a score, he doesn't do half measures. I feel like this company ruined Son's life. It took everything from him, and just when he was getting back on his feet, building a new life, he ran off the road into a flooded river." She said the last with bitterness. "How fair is that?"

Not at all. But someone far wiser than I said life isn't fair. He even put it on a bumper sticker. But repeating a cliché as if it were the only truth did no good and only sounded mean. Besides, I had a goose to cook when I got out of McFee Enterprises.

18

Zinnia sparkled in the morning sun like a fairy-tale city as we pulled into town. The winter air was crisp and clear; the sun a pale gold that highlighted the muted bricks of the older streets and the varying shades of brown earth. The hour-long drive had given me and Tinkie time to vent our spleen at Marco. Now we weren't seething, but we were ready to confront him.

We stopped at Millie's for lunch. We'd both skipped breakfast and though we could have eaten at a dozen wonderful places in Memphis, we came home. Home was where we'd find Marco.

The interview with Dorinda had confirmed our suspicions that Son had been unhappy at work. Nothing we learned informed us as to what had happened the night of the accident. The story behind Susan and Colin's lovefest played out just as we'd anticipated. Big deal. It amounted to nothing as evidence. We'd found useful information—and a lead as to why Son's life began to unravel—but nothing specific enough to use against Colin or Sister.

The bitter truth we had learned was that we were working for a snake.

My phone rang as we pulled into the diner's parking lot. Speak of the devil. I answered and put it on speaker.

"Those cameras you set up are perfect," Marco said. "Lorraine and I had breakfast in bed and reviewed some of the footage. Good job. I actually feel a little sorry for Colin. Susan is hormonal and nuts. They argued most of the night. And he's sleeping on the floor in the baby's room."

Just as Tinkie and I had discussed on the drive home, I put Plan A into action. We were going to act as if we knew nothing about Marco's visits to McFee Enterprises. We were going to take his money and pump him for information. "It's the only good job we've done," I said, sounding pitiful. "I'm sorry, Marco. Every time we hit a trail with a scent, it dead-ends." I told him about our visit to McFee Enterprises. I left out Dorinda's name and the revelation that I knew he'd been capering about with Colin. "Susan did set out to bust up Colin's marriage. She bragged to some of the other secretaries. Needless to say, she was successful, and she earned the dislike of many of the other employees."

"I'll bet before Susan got preggers she was into wild monkey-sex."

"Stop!" I dropped the phone and Tinkie covered her ears.

"Enough, Marco," she said. "Be prepared, Susan's determined to get a role in the movie. Frankly, you should at least give her a screen test."

I eyed Tinkie but didn't say anything. I couldn't tell if she was setting Marco up for trouble or if she was genuinely helping Susan.

"You have my word," Marco said. "I will audition her."

I chalked Tinkie's actions up to kindheartedness. She'd encouraged Susan to lust after a movie part in her ploy to gain information. I guess Tinkie wanted to hold up her end of the bargain. Unlike everyone else in this case.

"We're at a dead end," I told Marco. "All of the physical evidence is gone. The SUV, even Son's computers from McFee Enterprises. Of course, expecting to find any evidence there after more than five years was a long shot. I hate to concede, but I think we should refund your money, Marco." Tinkie nodded at my execution of the ploy. We'd give that money back when hell froze over.

"Don't be foolish. Keep looking. I'll go through the rest of the footage from the hidden cameras and see if I can't turn up something for you. A new lead. And by the way, you two should stop by Evermore this evening for dinner. Your friend is making something fabulous, and I want you to meet our screenwriter, Roon."

"Sure." I put as much perk into the word as I could, since I was feeling betrayed and snarky.

"Colin isn't going to be happy to see us," Tinkie said. Bazinga! Tinkie knew how to place a dart.

"I'm a thorn in his side he has to live with," Marco answered. "I've taken it on as part of my job description."

"We'll see you this evening," I said. "But we have to have a serious discussion about continuing on the case. I don't know that we can find anything useful at all."

"Don't give up just yet," Marco said. "Lorraine would be so disappointed."

Dinner would give us a chance to see the interplay between Colin and Marco. "See you tonight."

Tinkie and I entered the café and the smell of home cooking did wonders to pick up my spirits. I went with a vegetable plate, and Tinkie ordered homemade tomato basil soup and a grilled cheese sandwich. Comfort food. We both needed a bit of comfort.

Millie came out to hug us. We hadn't seen her since we'd gotten off the McFee property without incident with her help the night we hid the cameras, and I could see the renewed relief on her face. "We're fine," I assured her. "Safe and sound. And we're invited to dinner with the film crew this evening. I hear you're cooking something divine."

"Those California boys have never eaten Southern cooking. The screenwriter, Roon Talley, loves shrimp, so I'm having a friend drive some up from the Gulf. Should be here any minute." She smiled. "I'm glad you two will be there. You can help me in the kitchen beforehand. A little payback."

"Loving the idea," I said. "Loving it. Maybe I can pick up a few cooking tips."

My statement met laughter all around.

Tinkie propped her stilettoed feet on top of her desk and kicked back. We both held mugs of coffee, and if this had been a 1940s PI office, an oscillating fan would have ruffled the papers on our desks and someone would have walked in the front door smoking a cigar and holding a gun. But this wasn't 1940, and we had only our bitter disappointment in our employer to chew on.

"What a two-faced cheat," Tinkie said. We'd already used all the good descriptive words.

"Why hire us? I mean he's thrown away ten grand."

"As if Colin would care, and we have to assume Colin is funding this. Maybe he's trying to make things up to Sister."

"Then why pretend to oppose it?"

"Because he's a devious egomaniac." Tinkie sipped her coffee. "I don't want to go there tonight. I don't know if I can look Marco in the face without going off on him."

"Oh no, partner. We're going, and we're going to play this to the hilt. If I can do it, you can do it. And we're going to find out what happened to Son. Not because we're being paid, but because it's time for the truth to come out. A lot of people liked Son. And Cleo. If they were murdered, someone needs to pay."

"We have been thwarted at every turn, and I think Colin and his money are behind it." Tinkie put her feet on the floor and stood up in one fluid motion. The black suede pants and red bouclé sweater looked as fresh as when we left for Memphis hours ago. She picked up the remote control for the evil-looking rat I'd picked up for Pluto at Cat Emporium and set the little beast scurrying around the floor. Pluto came out of a dead sleep and gave chase. He loved the toy and had forgiven me my many transgressions.

"I agree. But we won't get payback if we quit."

She made the little rat run about two feet up the wall, and Pluto took a flying leap. The rat did a roll and took off across the floor with Tinkie working the control like a madwoman. I couldn't tell who was having more fun, her or the cat.

"Okay." She sent the rat scuttling across the room. "Then I'm going home to take a hot bath and get in the mood to put on an Oscar-winning performance."

"Not a bad plan." A soak would do me good, too.

"Now that we know this about Marco, I find it strange that he and Lorraine showed up at the bridge just after we'd been shot at. And that person you saw in your yard could easily have been Lorraine. Tall, athletic. Maybe they've been trying to spook us." Tinkie's chin jutted out, an indication she was well and truly pissed off.

"But why?" I kept asking the same question. "Why hire us just to torment us? Why bother?"

"To keep us busy. To make sure they know what we're finding?"

She had a point about that. If we were working for Marco, he'd know everything we did. But why the subterfuge of scaring us off the case—if Marco was behind that too. "Look, maybe we're getting all paranoid for no reason. What we'll do is reveal only what we choose to in the future. As long as we know about Marco's involvement with Colin, we're ahead of the game."

"What time do you want to head to Evermore?"

"Let's say six-thirty. We promised to help Millie."

"I'll pick you up." She jiggled the control toggle on the rat, and, before I could move, the dang thing ran up my leg and into my lap. Ten seconds later, fifteen pounds of Pluto landed on me so hard it knocked the breath out of me.

"Tinkie!" I said, gasping for air. But I was too slow. She was running out of the office. "I'll get you back," I called after her.

"Maybe, maybe not. Wear a dress tonight," she said. "Let's play this to the hilt."

"Okay." I much preferred my black jeans, but she had a point.

With Tinkie gone, I was at sixes and sevens. The only thing to do was take a horseback ride to clear my head. Because I was out of sorts with Marco, I didn't feel like pushing too hard on the case. I had five hours to kill, minus one to get ready for the dinner.

Miss Scrapiron was the first to come for a carrot, so I put a halter on her and ten minutes later had the lightweight English saddle on her back. I swung into the saddle and headed out across the open cotton fields I leased to a young farmer. He'd soon be out on his monster tractor, preparing the land for the spring crop. Now, though, it was Miss Scrappy, me, and the distant horizon. We set off at a ground-covering trot.

We neared a tree line where a small creek meandered through the land. Farmers had learned to leave the trees around the water sources. It helped with wind and rain erosion and also gave the wildlife a habitat. As we neared the trees, sweet birdsong floated out to me.

I rode along the edge of the woods, enjoying the winter day. I'd covered about three miles when I found a patch of sweet winter grass and stopped to let Miss Scrapiron graze. Sweetie Pie lolled in the shade of a sweet gum, a happy dog. She loved working on our cases, but she loved running with the horses even more.

The sound of hoof beats came to me at the same time Scrapiron raised her head, ears pricked forward, and turned toward the west. Over the crest of a small rise came my big black gelding, Lucifer. He was an Andalusian someone had abandoned on the grounds of a private home in Natchez. When no one claimed him, I took him home to Dahlia House where he fit right in with Miss Scrapiron and Reveler.

The surprise was the man mounted in the saddle riding my horse toward me at a canter.

Miss Scrapiron recognized her pasture mate and gave a deep-throated whinny that Lucifer answered with his own neigh. Not to be outdone by a horse, I lifted a hand in greeting. I loved seeing Coleman on a horse. He'd grown up riding and had all the skills of an accomplished horseman. He loved riding but seldom had the time.

And I loved watching him. There are men who demonstrate grace on horseback. They connect with the horse and become a unit. Coleman had that ability. I hadn't thought of it in years, but now I saw it in action. Coleman and I shared a past, a history, and a love of so much associated with Dahlia House and Zinnia. That common bond touched my heart.

"What are you doing riding a horse on a cold afternoon?" I asked, trying not to grin like the Cheshire cat.

"I followed your tracks in the dirt. Tracking is part of my job description." He too was feeling frisky.

"I didn't realize I'd been classified a felon."

"Not a felon, but surely almost as dangerous, Sarah Booth. Riding suits you."

I nodded. "It makes me feel alive, and I love it. The horses love it too. I believe that."

"Let's give them a run. Race you to the property line."

"What's the bet?" My heart was suddenly pounding. Without intending or planning it, I found myself in a dangerous place with a man I cared greatly about.

"The loser has to make breakfast in bed for the winner."

There it was. Coleman had come to a decision, and he put it right in front of me. The dithering was over. He offered a relationship, intimacy, and partnership. It was up to me to say yes or no. And he did it with a challenge I couldn't ignore. The fields were solid footing. There were no crops to disturb. If ever there was a time to race the wind, this was it.

"You're on!"

The horses bolted forward, hooves digging into the rich earth. As we sprang forward, clots of dirt flew behind us. Sweetie Pie wisely ran twenty yards to my left.

While Lucifer was the larger horse and had the longer stride, Miss Scrapiron was a Thoroughbred. I had no clue what her bloodlines might be, nor did I care. I judged her heart and temperament, which were big, generous, and true-blue. Lucifer took the lead, giving me a view worth contemplating as Coleman's strong legs gripped the saddle, and he held his weight at two-point to give Lucifer every advantage.

I grabbed a fistful of mane and steadied myself at two-point also. Miss Scrapiron knew the cue and surged ahead until I drew abreast of Coleman. We shared a quick look, and my heart thumped at the pleasure on his face. I hadn't seen him so open in a long time. I wondered if he'd noticed the same about me.

We ran across the vast field. Somewhere on the road a car slowed and finally stopped, the driver honking the horn while watching the impromptu race. When I chanced a look, I saw three cars stopped. The drivers and passengers had gotten out and were cheering us on. I could hear, "Go, black horse," or "Go, girl."

But we weren't running for the spectators, we were racing for the love of the ride. Lucifer climbed a small rise and gave a tiny sunfish buck as he let Coleman know how good he felt. I only prayed Miss Scrapiron had better manners. I could hang on, but I wanted to win. We edged past Lucifer and a laughing Coleman, and I saw the finish line in sight. There was no fence, only a dirt farm road that marked the edge of Dahlia House land.

Miss Scrapiron's right front hoof hit the dirt only seconds before Lucifer's. Our little cheering section at the road whooped and hollered, their voices tiny across the huge field.

We slowed to a walk, Lucifer prancing beside Miss Scrapiron as she preened.

"I would have won if Lucifer hadn't wasted his forward momentum on the buck," Coleman said.

"Woulda, coulda, shoulda," I answered. "Don't be a sore loser."

"Oh, I may be making breakfast, but I won't be a loser."

I couldn't get enough air to answer. My lungs felt squeezed by my pounding heart. The rapid pace of the blood thrumming through me left me light-headed. We'd come to the precipice. Coleman would not befuddle me with kisses or woo me with words and promises. This was a decision to be made with a clear head and full capabilities. It was one that would change the course of our friendship forever.

We turned to walk the horses back to Dahlia House. The wind whipping across the open land had a chilly bite I'd failed to notice earlier. Lucifer and Miss Scrapiron were content to walk, and Coleman and I rode in silence, the squench of the leather saddles and the clank of a stirrup the only sounds.

When he reached out and took my hand, I almost

burst into tears. I had wanted this for so long—and feared it. Coleman and I shared a love of the land that made me closer to him than anyone else. And this moment would change many things. I cared greatly for Harold and Scott, but I'd never truly allowed myself to fall in love with them. Maybe I'd always loved Coleman, since we were teenagers. I still didn't trust myself or my decisions, but life moved on and so would I.

19

We took our time unsaddling the horses and gave them a good rubdown before we turned them out to buck and snort in the pasture with Reveler. Happy to see his pasture mates, he reared and nipped at their butts until all three romped and squealed.

Coleman stood beside me at the fence, only inches away. Tension crackled between us, but he was not going to make this easy for me. He'd made his decision and made it clear. He was ready to take the next step. This wasn't flirtation; he hadn't come to tease and torment me with his kisses. It was four-fifty in the afternoon, and he should have been at work. Instead, he was at Dahlia House with me. I knew what that meant.

The navy winter night edged forward from the east,

and the first star glittered in the darkening sky. The west was an array of peach, mauve, lavender, and gold. A few clouds caught the darker hues of red and pink. The sky was alive with color.

"Make a wish?" I asked, indicating the lone star.

"I already did," Coleman answered. "What do *you* want, Sarah Booth?"

What did I want? I glanced back at Dahlia House and saw Jitty standing in the window of my bedroom, watching. I knew what she wanted. But what did I want? I had to be sure, because toying with Coleman wasn't acceptable. Playing the confused female was not a role I'd accept. Indecision was just another form of protecting myself, and it was time to fish or cut bait. What was my heart's desire?

I put a hand on Coleman's arm and felt the tension thrumming through him, though he gave no indication of it.

"What made you decide?" I asked. There was no need to pretend he didn't know what I was talking about.

"I was thinking about Krista Yost and how her life is over. She's your age, Sarah Booth. She thought everything was ahead of her. She came here for a business deal, as far as we know. Now she's dead. Her parents are coming to claim the body. She never married, never had children. They said she was totally focused on her writing career. Now her life is done."

I started to speak, but he continued.

"I looked out the window of the sheriff's office and I saw a man and a woman walking down the street. He put his arm around her and she stepped in beside him and they walked together. It was that simple. I knew then. It isn't grand or flamboyant, but it's very real. That's what I want, and I want it with you."

My heart yearned for the same thing. I wanted that easy connection, that sense of belonging to someone. I'd thought I had that with my ex-fiancé, but all of our dreams crumbled. Not because either of us betrayed the other or did a terrible thing. Events beyond our control wrecked us. I didn't know if I could survive that again, but I also couldn't live without trying. And I wanted to try with Coleman.

I leaned into him and he put his arm around me, yet still we didn't move from the fence. The simple act of walking into the house seemed beyond my ability. The horses raced across the pasture, over a slight hill, and disappeared from view. We stood looking at emptiness as the sky's display began to fade.

"Come inside," I said. My teeth chattered as I spoke, but it wasn't from the cold. My decision was made. Right or wrong, the heart wanted what the heart wanted. I couldn't protect Coleman or myself. The release was like a spring uncoiled. My chest literally opened, and the winter air was sweet and sharp and filled me with energy.

"Are you sure?" he asked.

"I am."

He held me close as we walked to the house and in the back door. The kitchen was warm and welcoming, and the paralysis was gone. What did I want? The question could only be answered in the moment, and I wanted Coleman. Next year or even next week wasn't guaranteed. There was only now. I turned into his arms and his kiss.

When the heart is truly engaged, there is a moment when a kiss becomes the only thing in the universe. Coleman's hands tugged off my jacket and his own, but his lips never left mine. My arms circled his neck, and I pressed myself against him, aware of how solid his body was, how I fit him in all the right places. His hands moved lower and cupped my bottom, pressing me into him as he lifted me and set me on the counter so that our lips were evenly matched. And then he really kissed me.

In the distance I heard the ticking of the oven, a sound that meant it was cooling. The old clock in the foyer chimed the hour. Five o'clock. The house sighed, and, to me, it sounded like my own breathy pleasure. Coleman took his time. So much so that I almost couldn't stand it. I wanted to tear his shirt open, to get rid of the clothes that came between us. We'd held back when I first came home because he was married. By the time he was divorced from Connie, I'd given my heart to Graf. Our timing had been off, but now there was nothing stopping us—except for Coleman's devilish determination to drive me mad with desire.

"Upstairs," I managed to say when his head ducked to plant kisses down my neck. Shivers made me weak.

"Upstairs?" He eased back so he could assess the level of my torment. "Are you sure?"

"Take me upstairs or I'll do something terrible to you." I didn't even have a valid threat.

"Just a bit longer." He pulled my shirt over my head and tossed it onto the kitchen table. My bra followed.

My fingers found his belt buckle and set to work. In a matter of minutes, we were both naked and clothes were scattered about the kitchen. He scooped me into his arms at last and pushed through the swinging door into the dining room. The house was cold and chill bumps danced over me, but Coleman had stoked an internal fire that demanded attention.

He was five steps up the stairs when the front door flew open.

Tinkie stepped into the foyer and stopped dead in her tracks. A gust of wind blew a whirl of leaves into the house as she gawked. "Oh my god," she said. "No wonder neither of you were answering your phones."

Coleman put me down in front of him. I tried to slip behind him but he was having none of that. He used me as a human shield from Tinkie's bugged-out eyes. I covered what I could with my arms and hands. Coleman and I remained speechless, though there was plenty I wanted to say to Tinkie.

"I cannot believe this is happening," she said. "I left a note on the kitchen table saying I'd be back in forty minutes. I put something in the oven to warm for the dogs." She made no effort to leave and the corners of her mouth lifted and fell as she fought a smile. She lost the battle and a huge grin lit her face. "So, what have you two been up to?"

"Tinkie!" Coleman and I said together.

"I gather you want me to leave," she said, at last closing the front door behind her, obviously determined not to leave at all. She took off her gloves and stuffed them in her coat pocket.

"It would be a . . . courtesy," Coleman said.

"I would if I could, but I can't." She took off her coat.

"Why not?" I asked.

"Sister has gone missing. Everyone in six counties is looking for the both of you. Glad to see you're armed and dangerous." She was so pleased with herself she almost wiggled.

"Sister is missing? What happened?" Coleman asked.

"If you took the time to read the note I left you, you'd know I put some pork roast and yellow rice in the oven for Sweetie Pie, and I said I'd be back to pick you up,

Sarah Booth. Coleman, DeWayne is frantic to get in touch with you. Colin McFee has gone berserk. He's called the FBI, Homeland Security, the CIA, and every other alphabet he can think of. I don't know who has the most people looking for them, you, Coleman, or Sister."

I glanced upstairs. I could find clothes there. Coleman would have to run past Tinkie to the kitchen. "Tinkie, would you *please* give us a moment. Maybe you could wait in the office."

Tinkie bit her lip to keep from laughing. "Oh, Cece is going to really enjoy this. And Millie. And Madam Tomeeka." She counted off on her fingers. "And photos would be excellent!" She pulled her phone from her pocket and aimed at us.

"I will wrestle you down and take that phone," I warned her.

"And I'll help her," Coleman added.

Tinkie put the phone away. "Sarah Booth, get your clothes. You both look like 'possums in the headlights. Seriously." She turned around so we could scatter. Coleman dashed to the kitchen and I ran upstairs to my bedroom. Before I slammed the door, I could hear her laughing. Oh, I was going to kill her when I got the chance.

Music from a long-gone TV show came from my bedside table where a 1960s tape recorder turned itself on. "Good evening, Ms. Delaney. The mission, should you choose to accept it, is to bed the local sheriff of Sunflower County and provide your long-suffering ghost, Jitty, with a new generation to haunt. If you're caught, it's my sincere hope it's after the sperm has left the . . . well, you know. In five minutes this tape will self-destruct." With a poof, it disappeared.

"Mission *not* accomplished." Barbara Bain as Cinnamon Carter stood in the middle of my bedroom, her hair perfectly coiffed with the little upswept flip. She wore a black-and-white minidress to die for. And she was up to no good.

"Leave me alone." I was not in the mood for Jitty's haranguing.

"You had the situation firmly in hand, and you blew it." Her grin was as wide as Tinkie's had been.

Oh, I was going to kill her. It didn't matter that Jitty was already dead. "Stop it with the sexual insinuations. It isn't my fault Tinkie burst through the door like a hurricane."

"That man is downstairs puttin' his pants *on.* After all these months of waitin', you finally got them off him, and now he's putting them back on. Nothin' happened. Nothin'."

"Do you think I don't know that?" I whispered in a seething tone. "What do you want me to do, fling him down with Tinkie watching?"

"I vote for that. Finish the mission." She reached under her chin and began to peel away her face. In one grand gesture, she whipped it off and revealed—me. She had assumed my image. The music of *Mission: Impossible* filtered softly through the air. "Let me at him. I'll show you how it's done."

I threw a boot at her, but it went right through her head and struck the wall.

"You okay?" Tinkie called out gleefully from downstairs. She was still standing in the foyer. She was not going to let this go with any degree of grace. I limped to the corner and retrieved my dress boot and laced it up. Finally dressed, I hurried down the stairs. If I could intercept Tinkie, I would distract her from further humiliating Coleman as he made his getaway. I would not be so lucky.

"Let's go to the office," I suggested, taking her arm.

"No need. Coleman took off out the back door. He's headed down the driveway now."

I ran to the sidelight and saw his taillights disappearing down the drive. "The coward." I would get him for this. He'd used me as a human shield and then run off and left with me a very self-satisfied Tinkie.

"Coleman certainly appeared ready to do the job at hand when I arrived."

Since we were alone, I rounded on Tinkie. "All I've heard for the past three months is that I had to let the past go and get on with my life. You and Tammy and Cece have done nothing but push me into bed with Coleman or Scott or Harold or . . . well, just about anyone."

"Yes." Her grin was enormous.

"So when I'm ready to do the deed, you come in here and won't leave. Ever consider the fact that two's company and three's a crowd?"

"Sarah Booth Delaney, don't you dare pretend you would have gone upstairs and had sex with Coleman knowing that he was needed on a case. I'm sorry, but there was no time for you to finish what you'd started. You know that's true. Sister is missing and Coleman had to get on the stick. Even if I'd left, the outcome would have been the same. I just had a little fun with the two of you." She giggled. "Make that a lot of fun. And there's more to come."

"Don't you dare tell a soul."

"This is too good to keep to myself. I make no promises."

"Tinkie, please." I was done threatening and had been reduced to begging.

She put an arm around my waist and gave me a hug. "Okay, enough is enough. I won't tell anyone. I promise. But just know that image of you two, frozen on the stairs, will give me a good laugh for the rest of my life. And a little tip: if you're intending to have late afternoon sex—or sex at any time for that matter—you should lock the front door."

"You have a key," I reminded her.

"Oh yeah, I do." She held it up. "Now that you have your clothes on, we need to get busy."

"Let me feed Sweetie Pie and Chablis." I looked around. "Where is Chablis?"

"She was so mortified by what she saw, she's hidden under the horsehair sofa in the parlor."

I peeked around the corner and saw Chablis under the sofa. I had scarred Tinkie's pup for life. But some pork roast and yellow rice might help her overcome her psychological abuse. "Come on."

When I went into the kitchen, Chablis followed, her appetite undeterred by seeing Coleman and me naked. Tinkie always played to the drama.

I fed the dogs and found some high-end cat food that Pluto deigned to eat. I gave him a taste or two of the pork. He'd put on a bit of weight, and he'd been portly to begin with.

"Looks like a clothes closet exploded in here." Tinkie held up my bra.

I snatched it from her hand. "Do not say another word." I picked up my scattered clothes. Beneath my panties I found her note and read it. She'd given fair warning that she was coming back.

Tinkie read over my shoulder. "See, I told you I would be back in forty minutes."

I crumpled the note and tossed it across the room toward the trashcan.

"Why in the world did you undress in the kitchen and then run through a cold house to the bedroom?" Tinkie put on a pot of coffee. She wasn't done having fun at my expense. She wouldn't be done for a long, long time.

"Uh, I don't know. Maybe because we started kissing in the kitchen and were carried away." I threw my shirt at her head. "Maybe because we were crazed with the idea of sex. Or maybe because I live alone and never considered that my best friend would come blowing through the front door like a desire-killing blizzard. You might be the newest, most potent form of birth control."

She laughed loud and hard, but not with meanness. "You should have seen Coleman's face. And the way he put you in front of him."

"So glad you find this funny. It isn't Chablis you should worry about, it's me. I've been scarred for life. I may never have sex again, and it's all because of you."

That really sent her into gales of laughter. "I can't believe I caught you red—well, you know. I don't want to get into mentioning specific body parts. I'm just wondering how I'll explain this to Cece."

"You promised not to tell. Can't we just drop it?" Tinkie was not malicious, but even I had to admit the scene she'd walked in on would be hard to keep quiet. The humor of it wasn't lost on me, if I looked hard enough.

"I said I wouldn't tell anyone and I won't." She gave me a hug. "And I'm sorry. If I'd had any idea you were about to do the dirty deed, I would never have come inside.

Certainly not on Sister's behalf. In fact, I hope they don't find her. Maybe the flying monkeys grabbed her."

"Coleman has to respond to a missing person's report, and, for his sake, I hope she's okay." I sank into a kitchen chair. Events were catching up with me. I'd been ready to take a big step in my relationship with Coleman, and the whole thing had been blown out of the water. I eagerly took the cup of coffee Tinkie handed me. I had to get a grip. The best thing to do was focus on why Tinkie was there—Sister was missing. It was ninety percent likely this was a mere bid for attention on her part, but it was the ten percent chance that we had to act on.

Krista Yost was dead. My assumption was that Sister might have killed her or had her killed. If that wasn't true, then whoever killed Krista might well be involved in Sister's disappearance. Her book might have stirred up trouble from a source we hadn't considered. "If Colin has called all the federal law enforcement agencies, Coleman needs to be on top of this. Damn Colin. He doesn't give a fig about Sister. Aliens could have taken her to the moon and he wouldn't give a damn. This is just publicity for him. So what happened to her?"

"What I got from DeWayne, who called me looking for Coleman because he wasn't answering his phone and neither were you—and now I know why—was that Sister had driven to Memphis this morning to do some shopping. She was due back after lunch but she hadn't returned by four. No one has seen her. She isn't answering her phone."

"Maybe she was trying to get laid," I said with some snap. "She'll be more successful than I was because she doesn't have any friends."

"Very funny." Tinkie never missed a beat. "Who in

their right mind would sleep with Sister? I heard that after sex, she pops the guy's head off and sucks his brains out." Tinkie grinned. "Then again, we were thinking you might not get laid until the Four Horsemen of the Apocalypse showed up."

I cocked an eyebrow, and she made a face. "I'm kidding you. But Sister doesn't have a boyfriend that anyone knows about."

"But is she really missing?" I asked. "She's been gone, what, eight hours? Isn't Colin jumping the gun?"

"DeWayne thinks it's a campaign ploy. If the TV stations from Memphis and Jackson cover this, it's free publicity."

"If it's an orchestrated trick, people are going to be furious." One lawman in particular. And one private eye who now had to deal with intimacy issues.

"Since you have your clothes on, let's make a few calls. We have to hurry."

"What about the dinner at Evermore tonight? Is it canceled?"

"Nope."

"Marco and Lorraine didn't cancel the dinner?" I was a little shocked. They might not care for Sister, but it was her book they were supposedly filming. I shouldn't be shocked. Marco was a Hollywood reptile. Maybe he was in on Sister's disappearing act.

Tinkie sweetened her coffee. "The dinner is on. And Colin is going to be furious."

"Unless the film crew is there because he wants them there." The potential understatement of the year. Delaney Detective Agency was ensnared in a case where the man who hired us lied, the man we were investigating was a professional liar and attention whore, and the man who was missing had likely been swept out to the Gulf of Mexico in floodwaters. We couldn't find a dry rock in a high tide. "Maybe Colin will entertain us with an after-dinner nipple-dance."

"I will not be able to hold my dinner down." Tinkie covered her mouth.

"Okay," I said. "Let's make some calls, and then I have to change." In my haste to dress, I'd put on jeans and a flannel shirt. Not exactly the attire for dinner at Evermore.

"I brought my dress. It's in the car. We can get ready together." Her face lit up. "We can do each other's makeup."

"Yeah, like high school." But I was happy to participate. Anything to keep from thinking about Coleman and what had almost happened between us. Besides, I enjoyed Tinkie's fashion sense and her grasp of the feminine. I always looked better when she had a hand in my choices. But before we got all gussied up, we had work to do.

Tinkie called the Memphis malls and upscale shops, of which there were a number Sister would have shopped in, because she had personal contacts there. Her description of Sister left no doubt. If the missing heiress had been in any of the stores, the clerks would have recalled her.

I made the phone rounds of Memphis hospitals, emergency clinics, and law enforcement to see if Sister had been injured in an accident, broken down somewhere along the road, or been picked up for speeding or abuse of an officer. If a cop had dared to pull her over, I felt certain she would have been abusive and might have landed in jail. Abusive was Sister's go-to behavior.

After all our calls, we both came up with zilch.

I tried wrecker companies. If something had happened

to her car in a dead zone, that could explain why she hadn't called anyone for help. But surely someone would have come along and helped her in eight hours. I hated to admit it, but by six-thirty, with no sign of Sister, I was a little worried, too. And I was late to help Millie. I sent her a text to let her know we'd been delayed.

When we called it quits, I asked Tinkie to report our findings to Coleman. Let her get that over with so she could have the pleasure of tormenting him for a few minutes. I ran upstairs and raided my closet for something to wear to the dinner. I found a long black skirt and a black silk jacket with slashes of bright red, yellow, and orange on the asymmetrical lapel that crossed over with one large art deco button. It would do. And just in time. I heard the front door slam twice and Tinkie come up the stairs. She was gleefully humming to herself, relishing what I could only assume was her recent devilment of Coleman. She was having way too much fun at our expense.

"You know payback is going to be hell," I warned her.

"Perhaps, but I am not about to give up this advantage."

I held out my makeup bag. "Do your worst!"

20

Evermore was aglow with lights as we turned down the drive. The closer we got, the brighter the house became. When we pulled up in front, I understood why. Colin McFee, with his very pregnant wife at his side, stood in front of a bank of microphones as he held a press conference about his missing daughter. The television lights created a glow worthy of a small city.

"If anyone has any information about my girl, Frangelica, please contact me. She's better known by the nickname Sister, and all of her friends are worried sick about her, as am I and her stepmother. I'm offering a fifty-thousand-dollar reward for information that leads to her safe return."

Tinkie pinched me hard, on the side. "Safe return," she repeated. "He won't pay if she's dead."

"And neither would I." This time I couldn't fault Colin. What was the point of paying that much money for a body? "If she has been abducted, that will encourage the kidnappers to keep her alive."

"I guess you're right. My daddy would pay for *any* information about me."

Tinkie was right about that. Avery Bellcase would pay, and then he'd find Tinkie's abductors and make them wish they'd never been born. "Your father loves you. I'm not sure Sister ever had that luxury."

To give credence to my words, Colin kept talking. "I believe my daughter's abduction is directly related to my attacks on the Russian bear, Vladimir Putin. He's behind this. He's feeling the wrath I've brought down on his head by exposing his nefarious plots. As your U.S. senator, I pledge that I won't let personal attacks—not even the abduction of my own daughter—stop me from doing what must be done to halt the Russian aggression. I have outmaneuvered Putin on every front, and his only recourse is to attack my family. But I will get Frangelica back, and I will win this election and go on to defang the bear. And today I announce further sanctions on Russia. When I am your senator, Mississippi will no longer export our cotton to the great bear's gins and looms."

"Oh, holy overblown egos," Tinkie said. We'd parked fifty yards away and stopped at the edge of the big crowd of reporters to listen to the press conference.

"Do the Russians even import cotton?" I asked. Tinkie was far better informed on economic matters than I was.

"They do. From Asia mostly. This is bull-hockey."

Colin finally noticed us in the back of the crowd. "Why don't we ask the two private investigators what they've found in regard to my missing daughter?"

The cameras immediately swung in our direction, but we ignored them and hurried past Colin and Susan, up the steps, and through the front door. We had nothing to say to the media.

Except for Cece, who met us inside. As always, she looked stunning in a winter white sweater dress offset with a red and black scarf and shoes that matched the scarf. She had an enviable fashion sense, and whatever she wore looked better on her than New York models.

"Do you think Sister's disappearance is real, or is this some game Colin and Sister are playing?" she asked.

"It's a mighty convenient disappearance," I said, "coming as it does on the heels of the murder of her writing partner." I didn't add especially since she was a suspect. "But it could also just be an opportunity for Colin to spout off."

I was about to tell Cece about Marco's deception, but Lorraine came into the foyer. "We've set up for the dinner in the main dining room," she said.

"Let me check with Millie in the kitchen and see if I can help," I said. "I'll be right with you."

Cece and Tinkie followed Lorraine to the dining room and I ducked into the kitchen where Millie and two helpers were putting the finishing touches on a salad.

"Sorry I didn't make it to help. Sister's disappearance threw a monkey wrench in my plans."

"We have it covered. I didn't need your help; I just enjoy your company."

"Same here. I was looking forward to it."

"We're all good. Everything is coming together."

And it was. The smell of the cooking seafood made my mouth water. "Have you met Roon Talley yet?" I asked.

"Delightful man, though he looks like he could use three squares a day for the next ten years. Painfully thin. He came to the kitchen and sampled everything as we were cooking." Millie gave the salad bowl to a helper to take to the table. "Go on, Sarah Booth. We're fine here."

I took her advice and went to the dining room where Marco, Lorraine, Cece, and Tinkie stood in a corner drinking wine and talking with a thin man whose long hair was pulled back in a queue. He had to be Roon Talley. He did look like some buttered biscuits would do him a world of good. I watched him for a moment, taking in his serious demeanor. I also watched Marco, duplicitous person that he was. A few crewmembers rounded out the dinner party, and they stood by a table that held an array of open wine bottles and crystal glasses.

Marco saw me and signaled me over. "Sarah Booth, please meet Roon Talley, our screenwriter. He's been eager to speak with you."

Roon's smile was slight, but his handshake was warm. "I've heard about you and your partner. The South's detective duo. I was glad to hear Marco took the initiative and hired you to look into what happened to Cleo and Son McFee."

"We haven't made a lot of headway on the case," I admitted.

"Marco said the physical evidence has all disappeared."

"We've been stymied by that. The SUV is gone. Someone stole it the day after it was recovered from the river. Law enforcement never really finished examining it."

"Did the thieves remove it from the courthouse lawn?"

"No, the recycle yard. Jimmy Deets, the wrecker owner who got the vehicle out of the river, said someone cut the chain that locked his gates, used the crane to lift the vehicle onto a flatbed, and drove it away. He also mentioned that the recovery of the SUV from the river might make a really dynamic scene for the movie. He had to use two wreckers."

"Great idea. None of that was covered in the book." He stepped back from the group so we could speak more privately. "Sister's book supports the theory that Son McFee was high or drunk and the accident was caused by him."

"Yes, and the heavy rainfall."

"Have you found evidence to support that?"

I told him about the tracks that were photographed at the scene—tracks that should have washed away in the ten inches of rain that fell.

"And there's nothing to indicate any other scenario?"

"There are suspicions. The problem is that without physical evidence, I can't prove or disprove any of our theories."

His interest was piqued. "Would you care to elaborate on your theories?"

Millie had already sent the salad in and two young waitresses were at the table filling wineglasses with a nice white to compliment the seafood dish. "Not at this time. Speculation is useless. Evidence is what I need to find."

He was about to say something else when Colin burst into the room. Wild-eyed, but with his shirt on, he spoke with disdain. "My daughter is missing and you're having a dinner party? You're drinking my private stock of wine! Eating the food I paid for. You people are on notice. I'll have you out of Evermore by tomorrow afternoon. Trash! You should move to Russia where you belong."

The room fell silent. He stormed out and slammed the door.

"That was awkward," Lorraine said. "But everyone please take a seat. Sister's shenanigans shouldn't impact our dinner. I assure you, Marco and I had the wine flown in from California. We picked it up when we retrieved Roon from the Memphis airport, and the seafood came from the Gulf Coast. We aren't mooching off Colin McFee." She waved at the table. "We have much to discuss, and Roon wants to talk about the screenplay. I'm hoping Sarah Booth has an update."

Yeah, I had an update—that our boss had thrown in with Colin. Or at least had secret meetings with him. I glanced at Tinkie and she shook her head. Her evaluation was correct. Better keep my mouth shut.

We took our places at the table, and I found myself sitting with Roon on my right. Tinkie sat on his other side. Lorraine was seated on my left. She leaned over to whisper in my ear. "The cameras you hid are giving us great footage. We're thinking of doing a reality show. The McFee Paranormal Activity show. That Susan is possessed. She's been doing cartwheels in her bedroom, and she broke another ThighMaster with her powerful legs. She's not really human."

"She's in damn good physical shape. I've never seen anything like it."

"She hates Colin, and he hates her. They fight something fierce and with great brutality. I thought one night he was going to smother her with a pillow, but her head spun around and her eyes glowed."

I almost choked on my wine. "Not a room of connubial bliss?"

"About as far from that as you can get. I wonder if that baby even belongs to Colin. They hate each other so much I can't imagine they actually had sex together. If Susan wasn't pregnant, Colin would leave her, I'm sure. Before that happened, though, I think she'd poison him."

"I can't imagine getting along with either of them," I said.

"At any rate, it's given me some great footage to splice into whatever we film."

"Can you do that? Use footage from a hidden camera?"

She grinned. "Once it's done, it's too late to stop it. Colin is such a media whore, he won't care. If he's elected, it will give him something to pontificate about. If he isn't elected, he'll use it for his next assault against the people of Mississippi."

"Has the camera in Sister's room yielded anything?"

"She snores like an old woman." She did an imitation that made my stomach hurt. "She's even boring when she snores. Who can be that vanilla?"

"You're not concerned with her disappearance?"

"Trust me. This is something Colin cooked up to get free publicity. Did you see the news crews outside? He's playing it to the hilt. Accusing Putin of kidnapping Sister. If Putin has her, he'll pay Colin to take her back. 'The Ransom of Red Chief.' "

Lorraine wasn't far off the mark. And no ransom request had come in, which led me to believe Sister wasn't being held anywhere. She was merely AWOL.

The meal progressed with the salad and lively conversation. Lorraine's dry commentary on Colin, Susan, and

Sister had me in stitches, and it also drew smiles from Roon, who was quiet and shy. Tinkie and Marco had their heads together on something. She was a far better actress than I was because I couldn't help but be angry at him. When Lorraine turned away to answer some technical questions from one of the crewmembers, I engaged Roon in small talk.

"Have you ever been to the South before?" I asked him.

"I've lived most of my life in LA, but I visited the South. A long time ago." One corner of his mouth quirked. "Good and bad memories."

"The Delta hasn't changed much since the sixties. In some ways, it seems timeless."

"In some ways," he agreed. "Nothing will really change in Mississippi until the education system is improved."

"You're not the first person to say that, but the politicos don't believe it, or they don't want things to change. How do you know so much about Mississippi?"

His half-smile flickered on. "The same is true about every place in this country. Only the truly elite can afford a quality education now. America once took public education seriously. No longer. Look at the McFees. Best education, best quality of life. The two go hand in hand." The half-smile again, as if he didn't take himself too seriously. "I read a lot of articles while I was working on the movie script."

"I would have thought the accident would have been the draw for a scriptwriter. I mean the philosophy of education is important, but it's the accident that's the heart of the story. It's a mystery and a tragedy."

He lifted one shoulder. "Of course, the tragic drama

is what compels a person to go watch a movie. But I didn't want the principals, Cleo and Son, to be reduced to victims. Cleo McFee was more than a woman who drowned in a flood."

"And Son? How do you see him?"

"A lot will depend on what you find out about the night of the accident. Was he high and simply lost control of the vehicle in the rain? Then he really is the ultimate victim who lost his life and also killed his mother. Or was there more to the story?"

"Sister's book promotes the former." I was pointing out the obvious.

"Yes, but Marco and I agree that's not necessarily the correct conclusion for the film."

"So you don't buy that sequence of events?"

That crooked little smile came again, as if he were too shy to talk. "I'm aware of the reasons Sister McFee came to the conclusions she did. And Mr. McFee, too."

"But you disagree?"

"I am open to new evidence. Until the final scene is shot, Marco and I both are. But I believe he said you'd have a report for us tonight. I'm looking forward to hearing what you've discovered."

I took a bite of my salad. I had nothing to report. Nothing. I returned to a safer topic. "Someone should have taken up Cleo's banner and finished what she started with her education initiative. You know, she left a ten-million-dollar insurance policy that was to be earmarked for that effort."

Roon's gaze found mine. "Did the McFee family follow her wishes?"

"I haven't completely finished checking out that aspect." The quick answer was no. Colin hadn't done anything to promote education, but I wasn't certain that he'd done anything else with the money either. It could just be sitting in an account.

"The book indicates Cleo was serious about her work. It was a calling, I guess you'd say. So what happened to the insurance money?" Roon demonstrated that he'd done his homework regarding the McFee case.

"An excellent question. Colin certainly didn't need the money. Then or now."

"I heard he hit a rough patch several years ago." He paused a beat. "Bad investment. Perhaps something illegal."

"Thanks for the tip." I'd really have to discuss this with Tinkie, who was the financial whiz at Delaney Detective Agency. "One of the things that puzzled me—and I've found no explanation—was why Cleo and Son were on the western side of the state. It was my understanding Cleo was driving from Ole Miss to Jackson. Cleo had given a talk in Oxford, and she was due to speak in Jackson. It seems Highway 55 would have been the direct route and much safer. It's a four-lane that's always well maintained."

"That wasn't addressed in Sister's book, was it?" He frowned.

"No, it wasn't."

"Wouldn't her husband know?" he asked.

"He made statements to the effect that he didn't. I read the sheriff's report in the county where the wreck occurred. In his statement Colin said he was puzzled by the fact his wife and Son were in Washington County."

"Interesting," Roon said. "I suppose the only people who know for sure would be Son and Cleo."

"Sadly, that's the case." I had a sudden thought. "Unless

Cleo was visiting someone or had a specific stop to make. It would have had to be important for her to go out of her way in that horrific weather."

"According to the book, Son met up with his mother at Clarksdale, which would make sense if he came from Memphis. But what was Cleo doing in that area?" He seemed excited by the question.

"It might be important." I knew it was important, but I didn't want to overplay my hand.

"I suppose so. From the research I've done, it rained over ten inches in a matter of a few hours. It would have come down in buckets. And as flat as the Delta is, it would likely flood. Some of those two-lane roads, according to Marco and Lorraine, who have been scouting locations, are level with the fields. High flood risk. It would take tremendous motivation to drive a longer distance in those conditions."

"The Sunflower River was high and wide that day. It was way out of its banks and treacherous. Gray rain, gray road, gray everything. I wish I could find out what Cleo was doing on that side of the state."

"Have you asked Sister? Maybe when she gets back." Roon checked his watch as if he had an appointment. "I do wonder where she got off to. I really wanted to talk to her. It was one reason Lorraine hosted this dinner, so I could spend some time with Sister."

"I'll ask Sister, as soon as she shows up." I was just as glad she wasn't there. She was certain to make it miserable for Tinkie. "She's pretty unpleasant. Just so you have a heads-up."

"Oh, I've met with her." He rolled his eyes. "She's acerbic. She has real control issues, and she tries to make everyone feel inferior."

"Understatements. But tell me about your screenwriting career." I knew his list of credits, but I wondered what he would say about his work.

"I've been really lucky. When I turned in my first screenplay, *Touched*, I got a lot of acclaim. From then on, I've never been without work, and I'm a fast writer. I've met and worked with some of the finest people in Hollywood, like Lorraine and Marco. It's been a terrific ride."

The door opened and Millie came into the room with the main course. Roon gallantly rose to help her and earned a dazzling smile. Millie loved all things Hollywood, but I could see Roon Talley was special to her.

Marco rose and lifted a glass. Roon put the giant bowl of shrimp étouffée on the table and a wineglass in Millie's hand. "Thank you, Millie," Marco said, "for cooking for me and my crew and friends. It smells wonderful. Welcome to the Black Tar Productions crew. To Millie."

We held our glasses aloft and then drank to the toast. "I'm happy to do it," Millie said. "Now we have homemade apple pie à la mode for dessert, so save room."

Marco caught her hand and kissed it. "You make me want to move to Zinnia, but Lorraine would have to get out her whip and chase me down the road or I'd become a round, pasty glutton."

When everyone stopped cheering, Millie said, "Maybe you could do film production here full time. Mississippi has the talent and plenty of great stories. Think about it." She left the room and we fell on the delicious shrimp étouffée as if we hadn't eaten in weeks. Millie brought in another basket of bread, and Tinkie pretended to swoon in her chair from the sheer joy of the food.

"This is wonderful, Millie," Cece said. "I'd forgotten what a great Cajun cook you are."

"I don't often serve New Orleans food in the café. Folks here like more traditional planters' or farmers' fare. Not everyone is a fan of spicy foods, but I love to cook New Orleans style."

"Add it to the menu," I begged. "It's fabu—"

The dining room door burst open and Sister McFee stumbled into the room. She was muddy and disheveled and smelled like a distillery. Her glare moved around the room like Medusa's, and we all stopped whatever we were doing as if we'd been turned to stone.

"You can't start dinner without me," she said, stumbling forward. "*I'm* the important one. It's *my* book. *My* book." She swept the room with a glare. "You're nothing without me."

"Shoot her now," Tinkie whispered fiercely. "Before she utters another word."

Sister rounded on Tinkie. "You're eating here? The stench!"

I rose, my hands clenched at my side. "I'm going to punch your teeth down your throat so hard they'll march out of your butt like little white soldiers!" I meant it too.

"Where the hell have you been?" Lorraine rose from the table and got between us. "You've had everyone worried about you. And you're the one who stinks. Did you fall into a vat of cheap bourbon?"

"Right. You look worried!" Sister waved her arm, indicating the table, the food, all of us.

Cece eased from her place at the table and began snapping photos. She was on top of the big story.

"What happened to you?" Roon left the table and went to her. "Are you injured?"

"I was kidnapped," she said. "And they're gonna pay. You just wait and see. They are gonna pay." She started to slump to the floor, but Roon caught her and eased her into a chair where Millie held a glass of water to her lips.

I left the room, giving her a wide berth. She stank of alcohol. I hurried upstairs to the suite of rooms that belonged to her father. When I knocked, Colin swung the door open with a grunt of anger. "I've had it with that film crew and with you and Mrs. Richmond. You'd be wise to pick your friends and employers with more care."

"Sister is home. You'd better come downstairs."

"Is she hurt?" Colin asked.

For a moment I thought I saw actual concern on his face, but it was quickly replaced by annoyance—the only expression he seemed capable of showing when it came to Sister or the memory of Son.

Susan, who'd been reclining on a chaise by the window, jumped up too. They both rushed past me to the dining room where a commotion ensued.

Sister had regained her feet, pushed Roon aside, and stood pointing a finger at Lorraine. "It was you. You had me abducted. I heard the kidnappers talking about how you'd paid them."

Lorraine picked up her video camera and began to film. "Smile for the camera, Sister. If you want to repeat your accusation that I'm responsible for anything regarding your abduction—if there was even an abduction—I'd love to have it on film."

Sister stumbled again, and Roon reached to catch her elbow, but she roughly jerked free. "I know you're trying to change the ending of my story. I'm not a fool. I can see what's going on."

"You're drunk," Roon said softly. "And you're exhausted. You've been through an ordeal."

"Don't condescend to me." She blew past him. When

she saw Colin and Susan frozen in the doorway, her demeanor changed. "Daddy, they hurt me. Lorraine paid those men to kidnap me and hold me hostage and they tied me up and hurt me." She rushed to him and wrapped her arms around him.

Colin didn't move a muscle to comfort her.

"You don't really look hurt," Susan said. "You stink like you spent the day in a Dumpster, but I don't think you're hurt. Maybe you should take a hot shower and have some coffee."

Sister sobbed against her father.

It was Millie who went to her and untangled her arms. Murmuring soothing things, Millie led her away.

Colin advanced into the room to stand directly in front of Lorraine. "If you had anything to do with my daughter's abduction, you're going to regret it. I don't like you here. I don't like the idea of your movie. You're only here because Sister insisted. Somehow, I think your invitation is about to be revoked."

At last Colin realized there was a new person in the room. He looked Roon up and down with a sneer. "The scriptwriter I've heard so much about. Enjoy your meal. It's the last you'll eat here."

He stormed out of the room. Susan was left standing in the doorway, hands holding her belly. She sighed. "For the record, I don't believe you had anything to do with Sister's disappearance, Lorraine. And don't worry. I'll talk to Sister and Colin. No one is going anywhere."

She left the completely silent dining room.

Tinkie turned to Lorraine. "Did you hire someone to abduct her?"

Putting her camera on the table, Lorraine sat down and picked up her fork. "I wouldn't hesitate if I saw a benefit. Sadly, Sister's ten-hour abduction, which by the way barely classifies as being gone, doesn't do a thing for me or Marco or the movie. If I'd been behind her disappearance, I'd have a confession by now. So no, I didn't."

I believed her. She was too much of a pragmatist to do something that would negatively impact the movie. I realized I had to call Coleman and let him know Sister was safe. I excused myself and went to the front door. Once outside in the clear, cold air, I felt my body relax. It had been a stressful day.

I didn't know what the heck was going on at Evermore, but someone was lying through their teeth. Krista Yost was dead, with all evidence pointing at Sister, who had a motive. Sister had been abducted—that I didn't doubt. She was far too vain to run around looking like a bag lady. But by whom? And what was accomplished by taking her for ten hours and then letting her go? None of it made any sense.

In fact, everything linked to the McFee family was a problem for Tinkie and me. And I had had about enough of dead ends and clues that led nowhere. Maybe Tinkie and I had been too passive. Maybe we'd been trapped in the past. Or maybe we'd been starstruck by the whole movie business. But that was over and done. It was time we found some answers and stopped spinning our wheels.

To that end, noticing Sister's car parked at the front of the stairs, I went down to investigate. Nothing was amiss in the interior, except for the awful smell that had rubbed off Sister. I popped the latch to the trunk and walked around to open it. There was only one thing there: a laptop computer.

Did it belong to Sister or Krista Yost? I picked it up

and hurried to the Cadillac. When it was tucked beneath some shoe boxes in the trunk, I called DeWayne and let him know Sister was safe. I returned to the dining room, where the dinner party was breaking up. Capturing Tinkie's arm, I pulled her into a corner. "I'm going to ask Sister what Cleo was doing on the west side of the state on the night she died. I want you to ask Colin the same thing. Someone has to have an answer. It's the clue we need to figure out what happened."

"Sure." She tilted her head toward the dining room. Cece was interviewing Roon and the St. Johns for another breaking story in the local newspaper. I'd heard that Cece's coverage of the McFees and the movie had boosted the newspaper's out-of-state circulation by twenty thousand. "Now's a good time to do it. Everyone is busy."

"Meet you at the car in twenty minutes." And I expected to have plenty to share.

21

I tapped on the door to Sister's room, very aware of the cameras I'd put in place. How ironic to be captured on video by the very spy devices I'd installed. Since I knew they were there, I'd refrain from threats or other aggressive behavior.

"What do you want?" Sister was her normal ungracious self, though she'd had a shower and was in clean clothes. She smelled tolerable and appeared to be sobering up.

"Why was Cleo on the western side of the state the night she died?"

Sister looked at me. "Have you lost your mind?"

"Nope." I tapped my head. "Still in there. It's a simple question. Why was your mother all the way across the state when she should have been headed down Highway 55 to Jackson?"

The look that crossed Sister's face told me she'd never given this any thought. "I suppose she had to pick up Son along the way. She'd do anything for him."

"The tail end of a hurricane was coming through. She drove at least four hours out of her way. Think about it, Sister. Why would Cleo do that?"

She swallowed. "I don't know. What does it matter, anyway? Mother is dead. Figuring out her reasoning for the things she did won't bring her back. Why did she insist on trying to save Son? Why couldn't she see he was beyond her help? Why did she let him in the car, especially behind the wheel? Those are better questions you might be asking."

For the first time, I saw a glimmer of the loss Sister felt over her mother's death. Her questions were those of a child abandoned. Had she and Colin not been so busy blaming Son, all of our questions might have been answered much earlier. Their obsession with fingering Son as the cause had impeded the initial investigation and contributed to the loss of physical evidence.

"Did your mother have a close friend or confidant who lived near Clarksdale? Someone she may have been visiting?"

"Mother had friends everywhere. She was always connecting and reconnecting with women she'd gone to college with or folks she'd met through her good works."

Sister's tone was derogatory, but at last I could see beneath it to the young girl who felt she had to compete with everyone and everything for parental attention.

"This is important, Sister. I—"

"What's important is that I was abducted from the

mall in Memphis. I was taken, and nobody came looking for me. I'm not stupid. I'll prove Lorraine St. John had me kidnapped, and when I do, I'll take control of this production company and film this movie my way."

"Sister, we might find the truth of what happened to your mother if you'll get onboard and help us."

"You just don't get it. You and that ditsy blond partner of yours. I have my conclusion. My book was published and hit bestseller lists. It tells the story exactly the way I want it told, and there is no one alive who can dispute it." She leaned into my face. "History is written by the victors, and in case you haven't figured it out, that's me. I'm alive. I'll inherit. *I win*."

My sympathy for Sister slammed into a brick wall. "Has anyone ever told you that you're eaten up with control issues?"

"Has anyone ever told you that your partner has issues of body odor?"

I didn't care that the cameras would nail me for this later. I grabbed the labels of her high-end terry bathrobe and twisted them until I held her so tightly I almost shut off her air.

"I don't care what happened in college. That was a long time ago. I care about right now, and if you don't lay off my partner, I am going to hurt you. Fair warning. I will come after you in ways you can't begin to imagine." I pushed her back into the room. "I've been hired to find out what happened to Cleo and Son, and I promise you I'm going to do it. So I'll ask you one more time. What was your mother doing near Clarksdale when she was supposed to be driving to Jackson?"

Sister inhaled, and she seemed to straighten her shoulders. "I don't know, and even if I did, I wouldn't tell you."

"High school, some? Grow up, Sister. What if someone deliberately killed Cleo? Aren't you the least bit curious?"

The features of her face froze in shock. "That's not possible. Mother went her own way, but she didn't have enemies. And she didn't consult with me or Daddy about her schedule."

"Can you be that naïve?" I didn't believe her. Something was off. She avoided eye contact, and Sister was confrontational if she was anything.

"My mother didn't confide in me. She was all about Son. I wasn't privy to her secrets."

She grabbed the door and started to shut it, but I blocked it with my foot.

"What happened to you tonight? You're blaming Lorraine. What's your proof? Or a better question is, can you prove you didn't set the whole thing up yourself to get sympathy?"

"What do you mean? I was taken and held hostage."

"The sheriff will be here any minute. You've wasted the resources of the county, the state, and the feds. You're in big trouble, Sister. If you were pretending to be—"

"I wasn't pretending, you poor excuse for a private investigator. I was walking to my car in the mall parking lot when someone ran up behind me and put a cloth to my nose and mouth. When I came to, I was tied up in an old warehouse. I managed, after hours of trying, to get free."

"And you somehow found your car and drove home." I laid on the sarcasm.

"They left the car outside the warehouse with the keys in it."

"Sounds really convenient." I could tell that got her goat.

"I saved myself because no one came looking for me. How do you think that feels?"

"Your father held a press conference and offered a reward."

Her face softened. "He did? How much?"

"Fifty grand."

"He really did that?"

A tiny grain of sympathy tried to creep back but I squashed it. "He did."

"He can save his money. I got free myself. Then I drove home."

"How come you smelled like a distillery?"

"I had a couple of drinks in one of the mall restaurants. Then whoever took me soaked my clothes in bourbon. I came to and I was wet and sticky and . . . gross. But they didn't hurt me."

It didn't make any sense that she'd make up such a preposterous story. "I'm glad you weren't hurt."

She looked at me. "I could almost believe you mean it, if I didn't know who you were and who your friends are."

There wasn't any point in further conversation. While she was busy playing the victim I had to use my time wisely and check out the laptop I'd found in the trunk of her car before she discovered it was missing. Now it was time to meet Tinkie and head home.

She was waiting for me in the car with the heater roaring. The night had grown cold and windy. "Any luck with Colin?" I asked.

"I was lucky he didn't hurl me down the stairs."

"Did he offer any theories about Cleo?"

"He said she probably had a lover in Clarksdale, but he couldn't offer any names. He was just being typical Colin, ugly and mean."

"The apple doesn't fall far from the tree. Exactly the same with Sister."

We left Evermore behind as we turned down the dark road toward Zinnia.

"Do you think Sister was really abducted, or is this some dodge to take the heat off of her for Krista Yost's death?"

"I don't know." I wanted to believe it was a dodge, but something about the way Sister had looked when she learned her father offered a reward made me believe otherwise. "There are forces at work here that don't make sense. Krista Yost is dead, but why? Sister abducted. Again, why? Who benefits from this? I don't see how Sister or Colin come out ahead. Maybe we need to rethink the whole business about what happened to Cleo and Son."

We were coming up on a sharp ninety-degree turn with no grade. Dead Man's Curve was always part of the driver's education test in high school. Coach Reid braved physical harm to teach high school sophomores to drive. The curve was a lesson because the temptation was to take the turn too fast. Tinkie applied the brake gradually, easing into the curve just as Coach Reid had taught us.

"Remember those driver's ed classes?" Tinkie asked.

Our thoughts often followed the same path, so I wasn't surprised. "I do. Remember Johnny Goff? He took this curve doing sixty on two wheels. Coach Reid almost had a stroke but Johnny held it in the road."

We laughed at the memory, and Tinkie slowed more. "We were foolhardy back then. And I thought you were a little weird. You were so quiet and you never talked. Except when you were on stage."

"Yeah, I was shy." Tinkie had been one of the popular girls. "I thought you were not very bright."

"I worked hard to hide my intelligence. It was high school. You would've been more popular if you'd pretended to be slow too."

I laughed because she'd only proven once again how smart she was. "No one sent me the memo."

"And Libby Delaney, had she been alive, would never have told you to pretend to be dumb so the boys would like you."

She was right about that. My mama didn't hold with women playing to a man's weakness. "Aunt Loulane wasn't up to speed on boy manipulation. She would—"

A loud noise was followed by the car jerking to the right. Tinkie grabbed the steering wheel with all of her might and tried to hold the car on the road, but it swerved and went off the shoulder. I was hurled forward against my seat belt, then thrown right. My head struck the passenger window with enough force to knock me loopy.

The car left the road and plowed through the deep, freshly turned dirt of a cotton field. We came to a dead stop. I heard the motor of the car ticking, and the headlights remained on, casting their beam across the empty field. The night was very quiet as I tried to shake the fogginess from my brain.

It took me several moments to gather my wits and figure out that somehow the car had blown a tire or had a mechanical failure that sent us off the road. Thank goodness we'd been going slow, or it could have been so much worse. I roused myself and realized Tinkie was slumped against the driver's window. A trickle of blood traced down the cold glass.

"Tinkie?" I unbuckled my seat belt and then hers. She was motionless, her head thrown back and to the left.

"Tinkie?" I touched her face. She was unconscious, and I couldn't tell how badly she was hurt, but I was worried this wasn't minor. "Tinkie?"

She moaned, and when I looked at my hand in the light of the dash, it was covered in blood. I had to get help for her, and fast.

"Don't move." I tried to open my door, but it was jammed. I searched the floorboard for my purse, cursing the long skirt I wore. I realized my purse was tangled up under the seat, and my cell phone was in my purse. I slipped over the seatback and down onto the floor of the backseat, at last finding the elusive phone. A minute later, I had Coleman on the line.

"Tinkie is hurt." I fought panic. "We're in Deadman's Curve on the Bullin Cemetery Road. Send an ambulance. And Doc. Tell him to come. Fast." My voice cracked.

"Are you okay?"

"I am."

"Stay in control. We're on the way."

I clung to that as I looked at my unconscious friend. I didn't know what to do. Should I try to lay her down? Should I drag her out of the car? I didn't have enough medical training to make a good decision.

I was able to open the back door. I slipped out of the car and got my bearings as I stood up. I was still a little woozy, but once I was upright, I examined the car. The right front tire was disintegrated, for all practical purposes. It was a blowout of epic proportions. Which didn't make a lot of sense because Oscar maintained the Richmond cars to perfection. Detailing, air pressure in the tires, oil changes, belt replacement—he was on top of it. Cars were his passion. And the Caddy was not even six months old.

I knelt to take a closer look. A bullet slammed into the front fender only inches from my head. I had no doubt it was a bullet, and I tucked and rolled, then crawled around the car to get on the offside from the shooter. The night was so dark, I had no idea where the shooter might be. Now I knew what had happened to the car tire. Someone had shot it out and caused the wreck. And they were coming to finish the job.

I had no way to defend myself. It hadn't occurred to me to take my gun to a dinner party at Evermore, so it was at Dahlia House. Truthfully, even though someone had shot at us at the Sunflower River Bridge, I hadn't taken the incident seriously. The figure I'd seen near the barn—I'd assumed it was just another scare tactic. More drama than danger. Now, though, I had to reframe my opinion. I should have taken it all way more seriously.

I had to come up with an action plan, a way to save myself and Tinkie—before the person with the gun decided I was a sitting duck. The only option was to make a run for it and hope the darkness gave me cover.

But Tinkie was helpless in the car. I couldn't leave her.

So I had better figure something out fast.

I made my way to her side of the car and opened the driver's door and pulled her onto the ground beside me. I couldn't leave her in the front seat, an easy target. She was breathing, but still unconscious. I tried to calculate how much longer before Coleman would arrive, but time had telescoped. It was impossible to guess how long it had been since I called. Ten minutes or an hour?

I used my jacket to cover Tinkie's upper body. I found

the trunk latch by the driver's seat and popped it. I doubted Tinkie's gun would be there, but it was at least something to try.

Raising the trunk lid the least amount possible, I fumbled in the interior. To my surprise, beneath the numerous shoeboxes I found Tinkie's Glock. Thank goodness. I brought it out and checked to be sure the clip was loaded. Now, if I had to, I could at least return fire.

Another slug slammed into the trunk with a sickening thud, and I saw muzzle fire from somewhere near the road. I sent four bullets in that direction. At least the bastard now knew I was armed and that I wouldn't go down without a fight. I was aware of the dangers of firing blindly into the dark night—and I figured the shooter had a night scope to be able to come so close to my location—but I had no other choice. I only hoped my hail of bullets would deter them from coming closer to finish the job.

I inched back to Tinkie, who had grown agitated. Her head moved from side to side and her arms and legs twitched. It was either a good sign or an indication that she had some kind of pressure building in her brain from banging her head. "Where the hell is Coleman?" I spoke the words aloud.

Movement only fifty yards from the car made me steady the pistol and pull the trigger. The shooter was moving in. A grunt of pain was my reward. Either I'd hit the person or come close.

Far in the distance was the sound of sirens. At last. I hunkered down, using my body to protect Tinkie as best I could just in case the shooter came for one last chance to kill us. I was ready.

The lights of two patrol cars and an ambulance cut the

black night and swept across the Caddy as the vehicles approached the curve. A blast of the siren told me Coleman saw us. He drove straight across the field to park not twenty feet from us so that his headlights would give Doc Sawyer light to examine Tinkie by. Doc hopped out of the patrol car, more spry than a man his age had a right to be.

"Someone is shooting at us!" I called in warning, and Doc and Coleman ducked, hurrying toward us.

Doc immediately went to Tinkie and began to examine her. Coleman pulled me against him and held me. "What happened?"

"I think someone shot out our tire in a deliberate effort to make us wreck. Then they started shooting at us. They meant to kill us."

Two paramedics rushed forward with a stretcher for Tinkie, and Coleman used his radio to let DeWayne know a shooter was on the loose. The deputy drove a second patrol car through the field, moving to the perimeter to scan the tree line with a powerful searchlight.

Coleman and Doc had it under control. I could relinquish my death grip on Tinkie's gun. When I did, I was glad Coleman still held me. One forlorn sob broke free before I regained control. "I'm okay. I'm just worried about Tinkie. Look, I fired back at the shooter. I may have hit them."

"Where?" Coleman eased back from me. He had his duties to perform.

"I thought back in that tree line at first, but then they angled around to shoot from this direction. They were about fifty yards into the field, that way."

"I'm going to call Oscar to bring Sweetie Pie. If you hit him, she can track him."

I nodded.

"Oscar can ride with Tinkie to the hospital."

I almost sobbed again, but I managed to hold it in. "Is she hurt bad?"

"Ask Doc." He gently maneuvered me to Doc's side. I knelt with him as he worked on Tinkie.

"Is she okay?"

"No bullet wounds, so that's a good start. She must have struck her head hard. We'll get her to the hospital where I can examine neuro-images. How long has she been unconscious?"

I swallowed my bitter fear. "Maybe fifteen minutes. Maybe longer."

He nodded and signaled the paramedics to take her. "The good news is that no bones are broken. Her spine and neck seem okay, but we'll take every precaution."

My hand on his arm shook with desperation. "She has to be okay."

"I know." He patted my hand. "I won't sugarcoat this, because I never do. Head injuries are serious. That she's been unconscious this long worries me. I'm glad Coleman called Oscar. He needs to be here, and you need to step back and let me work."

Coleman was searching the field with a flashlight in the direction I'd indicated where I might have hit the shooter. There was nothing for me to do but get out of the way and let Doc take care of my friend. And wait for Oscar to arrive with the dogs. I knew he'd bring Chablis, who, for all of her glamour dog grooming, was smart and a part of the Delaney Detective Agency team.

I called Cece to tell her what had happened, but before I could get any words out, I began to cry. Finally I managed to blurt out, "Wreck. Dead Man's Curve. Tinkie is really hurt." She didn't bother with goodbye but just hung up.

I considered calling Millie, but I didn't. She'd been at work in the café at five a.m., and then she'd served dinner at Evermore until ten. She's been on her feet for seventeen hours, and tomorrow would be soon enough for bad news. Or maybe, if the stars aligned, I would have good news and could spare Millie the anguish of waiting by Tinkie's side.

At last, headlights announced Oscar's arrival. He stopped behind the ambulance on the road and ran across the field, Sweetie Pie and Chablis streaking ahead of him. When the dogs arrived at Tinkie's unconscious body, Chablis let out a howl of dismay. Sweetie joined in, that strange, mournful hound-dog song echoing through the night. I only cried harder.

Oscar put a hand on my shoulder as he passed, but Tinkie was his concern. He knelt beside her, took her hand, and spoke softly to Doc. A moment later, the paramedics lifted the stretcher and Oscar walked with them, still holding his wife's unresponsive hand.

"We'll do everything we can," Doc said as he passed me. "When you're done here, come to the hospital. I want to check you out too."

As the sad little group tromped across the field to the ambulance, a cold resolve settled on me. I still had the Glock. I got another two clips from the trunk of Tinkie's car and saw the laptop I'd stolen from Sister's car.

"Coleman." He came to stand beside me and illuminated the trunk with a powerful flashlight.

"I took this from Sister's car. I think it belongs to Krista Yost. And I think it's the reason someone tried to kill us. They wanted it back."

Coleman put on a glove and transferred the computer to his patrol car. I took the dogs to the field and gave Sweetie the command to search. Not three minutes later Coleman was examining footprints and blood. I *had* hit the shooter.

And before the night was over, I intended to finish them off.

22

Sweetie Pie coursed across the field, giving voice to the fact she was on a trail. Chablis had more difficulty navigating in the raw, turned dirt, but she put her heart into the run. Coleman and I were right behind them.

"Stay behind me," Coleman ordered as we ran.

I didn't have the breath to argue, but I knew what I meant to do. This person had hurt my partner. The shooter had hidden in ambush with the intention of harming us both in an automobile accident. When I'd climbed out of the car, the shooter had come closer to finish us off. And to retrieve that damn computer.

Hoots Tanner believed that Son McFee had been forced off the road. When the SUV Cleo had died in was stolen, he'd lost every chance to prove his theory. Now I had plenty of physical evidence to show someone was adept at sending cars careening off the road. I had no doubt now that what everyone had accepted as a stormy-night tragedy was a lot worse—it had been orchestrated murder.

Sweetie Pie and Chablis hit the tree line and disappeared into the woods. Coleman had radioed DeWayne to call all of the sheriff's auxiliary and as many volunteers as he could round up to meet on Claymore Road, which was in the direction we'd headed.

My guess was the assailant had parked on Claymore, walked through the fields and brake line of trees, and set up to wait for us to leave the party at Evermore. The shooter had known where we were and the approximate time we'd leave. Someone at Evermore had been working with him. Or her. Somehow Sister's image kept popping into my head.

She'd been so furious with everyone. And if she'd killed Krista Yost—or had her killed—it wasn't a big step to commit additional murders. They could only execute her once.

But the why of it still made no sense. Sister inherited the entire McFee estate. Even if Krista Yost proved she'd penned the books Sister had put her name on, Sister had more money than she'd spend in twenty lifetimes. And scandal often enhanced celebrity.

There was no challenge to her claim of inheritance. Son had been declared dead, and Susan's baby wouldn't inherit. Aside from whether or not Son was portrayed as the guilty party in causing an accident, Delaney Detective Agency's investigation into the past could have no impact on Sister's financial future. Or Colin's, for that matter.

The truth hit with impact. Someone feared that Tinkie and I had stumbled too close to the truth. But what truth?

Coleman went into the tree line right where Sweetie had gone, and I was hard on his heels. The going was much tougher in the trees as brambles tugged at my clothes. Again I rued the silly dress I wore. I didn't care if I was invited to the Taj Mahal, I wasn't wearing another dress. It never failed that I ended up floundering around without the proper gear.

Fuming about my clothes kept my mind off the very dangerous truth I'd come to. When we found the shooter, I intended to make that person tell me everything I wanted to know. I was done with stumbling around in a cesspool of lies.

In the distance I heard men yelling. Shots were fired. Even though I was panting hard, I redoubled my efforts to run—and keep up with Coleman. Sweetie's strong bay led us unerringly toward a cluster of headlights and searchlights. We'd made it to the auxiliary road, and I hoped they'd been successful in a capture.

When we came out of the woods, I saw the men. One knelt beside Sweetie Pie, holding her collar and stroking her. Another held Chablis in his arms. There was no evidence of anyone in custody.

Junior Wells stepped forward. "It was a man in a dark sedan. He came out of the woods about a quarter mile up the road, and before we could get to him, he took off."

"You're sure it was a man?" I asked.

"Stout fella," Junior said. "Tall and muscular." He

took us down the road to show us a footprint he'd carefully marked off so Coleman could cast it. "Big foot."

And I had a sudden thought as to who it might belong to. Johnny Dan had been strangely absent from Evermore during the dinner—odd, considering he was supposed to be providing security at the house. Possibly because he was hiding in an ambush, waiting to kill Tinkie and me.

I would deal with him very soon. Tinkie was my first priority. And she had to be okay. She had to. We'd brushed up against danger numerous times, and a car accident wasn't going to be the thing that took Tinkie out of action. I found Coleman conferring with a group of the volunteers.

"I'm going to ask Junior to take me to my car," I told him.

His hands gently turned my face up so he could look into my eyes. "She's going to be okay."

I nodded because if I tried to speak I'd cry.

"And you? You're going to the hospital, right?"

He knew me too well. "Yes."

"I'll be there as soon as I can. Cece is already there, and Harold. I called him."

I couldn't hold the tears back any longer, and they fell silently.

Coleman drew me into his arm and held me tight. "Junior, will you take Sarah Booth home? She needs a car."

"Sure thing," Junior said. "If you don't need me here, I'll be glad to."

"The volunteers did a great job," Coleman said. "Everyone can go home. DeWayne and I'll finish up here, but there's not a lot we can do until daylight. Tromping around might do more harm than good."

My whistle was a little weak and wobbly, but I got Sweetie Pie and Chablis into the backseat of Junior's car and he drove us to Dahlia House.

The scene at the hospital was chaotic. Tinkie had been sent for an MRI, and Doc had uncharacteristically insisted that everyone leave, even Tinkie's husband. Oscar sat by himself in the waiting room while Cece and Millie rose to huddle around me and ask questions. That only added to my anxiety. No one knew if Tinkie had regained consciousness or not.

I told my friends what had happened, as I understood it. Oscar listened, but didn't comment. I'd never seen Oscar so quiet. He and Tinkie had been through hell with a previous case involving an infant that had been left on my doorstep. The Richmonds had taken the child in to care for her until we found the missing mother, but Tinkie and Oscar had fallen in love with the baby. It had been a hard reality check for all involved, and they were just recovering. Now Tinkie was injured.

When Doc came into the waiting room, I could tell by his face the news was not good. We stood back as he spoke quietly to Oscar. My heart thumped so hard, I sat down because I was afraid my legs wouldn't support me.

Tinkie had been unconscious for at least twenty minutes. She'd struck the side of her head on the window and possibly her forehead on the steering wheel. The airbags had deployed, but the wreck had been so violent I couldn't say exactly when she'd been injured. I'd been jostled and hurled and thumped around so much, I hadn't been able to watch Tinkie. We hadn't been going fast, and we'd both been wearing seat belts. But when the tire had been shot out the car gained velocity. When the vehicle rammed into the soft dirt of the field, we'd stopped too abruptly.

A million thoughts scurried through my brain. None of them gave me comfort.

At last Doc came over to us. He sighed. "We're sending Tinkie to Memphis by helicopter. She has bleeding in her brain, and the pressure has to be relieved. We don't have the expertise or equipment to handle that here."

Cece put a hand on one of my shoulders and Millie the other. "I know this is serious," Cece said, "but what's the prognosis?"

"The brain is a strange and remarkable thing," Doc said. "Once the pressure is removed, if she wakes up, I'd say it's a good chance she'll recover completely."

"And if she doesn't wake?" I hated that I had to ask. Sometimes not knowing was the best. But this was Tinkie. My best friend and partner. I had to know.

"If she doesn't wake up soon, the prognosis is not so good."

"How bad?" I couldn't stop myself.

"Let's not walk down the worst-case-scenario road," Doc said. He took a step back, but I stood and followed him.

"How bad?"

"If she doesn't wake when the pressure is relieved, she could be in a coma. For a while." Doc glanced at Oscar, who looked like he'd been hit in the head with a sledgehammer. He was stunned by the turn of events. His wife and I had gone to a dinner with a movie crew, and now his wife might not wake up. "Sarah Booth, you should comfort Oscar."

"Yes," I said, but my thoughts were far, far away. Comforting Oscar was something I should do, but I had other plans.

"Is Tinkie in pain?" I asked.

"Pressure on her brain is uncomfortable, but I'm not certain what she's feeling because she's . . . unresponsive."

"When is she leaving for Memphis?"

"They'll have the flight crew ready in five minutes."

"Can I see her?"

Doc once again glanced at Oscar. "It should be him," he said softly. "She's his wife."

"Tell her I'm taking care of everything." If I couldn't tell her myself, Doc could relay the message. "Tell her that when she wakes up, it will all be over. Tell her that I'm going to make her dream come true."

"I'll tell her."

Doc touched Oscar's shoulder, rousing him from his stupor. The two men walked into the ICU. Cece and Millie gathered around me. "Let's go to my house," Cece said. "You don't need to be alone, Sarah Booth."

"I have a terrible headache. I'm exhausted. I need to go to bed."

"You can sleep over."

"I haven't even fed the horses," I lied. "And Chablis is at my house. She's so upset. I need to get the dogs and crawl in bed with them. We're all wasted."

"Okay," Cece said reluctantly. "Should I call Marco and Lorraine and tell them what's happened?"

I shook my head. "Best to wait until morning. Why ruin everyone's night?"

"Good point." Cece gave me a hard look. "Are you sure you're okay?"

"No, I'm not okay. But I can't think of a damn thing

to do to make Tinkie or myself better. I'm going home. I'm going to make a very stiff drink, and I'm going to swallow it and go to bed."

"That sounds more like the Sarah Booth I know," Cece said, and I was happy to see I'd alleviated some of her worry. The passive Sarah Booth had not played well. My change of tactics had worked.

I took my leave and headed straight to Dahlia House.

I had one goal at Dahlia House. Additional bullets. And then I was going to Evermore to find Johnny Dan, and he was going to tell me who'd sent him to wreck us, or he would not like what I planned to do to him.

I'd been unable to get out of Dahlia House without the two dogs and one very determined cat. Blood continued to trickle down my forearm from the attempt to leave Pluto in my bedroom. Dogs could be willful, but cats knew no authority. So Pluto rode on top of the passenger seat, and I had no intention of trying to move him. Some things were better left alone.

I'd put my phone on automatic reply with a message that said I'd taken something to sleep and was tucked in at Dahlia House. I didn't suppose that would deter Coleman if he called more than three times and I didn't answer. He'd be by to check, and he'd figure out pretty quickly where I'd gone. I was racing the clock.

I understood my behavior was rash, foolish, dangerous, illegal—a long list of negative words. When I thought of Tinkie's pale face, the blood coagulating in her blond hair as she lay in the dirt beside her car, I didn't care how reckless my plan was. Someone was going to pay before the night was over. There was no secret, no fortune, no reputation worth the life of my friend.

I was clued in to the security system at Evermore, and I took the back road that Marco had shown us the night we installed the cameras. This would have been a lot easier if I'd had some inside help, but I didn't trust Marco. I didn't trust anyone.

I felt my phone vibrate in my pocket. When I checked, it was Coleman. The clock had started. He would soon be looking for me. I parked, left the critters in the car, and ran through the woods as fast as I could.

Once I made it to the lawn of Evermore, I hugged the dark shadows, avoiding the security cameras. When I was at the front of the house, I glanced inside. Family drama going down in the front parlor. Colin, Susan, and Sister were all in the room, along with Lorraine, Marco, Roon, and the members of the crew. And whatever was being said was heated. Marco and Colin yelled back and forth. Sister shook her finger. Susan tried to talk to Colin and then Marco—nobody listened. Everyone was talking, and from the expressions on their faces, there would be nothing left but scorched earth.

Susan walked over to Lorraine and slapped the camera out of her hands. Not a good move. Lorraine was tall, slender, and athletic. Susan was short, pregnant, and a dynamo of human fitness. Mayhem was about to ensue. To my surprise, Lorraine only laughed and turned away.

While my best friend was being airlifted to Memphis for a brain injury, the McFees and guests were at each other's throats. With any luck at all, they'd kill each other and put an end to the tragedy that followed behind all of them like the odor of decaying fish. Sister tormented

Tinkie about a smell, but it was the McFee family that had brought a stench to Sunflower County. The McFees and their henchmen.

I surveyed the room, searching for Johnny Dan. He wasn't in sight.

I considered forcing my way inside. I had Tinkie's gun and plenty of ammo, but I needed to be alone with Johnny Dan. Johnny had to be the shooter. He had motive, means, and opportunity. He'd been bragging about shooting the Swedish gun the night Tinkie and I broke into Evermore. One way or the other, I'd get the truth out of him about shooting out Tinkie's tire. Once I nailed him as the shooter, then he was going to tell me which McFee had hired him to cause the wreck. I suspected Sister, but, without a confession, I was afraid she'd escape punishment.

Coleman had Krista Yost's computer, and he'd find what Sister so desperately wanted to keep hidden, but even if the computer proved Krista was the ghostwriter for Sister's books, that wasn't enough. Johnny Dan was going to give me what I needed to make the guilty party pay.

To that end, I needed to slip around the house and enter from the back. I'd backed up about ten steps when I hit something very solid. Warm and solid. I reached a hand back and felt. Was that a thigh? Another thigh? A . . . My exploring hand was met with a harsh grip. I'd been discovered!

Another hand covered my mouth so I couldn't scream, and I was pulled deeper into the shrubs and out of the line of sight of the windows. When my captor spun me around, I drew in a breath to scream, but it was cut short when I recognized Coleman.

"What are you up to, Sarah Booth?" he asked.

"Actually, I was going home," I lied.

"Really?"

"You doubt me?" I feigned indignation.

"Come with me." Coleman had no time to waste. Tugging at my arm, he loped across the lawn and toward the path where I'd parked.

"How'd you know about this back road?" I asked.

"Cece figured where you'd be going. She sent me to be sure you didn't get your silly self shot. Or worse."

"Look, I really was leaving. I realized it was a bad idea and I was going home." I looked him dead in the eye and lied.

"It looked to me like you were peeping in their window. With a gun and enough bullets to take out a platoon. That's trespassing and possibly worse." Coleman opened my car door. "Get in and drive. Straight to Dahlia House. Right now, and don't you dare take a detour."

"What are you going to do?" His cruiser was parked at the front door. He'd come on official business.

"It was Krista Yost's computer you found in Sister's trunk. There's detailed correspondence between Krista and Sister revealing how Krista had written all of Sister's books. And she was threatening to go public unless Sister included her as a cowriter on the YA fantasy series. Sister pretty much told her to go to hell. Krista promised retribution and that she'd go public. That was the last correspondence. I'm bringing Sister in for questioning in Krista's murder. I don't need you on the premises to screw this up. Now get out of here or I'll arrest you. Maybe you two could share a cell."

"And Johnny Dan? What about him? He shot out Tinkie's tire."

"And he'll pay, but we have to do this legally. We need proof. You know that."

My cell phone vibrated in my pocket and I pulled it out as a distraction to give myself a moment to think. Dorinda Posey was calling. I held up a finger, answered, and put the phone on speaker.

"Ms. Delaney, I need your help." Dorinda started to cry.

"What's wrong?"

"Someone is trying to hurt me. A man called not ten minutes ago and claimed he was Son McFee. He said he wasn't dead, that he'd been saved from the river, and he wanted to see me. He said he would be in Memphis tomorrow."

It was a little more than I could take in. "This caller said he was Son McFee? That he was alive?"

"Why would someone be so mean?" Dorinda asked. "It's Colin. I know it's him. He knew how much I cared for Son. He must have found out I talked with you. He's letting me know how cruel and horrid he can be. He'll hurt me."

"Dorinda, call a friend and go there right now. Don't tell anyone what's going on, just get out of your apartment." I didn't get to finish because I was interrupted. Coleman took the phone.

"This is Sheriff Coleman Peters. I'm calling the Memphis police. I'll ask them to keep an eye on you once you've decided where you're going."

"You're scaring me." Dorinda's voice shook.

"Be scared," I said. "I want you to be afraid because you're in danger. Now get moving. I have no idea how far these people will go. The sheriff here will tell you."

"Do exactly what she said. Now!" Coleman left no room for argument.

The line disconnected and I hoped we'd scared her

into immediate action. If a dead man was calling her, she was in a lot of danger.

"What do you think that was all about?" I asked Coleman.

"Someone is sending her a message, and I hope she listens." He made a quick call to the Memphis police and explained the situation. "They're going to her apartment now to make sure she's safe. They'll escort her wherever she wants to go."

It was a tiny bit of relief, enough to give me some breathing room—and to allow me to gather my wits. "Coleman, you can't go in there alone. You have no idea who is up to what. There's not a person in that house who can be trusted. There are guns all over the place. Show guns, personal weapons. It's dangerous."

He glanced back toward the house where light spilled out across a portion of the lawn. The front door flew open, and Lorraine rushed outside. "Security! Security! Open the front gate. We need an ambulance."

Coleman took off running toward the house, and I was hot on his heels.

23

When Coleman barged through the door, I was so close behind I went in with him like his shadow. To be honest, no one was interested in whether I was there or not. Everyone was gathered around the staircase, and when Coleman shouldered our way through, I could easily see why. Susan lay at the base of the stairs. Sister reclined beside her, moaning.

"She pushed me," Susan whimpered, scrabbling away from Sister on her elbows and heels. She looked like an ungainly crab. "She's trying to kill me and my baby."

Sister pushed up on her elbows. "I did nothing of the kind. You grabbed me and pushed me. Then you lost your balance because you're pregnant."

"I didn't lose my balance. I'm in excellent shape. She

tried to kill me, just like she killed that writer woman." Susan's complaint was cut short with a howl as a contraction hit her. "Oh, damn," she gritted. "I'm having the baby. Someone get a doctor."

Roon spoke up, "An ambulance and doctor are already on the way."

I looked behind me and Lorraine had her camera up and recording. She was either dedicated to her job or dedicated to ruining the McFee family. I liked it either way.

"Help is coming." Colin knelt beside Susan, but, strangely, he didn't touch her or comfort her. "It's going to be okay. You took a tumble, but it's going to be okay." He actually looked worried.

"You don't know a damn thing," Susan snapped. "The baby is coming early. Four weeks early. If my baby dies, it's on Sister's head."

"You're a fruitcake." Sister pushed herself to her feet and finally realized she was the center of attention for a roomful of campaign workers, movie people, the sheriff, and me. I was the one she zeroed in on. "Why are you in my house? Get out." She looked at everyone. "Out! All of you. Off the premises right now or the sheriff will take you to jail."

The campaign workers grumbled and began to move away. Lorraine never budged.

"Did you get our fall down the stairs on film?" Sister asked, and it was the first civil tone I'd heard.

"Maybe," Lorraine said. She edged back, as if Sister might take a leap at her. She lowered the camera, protecting it.

"I'll pay you fifty thousand for it." Sister steadied herself with the handrail, completely ignoring Susan, not six feet away, howling with another contraction. Roon got blankets and pillows and worked to make Susan as comfortable as he could. Colin seemed frozen in place. He knelt beside Susan, but he offered no help.

Lorraine cocked an eyebrow. "Really, Sister? Fifty grand? Why?"

"It will prove I didn't push Susan. She hooked a leg around my ankles and pushed me. When I lost my balance, I grabbed her." She had everyone's attention. "Susan has been up in the gym taking private pole dancing lessons from some guy from Memphis. She's strong as an ox. She pretends to be all vapid and exhausted from carrying the baby. It's all fake. She tried to kill me and now she's trying to blame the fall on me. I get all the blame. All of it. No one ever takes my side."

I felt like a rabid ferret was clawing the inside of my skull. The McFees were stark, raving mad. There wasn't a sane one in the lot.

Susan started to push up off the floor but a contraction hit and her features squeezed into a grimace. When she could talk, she said, "Those two, Sister and Lorraine, are in cahoots."

"In your wildest dreams," Sister said calmly. "I don't partner with anyone."

"Except your ghostwriter," Coleman said. Before Sister knew what had happened, he had her handcuffed. "Frangelica McFee, you're wanted for questioning in the murder of Krista Yost." Just to be on the safe side, he continued with her Miranda rights and not even Susan interrupted.

"You're making a mistake," Sister said. "Daddy, aren't you going to do something?"

Colin looked up at her. "If anything is wrong with this baby, my son, my only real heir, you'll regret it. You've always been a greedy, desperate person. Grasping at everything, taking it all. And it was never enough."

His words knocked the breath out of her. I could only imagine the punch Sister felt. Despite her meanness and cruelty, I felt for her. All she'd done for her father, all she'd lost—and it had been for nothing. Colin would never love her because she was a girl. He knelt with his back to me, and I drew back my foot to give him a kick he'd remember. Coleman intervened, stepping between my foot and Colin's bottom. "No," he said. "No. He'll get his, that I promise you."

Before I could react, Susan let out another series of cries mingled with curses. Lorraine handed me her camera. "Keep the focus on her face. I'll deliver this baby." She pushed Colin out of the way and reached under the blankets. The next thing I knew, yoga pants flew up in the air.

"Do you know how to deliver a baby?" I asked her.

"I've filmed it before. When I did a documentary on natural childbirth back in the nineties. I filmed five or six deliveries. Besides, there isn't an alternative, unless you want to deliver it. I don't think Marco or Colin would be much use. This baby is coming now."

"It's four weeks premature," I whispered in her ear. From what I knew, we needed life support, incubators, whatever they did for babies with undeveloped lungs.

With Roon's assistance, Lorraine set to work. I cleared the area of all unnecessary spectators. Doc and the ambulance would be there any moment, but Lorraine was right. The baby wasn't going to wait. When I had Colin seated in the parlor with a stiff drink, I realized Coleman was in a corner of the room talking to Sister. Why hadn't he taken her to jail already?

I signaled him for a word, and he came over, his gaze never leaving Sister.

"Aren't you taking her in?"

"She asked to stay until the baby is born. I need to talk with her and I can do it here as well as at the courthouse." He finally looked at me. "She says she didn't kill Krista or push Susan. She says you and Tinkie were snooping in her room and were set up to find a manuscript that showed Krista had been ghostwriting Sister's books."

"That's true. We were in her room." I hated admitting it, but there was no way around it. As Aunt Loulane, a true Shakespeare fan, would say, truth will out. Better now than in the future when Coleman would not have a prisoner to distract him.

"Sarah Booth, she can charge you with trespassing, robbery, a dozen other things. Tampering with evidence."

"We didn't touch anything. Of hers." I wasn't about to confess to planting spyware. "Besides, Tinkie and I were invited into the house by Marco St. John." I doubted that would save me from the fire, but it was at least worth an effort.

Coleman scowled. "I'll deal with you and Tinkie at a later date. What's important here is that Sister insists someone is setting her up. She swears she never took Krista's laptop from her hotel room and that she had no idea it was in the trunk of her car. She believes she was abducted in Memphis so the laptop could be put in her possession."

"And you believe her?" I was stunned.

"It's making a lot of sense to me."

"Does Sister know who was shooting at us or why?"

"She didn't know anything about a shooting or the wreck. Either she's the best actress around or she's telling the truth about that."

"If Sister didn't send the marksman, who did?"

Coleman looked at Colin, who seemed like a deflated version of himself. There was something more going on with him.

A bloodcurdling yell from the foyer had us all on our feet. Colin seemed to revive. "My son, is he okay? My son has to live. He's the McFee heir."

"What about me, you buffoon?" Susan snarled from the floor in between panting. "Your heir is about to tear me apart. Not that I'll get any credit for carrying and delivering the baby. Only those with true McFee blood count in Colin's world. I'm just a vessel for the sacred heir."

Colin ignored Susan's sniping and put a hand on Lorraine's shoulder. "Will the baby live?"

"I don't know," Lorraine said.

Susan tried to sit up. "Get away from me. All of you. You don't have a clue what you're talking about. I'm not having this baby here. It isn't due yet."

Thank goodness the front door opened and Doc rushed in with his medical kit. "The ambulance is right behind me," he said. He shooed us away from Susan and in a few moments he was talking to her soothingly. "One big push," I heard him say, and then the sound of a baby crying—a loud, lusty, wailing cry. The lungs sounded fully developed to me.

I peeked around the corner to see Doc wiping clean a baby that had to weigh at least eight pounds. Premature my eye. That baby had the lungs of an opera singer. He was going full blast and Doc was pleased as punch, if his expression was any indication.

The door opened again and two paramedics rolled in a gurney. "Load her up," Doc told the medics, pointing at Susan, who amazingly looked none the worse for wear.

Doc came into the parlor with the infant in his arms and handed him to Colin. "You've got a fine, healthy son," Doc said. "Eight pounds if he's an ounce."

Colin handed the baby back. "I don't think so."

Like characters in a soap opera, everyone stopped and turned toward Colin. Even Coleman and Sister drew near. "Colin! Colin!" Susan called from the gurney. "I can explain."

Colin stood, his face cold and hard as granite. "Jeremy!" He called out to his campaign manager, and he motioned to Lorraine. "Jeremy, call a press conference. You, Lorraine, get that camera rolling." Lorraine had already been filming him so she just kept going.

"This is better than any trashy melodrama on reality TV. I can build an empire with the footage just from today. The McFees are the gift that keeps on giving," Lorraine muttered.

Colin straightened his shoulders, a man carrying the weight of the world rising to the occasion. When Lorraine had him dead center in her lens, he began. "My wife has betrayed me. This isn't my son. It couldn't be. Last April and May, I was in the Soviet Union learning the devious secrets of Vladimir Putin and his plan to overtake the United States from within. I didn't have conjugal union with my wife for nearly three months, and I know for a fact this baby wasn't conceived by immaculate conception.

"This baby was conceived during my absence." He walked to the lobby and Lorraine followed. He pointed at Susan, who was tucked beneath blankets on the gurney. "She is a Jezebel. She is not the mother of my son. That is not my child." He looked at the paramedics. "Take her!" He thundered like Moses on the Mount.

In a perfectly executed quarter turn, Colin faced Lorraine's camera head-on. He spoke to the lens, to his audience, to the only people who really mattered to him. "My family has completely betrayed me. I am alone now, without an heir."

"What about me?" Sister said.

Colin made a motion with his hand for her to be quiet. "My first son, Daryl McFee, is dead. His sister, Frangelica, is facing murder charges in the death of her ghostwriter, and though I've tried hard to protect her from her own actions, I'm fearful she was involved with her own mother's death. I was able to protect Sister five years ago. When my private investigator got on her trail, I paid him off and made all the evidence against her disappear. But she has betrayed me again."

"Daddy! I didn't—" Sister nearly collapsed.

"Now my wife has just delivered a male baby, a child I thought to be my son, but a DNA test will show that Susan has been unfaithful to me."

"Who could be faithful to you, you preening old goat? I'd rather be faithful to a one-eyed Cyclops!" Susan yelled from the gurney at the doorway. The paramedics, like the rest of us, had stopped, transfixed by the show.

"The cries of a Jezebel," Colin said without missing a beat. "So as it comes to pass, without a viable heir, and since Frangelica is facing a murder charge, no make that multiple murder charges, I am now in line to inherit the McFee Estate, which will transfer to my name on February 5."

"You can't do that." Sister tried to get away from Coleman, but he held her fast. "I'm alive. By the terms of Great-grandpa Jamie's trust, I inherit."

Colin turned a cool eye on his daughter. "You didn't

read the trust thoroughly, Sister. A felon can't inherit. The only thing that old prude hated more than a fornicator was a murderer. Looks to me like you'll be in prison. It would be a shame for this grand old house to be empty."

I slipped out my phone and sent a text to Cece. She had to get here fast or she would miss the entire show, and I had no doubt that Colin, who'd found his ultimate soapbox as the betrayed and abandoned patriarch of the McFee tribe, had every intention of sealing the deal on inheriting the kingdom as fast as he could legally make it happen. He didn't care that Sister might go to prison, or that Son was dead, or that the baby he thought was his had been born. He didn't care about anything except himself.

"Jeremy, bring me the copy of Jamie's will, please," Colin said, making my prediction come true.

The staffer handed Colin a document in a blue folder, which he smoothed out. "According to the will left by my grandfather, Jamie McFee, 'the children of Colin and Cleo McFee shall inherit and share equally the entire McFee estate.' " He lowered the paper. "That would be Son, who is dead, and Sister, who is in handcuffs. Lorraine, zoom in on those handcuffs."

I was surprised when Lorraine did as she was bidden. But it was all damn good melodrama.

"Now, a codicil to the will made several months after the original adds, 'Shall Daryl or Frangelica not survive to inherit, the estate will transfer to the next McFee heir.' " He lowered the page again. "That would have been the baby Susan carried, *if* that were truly my child. It is not." He turned back to the document. " 'Should the great-grandchildren not survive or be unqualified to inherit due to felonious conduct, the estate shall pass to the next living relative.' " He cleared his throat. "That would be me."

"That wasn't in the original will!" Sister was beside herself.

"You thieving old bastard!" Susan was coming off the gurney. She'd apparently recovered from childbirth in a flash. I remembered the way she kept her body toned and all of the stories I'd heard about her sexual prowess. It paid to stay in shape! I had to say, she appeared to be in fighting form. Now that she wasn't weighed down by the baby, she would be a force to be reckoned with.

"Who is the father?" Colin asked, looking down his nose. "The milkman?"

Susan stood up, wrapping the sheet around her. "A real man. Not someone who relies on those little blue pills. Someone who knows how to treat a woman." She whipped around to confront Sister. "This is all your fault. I had everything set up in Memphis, but you had to force me into labor."

"If you hadn't tried to kill me, you wouldn't have fallen." Sister was giving as good as she got.

Susan was almost sputtering as she rounded on Sister. "You were the only thing in the way of my child inheriting. It never occurred to me that a murder charge would knock you out of line."

"And it won't, you breeding heifer, you malevolent sow, you—"

"Jezebel!" Colin threw in.

Susan pushed past Colin and climbed the stairs still clutching the sheet around her. "I need to get dressed. I'm leaving this madhouse."

Doc, who held the baby, motioned the paramedics to

leave. "Doesn't look like she needs a ride to the hospital," he said. "You can go."

"Uh, in a few minutes," one of them said. "This is too good to walk away from."

"As the heir of Evermore, I demand that all of you get out." Colin was beside himself with glee. "Every last one of you. Pack your things and vacate the premises. You have an hour. Except you, Lorraine. As long as you're filming, you can stay. Sheriff, take the criminal away."

"Daddy!" Sister looked like a spear had pierced her gut. "I didn't kill Krista. I didn't kill anyone. You can't let them charge me." She tried to go to her father, but Coleman had a grip on her. "Did you really fire the PI to protect me?"

"To save the McFee name from disgrace. You were always a disappointment. You and Son. He had everything. Everything going for him and he threw it all away for a drug high. And you, you couldn't even write a book without help." He shook his head. "I'm the last real McFee, and I'll take over the estate and rebuild my empire."

"Rebuild?" Coleman asked calmly.

"He's squandered everything," Susan said from the top of the stairs. She'd put on slacks and a sweater, and I was google-eyed at the way her body had simply sprung back into form. If the woman didn't get a part in Marco's movie, she could start her own fitness empire and make a fortune. "That's why Son was using drugs. He couldn't deal with the fact that his father was cheating the corporation, inflating building contracts, skimming off the top, stealing tax payments and pocketing them." Susan stood at the top of the stairs. "I'm not a fool. I have proof."

"Who can believe the word of a lying, cheating, Jezebel.

Ignore the fallen woman," Colin said. He frantically signaled for Lorraine to focus the camera on him.

"Hey, Marco, watch this!" Susan called out, and I knew this was her moment, her real audition for a part in the movie. Susan was going to do something spectacular.

24

Before anyone could move, Susan ran down several stairs. "Aaaaarrrrghhh!" she screamed as she vaulted into the air and landed on Colin's shoulders. She wrapped her legs tightly around his neck and her momentum took them both headfirst down the few remaining steps. She flipped in midair and landed on her back, her legs still tight around his neck.

"I'm going to choke the truth out of him. I don't care if it kills me," she vowed, exerting even more pressure. "He'll talk or I'll pop his head off."

I inched back from her in awe. She was like an Olympic athlete on the biggest endorphin high in the universe. I had no doubt she was in pain, but her honed body had reached beyond the pain to . . . feats of endurance. "Shoot her with a rhino tranquilizer," I suggested. "It's the only thing that will stop her."

Coleman started forward, but Susan gave another little squeeze. "Come any closer, Sheriff, and I'll break his neck. I can, you know. This is why he loved me so, my athletic abilities. Especially my thighs. He didn't have to do anything but lay there. I did all the work. Every single time. Being married to Colin, I've learned to endure pain."

It was truly like watching a natural disaster. I couldn't look away. No one could. I had no desire to stop whatever came down, and while Coleman might want to, he realized that Susan wasn't kidding. One tiny twist of her pelvis and Colin's spine would be snapped. I definitely needed to know her exercise regime—and what kind of drugs she'd gotten hold of.

The sound of a holster unsnapping was as loud as a gunshot. Coleman drew his weapon. "Susan, I can't let you hurt him."

"Sheez strannling me," Colin wheezed.

My theory was that if he could talk, he could breathe. No worries of his imminent demise. Yet.

"Tell them how you blamed the missing funds on your own son," Susan said. "How you robbed McFee Enterprises blind and set Son up to take the fall. How you used your children as collateral in your twisted view of your superiority."

Colin's face went a little redder. Was it embarrassment at how his fiscal shenanigans had been revealed? Or was Susan choking him to death? I was willing to wait to see.

"Susan, I'm warning you," Coleman said. "Let him up."

"Confess first." Susan seemed capable of applying the

pressure until the cows came home. She had inner thighs of iron.

"I confuzzz." Colin gasped for air when she released him.

"Everyone heard it. He confessed." She was on her feet. "It doesn't matter if he confesses or not. I have the records."

Colin sprang to his feet and grasped Susan by the throat. "You conniving piece of secretarial trash. I'll throttle you."

Coleman landed a roundhouse punch on the side of Colin's face and he went down hard. "Enough!" Coleman roared. "Colin McFee, you're under arrest for assault on your wife and the murder of Cleo McFee."

"You don't have any evidence," Colin said. "You can't arrest me."

Pulling a second pair of handcuffs from his back pocket, Coleman hooked Colin up. "You people are unbelievable," Coleman said. "I've never seen the like."

"I didn't murder Cleo," Colin said. "Hell, I needed her alive to keep that barracuda off me. I never wanted to marry Susan. Never. Once Cleo was dead, marrying Susan was inevitable. She knew all of my weaknesses. She plied me with sex and attention and pretended to care about me. But it was all a lie. And then, when I was preparing to divorce her, she got pregnant. All this time, I thought it was my child." He shuddered. "Those commercials, where I touted the next McFee." He moaned. "I've humiliated myself. Putin is going to have a heyday mocking me. I challenged his manhood, and now I'm a man without a viable heir."

"Hit him again!" Susan begged. "Greedy old fartbag

egotist." She'd edged away from Colin and toward the door. "Give me my baby," she said to Doc, who still held the surprisingly quiet infant.

Doc made no offer to give up the infant. "Ms. McFee, you should come with us to the hospital. Get the baby checked out and you too. I think you may have some hormone irregularities. An overload of testosterone. I've never seen a woman give birth and do a vault onto a man's shoulders." Doc eyed her with worry and perhaps a degree of terror and respect. Her recovery from childbirth was impressive.

"Yes, an overload of testosterone. Or human growth hormone. Or blood doping. Or maybe," Cece came in from the kitchen entrance, her eyes wide with possibilities. "She's gene doping. That would explain her rapid recovery."

"Screw you," Susan said. "I've been pregnant. I haven't taken anything. Not even a glass of champagne."

"Then I applaud you on a natural delivery," Cece said. "Your recovery is one for the Guinness Book of World Records." She snapped a photo.

"I'm fine, and there's nothing wrong with my hormones. I keep my body in tip-top shape, which is more than I can say for any of you sofa slugs. Now give me the baby. I've had enough of the McFee family. I'm out of here." Susan reached for the child.

Doc took two steps back. "In good conscience, I can't release this baby until he's been thoroughly checked by a pediatrician."

Like a comedy where the entire cast appears on stage at the conclusion, Johnny Dan came out of a door beneath the stairs. He held a gun, and it was pointed at Doc. "She said give her the baby." He glowered, waving the weapon. "Get the kid, Susan. Make it fast."

Coleman tensed, but Colin and I were between him and Johnny. The situation could quickly turn into a bloodbath.

Johnny came forward, tracking some substance from the basement across the beautiful black-and-white tile floor. I took one look at the waffle design of the boot print and knew Johnny Dan was indeed the shooter in the field. On top of the footprints he left, he limped slightly on his right leg. Very probably where I'd winged him.

A whole different scenario began to play out in my mind. If Colin had been the cuckold this whole time, and Susan intended to pawn Johnny Dan's child off as heir to the McFee estate, who stood to gain the most by the death of Cleo and Son? I swiveled to see Susan at the front door.

"Listen, old man. Give me the baby or Johnny will shoot you." Susan was half out the door.

"Let's go to the hospital," Doc said as if speaking to a child. "We'll get everyone checked out and make sure this young man has a healthy start to life."

"Keep the freaking baby," Susan said. "I never wanted a child." She and Johnny Dan bolted through the front door, slamming it shut.

"They're getting away," I said to Coleman, who seemed completely unfazed by the turn of events. "Stop them. They're behind Cleo and Son's death. Johnny Dan caused the wreck that hurt Tinkie. And they're getting away."

"No, they're not," he said. "DeWayne pulled the spark plug harnesses on all of the cars out there. No one is going anywhere." He climbed two steps and addressed the crowd. "Let's make this simple. Everyone here is under arrest. I'm taking you all in."

Five hours later, Oscar, Cece, and I sat in the waiting room of the Mercy Medical Hospital in Memphis. We'd managed to get to the hospital before Tinkie came out of surgery so we could wait with Oscar. Colman had relented on charging me for trespassing until Tinkie could face the music with me.

A doctor came over to our group and introduced himself as Martin Gwinn, head of neurosurgery. He looked haggard, and I held my breath and squeezed Oscar's hand.

"We were able to stop the bleeding, and the swelling is going down," he said. "It's still touch and go, but I believe we're looking at a good prognosis."

"Oh, thank heavens." Cece threw her arms around the doctor and kissed his cheek. "Thank you, thank you."

"Yes!" Oscar pumped his hand. "Thank you, Dr. Gwinn. Thank you."

I merely swallowed a lump of raw emotion and nodded. "Can we be with her when she wakes up?" I asked.

The doctor considered us, each in turn. "When she starts to regain consciousness, I'll send a nurse to get you. The hospital frowns on more than one visitor, but somehow I think you three might be better for her than any medicine I can prescribe."

I had something even better for Tinkie than all three of us rolled together, but I had enough sense not to let on that Chablis was secretly tucked in my overlarge handbag on the floor beside my chair. I swear the pup understood she was on a mission of mercy to nurse Tinkie back to health, because she never uttered a sound.

"We won't tire her," I promised. "Cece and I will only stay a minute."

"I'm glad you're here," Oscar said, putting a hand on each of our shoulders. "Let's just hope this is as rosy as the doctor thinks."

"It will be," Cece said. "I feel it in my bones."

Two hours later, we huddled around the bed of my partner, who looked as if she were auditioning for a role in *The Mummy*. Her head was swaddled in gauze. She was going to have a conniption when she realized they'd shaved one side of her head. She set a great store by her sun-glitzed mane.

When her blue eyes blinked open, Oscar kissed her lips lightly. "You have to stop doing things that put you in the hospital," he said, but he wasn't really scolding her.

"Sorry." She lifted a hand and felt her bandages. "My head is pounding."

"I'll bet." I kissed her cheek and whispered. "Someone is missing you." And I slipped Chablis onto the bed with her. The little dust mop ran up the sheets and licked the tears that squeezed from Tinkie's eyes.

"What in the hell happened?" she asked.

"Tire blew. Well, someone shot it out. We hit that newly turned dirt in the field and came to a dead stop. A very abrupt stop. You hit the steering wheel and the driver's window. Brain bleed. Airlifted to Memphis. You're fine." I said it all at once—got it out of the way.

"Okay," Tinkie said. "*Who* shot us?"

"Johnny Dan."

"Colin's security man?" Tinkie was puzzled. "Why?"

"That's still up in the air. Johnny, Colin, Sister, and Susan are all in jail, but right now, no one is talking. Oh yeah, Susan had the baby but it didn't belong to Colin. Johnny Dan was the father."

Cece leaned in. "After all of those awful commercials where Colin used a laser pointer to highlight the baby's man parts to prove his masculinity to Putin, the baby doesn't even belong to him. It belongs to Johnny! Isn't that delicious?"

"Hold on!" Tinkie motioned us to stop. "I can't take all of this. My head is pounding and I need to be alone with Oscar."

"Girls, you should let her rest." Oscar had been tolerant, but now he was in charge.

"You got it," I said. Chablis was reluctant to return to the purse, but she knew the drill. She had to be quiet or we'd get in big trouble. "We're going back to Zinnia. Now that you're okay, I have some things to finish up."

"I want to go home, too." Tinkie looked at Oscar as if he held the answers to all the questions of the universe.

"And you will," Oscar said, picking up her hand. "As soon as the doctor says so."

Cece and I blew kisses at the door and then hauled it for Zinnia. There were a lot of loose ends to tie up and questions to be answered. Now I could attend to my work with a joyful heart. Tinkie would recover. It didn't matter that I'd failed to uncover the truth of Son's disappearance or even if the wreck that killed Cleo and Son was accidental or caused by someone.

Son and Cleo's deaths were in the past. Marco, with the footage Lorraine had shot, had the makings of a true-crime documentary that would sweep the awards about a Southern family eaten up with criminal tendencies. What really mattered to me was that my partner would fully recover, and my life would return to normal without any losses. I couldn't take it if anything bad happened to Tinkie.

By the time Cece pulled up in front of Dahlia House, Chablis and I had been snoring away for at least thirty miles. Cece was kinder than I might have been and had let me sleep. I stumbled inside and up the stairs. Tucked in bed with Sweetie, Chablis, and Pluto for company, I gave myself to the sweet release of slumber.

The sound of someone else breathing in the room woke me. It wasn't Sweetie Pie—she was a snorer. Or Chablis, who was tucked against my hip. Not even Pluto, the sassy black cat who slept soundly on my head. This was a strange and alien breathing pattern.

I opened my eyes and let out a scream. One single giant eye, big as a softball, glared down at me. It took me a minute to realize a young girl was staring at me through a magnifying glass. "You mumble in your sleep. I have to write that down," she said.

"What the hell? Are you counting my pores?" I pushed back in the bed away from her.

"I deduce that you don't get enough sleep." She grinned, and there was something sharkish about her. "And you need more sex."

I was horrified. "You are too young to be thinking about such things." She looked to be twelve or so with her braided hair, glasses, and rain slicker, though I couldn't recall any indication of rain in the area. "Why are you wearing a rain slicker inside? Who are you?"

"Harriet."

She said it as if I should instantly know her. "Harriet who? And you'd better have a damn good answer."

"Harriet M. Welsch. I'm a spy."

I sat up. When I was in grammar school, before my parents died, I'd loved the adventures of Harriet, the girl spy. She'd been a role model for choosing the road to adventure, for asking questions, for observing people, and for justice. In fact, she'd helped shape me into who I was today. "What are you doing here, Harriet?"

"Writing down all the things I see."

Indeed, she had a tablet on my stomach and was pressing down hard with a Number 2 pencil. "I saw a woman kissing a man in the kitchen. I saw a shirt go flying over her head."

Oh, I knew what was happening. The innocence of one of my childhood icons was destroyed. "Jitty, this is wrong. You can't take someone like Harriet and bend her to be your minion to promote carnal knowledge between me and Coleman." I yawned because I'd been dead asleep before Jitty's nocturnal arrival. "Go away. I'm exhausted."

Harriet sat up. "You don't know what you're missing. I wrote down some things about that sheriff. He has broad shoulders and a lean waist. His legs look strong, and so does his back."

"Stop it! Jitty, you are my Marion Hawthorne."

"I know." Harriet began to shift into the features of my beautiful haint. "I'm the ghost of sexual encounters past," she said. "Here to remind you that once upon a time you enjoyed getting it on."

"Jitty, shut up." I was too tired to argue with her. "Let me get some sleep. Perhaps if I had more sleep I'd have more energy to pursue a man."

"Promise?"

She sounded so hopeful I had to chuckle. "No promises, but if you don't let me sleep, I'll never be able to catch Coleman. Or anyone else."

"Time's a-wastin. I hear those eggs aging, Sarah Booth."

I'd had more than I could take for one day. I pulled the pillow over my head and went back to sleep. The bad guys were in jail—at least for right now. Tinkie was healing and might be home from Memphis within the next twenty-four hours. Things could have been a whole lot worse than they were.

Two weeks passed in a blur as I helped Coleman sort through the elements of the case and hauled food from Millie's Café to Hilltop for Oscar, Tinkie, and Chablis. My partner had fully recovered and was healing nicely. Susan and Johnny Dan remained in the hoosegow charged with a variety of crimes. Colin was out, pending an investigation of McFee Enterprises, and Sister was under house arrest at Evermore.

Tinkie was coming over for a small gathering—a simple celebration of friends for movie night. I shook the popcorn, the kernels exploding softly in the big cast-iron pot. I poured the fluffy white snack into a big bowl and started another pot. I already had a pitcher of Lynchburg Lemonade made and waiting on the table in the den.

The doorbell rang just as I poured the last kernel, and I hurried to escort Tinkie and Oscar to the den. Tinkie wore a much smaller white bandage around her head. She curled up with Oscar in the oversized recliner. I covered them with a plush throw, plumped up their pillows, and hurried back to answer the door again. Cece, Marco, Lorraine, and Millie came in a group. Lorraine had several discs that she handed me. Since Tinkie had missed the big scene at Evermore, we decided to preview the footage of the staircase event. And some other choice footage. Lorraine and Marco had moved out of Evermore to the Prince Albert Hotel, but they were leaving for Hollywood early in the morning. Before Coleman confiscated their film footage.

Lorraine leaned to whisper in my ear. "The discs are for that handsome sheriff. Just don't give it to him until I'm on the plane for LA. I can't be embroiled in a trial here, and neither can Marco. We've got a studio interested in our movie and we have to be in Hollywood to work."

When everyone was settled in the den and Lorraine put the disc in the player, I poured more drinks and passed out bowls of popcorn. "Enjoy!" I said.

"Before we start, why don't we each posit our theories of what happened the night Son disappeared, and what happened to Son," Marco suggested.

"Good idea." Cece sat on the plush carpet beside Millie. She tilted her head. "I think it was raining so hard, his wheel went off the road and Son lost control and plunged into the river. He was pulled out of the car by the current and drowned."

"Tinkie and I think someone must have forced him off the road," I said as I refilled a bowl of popcorn on the table in front of Marco and Lorraine. "The impact knocked him unconscious and the river took him."

Millie was the last to speak. "I always had a soft spot for Son. He was a kind young man with wonderful manners, and Cleo adored him. I hate to say it, but I think someone shot him and killed him. He was dead before the car ever hit the water. Cleo was collateral damage."

"How are you going to end the movie?" I asked Marco.

"I can't say, but I promise you, it will be a surprise.

Now, let's show our little invalid what happened at Evermore while she was fighting for her life."

Lorraine hit play. We watched transfixed as Sister started down the stairs. She was blasting Susan and Colin with promises to throw them all out of Evermore the minute she came into the trust. Whatever hope Sister had ever had of winning her father's heart, she'd finally given up. She mocked his political aspirations and tore into Susan for being a gold digger.

Sister was in the middle of a rant when, just as she claimed, Susan snaked a leg out and tripped her. It was clearly deliberate, and when Sister lost her balance, Susan gave her a push. Sister twisted to grab the handrail but caught Susan instead. And the two went tumbling. It was a wonder one or both of them weren't dead.

"There's no doubt about it. Susan deliberately tripped Sister. The fall could have killed her." Lorraine eased to the edge of her seat. "And there it is, right on film."

"I can understand why someone might want to kill Sister," Tinkie threw in. "She's a vile human being."

"It's the inheritance." I sat up taller. "Since Son is dead, if Sister died, then Susan's baby would have inherited everything." I felt like lightning had sparked in my spine.

"If the baby had actually been a McFee," Tinkie said.

"It was my understanding Jamie left the estate to Son and Sister. There were no codicils or amendments." I finally caught the big picture. "This is what Hoots Tanner uncovered. That's why Colin paid him off so handsomely. Colin added codicils to Jamie's will so any child of his and Susan's son could inherit and a felony charge would be grounds for disinheriting. Colin had stacked the deck to be sure he got everything, and Hoots caught him out on it."

"He said he did it because he thought Sister was behind the deaths of Cleo and Son and he didn't want the estate tied up in court," Cece said. "Do you think there was a shred of truth in it?"

"I don't know," I finally said. "Lies are piled on top of lies. I wish we'd been able to prove what really happened that night."

"Maybe one of them will turn on the others," Cece said. "Colin and Susan hated each other, but the baby was the ticket to wealth for both of them. It's all falling into place now. The only thing that stood in their way was Sister."

"You are a genius, Tinkie." I hated to say it. I really did. Sister should do prison time based on the fact she was a horrid human being. "I don't think Sister killed Krista Yost." I went to my partner and put a hand on her shoulder. "Someone knew we were in Sister's room. They deliberately came in and showed us where that manuscript was so that we would discover Sister had a ghostwriter. Because they intended all along to kill Krista and pin it on Sister."

Tinkie sighed. "You're right. Someone was setting Sister up."

"It was Colin," Marco said. "He's a devious bastard."

I still wasn't over Marco's secret meetings with Colin. I'd have the answer to that before the night was over, but first things first. "I'm not so certain about that." I had everyone's attention. "I think Susan is behind all of it. But Marco knows something he hasn't told any of us."

25

When I had everyone's attention, I pulled the check I'd written for eight grand from my pocket and gave it to Marco. "We spent two thousand on expenses, but Delaney Detective Agency is returning the balance of your money. We didn't find out what happened to Son. We failed. But you haven't been honest with us. You met secretly with Colin."

Marco looked at the check. "I haven't played exactly fair with you ladies."

No kidding, I wanted to say.

"What do you mean? How can you expect someone to solve a case if you don't tell them the truth?" The red that climbed Cece's neck told me she was pretty hot under the collar.

Marco was unflappable. "I hope you don't mind, but I invited Roon over. He's bringing a guest. When they arrive, I think everything will be clear."

"Sure." I didn't have a feel for the screenwriter one way or the other. He was quiet, but he'd been the only one to show any compassion for Susan.

The knock at the front door let me know our screenwriting guest had arrived so I padded there in my socks to let him in. Sweetie Pie followed to be sure he was one of the good guys.

When I opened the door, Roon stood there with Dorinda Posey. I stepped back, but I didn't invite them in. I simply stared. Why was Dorinda Posey with the screenwriter? When it hit me, I swallowed. "Son?" I asked. He looked nothing like the young man I'd known in college. Sure, he was the same height, but Roon was lean to the point of starvation. The aquiline nose so characteristic of the McFee lineage was missing. Only his eyes were the same, and now I saw it. "You're alive."

He nodded. "It's me."

"What the hell?" I couldn't decide if I should be furious or excited.

"It's a long story, and I owe you and everyone else an explanation. Especially this woman." He drew Dorinda close to his side. "May we come in?"

I ushered them to the den and waited for everyone else to grasp the obvious. Marco and Lorraine already knew the truth—the liars. Marco had hired me to solve a case when he already had the answer. He would pay for that.

Son took the initiative. "I'm sorry I had to deceive everyone for so long. I know I hurt a lot of people. Without meaning to, I put some people in danger. I didn't do this for a selfish purpose. For a lot of reasons, I had to remain dead, until now. And I couldn't have done it without the help of my friends Marco and Lorraine."

"Son!" Tinkie stood up, shedding popcorn kernels like a chipmunk. "You're alive." I saw the change come over her face and I knew she was about to break bad. "People have been hunting your remains for *five years*. You broke Dorinda's heart because she believed you were dead. And even Sister. I think she was glad you were dead, but still, she's been living a lie, planning for all of that McFee trust money to come into her hands." She started toward Son with clear intention to cause harm. She looked like a badass with her mummy head and glaring blue eyes.

I put a hand on her arm, but it was Oscar who circled her waist and held her firm.

"You can't excite yourself like this, Tinkie," Oscar said. "You're just recovering from a serious injury."

"I might have to wait another week or two, but I'm going to kick his butt from here to tomorrow," she said. "I almost died because I was trying to figure out what happened to you. You were hiding out in Hollywood the whole time. Damn!"

"I'm so very sorry, Ms. Richmond, Mr. Richmond." Son looked so hangdog I almost felt sorry for him. "Let me tell you what I know and maybe you'll understand. I had to try to find out who wanted me dead before I revealed that I was alive. That's why I gave Marco the money to hire Delaney Detective Agency. You two have a great reputation, and I thought if anyone could figure out who was after me, it would be you."

"Why didn't you just tell us that?" Tinkie was mad, and I didn't blame her. She was the one with a half-shaved head and a cracked skull. Luckily, she had a very hard head.

"I needed you to approach the case as if I were dead. And call me paranoid, but if word had leaked that I was alive, I feared someone would try to finish the job. Marco and Lorraine and I have been friends for a while, and he agreed to hire you on my behalf."

"Tell us everything." Millie poured drinks for Dorinda and Son. "Take a seat and talk. You owe us an explanation."

Son nodded. "I didn't plan any of this. Please understand that. At first, I didn't have a choice. A lot of what happened was because of how badly I was hurt when the SUV went off the road. I—"

"Whoa! Back up." At last we had the person who could tell us what really happened on that storm-swept night. "What made you go off the road?"

Son looked down at the floor, and Dorinda picked up his hand and held it, giving him strength. "Just tell them, Son. Now's the time. Just the way you explained it to me."

Son nodded. "I was living in Memphis and working at a halfway house, working hard to stay clean. Mother called me and told me she had physical evidence that Father was stealing from McFee Enterprises. I'd known for a long time that Father was committing crimes. He used me to lie to the investors, to the board of directors, to everyone. Illegal things were happening at the company, but I couldn't put my hands on the proof. Father refused to discuss any of it. He told me to do my job or else."

"It's why Son started using drugs," Dorinda said. "Colin was careful. He kept one set of books at McFee Enterprises and the real books were hidden. He never suspected Cleo was on to him, but she found the hard physical evidence in a secret safe at Evermore. I think Jamie must have helped her. Anyway, she copied some documents and photographed the rest. Tell them, Son."

"That's why she called me to meet her in Clarksdale. She'd been collecting evidence, and she'd left it in a safe deposit box at the First National Bank of Clarksdale under a college friend's name. That's why we were on that side of the state. Mother's friend had retrieved the evidence and Mom waited at her house for me to arrive. I was clean and sober and determined to help her stop the things Father was doing. After we connected in Clarksdale, I was to drive her to Jackson and then catch a flight to Atlanta, where I had an appointment with an investigator for the Securities and Exchange Commission."

"But Colin found out your plan, and he tried to kill you both." Oscar had maneuvered Tinkie back in the recliner, but she leaned forward and forced the chair upright. "Did he shoot out your tire? That's what happened to me and Sarah Booth."

"I can't prove who was responsible for the wreck. Let me tell you what I remember." Son continued his story. "The rain was relentless. It came down in sheets so heavy I couldn't see anything. I pulled off the road, but I realized it was more dangerous to sit on the side of that flooded two-lane than to keep moving along. I had a sense we were being followed, and Mother was very upset. She said something was wrong. Someone had been in her room at Evermore going through her things."

"Was Colin on to her?" Millie was as caught up in the story as the rest of us.

"I can't prove it was Father." Son swallowed and looked down at the floor. Dorinda rubbed his back, and

I couldn't help but think that for all he'd lost, Son had found someone who truly loved him.

"What happened?" I asked.

"We came up on the approach to the bridge. The rain had finally let up. Even with just the headlights I could tell the river was higher than I'd ever seen it. I was going slow, because the bridge is narrow and it had been raining so hard. When I was twenty yards from the bridge, a tire blew and the vehicle went onto the shoulder. I fought hard to bring it back on the road, but a bullet came out of the darkness and hit me in the shoulder. I lost control. I remember going over the side and into the cold black water. The SUV rolled. I tried to force a door open, but I was shot and weak and the current tore the door off." He stopped and closed his eyes. "I looked over at Mother, and she said, 'I love you,' and we hit something in the river and the current pulled me out of the car."

It didn't take a big imagination to re-create the horror of that night. I'd had enough drowning dreams to feel the press of suffocation, the confusion of not knowing which way was up or down, of tumbling into debris and hurtling along with the water always tugging, tugging.

"It was the last time I saw my mother."

"And what happened to you?" Cece asked, but there was a gentleness in her tone I didn't normally hear.

"I found part of a dock that had been knocked free and was drifting down the river. I held on as best I could. My left arm was broken and both legs. I was shot in the shoulder. Something sharp, probably from the car, sliced my face open and took part of my nose. Anyway, the dock caught up in some debris and an older couple happened to see me. They rescued me. They had a place in Arkansas and they took me to the hospital there."

I thought back to the people Tinkie and I had interviewed. "Grant Pennebaker had said he had relatives in Arkansas. He'd claimed that he and his wife hadn't been on the Sunflower River during the flood. I believe he lied."

Tinkie signaled for a refill on her glass of tea and I was happy to oblige. I filled my own glass too—with more medicinal lemonade. We'd been very close to the truth. The Pennebakers had been on the river that rainy evening. And they'd rescued a young man and helped him reinvent himself.

"Don't blame them," Son said. "They meant to take me to Memphis, but there was an accident and the northbound lanes were closed. Highway 1 is built up higher than some of the county roads, so they drove up to Highway 49, crossed the Mississippi River and took me to Marvel, Arkansas, where they had a friend who was a pilot. The storm was moving to the east, and the weather was clearing, so the pilot flew me down to Little Rock to the hospital. I was there for three months, mostly in traction. Plastic surgery. By the time I realized what had happened and who I was, it was weeks later. I'd been declared dead by my father and sister, and Mother was long buried. It was just easier to become someone completely different than Daryl McFee. I knew if I resurfaced, I would be killed."

I was like a dog with a bone. I hated to be lied to. "The Pennebakers never knew who you were?"

"Later, they figured it out. But they protected me. My life was in danger. Someone had tried to kill me and succeeded in killing Mother. Grant and his wife, they're good people. They saved my life."

Millie looked like she was going to cry. "Son, you could have shown up and told everyone what happened. You could have—"

"Believe me, I wanted to. But someone very powerful was at work. The SUV that Jimmy pulled out of the river disappeared. All of the evidence Mother had collected was washed away. I had nothing but empty accusations and a record as a drug addict."

"You had a bullet wound in your shoulder," I pointed out. "That's evidence."

"A lot of good it would have done me if I'd been killed. I was a sitting duck in the hospital in traction. Anyone could have come in and smothered me. I had to fight hard just to live. The endless surgeries, the work to give me back a face, any face."

"He has a point," Cece said.

"And so you ran." I sounded harsh even to my own ears.

"Yes. I healed and the hospital took up a collection to buy me a bus ticket to Los Angeles. I became Roon Talley, screenwriter. I did a couple of scripts, hit it lucky with one, and managed to get steady work. Marco and Lorraine befriended me. But I never gave up the idea of finding my mother's killer."

"And Sister's book about the McFee family was the perfect opportunity."

"Yes." Son held his shoulders back and refused to show any remorse. "In the guise of a screenwriter, I could return to Evermore. I hired the best PIs I could find, and I waited for all the chickens to come home to roost. I knew someone in my family had caused the accident that killed my mother, and I meant to find out who it was."

"Did you?" Tinkie asked. "Did you find evidence?"

Son's lips pressed together. "Ballistics will tell me that." He looked at his watch. "And I should know at any moment when Sheriff Peters gets back to me. You see, I kept the bullet the surgeon removed from my shoulder. I believe it will match the bullets that were shot at you and Sarah Booth."

"The same shooter?" I asked.

"I believe so."

"Johnny Dan," I whispered. Even nearly six years ago he was using a gun to remove anyone who stood in . . . Susan's way. "It was Susan all along. It was never Colin. Or Sister."

Son nodded. "That's the same conclusion I came to. Johnny Dan worked for my father as head of security at McFee Enterprises back when my wreck happened. Prior to employment at McFee, he was a military sniper, and he really enjoyed firing some of Dad's expensive weapons. If he was sleeping with Susan, and we know he was, it was in his best interest to make sure she inherited everything. I believe Johnny set up on the other side of the Sunflower River with a thermal scope and caught me just as I approached the bridge."

"How would they know you were headed that way?" Tinkie asked. She might have bumped her head really hard, but she still had plenty of brain power.

"Someone was following Mother. That's why we didn't lay over in Clarksdale," Son explained. "We thought we'd given them the slip, but Highway 12 was the only open road to the east. We had to go that way. We both thought the person following us was after the documentation Mother had. We were wrong."

"So Cleo was the target," I said. "Not just because she had something on Colin, but also because she was in the way of Susan's plans to marry Colin."

"And Johnny Dan had switched his allegiance to Susan. But would he want his lover to marry another man?" Tinkie asked.

"The long-range goal was billions of dollars. Johnny Dan saw the future. He and Susan shared that trait. Lay the plans and wait for the intended outcome. My family seems to attract bloodsuckers. A lot of people have said the McFee inheritance is cursed because of the blood on my family's name." Son was pensive. "I believe it."

"And Sister was merely a pawn of Colin. She said and did whatever he wanted to win his approval," I said.

"I think that's come to an end," Son said. "Sister finally realized that nothing she does will ever be enough. She doesn't have to hate me or anyone else any longer. If nothing else comes of this, I believe my sister will find freedom from her misery."

"Does she know you're Son?" I asked.

"Not yet. I'll tell her when I leave here. I owe her that."

"Does Colin know?" Tinkie asked.

"No. It's going to wreck his inheritance plans." Son laughed, a full-fledged, deep laugh. "And Sister didn't have that writer killed. It was Susan. She had to frame Sister to get her out of the line of inheritance. Only Father and Susan knew about that felony clause, because Father added it. He can't help himself," he said with more pity than I could have mustered if my father had tried to screw me out of my inheritance. "McFee Enterprises was once great, but

Father's ego has run the company the last seven years. Pride, arrogance, an unwillingness to listen to others. Eventually the piper had to be paid. This run for the Senate was his gamble to gain power and influence. A lot of Mississippi senators have gone to Washington as members of the middle class and come home multimillionaires."

My cell phone rang, and it was Coleman calling. I stepped out of the room and answered.

"Are you busy tonight?" Coleman asked, and the sound of his voice made me flush.

"A little. Son McFee is here, along with my friends and the footage Lorraine captured at Evermore. She has copies for you."

"So Son has told you the truth."

"At least a portion of it. He says Sister is innocent of Krista's death and trying to kill Tinkie and me. He also believes it was Johnny Dan that Harold and I saw by the barn. Son believes the sniper was scoping out a possible location to set up—should it be necessary."

"And I believe Sister is innocent. The bullet from Son's shoulder matched the slugs in Tinkie's car. It was the same gun, and I believe the same shooter. Johnny Dan. He took the shots at you on the banks of the Sunflower and in that curve at Susan Simpson McFee's behest. Colin is guilty of financial crimes, but I don't think he was involved in Cleo's murder or the attempt on Son's life."

"Can you prove it was Susan?"

"I think Johnny is ready to talk. I've made him an offer that could keep him off death row. If he's smart, he'll take it."

Was it possible this dreadful case was actually coming to an end and I would be done with everything McFee? "Will you let me know?"

"I'll drop by."

Three simple words that sent my world into turmoil. I had a split second of terror when my voice and body failed to respond to my commands—short circuited by the mere thought of Coleman. At last I managed, "I'll be sure Tinkie *isn't* here." It was the best I could offer.

Coleman's tone was dry. "Good plan, Sarah Booth. Good plan."

When I returned to the den, Tinkie and Oscar were already preparing to leave. I relayed the ballistics information from Coleman and promised if I learned anything new I'd call everyone. Millie and Cece left with the Richmonds. Lorraine and Marco hung back.

Marco scrutinized me, assessing the level of my anger. "I wanted to tell you the truth, Sarah Booth, but I didn't want to do anything that would affect your investigation or endanger Son. We had to find the truth, for Son's sake."

"I get it." I hated to admit it, but I did. Knowing Son was alive would have impacted the investigation. Inevitably, we would have tipped our hand. "All this time, though. Everyone thought he was dead."

"And they were safer believing that," Marco said. "Until we were able to flush out the killer, Son didn't know if his father, his sister, or someone else was behind the attempt on his life. We couldn't risk it. When Son decided to come home as Roon Talley, it was with the sole purpose of finding out who was responsible for his mother's death. This was a plan he put into action years back. And I think we've almost completed the mission."

"Coleman said he would call me if Johnny Dan confessed. I'll let you know."

"I'll bet that sheriff will call you." Lorraine put her

arm around me. "You have something very special, Sarah Booth. You have a place in your world, a secure place. You and Tinkie have found where you fit perfectly, and you have a network of friends who nurture you."

Lorraine's words struck me with the hammer of truth. I did fit in Zinnia. "And you and Marco are the Hollywood power couple."

"A transitory title at best," Lorraine said. "If you hear anything from the sheriff, you'll let us know? We have a flight to catch in Memphis, and we must be leaving now."

"Taking a runner before you get pulled into a trial?" I asked.

"Absolutely. We can't be trapped here, and we don't want to testify. We have enough footage for a documentary on the McFee case. True crime. A new genre for us. Cece has agreed to cover the initial hearings for the film. We have to get busy editing. If we're fast, we can release the documentary in time for Oscar consideration."

"Good luck," I said.

Marco reached into his pocket and brought out my check and another. "I'm returning your check and here's another ten thousand. The work you did was well worth it. You brought the guilty parties to light and gave us the perfect ending for the movie."

"Take the check," Tinkie said from the doorway. She had come back inside the house to retrieve her coat. I wondered if she might try to hide in the closet on the off chance Coleman came by and she could impede another romantic encounter. "I'll take that check. I have to buy a new car."

"Thank you, Marco." But I had another question. "Your meetings with Colin at McFee Enterprises?"

"I had to be certain he believed Son to be dead before

I would risk telling Roon to come home. All of us wanted to find the truth, but not at the cost of another life."

My last doubt about the St. Johns vanished. "Good luck with the film."

"We'll be back," Marco promised. "I can't go too long without some of Millie's cooking."

When the St. Johns and Tinkie were finally gone, I closed the door and leaned against it. I was alone at last.

From upstairs, horns blared the opening sequence from every James Bond film I'd ever watched, followed by the guitar theme. I couldn't believe it. I'd just cleared the house in the hopes Coleman would stop by and now Jitty was on the warpath. James Bond? Who was she going to be now, Doctor No? Pussy Galore? She was capable of anything.

Eva Green materialized on my staircase in a classic and sexy black pants suit, descending with all the grace and beauty of the financially talented Vesper Lynd. Jitty had transported us into the heart of *Casino Royale,* the only Bond movie that had ever made me cry.

"Dammit, Jitty. Stop right now." I took a stance at the foot of the staircase. After the day I'd had, I wasn't about to participate in one of her crazy spy charades.

"I'll be keeping an eye on our government's money, rather than your perfectly formed arse." Jitty delivered the line with the aplomb of a seasoned actress, and I instantly recalled the scene with Eva Green and Daniel Craig and the heat between them.

"Stop line stealing from a movie. What are you doing? You have to stop. I'm serious. How can you expect me to pursue a romantic interest if I have to worry that any minute you'll pop up?"

"I've never popped up in the middle of sex. Oh, wait, how long has it been since you had sex? And by the way, you never found out why Sister insists on calling Tinkie Stinky."

If I could get my hands on her throat, I'd throttle her. Being dead, she had the advantage. "I know that. Tinkie will tell me when she's ready. I'm her friend, not a paparazzi. I don't have to dig out her secrets. Now skedaddle. Please. I'm nervous enough. And remember, Vesper Lynd broke Bond's heart. That's not comforting to me at all."

"Yes, I embody the one love that nearly destroyed James Bond." Jitty still spoke with Vesper's voice, but they were my haint's words and not lines from a movie, and that worried me.

"Why are you doing this? Am I the person who might destroy Coleman? Is that the message?" My heart was pounding.

"You know I can't predict the future, and even if I could, it's against the rules of the Great Beyond to tell you anything."

"Then why torment me?"

"Before you let Coleman take a risk, be sure you're ready to take one too."

And there it was. The issue I'd been struggling with since my heart had begun to heal from Graf's rejection. I wasn't a person who would take another's heart callously. But how did one truly know when the spirit was willing to try again? What if I opened the door to Coleman and let him into my bed and my life, only to discover my heart was still impaired?

Jitty had hit upon my greatest fear. Vesper Lynd embodied the nightmare I never wanted to be, for Coleman or anyone else. She had come to love James Bond, and yet she'd damaged him irreversibly. It had cost her plenty, but he was the one left to suffer.

"Why are you doing this, Jitty?" She had to have some foreknowledge. "All you do is devil me to get laid, and when I finally decide I'm ready, you terrorize me."

"Not nearly as much as you'll terrorize yourself if you hurt Coleman."

"And you believe I'll do that." My heart was a lump of black coal. I wondered how it continued to beat. "You believe I'll hurt him."

She came down the stairs and with each step, she shifted more and more to my beautiful haint, the one presence I could count on in my life. "I don't know the future. And I don't know your heart. Only you can answer that question."

But I couldn't. I was as uncertain of the future as I'd ever been. "The heart is a fickle beast." I knew that much.

"Sarah Booth, you can't know how you'll feel in ten years or even ten months. All I'm saying is that you should act now only if your heart is truly unencumbered. If you have any doubts, hold off. But if you feel you want to try for love, then you have to take the risk."

She was right. Love was always a risk. Every day. Not just in this moment, but far into the future. Nothing in life was guaranteed. That was what I had to accept before I let Coleman into my life.

Jitty faded into the gloom of the foyer as Coleman's footsteps crossed the porch of Dahlia House. The moment of decision was upon me, and I opened the door before he could knock.

"Johnny Dan confessed," he said. "He shot Son and caused the wreck, and he shot Tinkie's tire. Susan was behind all of it. It's over."

But I knew differently. I knew it was only just beginning.